"I'm not your wife!" she shouted furiously. "It was all a trick. Let me go, Evan!"

He didn't answer. Couldn't answer. Her nearness was intoxicating, and he couldn't stop himself. Bending his head, he kissed her.

The touch of his lips was like fire. Cynara struggled against him, her hands pushing vainly against his chest. His mouth was demanding, and despite her fury, she felt herself responding. Suddenly she was caught up in a wave of desire so strong that she pressed her body into his and wound her arms around his neck.

This, she thought dazedly, this was what it was like to be loved. She felt lifted, transported, breathless, and she wanted to prolong this moment forever. "Evan," she whispered, "wait . . ."

But he was beyond hearing her. Caught up in his own delirium, he was conscious only of her slim white body under him . . . he was lost in her, drowning in the touch and scent of her. He had denied himself too long; all his senses screamed at him to take her, and he didn't hear her second, frightened protest. . . .

Cynara

Janis Flores

ace books

A Division of Charter Communications Inc.
A GROSSET & DUNLAP COMPANY
360 Park Avenue South
New York, New York 10010

CYNARA

An ACE Original

First Ace Printing: April 1979

Published simultaneously in Canada

Printed in U.S.A.

To Eldon and Dorothea Overholser
for what was important —
then, and now . . .

PROLOGUE

THE LYREBIRD GARDEN was as Cynara remembered it. She was almost offended at the sight, for during the long walk toward the rise from which the garden and the Lyrebird Manor itself could be seen, she had convinced herself that it would have changed in some way, as she herself had been changed in the three years since she had last seen it. But it was the same, as she was not, and where once she had actually admired its wild beauty, now she hated the sight of it and all it represented.

She stood side by side with Evan, and they both stared down on the scene from their high vantage point. Evan's face, as it was so often, was unreadable, but she knew her own expression betrayed her turbulent emotions, and she wanted to run, run away from the sight below and the memory of what had happened there.

So strong was the desire for flight that she actually took a step back. She looked toward Evan again, and was surprised to see that he had moved off a short distance from her. As she watched him, his glance swung away from the garden toward the house, and when she saw his expression change, she knew he was thinking, as was she, of Myles. Myles. His face flashed into her mind, and she shuddered.

"Evan?"

He did not hear her, or if he did, he paid no attention to her call. He stood alone, the wind ruffling his black hair, lifting it away from his face. His eyes were shadowed again, his mouth a thin, bitter line. Cynara took a step toward him. He tensed at her movement, and turned to look at her. Their glance held angrily.

"I hate you for bringing me back, Evan!"

"You wanted it as much as I," he answered, his voice hard.

She stared at him a moment longer, and then with a cry, she turned and started down the hill without looking back. By the time she had reached the bottom, she was running, her skirts lifted high.

Evan watched her go. Only when Cynara disappeared around the curve of the hill did he turn back to his contemplation of the house below him. Now that he was alone, he allowed his feelings to surface. Pain flickered briefly in his eyes, but it was instantly replaced by a look of such hatred that his lips actually drew back from his teeth. Bitter memories came back to him, unbidden, but he let them come. He wanted to remember all of it, savoring the full depth of his hatred, so that the final victory over those who lived below would be that much sweeter when it came.

For the first time, he smiled. It was a savage smile, and he gloried in the feeling it brought with it. He did not realize that that smile betrayed a deep hidden anguish as well.

Cynara ran until the curve of the hill hid her from sight. Only when she was sure that Evan could no longer see her did she stop. A shuddering sob escaped her, and she threw herself on the ground, burying her face in her arms as she began to cry. She had told herself that this was what she wanted; she had been so sure, until now. But her first glimpse of the garden and the house beyond had brought the memories rushing back at her, and she knew now that she had been a fool to return. She hated the house and those who lived there; she hated them all for what they had done to her. She would never forget; the memories would be with her always.

PART I

CHAPTER ONE

"BUT THIS IS my home! Certainly I will remain here!"

The words were delivered in a clear tone, but the slight note of panic in the girl's voice made the solicitor, Mr. Abel Bertram, hesitate again. He had dreaded this interview from the first moment he had been notified of her father's death, for it had then become his responsibility to settle the Rosslyn estate, and to make arrangements for Henry Rosslyn's daughter according to Henry's last wishes. The person in question, Cynara Rosslyn, was staring at him defiantly, and he must try to explain once more without arousing her suspicions.

Mr. Bertram shifted his gaze away and looked down at the papers in his hand. He was exasperated that this girl could discomfit him so, because it made this chore even more difficult. She was only sixteen, he believed, but already she had a will and a presence of her own, which was most disconcerting. And she was a beauty, there was no denying that. Something stirred in him as he looked at her, and under the pretext of arranging his papers, he observed her more closely.

She had gone to the window and was staring out. As she lifted her hand to pull back the curtain, a ray of sunlight entered, outlining her body in soft gold. Abel swallowed. Even at her young age, she had the figure of a woman, and he found himself imagining her naked, standing in the sunlight, beckoning him out to the garden. Dreamlike, his fantasy rolled on, and he could see her, her flesh white and unblemished, her breasts high and pointed, the line of her torso molding into slender hips and long legs. She would laugh, softly, reaching up to pull the pins from her hair, allowing the tresses to tumble in a rich auburn fall down her back. Green eyes would gaze at him with longing, and she would pull him down to lie with her on the grass. They would make love, there in the garden, her legs parting eagerly for him, her mouth open for his kisses. Her slim arms would encircle his neck, her lithe body would writhe under him in ecstasy, and she would moan his name again and again as he drove into her. So strong was the image in his mind, that Abel could actually feel the firm flesh of her breasts under his hands, the rising of her nipples as he caressed her, the sensuous movements of her legs as she gripped him, holding him close.

"Well, Mr. Bertram?"

He came out of his reverie with a start. The throbbing in his loins receded, reluctantly, as he forced control of his wild emotions. He could not allow himself to be affected by her, he reminded himself; if he did, all would be lost. There was business at hand—profitable business, if he watched his step. Clearing his throat, he tried again to make her see reason.

"Miss Rosslyn," he said, in what he hoped was a patient, fatherly tone, "I fear that I have not made the situation clear to you. It is impossible for you to remain here—" he raised his hand as Cynara moved angrily away from the window— "not only because it would be extremely improper for you to live alone, unchaperoned, but because this house is no longer in your father's possession. I'm afraid—" here his tone became gentle, for he wanted her to believe his sympathies were all for her—"that your father was unwise in his investments, with the result that . . . um . . . the house and all its contents will have to be sold to pay his debts. However—"

"I don't believe it! My father would never have been so careless. I know he wouldn't! There must be some mistake."

Bertram sighed. This was even more difficult than he had anticipated. "There is no mistake, Miss Rosslyn," he insisted, praying that she would believe him. "But as I was about to say, he did provide for your welfare. He made arrangements for you to go to a distant cousin . . ." He looked down, pretending to search for the name he knew so well." Her name is . . . let me see . . . Here it is. Mrs. Cornelia Ward, of Lyrebird Manor. You—"

"I won't go."

"I beg your pardon?"

"I said, I won't go."

"But, my dear Miss—"

"No."

Cynara stared at him defiantly for a long moment as he gaped at her, nonplussed. With an abrupt toss of her head, she resumed her pose at the window, but her emotions were in such turmoil that she was unaware of the pleasant garden scene outside. Unknowingly, her hand crushed the drapery she held as pain and anger rose swiftly inside her. How could this have happened? How could her father have done this to her? It seemed impossible to believe that only a short time ago she had been the center of her father's life, as he was of hers. They had grown so close since her mother had died four years ago, or so she had thought. It seemed now that she had been mistaken. She shut her lids tightly, forcing back tears. Taking a deep breath to steady herself, for she would *not* cry in front of this man, she faced Bertram again.

"I won't be a poor relation, dependent upon charity," she declared stubbornly. "I'm well educated; my father, for all his apparent weaknesses, at least saw to that. I can take a position as governess, or—"

The solicitor shook his head. "Impossible."

"But why?" she cried. "There must be something I can do!"

"There is. I've already written to Mrs. Ward. She is expecting you within the week. I might add that the reply I received from her was . . . favorable. She expressed her regrets that she is unable to send someone to accompany you, and cannot come herself. I gather she is somewhat of an invalid. But she assured me that you would be met at the station. Everything is arranged, Miss Rosslyn. You must remember that this was your father's last wish, and obey him."

Cynara was silent at this last thrust, and Bertram took the opportunity to conclude the distressing interview. She watched him quickly shuffle his papers into his case, take his hat and coat from the chair, and depart swiftly into the waiting cab.

Only after he had gone did she surrender to her conflicting emotions. Throwing herself into the chair he had vacated, she put her hands over her face, and this time when the tears sprang into her eyes, she let them come, for she had no will to stop them.

Cynara was dry-eyed three days later as she stepped off the train. She had stared unseeingly out the window during the long ride, her hands clasped tightly in her lap, trying to reconcile herself—as Bertram had insisted she must—to her new situation. She had failed utterly. Deep within her, warring against the sorrow and grief she felt over her father's death, was a burning resentment against him. She knew that she could never accept the circumstances that had thrust her so unwillingly into another's care.

It was ominous, she thought grimly, that Cornelia Ward, in responding to Bertram's letter, had failed to include a missive for her. She wondered if the omission was significant, and bitterly concluded that it must be. Cornelia. She had always disliked that name, for to her it conjured up a picture of a harsh and unyielding woman. And there was a husband and a son to wonder about, too. How would they feel about a penniless relation pushed so suddenly upon them?

It was impossible, she thought rebelliously. She simply couldn't go on with it, knowing that she would be dependent upon them for everything. The soundless, bitter cry rose in her again, as it had so many times over the past days:

What was she going to do?

The train lurched to a stop, and as Cynara resentfully gathered her things, she wondered what would happen if she simply chose to ride on. But she knew what would happen; she had little money, no place to go, and in the end she would be forced to return. Far better to arrive with her head held high, than to slink back in ignominy. And since she could not alter her penniless state (only for the time being, she assured herself) she could at least rely on her pride to see her through.

The station platform was deserted. Perhaps they had forgotten about her and she would be forced to return! Her spirits rose at the thought, then fell dejectedly. She had nothing to return to; already the house had been sold, and she knew she could not ask Bertram to supply lodgings until she could find the means to support herself. He had been adamant in insisting that she fulfill her father's wishes for her future. Future! What future did she have?

She thrust the thought from her mind and glanced around dispiritedly. The road that led away from the station was empty except for a heavy wagon lumbering toward her. A boy—a farm lad, judging from the rough clothing he wore—was driving it, and she prepared to call out to him and ask if he could send a message to the Manor to tell the Wards she had arrived. To her surprise, the wagon pulled to a halt as it came abreast of her.

"Are you Cynara Rosslyn?"

His voice was deep, startling her. She looked closely at the face under the cap carelessly pushed back onto his head, and saw that he wasn't a boy at all, but a young man, about two years older than she. He was waiting impatiently for her response, his dark eyes holding hers in an insolent manner that annoyed her immediately. She nodded haughtily.

"Yes, I am Miss Rosslyn," she answered. Was it possible that Cornelia Ward had actually sent this—this conveyance—to fetch her from the station? She allowed her glance to rest scornfully on the wagon before she raised her eyes again to the driver. "Are you from Lyrebird Manor?" she asked curtly.

"I wouldn't be here if I wasn't."

She glared at him; he stared back. To her fury, it was she who dropped her eyes first. She gestured to the trunk that had been placed on the edge of the platform. "My trunk," she said, and waited.

His expression mocked her high-handed attitude, and she felt herself flushing as he sprang easily from the high wagon seat to the ground. She watched him shoulder the chest as though it were no more than a featherweight, and suddenly ashamed of herself, she attempted a conciliatory smile as he passed her again to deposit the trunk among the bags and parcels in the body of the wagon. The smile faded when he ignored her, and she was angry again.

"I don't care to ride with a perfect stranger," she said coolly. "What is your name?"

He went to the other side of the wagon, looked at her across the seat, and said, briefly, "Evan Calder," before he sprang up again. He reached down a hand to help her inside.

Pointedly ignoring his outstretched hand, she put one foot on the high wheel, grasped the railing, and lifted herself up without his assistance. She landed ungracefully beside him, which did not improve her temper, and as she made a great business of arranging her skirts, she glanced covertly at him to see if he was laughing at her. He wasn't. In fact, he was busy unwinding the reins from the brake, and he took no notice of her at all. As soon as she was in, he touched the horse lightly with the reins, made a circle in the road, and started back the way he had come.

They rode in silence for some time. He had not spoken since his terse admission that he was from the Manor, and Cynara was annoyed, both with him for ignoring her, and with herself for wondering why he did so. Why should she care what he did or didn't do? She had obviously been correct in her first assumption; he *was* an ill-mannered lout. Why else would he continue to stare straight ahead, oblivious to her presence beside him?

All the same, she was uncomfortably aware of him. She stole another look at him, and saw that his jaw had an arrogant set to it, as did his mouth. The profile he unselfconsciously presented to her was not that of a coarse farm lad, and she felt her confusion deepen. Even his hands proclaimed fine blood, for tanned as they were from the sun, and calloused from hard work, the fingers were long and strong and supple. But relaxed as those hands were on the reins, there was about the rest of him a tension that communicated itself to her, and she was uneasy.

If he was aware of her scrutiny, he gave no sign of it, and because his continued silence irritated her, she finally asked, "Is it much further to the Manor?"

"Not far enough."

She saw that his hands had tightened on the reins at her question, causing the horse to lift its head in surprise, and his curt answer dismayed her, for the words held such a note of bitterness that her uneasiness increased. The feeling intensified when he turned to her for the first time and asked curtly, "Why did you come here?"

She felt herself retreating from the intensity in his hard, dark eyes, and she responded stiffly, "I'm afraid that is none of your concern."

He stared at her a moment longer, and though she wanted to look away, she could not. For a horrible instant, she thought she saw pity in his expression, and she began to say indignantly that she had no need of his sympathy, but he interrupted her curtly. "You're right. It is your own affair—isn't it?"

He turned back to his contemplation of the road, and she knew that his almost contemptuous tone had been one of dismissal. It appeared that he had already forgotten her again, and his indifference made her angry. She shifted as far away from him as she could, and pretended to examine the countryside as though she, too, had forgotten him.

It was close to an hour later when the high stone walls

appeared alongside the road. The wagon had turned off the main track at a small village, and they had been following a smaller path that wound down and around the edge of a forest for some distance before Cynara became aware of the wall that obviously encompassed a large estate. She had been determined to maintain frozen silence as long as her companion did, but at the sight of detailed wrought-iron gates that the wagon was approaching, she cried out with pleasure.

"Oh, do stop for a moment," she begged.

The gates were set into pillars that angled out slightly from the walls on either side, and as her companion wordlessly pulled the horse to a halt, Cynara saw that they formed an arch framing a gravel drive that began on the other side. The gates themselves were a work of art, for the iron had been forged with such delicacy that the form of a lyrebird was easily discernible. It was a stylized rendering, but even so, she could see the graceful curves of the lyre-shaped feathers, for which the bird had been named, fanning out and away from either side of its head. So finely drawn was the iron that every detail was clear, and Cynara exclaimed with admiration, not caring that her companion muttered impatiently as he lifted the reins again.

Further down the road was another gate standing open, and as the horse turned into it of its own accord, Cynara realized with apprehension that she had arrived at her new home. She glanced anxiously at her companion, but again he ignored her. Fifteen minutes later, they entered the stableyard of Lyrebird Manor, and her misgivings increased when she saw that the young man's profile was suddenly so rigid that it could have been made of marble. His tension communicated itself to her, and she glanced distractedly around the yard and then toward the house, which seemed to tower over her.

"Evan! Where in bloody hell have you been?"

Her companion tensed, and as Cynara looked in surprise at the burly man who had erupted from the stable and was rushing toward them, she also saw that a groom had paused in his currying of a horse and was regarding them gleefully.

"Evan! Did you hear me?"

"I heard you, Jacob," came the deadly quiet response from beside her. "And you know very well where I've been, since it was you who sent me in your stead."

Jacob's beefy face flushed with anger. He took a threatening stance in front of the wagon, raising his fist. "Don't you take that tone with me, you young bas—" He stopped, his eyes going to the white-faced Cynara.

His manner changed abruptly as he looked at her, and he actually leered at her before his head swung again to Evan and he shouted, "Those horse boxes need muckin' out, and the master has been wantin' his horse this past half hour! And you there, Jimmy," he roared suddenly over his shoulder, "get on about your business afore I box those big ears of yours!"

The virulent look that flashed from the groom's face toward Evan startled Cynara; she drew back from both of them and glanced nervously toward her companion.

Evan seemed unmoved by either Jacob or the groom. He had already climbed down from the wagon and was reaching up calmly to help her descend. Strong hands closed around her waist as she stood up shakily, and he lifted her down without effort. Their eyes met for an instant, and Cynara wanted to say something to him, but he had turned away abruptly. She watched him walk swiftly across the stableyard, Jacob following closely on his heels. Both disappeared into the stables, and an instant later there was the sound of fist meeting flesh. Involuntarily, she took a step forward, and then stopped at the knowing look in Jimmy's eyes as he giggled.

"You there! Cynara Rosslyn!"

Cynara turned at the peremptory call. A tall, heavy-set woman was standing in the doorway, beckoning imperiously to her. "Come here, girl. The mistress is waiting for you. Be quick about it!"

Cynara tensed. Never in her life had she been addressed in such a manner, and she would not have it now. "Are you speaking to me?" she asked haughtily.

The woman answered her in almost the same words Jacob had thrown at Evan. "Don't you take that high tone with me, miss. You can leave those fancy airs back where you came from, and get yourself over here."

Her face burning, uncomfortably aware that Jimmy's smirking attention had swung from Evan to her, Cynara approached the woman. Short of creating an unseemly scene in the yard, she could do little else, she thought angrily; but Mrs. Ward would certainly be immediately informed of this woman's appalling rudeness!

"Follow me." The woman, who was the housekeeper, judging from the heavy ring of keys fastened about her waist, whipped around and started off without looking back.

Her anger mounting with each step, Cynara followed her guide through the kitchens, up a steep flight of stairs, down a wide corridor to another staircase, and finally along a carpeted and paneled corridor, to a door before which the housekeeper paused.

"Mind your manners, girl. The mistress is having one of her bad days, but she would insist that you be brought to her as soon as you arrived. If you disturb her in any way, you'll have me to answer to."

The threat hung in the air, leaving Cynara speechless with anger. Before she could collect herself and respond to this outrageous attack, the housekeeper knocked briefly on the door, opened it at a faint response from within, and ushered Cynara roughly across the threshold.

The room was so dim that it took Cynara several seconds to adjust to the gloom. Heavy velvet draperies were pulled tightly across the windows, and a fire burned in the grate, adding its heat to the already oppressive stillness. Cynara felt a hand at the small of her back, and she threw a furious look over her shoulder at the housekeeper.

If Cynara had expected any offerings of sympathy for her recent bereavement, she was disabused of the idea at once, for from the couch came a sharp, "Come here and let me look at you."

Unwillingly, Cynara stepped forward, her nostrils contracting from the overpowering wave of eau-de-cologne that emanated from the handkerchief Cornelia Ward wafted delicately in front of her face. "Mrs. Ward, I—" she began.

"Kindly do not speak until you are spoken to," the woman snapped. She shifted position on the couch and added, "I think we should have one thing clear between us from the outset, and that is that I do not harbor any affection for the Rosslyns. I was not acquainted with your father, and did not know of his existence until I received the information from his solicitor. Indeed, I only consented to take you because that ridiculous man preyed upon my sense of duty. And I believe in doing my duty, however onerous or inconvenient."

Cornelia sniffed and fixed the bewildered Cynara with a grim stare. She raised a white, languid hand to press the handkerchief to her mouth before continuing. "Come closer," she commanded.

When Cynara obeyed, Cornelia surveyed her with such a disdainful expression that Cynara felt herself tensing under the scrutiny. In the silence that followed, Cynara observed the woman, and what she saw did not augur well for the future.

Everything about Cornelia Ward was thin and sharp. Her long body reclining on the chaise longue was draped in a peignoir of the finest silk, trimmed with feathers, but even the softness of the material could not modify sharp bones and meager flesh. Her face, framed in dull blond hair streaked here and there with threads of gray, was angular and pointed, her cheekbones seeming to cut into the skin of her face. Her nose was long and pinched, her mouth a narrow slash. Gray eyes, which could have been handsome for their deep color, were remarkable only for their expression of cold disdain and discontent. The eyes now regarded Cynara icily.

"Well!"

The single word was like a small explosion in the stultifying quiet of the room, and Cynara jumped. "Mrs. Ward," she began. "It is obvious that my coming has been"— she bit back the word mistake and substituted instead— "an inconvenience. Perhaps it would be—"

"Oh, it is definitely an inconvenience," Cornelia interrupted, "but we must manage as best we can." She motioned with one hand, and a woman Cynara hadn't noticed before stepped forward with a simpering expression as she looked at Cornelia. Cornelia ignored her and said, "I've decided that you may assist Briggs, here. She's getting on in years, and not quite the help she used to be to me. Perhaps if you apply yourself, girl, you may take her place when she is unable to continue."

"But, madam!" Briggs's voice was hoarse with shock, and Cynara herself was speechless. Did the woman actually mean that Cynara was to act as her *maid*? Briggs's expression was no longer simpering; the look she flashed at Cynara was pure hatred, and Cynara drew back.

"I've not finished speaking with you, girl!" Cornelia snapped.

"Mrs. Ward, I don't think you—" Cynara began angrily.

"Silence! How dare you interrupt me! I see that your father, whoever he was, failed to—"

"I won't have you speak of my father!" Cynara cried. "It was obvious that he had no idea what kind of—"

"Did you hear me?" Cornelia did not actually bang her fist on the arm of the chaise, but she gave the impression of doing so. Her face was livid, and she choked, "I told you not to interrupt me, girl. I won't have it! Apologize at once!"

"Apologize!" Cynara repeated incredulously. "For what?" She was so angry that her voice shook. She looked away from the sudden gleam in Briggs's eyes and took a deep breath. This entire situation was outrageous, but it wouldn't help if she lost her temper. She said as calmly as she could, "I said before that my coming here was an inconvenience, but I was in error. It was a mistake. I have no intention of remaining here, of that you may be sure."

"Your intention is of no importance to me, miss. If you expected to be treated as a member of the family, simply because your foolish father wished it so, that was your mistake."

Cornelia paused to give her words the desired effect, but again she had underestimated Cynara. Cynara, her eyes flashing, responded furiously, "I have no desire to become a member of this family. In fact, I—"

"That's just as well, then, isn't it? It might be wise for you to remember that you have no prospects, other than what I choose to arrange for you. I have offered to provide you with training that is suitable for your position. But there is, of course"—Cornelia's eyes snapped up to Cynara's face"—another alternative. Perhaps there is a farmer or other laborer hereabouts who wouldn't mind taking a wife who has no dowry."

Cynara was incredulous. "You don't mean to suggest that I marry—"

Cornelia Ward cut through Cynara's protest as though she hadn't spoken. "I've heard that the farmer's life is a hard one, but you appear strong enough; you might become accustomed to it in time."

"But I don't want to marry! And certainly not—"

"Your wishes don't concern me, girl. However, because I believe in being fair, I will allow you your choice: you may stay here, or . . . I can begin casting about for a marriage prospect for you. Which is it to be?"

Cynara was so outraged she was unable to speak. Cornelia continued smoothly. "Excellent. You may begin your duties by bringing me a soothing tisane from the kitchen."

As Cynara tried to speak over the indignation choking her, Briggs moved from behind the chaise, and almost dragged her out into the corridor.

"Don't think you can take my place, girl!" she hissed when the door was closed behind them. "I've worked too long and too hard to be put aside now!"

Cynara jerked away from her. "Don't be ridiculous!" she snapped. "I have no intention of usurping your position!"

"Just remember what I said, girl," Briggs warned, as she pushed Cynara toward the staircase. "I can make trouble for you if you try!"

It was impossible, Cynara thought angrily later that night. Utterly impossible. The woman was a heartless, cruel monster, and Briggs was no better. The two of them had found fault with whatever they sent her to do, until she thought she would scream with frustration. Only her pride had enabled her to get through the day, and by nightfall, even that was ragged. The strain had taken a toll on her nerves, and now, safe in the room she had been assigned, she paced back and forth. She wanted to break something, smash something; anything to give vent to the anger she felt. There must be somewhere else she could go; something else she could do beside waiting on that woman! And she would *not* marry anyone whom Cornelia selected for her. She would not. She could just picture the sort of man Cornelia would choose: a big, dull lout whose only interest would be in working his wife to death while she had one child after another. Oh, after today Cynara had no doubts about Cornelia's character, and she would not endure it. She wouldn't! Surely no one, least of all her father, would expect her to suffer this degradation, this humiliation. Even Mr. Bertram, if he knew of this situation, would not insist that she remain. She would write to him without delay and tell him that it was impossible for her to stay here.

Hot tears of self-pity slid down her cheeks; she brushed them away furiously as she looked about the dismal chamber the housekeeper, Mrs. Bascomb, had led her to earlier. Her trunk was in the middle of the room, its lid open, and Cynara went to it and slammed the lid down. Since she wasn't going to stay, there was no need to unpack.

Feeling considerably cheered by this defiant decision, she went to the small window that overlooked the stableyard. Opening the window, she leaned her arms on the sill and rested her head against the casement. It was nearly nine o'clock, but tired as she was, she knew she could not sleep. Looking down, she saw that the yard was deserted and dark, except for a single lamp that burned by the stable door, and she decided she would go out for a short walk. No one would notice if she stepped outside for a breath of air.

She had turned away from the window and was reaching for a shawl when there was a soft tap on her door. Her thoughts went immediately to Briggs, and she paused, bracing herself for another unpleasant confrontation with the woman. Her voice had an edge to it as she called permission to enter, and she vowed that whatever Briggs had come to say, she would not remain long. But the door was already opening before she finished speaking, and Cynara felt a flash of anger at Brigg's rudeness.

"What is it?" she asked, annoyance sharpening her tone. It was not the angular maid who stepped into the room. Cynara stared in surprise at the man who had entered and was standing there, appraising her silently, before he shut the door behind him. He was of medium height, scarcely taller than she, and it seemed that everything about him was some shade of brown. Thinning brown hair on a round, bullet-shaped head, bulging light brown eyes, a skimpy brown moustache valiantly attempting to embellish his thin mouth. He was even dressed in a tan suit, and Cynara's first impression was of a dull, nondescript, almost harmless man. When he began to speak, she knew she had been mistaken.

"So. You are Cynara Rosslyn," he said softly. The snuff-colored eyes bulged even more as his glance traveled slowly from the top of her head to the hem of her dress, and Cynara instinctively pulled the shawl closer. "I meant to visit you earlier, but alas"—the moustache twitched, and Cynara watched in horrified fascination as it lifted to expose his large teeth—"pressing business matters claimed my attention. Do forgive me, my dear."

Cynara suddenly wanted to shout at him to leave, for although he hadn't moved, it seemed that he had somehow stepped closer to her, and she was alarmed. Who was he? What did he want?

He anticipated her first unspoken question by bowing slightly. "I'm John Ward, the master of Lyrebird Manor. Are you frightened?" Cynara shook her head dumbly, unable to take her eyes away from his mouth, which was beginning to glisten with drops of saliva. "You shouldn't be frightened," he continued softly, insinuatingly. "I just thought we should become aquainted. After all, you are my . . . my ward—aren't you?"

He laughed to himself at the intended pun, and Cynara took advantage of his slight humor to say hesitantly, "Mr. Ward, it's very late, and—"

"John," he said.

"I . . . I beg your pardon?" she stammered.

"Call me John. I believe we're going to be friends—good friends—and it would only be natural for you to call me by my Christian name. Don't you think so?"

Cynara most definitely did not think so. She did not wish to be friends with this man, and certainly not in the way his tone implied. She didn't really know *what* his tone implied, but whatever it was, she wanted nothing to do with him.

"I'm afraid that's impossible," she said, striving to control the tremor in her voice. She saw him raise an eyebrow, and she plunged on, "Mrs. Ward has decided that I'm to act as her maid, and so . . . and so . . ."—she swallowed hard before continuing—"it certainly wouldn't be proper for me to call you by your given name, would it?"

"Ah, Cornelia!" he said, waving his hand negligently, and taking the opportunity to move a step closer to her. "Cornelia wouldn't have to know. It can be our little secret."

To her horror, he winked conspiratorially at her, and this time, in spite of her efforts, her voice shook as she said, "Mr.

Ward, really, I don't think—"

She started violently as his fingers closed around her wrist. In spite of his innocuous appearance, he was strong. She was imprisoned in a viselike grip.

"You have such beautiful hair," he murmured, raising his hand to touch the knot at the back of her neck. She tried vainly to cringe away from him, but his grasp tightened, and now, rigid with shock, she heard him say, "Such tresses should never be hidden from view . . ."

Helpless, she felt him pull the pins from her hair, and when it fell down her back to her waist, he grabbed a handful of it and twisted her head toward him. Panic-stricken, she saw the peculiar light in his eyes, and she tried to scream for help.

The scream was choked back into her throat as he clamped his hand over her mouth. "I wouldn't do that," he whispered. "You don't want to raise the whole house, do you?"

Her eyes wide with fear, she looked at him. "*Do* you?" he asked again.

She shook her head and he seemed satisfied, for the pressure against her mouth and nose abated slightly. She could breathe again.

"If you scream, I'm afraid I'll have to hurt you," he said. "Do you understand?" He waited for her nod, and then continued, "Now, I'm going to take my hand away, and you'll promise to be quiet—won't you?"

Cynara had never been so frightened in her life. When he released her, her eyes measured the distance to the door, and she wondered frantically if she could even command her legs to run. She was shaking so violently that she was afraid she would fall and not be able to get up again.

John Ward put an arm around her shoulders and hugged her to him. "There. I told you not to be afraid, didn't I?"

Woodenly, she nodded, not daring to look at him again for fear that he would do something worse. She shivered at the contact of his body against hers, and she closed her eyes, praying that he would let her go.

John had no intention of letting her go. He had wanted her from the moment he had first seen her, and he would have her, willing or not. In fact, he thought, his pleasure would be greater if she resisted him a little. He grinned to himself. He had always preferred a spirited chit to one who dumbly spread her legs for him, and he had an idea that the battle was just beginning with this one. His grin broadened as he held her hard against his side, enjoying the contact. She was trembling, frightened . . . and too proud to show it. Good, he thought. It was always more exciting this way. In the end, her pride would avail her nothing, and she would be forced to surrender to him.

The throbbing in his loins was becoming almost painful as he savored the moment before he would take her; he couldn't wait much longer. But he had to see all of her first. It was always better when he saw them. . . .

Before Cynara could defend herself, he grabbed the neck of her dress, ripping it down the front, tearing it away from her. God! she was even more beautiful than he had imagined. He gazed at her, sweat breaking out on his face as she tried vainly to cover herself. He gripped her arms, holding her as she tried to struggle away from him. He didn't hear her cries of fear and outrage; he was aware only of the sight of her.

He was accustomed to the stocky farm girls, the frowzy prostitutes in the city, the sturdy young maids at the Manor—but this girl! To compare her to the others was to compare a thoroughbred to a cart horse! He stared at her in fascination, admiring the long, clean, delicate lines of her body. She was slender, fine-boned; nothing about her was coarse, from the line of her neck to her small waist. Her skin was pearl-like, soft and luminous; her breasts were round, with a rosy aureole circling the nipples. He drew in a sharp breath at the sight, reaching out to touch her, to feel that smooth flesh under his fingers.

Frantic, Cynara tried to shove him away. He held on to

her, almost lifting her off the floor as she fought him. Dimly now he heard her cries, but he was too excited to heed them. Her body went taut with her efforts to escape him, to cover herself, and his blood drummed in his ears as he grabbed her by the waist. He wanted to see every bit of her, and he now tore away the remnants of her shift, propelling her toward the bed in the same motion. His passion for her was like a red tide, blotting out everything but his need. He could wait no longer.

Cynara beat at him with her fists, screaming for help. When she felt the edge of the bed against her knees, her terror was so great that she heaved upwards and broke away from him.

"Damn you! Come back here!"

He snatched at her, but his hands clutched air; she had already leaped the distance to the door.

"Let go of me!" she cried, flailing at him as he caught her again. "Stop! You can't do this! Let me go!"

His hand lifted to strike her; she cried out again and managed to get away from him a second time. Throwing herself forward, she strained toward the door. He had her again; she felt those hateful hands on her body, and she screamed. She couldn't see him for the tangle of hair in her eyes; she struck out blindly, felt her hand hit his face, heard him curse again.

Her attack had been futile. Lifting her from the floor, he carried her, kicking and screaming, to the bed. "I won't let you—"

He threw her onto the bed. As she fell, her head hit the bedstead, and she was dazed for the few precious seconds he took to unbutton his trousers. By the time he had flung himself on top of her, there was no escape.

His mouth sought her breast; the pain of his teeth on the nipple shot through her, making her arch her body, almost throwing them both off the bed. Distraught, she heard him laugh, as though it were all a game, and then, to her horror, she felt a hardness against her naked thighs. His legs were pushing hers apart in spite of her frantic efforts. He thrust himself against her, and she screamed in pure terror.

He grabbed her by the throat, choking her into silence. She clawed at his hands, trying to pry his fingers away from her neck. Bright lights flashed before her eyes; she couldn't breathe. His face was above hers, unrecognizable, distorted with passion. He bent his head, his mouth closed on hers, his hands gripping the soft flesh of her breasts, and in that instant a blinding, agonizing pain shot through her as he entered her. Her body went rigid with the shock of it, and she uttered a strangled cry that was lost in the harsh rasp of his breath as he thrust deeper and deeper.

The pounding of his body against hers seemed to go on and on. He thrashed above her, moaning, and she closed her eyes, waiting for it to be over, her mind a blank wall of shock. At last, a sound that was half sob, half groan, escaped him, and he stiffened on top of her before he collapsed, panting.

Was it over? It must be, because he was so still. She wanted to cry, to curse, to scream, but she could do none of those things. She could only stare, dry-eyed, at the cracks in the ceiling until he rolled off of her.

Her hearing seemed to have become acute. She heard him take a few steps away from the bed, heard the rustling sound his clothing made as he adjusted it. Only when she believed he did not intend to attack her again did she force herself to a sitting position. Wrapping the blanket around her, she clutched the edges of it with both hands. She was numb; the horror of the experience had not yet fully penetrated.

John Ward cleared his throat as he turned toward her. She saw the movement from the corner of her eye, and she started visibly, shrinking away from him as he approached her again. She would not look at him; if she did, the hysteria that hovered at the back of her mind would break free. Carefully, she kept her eyes averted as he began to speak.

"I'm sure you realize that this little incident will be kept between us? It would be a pity indeed if you were turned out simply because you failed to be discreet," he continued casually. "Terrible things can happen to a young girl who has no money, no place to go . . . ."

She closed her eyes, willing him to go away, to leave her alone.

"Do we understand each other?" He seemed to take her silence for aquiescence, for he continued approvingly, "Excellent. I'm glad you have decided to be reasonable."

Reasonable. Reasonable. The word echoed in her mind as he went to the door, opened it, and then shut it behind him. His going released something in her, and she sprang off the bed and ran to the door. Hysteria rose in her again as she realized that there was no lock, no bolt. How could she stop him if he came again? Wildly, she looked around the room, her eyes leaping from object to object until they came to rest on the dresser. It was not very big but she flung herself toward it and dragged it to the door. Panting, she pulled and shoved until finally she succeeded in pushing it solidly against the door.

Gasping, she bent over the top, leaning on her elbows with her head hanging down between her arms. She forced herself to take one deep breath after another, trying to calm the nausea that churned her stomach.

Sweat broke out on her forehead and she raised a shaking hand to wipe it away. It hadn't happened, she told herself over and over; it had only been a nightmare.

But she knew it had been no dream when she felt the blood between her thighs. Sobbing, she threw herself toward the washstand, and like someone possessed, she grabbed a cloth, plunging it into the cold water from the pitcher, scrubbing herself again and again, until her whole body felt raw.

She threw the cloth down and ran to the trunk. All the carefully packed articles of clothing were flung to one side as she searched wildly for a nightgown, and when she finally found it and pulled it over her head, she dropped into the chair, her knees drawn up close to her body to stop her shivering.

She would never be warm again; she would never forget that man's horrible touch, his violation of her body. Slowly, her head dropped until her forehead rested on her knees. To think how naively she had dreamed of her first time with a man! She had pictured a tender, loving scene, and herself responding to his caresses, returning his kisses. Never— *never!*—had she imagined a terrifying, brutal assault that left her degraded and humiliated, feeling nothing but disgust and revulsion. Was this what it was like being with a man? Every fiber of her body denied it, and she clung to her romantic dream in desperation, as if by picturing another time, another man, she could erase this night's horror. The fantasy, once conjured by her frantic mind, continued to grow, until it was so real that she could actually see the young man reaching out toward her.

The image in her mind was soft and blurred, as though she were looking at him through a veil. Sunlight touched his dark hair, the lean planes of his face, his broad shoulders and strong arms under the white linen shirt he wore. She could see his chest, for in her imagination, his shirt was unbuttoned; she could see his muscular legs under the tight breeches he wore. She could see . . . she could see the bulge of him, the unmistakable maleness of him, as he turned toward her, holding out his hand. It fascinated her, this outward manifestation of his maleness, and she wanted to learn more, much more. She wanted to see him naked, to see that masculinity revealed, she wanted . . . him.

She placed her hand in his, and his fingers were warm as they entwined with hers. She felt the hard, supple strength of his arm rubbing against her as they walked, and suddenly, they were in a forest glade, the sunlight slanting through the trees, a small brook trickling nearby. It was a place made for love, quiet and peaceful, with only the two of them to share, to unfold the dream.

She felt no fear as he gently pulled her down beside him on the grass, and his lips were firm and soft when he kissed her. She wanted him to kiss her again, to initiate her into the intimacy she longed for, but he embraced her instead, holding her head against his chest so that she could hear the hard pounding of his heart.

Slowly, tantalizingly, he began to caress her, his fingers following the line of her throat, tracing the contours of her shoulders, stopping just above the swell of her breasts. She wanted his hand on her breasts, stroking her, fondling her, kneading her flesh until she moaned with the sheer pleasure of it.

But his hand moved away again, cupping her chin instead, lifting her face to his. Now he brushed his lips across each eyelid, murmuring her name again and again.

Her need for him grew with each gentle kiss. She could feel desire surging through her, spreading like a white heat that demanded fulfillment, and still he held her, as though comforting a child. But in this dream she was no child; she was a woman, with treacherous longings, intolerable need. Her arms encircled his neck, bringing his mouth to her own trembling lips.

This time, as if he recognized her yearning, he kissed her—a man's kiss, hard and demanding, his tongue thrusting against her teeth, parting her lips, probing her mouth.

She felt like she was drowning in that kiss, in the shuddering waves of sensation it evoked, and she clung to him, unwilling to let him go.

Now his hand was at the buttons of her bodice; he loosened a few, slipped his hand inside. The touch of that hand against her bare skin set up a clamoring inside her that would not be denied, and still he did not move his fingers to her breast. That white heat was spreading, a pulsating tremor that heightened all her senses. She *wanted* him to touch her, longed for it, demanded it with every move of her body, and still he did not.

Every sense screaming, she pressed against him, her own

hands inside his shirt, kneading, rubbing, caressing him. This time it was she who pulled him down, and then suddenly, they were both naked, and she gloried in the ecstatic sensation of his flesh against hers.

But there was more she needed, much more. She wanted to feel him inside her, and she opened her legs as he slid over her. This time there was no searing, agonizing pain as he entered, but only a sweetness, a nameless joy of being truly united with him. They moved together, desire and passion mounting with each thrust, each motion of her hips and his bringing them ever closer to fulfillment. When he lowered his head to kiss her nipples, she held him there, her body throbbing with every touch of his tongue and lips on her tingling skin. His hands slid down her torso, to her waist . . . and beyond, and she arched against him, increasing the tempo of her movements.

The climax, when it came, shuddered up from deep within her, spreading in vast, pulsating waves through her entire body, calling her to ecstasy and beyond, causing her to hold him fiercely to her, laughing and crying at the same time with the utter abandoning of her self to him.

The dream disappeared abruptly, dissolving in the mist of her tears, and she looked around the dismal room dazedly, trying to remember where she was. Reality hit her with the force of a blow: she saw her torn clothing, the rumpled bed, and she remembered.

Huddling into a tight ball, she began to cry in earnest, and couldn't stop. It was some time before she recalled the face of the man in her dream, and when she remembered, her tears came even harder. The man had been Evan.

CHAPTER TWO

HOW LONG THE storm of weeping lasted, Cynara didn't know. She was exhausted, her eyes swollen and her head throbbing, when she finally lifted her head. For the first time, she was aware that she was shivering, not with fear, but from the cold. The room was icy, her hands and feet frozen. She looked toward the bed and shuddered, deliberately shutting her mind to what had happened there. Stiffly, she uncoiled herself from the chair and stood up. She must think what to do; there wasn't much time before morning.

She found her slippers and slid her feet into them. Then, lifting her shawl from the floor where she had dropped it, she wrapped it closely around her chilled body and tucked her hands inside its folds for warmth. Pacing back and forth, her glance carefully averted from the sight of the rumpled bed, she tried to think. She couldn't stay here after tonight; the idea was even more impossible than before. But if she left, where would she go?

She shook her head. What did it matter where she went, as long as she was away from this horrible house and the people in it? *He* had said that terrible things could happen to a girl on her own, but what could be worse than what he had done to her tonight?

Cynara stopped suddenly, her body rigid, as a hideous thought struck her. What if she were to have a child? Unconsciously, her hand went to her stomach, as though the unwelcome life was already within. What would she do if she had to take care of a child? How would she manage to support both of them? And worse yet, who would employ her after seeing that she was burdened with a baby?

Cynara resumed her agitated pacing, asking herself what she was going to do. She was not yet willing to accept the helplessness of her position, because to do so would admit the possibility of John Ward's return to her room, and she refused to think of that at all.

She was no closer to an answer hours later when the sound of activity in the stableyard drew her to the window. Surprised, she noticed the red and purple streaks of light in the sky, and realized that it was almost morning. As she looked down, she saw Evan harnessing two horses to a carriage, and several minutes later, John Ward appeared in the yard. Behind him was a servant carrying a bulging portmanteau, which he proceeded to put inside the carriage.

Moving away from the window, Cynara stood with her back to the wall, not daring to believe her good fortune. If only he would stay away for a few days, she would have time to send a letter to Mr. Bertram and beg him to rescue her from this house.

Before the carriage had clattered across the yard, Cynara had already found her writing case and was scribbling busily. Her pen fairly flew over the paper until she came to the reason she wanted to leave the Manor. She hesitated, biting the end of her pen. She couldn't possibly tell Bertram what John Ward had done to her; she would die of shame. And yet, would any lesser explanation cause the solicitor to act in her behalf? Bending over the half-finished letter, Cynara fought back tears. She couldn't tell Bertram the truth; he would just have to believe her when she told him it was impossible for her to remain here. Dashing the tears from her eyes, she wrote rapidly, begging him to understand.

She had almost finished the letter when a heavy knock on the door startled her. Wildly, she looked from the door to the window, telling herself that it couldn't be John Ward; she had seen him leave. But what if he had returned and she had been unaware of it? No, no, she was being ridiculous, allowing her fear to run away with her.

The doorknob turned as someone took hold of it. Cynara jumped up, clutching the writing case, and stared as the door rattled against the frame. But of course it wouldn't open, she told herself; the chest blocked the way and she was safe.

"Rosslyn! Open this door at once!"

Cynara recognized the housekeeper's voice, but still she couldn't move. The command came again, even harsher this time, and Cynara realized the folly of refusing to obey. Mrs. Bascomb could easily order the door broken down, and while John Ward might hesitate to do so simply because of the noise it would create, the housekeeper would have no such compunction; she would only consider it her duty. Reluctantly, Cynara went to move the chest out of the way.

"Just what is the meaning of this?" Mrs. Bascomb's face was livid as she was forced to squeeze through the partially open door. With a heave she shoved the chest toward the wall, surveyed the chaos in the room, and stared in outrage at Cynara. "Well?"

Cynara felt the blood rushing to her face. How could she explain? How could she even speak of the fact that John Ward had been in her room? She hesitated, searching for words, and finally muttered, "The door had no lock."

"The door had no lock," the housekeeper mimicked. "And for what reason, may I ask, do you need a lock on your door?"

There was no answer Cynara could give that would not lead to further questions, additional explanations; she remained silent, biting her lip.

"What is that you're holding?" Mrs. Bascomb asked abruptly.

Cynara looked down; she had forgotten that she still held her writing case. The letter was inside, and she knew that the housekeeper must not see it. Instinctively, she held it closer.

"Give that to me at once!"

"I will not! This is my private correspondence, and you have no right to see it!"

To her utter disbelief, the housekeeper's arm seemed to

shoot out across the short distance that separated them, and before Cynara could protect herself, the woman delivered a stinging slap across her face.

Gasping as much with surprise as with pain, Cynara put her hand to her cheek. Frozen, she watched Mrs. Bascomb retrieve the letter from the case she had dropped, and she was still unable to move when the woman read it.

"That Mr. Bertram isn't going to help you," the housekeeper said calmly as she tore the letter into small pieces.

"You can't be sure of that," Cynara snapped. "He was my father's solicitor, and—"

"Oh, I know who he is," Mrs. Bascomb said. She glanced contemptuously at the scraps of paper she held, opened her fingers, and allowed the pieces to drift to the floor. "Your Mr. Bertram has other interests, girl. It isn't wise to pin your hopes on someone who was willing to trade his integrity for a small share of your father's money."

"I don't know what you're talking about! My father left no money!"

"Didn't he!" Mrs. Bascomb shook her head pityingly, trying not to smile and ruin the effect. "And you believed Bertram when he told you that?"

"Of course I believed him!" Cynara said hotly. She stopped. There was something about Mrs. Bascomb's expression that made her pause. Was it true that Abel Bertram had lied to her? She shook her head, denying the possibility. It couldn't be; her father would not have trusted the man if he suspected him to be corrupt.

"Well, you can think what you like," the housekeeper said condescendingly. "Especially since it's too late now. Here you are, and here you will stay."

"Not necessarily," Cynara answered sharply. "You can't prevent me from writing to Mr. Bertram."

"Oh, can't I? I don't think the mistress would approve of your carrying on correspondence with her cousin."

"Her cousin!" Cynara was shaken, and she knew her expression showed it.

"Oh, you didn't know?" Mrs. Bascomb asked, smiling slyly.

"No . . . I didn't know."

"Well, that explains quite a bit then, doesn't it?"

"Does it?" Cynara hoped that she sounded calmer than she felt.

"I think it does. Enough to suggest that you accommodate yourself to your new position, since there isn't anyone to help you."

"Why are you telling me this?" Cynara demanded.

The housekeeper took a step toward her. "Because you're too cheeky by far, girl, and you needed to be put in your place. Since you're going to stay here, you might as well know from the first that I won't tolerate your fancy airs. Mrs. Ward might be the mistress, but I run this house. One word from me and you'll be out. Do you understand? And if you don't believe me, just try!" She glared at Cynara, almost daring her to make a reply, but Cynara said nothing; it was impossible for her to speak.

Mrs. Bascomb waited a moment more before going to the door. She paused with her hand on the knob and said curtly, "See to this room immediately. I do not allow slovenly habits in this house, and I will thank you to remember that."

Cynara nodded blankly without turning around, and when the door banged shut behind the housekeeper, Cynara closed her eyes, thankful to be alone again. She fumbled for the chair and sank into it, trying to convince herself that this was all a horrible dream from which she would soon awaken. Fighting panic, she gripped the arms of the chair and tried to think calmly about Abel Bertram. What did she know of Bertram. He *had* seemed relieved when he put her on the train, she remembered suddenly. But she had been too preoccupied, too absorbed in her own troubles to pay much attention to him. Now it was too late to wish that she had.

Was Mrs. Bascomb telling the truth? Of course she was,

Cynara thought bitterly. It had taken only those few words for Cynara to recall Bertram's uneasiness, his furtive shuffling of papers, his refusal to meet her eyes. And he had dared mouth those platitudes about duty and respect for her father's last wishes!

She sprang out of the chair, infuriated at the thought that she had been played for a fool. And she had been, she told herself, to believe that what that man had told her was true. Against all her instincts, against her own knowledge of her father and his methodical habits, she had believed Bertram. That he had taken advantage of her youth, her inexperience, her grief over Henry Rosslyn's death, was beside the point. She should have questioned, she should have demanded proof. She had only herself to blame.

And what was she going to do now? Angrily, knowing that the decision had already been made for her, she kicked at the clothing scattered on the floor. She had to stay here; there was no other choice. Savagely, she reached down and snatched up an armful of undergarments from the trunk. She would stay, she told herself, as she went to the dresser and jerked open a drawer, but only until she could think of a way to find a position—any position—elsewhere.

She threw the clothes into the drawer and slammed it shut. She would remain at Lyrebird Manor, but if John Ward came to her room a second time, she would be ready for him. Finding a weapon of some kind shouldn't be difficult, she thought fiercely. And if the chest in front of the door wasn't enough to keep him out, she wouldn't hesitate to defend herself with whatever came to hand.

Smiling grimly at the thought she turned to finish emptying the trunk. As she did so, she happened to catch sight of herself in the small cracked mirror over the commode. She went to it, staring at her reflection as if she had never seen herself before. And she hadn't, she thought; she had never seen the girl who had endured that hideous experience with John Ward.

Still staring at herself, Cynara slowly unbuttoned her nightgown and let it drop to the floor. Naked, she stood in front of the mirror and examined her body as though it belonged to someone else. Her hair fell over her shoulders, its dark, burnished color contrasting sharply with her skin. Bemused, she raised her arms, lifting the heavy mass of hair, noting the rise of her breasts as she did so. Still in that position, she turned sideways and looked over her shoulder, seeing the long slender line of her back, her round small buttocks, her slim legs. Her feet were small and narrow; her ankles delicate. Like the rest of her, she thought wryly, turning forward again. She had never needed stays, for her hips swelled gently from a tiny waist, and her breasts were naturally high and firm. She had none of the voluptuousness of figure that was so fashionable, and yet it had never mattered to her. Until now. What was it about her that had caused John Ward to become so impassioned?

Leaning forward, she looked critically at her face, wondering if the answer was there. She knew she was not pretty in the conventional sense—little bow mouth, round eyes, dimpled chin—for her features were too strong for fashion. Wide-set deep green eyes, slanted slightly at the outer corners, stared back at her from under arching black brows, and she shook her head. She had always secretly bemoaned her nose, for it seemed too straight to her, the nostrils flaring, just a little, instead of the cute button that was so desirable. And her mouth was too large, she thought, the lower lip pouting slightly; her chin was not dimpled, but determined.

Stepping back from the mirror, she assumed a haughty expression, as if disdainful of all the dimples and round eyes and cupid mouths found so readily on cuddly young girls. She might not be pretty, but there were other attributes that were even more important, she told herself stoutly—character and dignity and poise. Perhaps one day she would learn these, and more.

Somehow heartened by this searching, if inaccurate scrutiny, Cynara moved away from the mirror. She did not know, nor would she realize, for a long time to come, that she was indeed a beautiful young woman, and that many men would be impassioned to the point of madness by that beauty she refused to recognize.

CHAPTER THREE

"I'VE TOLD YOU before, miss, that frock is entirely unsuitable for your position. Go to your room at once and change!"

Cynara thought of the day Mrs. Bascomb had entered her room and searched the contents of her wardrobe. In the end, she had taken almost all of the gowns Cynara had brought with her, leaving only two plain wool frocks, and one sprigged cotton. When Cynara had protested angrily, the housekeeper had told her in a cold voice that she would not be needing the others, and she had whisked them away before Cynara could stop her. Cynara was wearing the green wool now, since Cornelia had objected to the lavender the day before.

"Why are you standing there, girl? Didn't you hear me?"

Cynara's eyes flashed as she responded to the sharp tone in Cornelia's voice. "I cannot, Mrs. Ward. I have nothing else, and the seamstress has not finished the dresses you ordered."

"Send her to me then—immediately. And take those gowns to be pressed."

Cynara snatched up the garments the smiling Briggs indicated. Turing on her heel, she left the room, seething with anger. Even after a week, she could not accustom herself to being treated as though she had no mind or will of her own, and must obey the slightest whim of the mistress without question. Mistress! Her lip curled at the word as she glared at the door she had closed behind her. And Briggs—*Miss* Briggs, Cynara corrected herself almost savagely—was no better. She was a petty tyrant when Cornelia's back was turned, completely self-effacing and meek when in Cornelia's presence. Cynara almost kicked the door in fury.

The seamstress, a timid little woman named Violet Harris, looked up fearfully as Cynara entered the small, cluttered room set aside for Violet when she was summoned to the Manor. She was working on an ugly black gown that Cornelia had ordered for Cynara, and Cynara, glancing at it, grimaced.

"It's almost finished, miss," the seamstress said anxiously. "And I can start the other one this afternoon." She gestured hesitantly toward the neatly folded pile of undergarments at her side, and continued in a frightened tone, "I would have had them done before, but Mrs. Ward wished me to complete those chemises first."

Cynara tried to smile reassuringly at her. The woman reminded her of a bird about to take flight. She spoke quietly, trying to quell the alarm her words would bring. "Mrs. Ward would like to see you, Violet."

Violet sprang out of the chair, dropping the uniform to the floor as she put her hands to her cheeks. "Oh, no!" she cried. "What have I done? Is she displeased?"

Cynara shook her head, reached down, retrieved the garment and put it on the worktable. She glanced around quickly, lifted the beautifully stitched chemises from the chair, and held them out. "Here. Take these to her. She can't help but be pleased, Violet. The workmanship is exquisite."

Violet rushed out, clutching the garments to her meager bosom, almost in tears at the idea that Cornelia might be dissatisfied. Cynara stood at the door, watching her go. Would she ever be like Violet Harris? So anxious to please, so terrified at the thought that she might have offended? She shook her head, denying the possibility of ever allowing herself to be so intimidated.

But the thought stayed with her all day, and as she ran back and forth for Mrs. Ward, each time growing more resentful and rebellious, she wondered if, in time, she would become so accustomed to taking orders that her pride would be beaten down and she would become another Violet Harris. Mrs. Harris was a widow, her only means of support was what she could earn by her sewing. What would she do if that support was denied her? How would she live? The thought was sobering, for Cynara realized that her position, while not the same as Violet's, was similar. If she offended or displeased Cornelia too many times, would she be turned out and forced to marry the farmer Cornelia threatened to find?

Cynara could not eat that night. The cook, a fat, comfortable-looking woman named Bertha, gave her a searching glance as she took Cynara's untouched plate away. Cynara smiled at her in apology. She liked Bertha, for the woman had been kind to her from the first. As she pushed back her chair and stood, Cynara said, "I'm sorry, Bertha. I'm just not hungry tonight."

"Huh! And no wonder, the way you've been running up and down all day!" Bertha looked at the plate she still held, and added, "Why don't you go out for some air? This meat pie will keep in the oven; you can have it when you come in again. Go on, now. It'll do you good."

The night air was cool on her face as Cynara stepped outside. She stood, indecisive, for a few minutes, and finally walked across the courtyard toward the garden. She had glimpsed the garden a few times from the upstairs windows and had admired it each time.

From her vantage point on the second floor, the garden had swept down and away from her, and as she had stared at it, she had begun to see the lyre shape that had been repeated on the entry gates. But here the form was living: two lines of yews fanned out gracefully at the borders, forming the arms of the lyre, while inside flowers blazed with every color imaginable. Gravel paths and walkways followed the curving yews, and all seemed to lead eventually to the four birch trees that formed the focal point of the garden. Tall, very old, the largest was surrounded by three slightly smaller trees; all were encircled by a short stone wall made for sitting upon. The branches of the trees bent and swayed in the breeze, at times almost touching the top of the wall that surrounded them, forming a living wall of green that hid their trunks.

As she gazed at the brilliant expanse of color, she realized suddenly that it had been some time since the garden had been cared for. The paths were overgrown with weeds, the yews needed clipping, and the froths of flowers that bordered every walkway were crying to be trimmed back. Still, the overgrowth gave it a wild beauty, and Cynara thought she would like to walk there sometime.

But now it was growing dark, and Cynara turned away; she had no desire to become lost in the garden, for as she had observed earlier, the paths curved over and back upon themselves, and the yews had grown so tall that, once inside, it would be difficult to see her way out if she became confused.

A sound from inside the stable caught her attention. Curious, she moved closer to listen. She heard a low murmuring followed by the nicker of a horse. She was about to walk away again, having no wish to confront Jacob or that grinning Jimmy, when a sharp exclamation made her pause. Without knowing why, she stepped inside the stable to listen.

The stable was dark, but there was a small lantern hung on one of the doors to a horse box. It was from inside this box that the sound came, and she moved closer to peer inside.

Evan was bent over a horse lying on the straw. The animal's coat was dark with sweat, and as Cynara watched, a powerful ripple of muscle contorted the smooth side of the mare. The horse struggled briefly, and Evan reached out a hand to soothe it. The mare lay back, breathing heavily.

Carefully, quietly, Evan moved toward the mare's head, and this time, when the contraction came, the horse heaved violently, trying to get to her feet. Evan held her head down, his face grim as the animal tried to fight him. Watching, Cynara must have made some sound, for Evan's head swung around and he looked up to see her standing there. Their eyes met, Evan's challenging, Cynara's wide with surprise.

"Something is wrong, isn't it?" she whispered.

"The foal's leg is caught," Evan replied briefly. He bent over the mare again as she began to fight the pressure of his hands on her head.

"Shall I . . . shall I fetch Jacob?"

"No."

"But—"

"I said no! Jacob can't be bothered; he's off somewhere with his bottle. Now, get out of here and leave me alone!"

"Can you . . . can you do anything?" The horse was lying quietly now, but Cynara could see that it was only gathering strength. Another contraction came, and the mare's legs flailed the air, narrowly missing Evan's head.

Cynara bit her lip, wondering what to do. The idea of trying to assist in the birth of a foal frightened her, for never had a horse seemed so huge, so powerful, as the mare lying in the stall. She wanted to turn around and leave, but the sight of Evan struggling alone made her hesitate again. Before she could think about what she was doing, she lifted the latch and gingerly stepped inside the horse box. Her eyes on the horse, she crept around to where Evan was kneeling, and whispered, in a voice that shook, "What can I do to help?"

It was Evan's turn to hesitate as he glanced quickly at her white face and frightened eyes. He began to tell Cynara to leave, but the mare strained again, fighting his hands. "Hold her head," he said curtly. "She mustn't get up until I've moved the foal."

"But what—"

"Just hold her—like this." He grabbed her hands and put them on the animal's head, pressing them down hard. "Can you do it?"

"I . . ." Cynara swallowed. "I think so."

He had already crawled away from her, and to her horror,

was reaching inside the mare with one arm. She bent her head quickly and saw the glazed eyes of the horse underneath her trembling hands. Without knowing what she was doing, she began to talk softly to the mare, as much to still her own panic as to soothe the horse.

Several long minutes later, she dared to raise her head again. To her relief, Evan had withdrawn his arm and was sitting back on his heels, watching intently. The mare gave one last groaning sound and, before Cynara's eyes, the foal slid from the birth cavity. Evan ripped away the membrane that covered it, and as the foal's head emerged, wet and shining in the lamplight, its ears plastered to its head, Cynara forgot her fear and gave a soft exclamation.

"It's alive!"

Evan nodded. "Let the mare go now."

Released from the pressure of Cynara's aching hands and arms, the animal lifted its head and gave a nicker. Reaching around to where her foal lay, the mare touched her nose gently to her baby.

"Come away," Evan said softly.

Outside the box, Cynara and Evan watched as the foal struggled to its feet. Seconds later, it was standing, bumping its mother's side, trying to find its source of nourishment.

Cynara whispered, "It will be all right now, won't it?"

"Yes."

Cynara kept her eyes on Evan's face as he gave his attention to the mare and foal. She couldn't believe this was the same young man who had kept his silence during the long ride to the Manor. His face was shining with sweat, his hair clinging damply to his forehead, but as he watched the mare nuzzle her baby, his expression was tender. In that moment, he looked young and happy, his face without the bitterness that added years to his features.

Together, they watched the foal. It was tired now, its eyes almost closed in exhaustion as it folded long legs and plopped down ungracefully on the straw. Cynara uttered a soft sound of delight at the picture of the mare standing careful guard over her sleeping baby, and when she lifted her eyes to glance at Evan, she saw with surprise that he was watching her instead of the scene before them. Before she could speak, he put his hand over hers and said quietly, "Thanks for your help. I couldn't have done it alone."

His fingers tightened, and Cynara was alarmed at her response to his touch. She was too aware of him, standing so close to her there in the darkness and warmth of the stable, and she wanted to withdraw her hand from his. She could not. To her horror, she actually wanted to move closer to him, to feel more than the slight pressure of his hand. She glanced away from him, knowing that he was still staring at her intently as if caught up in some emotion of his own.

The silence vibrated between them, and her feelings were chaotic. She did not understand what was happening to her, and she was both frightened and excited by it. A picture of herself in Evan's arms, of his mouth on hers, and his body pressing against her flashed into her mind, and abruptly she pulled her hand away, her face flaming at the powerful image her thoughts evoked. What was she thinking of? But as much as she tried to ignore her turbulent feelings, her fingers seemed to burn where Evan had touched her.

"Cynara—"

There was a clattering of hoofs on the cobblestones outside. At the sound, the mood, whatever it had been, was lost. When she looked at him again, Evan's face had lost its tenderness and had become shuttered once more. Seconds later, a high, shrill voice rang out. "Evan! Come and take my horse!"

Evan stiffened. He turned abruptly from her, and Cynara, bewildered at the sudden change in him, ran after him. "What is it?" she asked, pulling at his sleeve.

He jerked away. "Get out of here before he sees you!" he hissed. "If he catches you in the barn, there will be trouble!"

"But why? I haven't done—"

"Go!"

But it was too late. A shadow filled the doorway, and

both Cynara and Evan turned toward it.

"Evan! Did you hear me? I said—what's this? Well, well . . ."

The shadow became a young man, limping badly as he advanced. He surveyed them both, his eyes lighting maliciously as he looked past Cynara to Evan.

Cynara watched the newcomer warily. He did not appear much older than Evan, but they were opposites in every way. Where Evan was tall, and lean to the point of thinness, this boy was short, scarcely taller than she, and so round that his waistcoat strained across the bulge of his stomach. He had a barrel-shaped chest that tapered to skinny legs, a large, round head topped by tightly curled blond hair, a complexion so fair that his brows and lashes seemed almost nonexistent. His eyes were mere slits in folds of fat, but they glittered evilly as he stared at Evan. He frightened Cynara, and when he spoke again, she started nervously.

"Well! So the mighty are fallen at last, are they?" he addressed Evan with a sneer. "I wouldn't have believed it if I hadn't seen it with my own eyes. How very interesting!" His pale eyes gleamed in the lamplight as he swung back to Cynara. "Come here, girl. I haven't seen you before, but if you have caught Evan's fancy, perhaps it would be well for me to sample your charms also."

Cynara sensed, rather than saw, Evan's violent movement forward, and she stepped in front of him quickly. She had no desire to be the cause of a confrontation between Evan and this horrible young man who could only be Cornelia's son, Myles. Frightened as she was of him, she forced herself to regard him coldly. "I would prefer," she said, "that you did not speak to me in such a manner. I—"

"What is your name, girl?"

"Stop calling me girl!" Cynara said sharply. Again, she was aware of Evan's quick movement behind her, but she continued. "My name is Cynara Rosslyn, and I won't stand here and listen to your rudeness. Now—let me pass!"

That Myles was taken aback by this attack was clearly

evident in the almost comical look of surprise on his face. He stared at her in pure amazement as she glared back at him, but his astonishment was short-lived. The look of surprise was quickly replaced by outrage, and he raised the cane he carried with a threatening gesture. "How dare you!" he cried in a choked voice. "Do you know who I am?"

Cynara raised her chin. Their faces were almost on the same level, and she looked directly into his eyes as she replied clearly, "Certainly I know who you are. But that does not excuse your ill manners. I won't be intimidated by your threats."

Myles's face was crimson. His fingers tightened around the stem of the cane as he gripped it in sudden rage, and Cynara thought for a horrified instant that he would actually use it against her. The wild look in his eyes frightened her, and just as she tensed to run by him, Evan stepped in front of her.

"Stop it, Myles," Evan said, his voice low and threatening.

"Get out of the way, Evan! This isn't any of your concern!" Myles stopped abruptly, his glance swinging from Evan to Cynara and back again. "Or is it?" he asked insinuatingly. "Are you actually championing this girl, Evan? Have you forgotten what happened the last time?"

Evan went rigid, every muscle in his body taut, as though he would spring on Myles.

Myles saw the movement and his sneering expression disappeared. It was with real fear that he raised the cane even higher and waved it wildly in Evan's face. "Don't you come near me!" he shrieked.

"Myles? Myles! What's all the shouting in here?"

Cynara started violently at the sound of the voice from the doorway. It couldn't be he, she thought frantically; Jacob had returned several days ago with the empty carriage and had not been sent out again to bring John Ward home. But the hated voice continued, and Cynara knew she had not been mistaken. "Where's that damned Evan? I want these horses taken care of at once!"

Myles had lowered his cane after a quick glance at Evan to make sure he hadn't moved. As he swung around to reply, Cynara noticed for the first time the misshapen foot that hampered his movements and made him appear clumsy. Pity stirred briefly in her, but was gone the instant Myles turned back to her again. "Come here a moment, Father," he said, over his shoulder. "There's something here I think you should see."

"What? What are you talking about?"

John Ward stepped impatiently inside the stables. "What's this, Myles? It's damned late, and I—"

He stopped at the sight of Evan standing protectively in front of that girl—what was her name? He couldn't remember, but the picture of long, slender legs flashed into his mind—and his eyes narrowed. He glanced again at her, speculatively, and wondered if he had misjudged her. Was she really a sly little baggage instead of the terrified innocent she had pretended to be? Was she after something more than a romp with the master? He thought of Cornelia and the trouble this girl could cause should she let something slip about that night. He wasn't in the least afraid of his wife, but it was a bother when she discovered his infidelities, especially when they occurred under her own roof. Cornelia always expected to be rewarded in some suitable fashion after these incidents, as though a new trinket or gown would make up for the suffering she endured at the hands of her philandering husband. As if it mattered a damn to her anyway, he thought irritably.

He forced his thoughts away from his wife and focused again upon the defiant pair in front of him. Myles was saying something, and he turned to listen to his son.

". . . seems that Evan discovered her first. I found them together when I came in."

Cynara had recovered somewhat from the shock of John Ward's sudden appearance. Seeing him again had caused her to relive the terror of her experience once more and although she was afraid of him, she could not allow Myles's insinuation to go unchallenged. She stepped out from behind Evan and, praying that her voice would not shake, she said, "Your son judges too hastily. It was not as he thinks."

"Are you calling me a liar?" Myles shrilled.

"No," Cynara answered as calmly as she could. "It is just that you are mistaken."

"Oh, I wasn't mistaken! Father—" Myles turned triumphantly toward John Ward, but Evan's voice cut harshly into whatever he had been about to say.

"The girl helped me with the mare. That was all."

"Indeed?" John Ward's voice was heavy with sarcasm as he continued. "And in my absence, is it your habit to lure my servant girls to the barn to assist you in your chores?"

"He didn't lure me into the stable!" Cynara cried as Evan flushed angrily. "I was taking some air, and I heard—"

John Ward turned a forbidding glance on her, and Cynara fought the urge to shrink back. He said sharply, "And you, girl, had no business being outside at this time of night. I will discuss your behavior at some other time, but in the future, I will expect you to attend to your duties, and—" he looked across to the grimly silent Evan "leave others to theirs. Is that understood? You may go."

Cynara was angry and frightened at the same time. How dare this man assume that she . . . that she and Evan . . . She couldn't complete the thought even in her own mind. And what did he mean when he said he would discuss her behavior with her at another time? She felt a sharp stab of fear at the thought that he intended to visit her room again, and it took a fierce effort of will for her to walk calmly past him and out of the stable.

Once outside, she didn't look back. Picking up her skirts, she raced across the yard, and didn't stop until she had reached her room and slammed the door. She shoved the chest across the door again, but all that night she couldn't sleep; the slightest noise in the corridor startled her awake, her fingers tight around the fireplace poker she had taken from an unoccupied guest bedroom. John Ward didn't come that night, but she had seen the look in his eyes, and she knew it was only a matter of time before she heard him at her door.

CHAPTER FOUR

MYLES WAS WITH his mother when Cynara entered the sitting room carrying Cornelia's tea tray. Cynara hesitated on the threshold when she saw him, but Cornelia turned toward her and snapped, "Well, bring it in, girl. Why are you standing there?"

Unwillingly, Cynara crossed the room to deposit the tray on a table. She was aware that Myles's pale eyes followed her as she did so, and she kept her eyes averted from him. She had tried to avoid him as much as possible after their first encounter, but when he stepped in front of her, blocking her way, she glared at him. He pretended to examine the contents of the tray, lifting the silver covers with a casual air that immediately annoyed her. She went to brush by him, but as she did so, he reached out and pinched her on the arm.

Cynara gave an exclamation of surprise and pain, and the dishes tilted alarmingly on the tray. Furious at his childish trick, she glared at him again, but he had already moved away, an exaggerated expression of innocence on his face.

"Really, Mama," he said, with a sideways glance at Cynara, "is she always this clumsy?"

Cornelia glanced lovingly at her son as he went to stand beside her, and Cynara fought down the urge to hurl the tray straight into their faces. With a great effort at control, she set the tray on the table in front of Cornelia, and stepped back. She was aware of Myles smiling slyly at her over his mother's head.

"Is there anything else, Mrs. Ward?" she asked stiffly.

"Yes," Cornelia said sharply. "There is. You may bring another cup for my son. And take my lilac silk from the wardrobe and press it. I will be needing it tonight."

Cynara, her mouth a tight line, went to fetch the gown, and Myles said, "But Mama, surely you don't intend going out tonight? You must think of your health!"

Her back to them, Cynara grimaced at the honeyed sweetness in Myles's tone, but Cornelia, hearing only the concern in his voice, answered bravely, "I know, dear. But your father insists. After all, Hiram Brakewell *is* a banker, and I suppose I must take that into consideration, as your father suggests." Cornelia paused, and when she spoke again, there was a pleading note to her voice. "Myles, would you come with us? I would so love to have you join us—and that darling Eloise will be there. I hear that that French school has done wonders for her. Why, she will be the life of the party!"

"Eloise!" Myles scoffed. "The most expensive school in the world will not alter that doughy face of hers!"

"But she will have a handsome dowry, Myles. You must think of—"

"Hush, Mama," Myles interrupted as Cynara took the gown from the wardrobe and turned to leave. He watched her walk to the door, and then said abruptly, "I cannot have tea with you after all, Mama. Excuse me, please."

"But, Myles—"

"I will be in later, Mama."

Myles followed Cynara out the door, in spite of his mother's protestations. Cynara ignored him as he came down the corridor after her, the memory of that painful pinch still fresh in her mind, and when he reached out and pulled her around to face him, she regarded him coldly.

"What do you want, Myles?"

Instead of answering, he forced her back against the wall, his hands on either side of her, pinning her there. Cynara was so surprised that for an instant she couldn't move, but when he leaned forward, his body pressing against hers, she dropped Cornelia's gown with a cry, and raised both hands to push him away.

"Myles! What are you doing? Leave me alone!"

"What's the matter, Cynara?" he asked. "Or is Evan the only one to be favored with your attentions?"

"I don't know what you mean!" She beat at his chest with her fists, but he seemed impervious to the blows, and she was beginning to be frightened.

"Oh, I think you do," he continued. "After all, I did find you in the stable together that night, didn't I?"

"I told you you were mistaken! Myles, if you don't let me go—"

"Oh, so nothing happened, did it?" He shook his head, smiling slyly. "That's not what Evan says."

Her shock was so great that she paused. "I don't believe you," she said harshly. "And if you don't leave me alone, I'll—"

"You'll what?" he challenged. "Tell my mother? My father?"

He grabbed her suddenly. His arms went around her and he pulled her away from the wall toward him. She wouldn't have believed him to be so strong, she thought in a panic as she fought to get away from him. She was trapped in the circle of his arms, and she could not break away. His face came closer and closer to hers, and when his mouth covered her own, she gave a strangled cry of revulsion. The next instant, she felt his hand on her breast.

His touch seemed to burn through her gown to her bare skin, and she reacted violently. She reared back with such strength that he was almost flung from her. Staggering on his lame foot, he lost his balance and crashed to the floor. She stood over him, gasping, and when he looked dazedly up at her, she hissed, "Don't you ever touch me again, Myles! Do you hear me? Never!"

Without waiting for him to respond, she whirled around and ran blindly for the stairs at the end of the corridor. It wasn't until she was almost at the top that she saw the flicker of a black wool skirt disappearing around the corner, and she stopped, her hand going to her mouth in dismay. Black wool. It had to be Briggs, she thought, and if Briggs had witnessed that horrible scene, Cynara knew she would waste no time reporting it to her mistress. But Cynara couldn't think of that now; she must get away from Myles.

Throwing a hurried glance over her shoulder, almost expecting Myles to appear suddenly behind her to attack her again, she saw that the stairs were empty. Lifting her skirts again, she dashed along the corridor to her room.

Cynara slammed the door behind her and stood with her back to it, panting. Her mouth burned where Myles had kissed her, and she took out her handkerchief and rubbed it furiously across her lips. Evan's darkly handsome face flashed before her eyes, and the contrast between Evan and Myles with his pale eyes and fat cheeks and fleshy lips was so great that she uttered a cry, putting her hand over her eyes, trying to shut out the repulsive picture of Myles.

Treacherously, now that she had thought of him, her mind fastened on Evan, and she knew that if it had been he who stopped her in the corridor, he who tried to kiss her, her reaction would have been entirely different. She would not have been frightened or repulsed then; she would have desired his kiss, thrilled to the press of his body against her.

Her cheeks flamed at the picture conjured in her mind—a picture of Evan's strong arms on either side of her, of his face close to hers. She imagined him kissing her, a long and deep and demanding kiss, his tongue hot inside her mouth, his hands roaming her body, his touch burning even through her clothing. Her legs became weak at the thought, and she wondered wildly what was the matter with her, that she could think of Evan at a time like this.

Wrenching her thoughts away from Evan and her trembling response, she passed a hand over her eyes, trying to get control of herself. She mustn't think of Evan now; she must decide what to do.

Moving away from the door, she fumbled blindly for a chair and sank down into it. She had managed to escape Myles this time, but what if he tried to attack her again? How could she possibly be on guard against both Myles and his father? She shuddered and rocked back and forth on the chair, trying to think. Disgust and revulsion swept through her as she remembered the way he had kissed her, the horrible touch of his hands on her, and for a hideous moment, she thought she would actually be ill. The memory of that night John Ward had raped her rose up in her mind, and she thought wildly that if Myles tried to do the same, she would kill herself. She would, she would!

A soft tap on the door brought her to her feet with a rush. She whirled to face it, expecting Myles to burst through and confront her. The tap came again, this time followed by a "Miss? It's me, Rosie. Are you in there?"

She was so relieved that she almost stumbled in her haste to open the door. Rosie, one of the chambermaids, a girl about her own age, to whom she had spoken several times, stood on the threshold, almost hidden by the voluminous folds of Cornelia's gown.

"Did you drop this, miss? I found it in the corridor, and—" Rosie hesitated, her eyes going to Cynara's white face. "What is it, miss? You look—" She hesitated again, and to her surprise, Cynara pulled her inside the room, slamming the door behind her.

Rosie looked closely at Cynara as she stood with her back to the door. "Something happened, didn't it, miss?" she asked quietly.

Cynara's head jerked at the question, and Rosie nodded to herself. She put Cornelia's gown on the bed and led Cynara away from the door and to the chair. Gently, she pushed the unresisting Cynara into it.

"Oh, Rosie!" Cynara said in a choked voice. "What am I going to do?"

Rosie looked down at the bowed head, and was amazed at herself for actually putting her hand out and stroking the bright hair. Until this moment, she had been a little in awe of Cynara Rosslyn, for she had realized from the first that this girl was not of her own class. She didn't act it, Rosie admitted to herself; oh no, she never put on airs, but still . . .

"You mustn't upset yourself so, miss," Rosie said quietly.

"Oh, Rosie!" Cynara said again. "You don't know what—"

"I know, miss. I know. Yes," she added, as Cynara raised horrified eyes to her face, "He's tried it with me, too." She paused, and then said, even more softly, "Both of them have. Which one was it with you?"

Cynara shook her head. "It . . . it doesn't matter. But, Rosie—" She swallowed painfully. "What did you do?"

"Do, miss? What could I do?" Rosie's voice was bitter as she added, "I wanted to keep my position, miss. My ma has six others to care for, and she needs the bit I can send her."

"But Rosie!"

"Aye, you can say, 'but Rosie'—that doesn't alter the facts, miss. I did what I had to do, and after it was over, I kept my mouth shut."

Cynara shuddered. "How horrible for you," she said, her voice low.

Rosie nodded. "Aye. And for you and all, miss. There's not a one of us that hasn't had to put up with that business." Her tone hardened as she added, "The mistress doesn't care about the master, but it's a good job she hasn't discovered her son's playin' about, for you can bet it would be us she'd send packin', and not him. Oh, no; the sun shines out of Master Myles, and that's the way it's goin' to stay." She saw Cynara's shocked expression and continued quickly, "It's best that the mistress doesn't know what he's up to, miss, believe me. There'd be hell to pay, and we would be the ones payin' it. So don't you let on—"

"But—"

Rosie shook her head fiercely. "No! There was a lass afore I came that young Master Myles dropped—"

"Dropped?"

"She was goin' to have his child," Rosie said, with a trace of impatience at Cynara's ignorance. "And she made the mistake of tellin' the mistress about the high jinks her son was up to—"

"And?"

"She was out of the place within the hour, bag, baggage, and no wages for the time she had comin'."

"How awful!"

"Aye. So you can see that it's best for you to keep this business to yourself . . ." Rosie paused and looked closely at Cynara. "He didn't . . . ?"

"No, no." Cynara shook her head quickly, unable to meet Rosie's eyes. She could feel the color flooding her face and she turned away, only to turn back again at Rosie's next words.

"Well, if he does, you go to Cook. Sometimes, if you aren't too far gone, she can do somethin' for you."

Rosie bit her lip as Cynara looked blankly at her. She felt a rush of pity for this girl who, despite her education and class, did not understand what she was trying to say. She hesitated, seeking the right words, and finally finished weakly, "If somethin' happens, you go to Cook. She'll know what do do—understand?"

Cynara wasn't sure she understood, and what was more, she didn't know if she wanted to understand. How could she go to the cook and tell her what had happened, let alone ask for her help? It was impossible; she couldn't make herself confess her shameful secret to anyone. But Rosie was looking at her expectantly, and so she nodded. Rosie seemed satisfied, for now she gestured toward the bed where Cornelia's gown lay in a heap, and she said, "I'll take that and press it for you. Maybe it would be best for you to rest for a while."

When Rosie had gone, Cynara went listlessly to the window. Her head resting wearily against the casement, she stared across the roof of the stables to the woods beyond, and thought that she would like to lose herself in those green shadows and never return. Scraps of Rosie's conversation flickered through her mind, and she felt weighted down by the hopelessness of it all. She had no doubt that Rosie had spoken the truth about Cornelia shielding her son against any accusation, and she knew that John Ward would protect

Myles, as he protected himself. What could she do—who could she turn to—if either of them tried to attack her again?

She was about to leave the window when she saw Evan come out of the stable. Her eyes narrowed as she watched him stride quickly across the yard, for now she remembered Myles's sneering remark about her and Evan. Had Evan really lied about her? She thought of the warmth they had shared in the success of the foal's birth; that moment of companionship in which he had appeared almost happy. Why had he lied?

Evan paused to glance swiftly up at the house, and Cynara moved back from the window. Hidden from view by the curtain, she watched him disappear around the corner of the stable and reappear a few minutes later heading into the woods. When he was lost from sight, she turned away.

Bitterly, she thought that until now she had been an innocent where men were concerned; she hadn't realized that her father, who had been kind and honorable, was an exception. It was clear to her now that men were liars, determined to have their way with women, strong and ruthless enough to seize what they wanted without compunction. Even Cornelia, who seemed so formidable, could not demand faithfulness from her husband; John Ward took what he wanted here in her own home, and his wife was helpless to prevent it. And if Cornelia was helpless, how much more vulnerable was she?

When Cynara was summoned that evening to assist in Cornelia's preparations for the party that night, she entered the room almost defiantly. If Mrs. Ward mentioned the incident with Myles, Cynara was prepared to defend herself, despite Rosie's warnings to the contrary. But Cornelia said nothing; after giving her a single sharp glance that Cynara was unable to interpret, she turned back to her dressing table and the minute inspection of her face in the mirror, leaving Cynara to wonder if she knew.

But of course she knew, Cynara thought as she saw Briggs emerge from the dressing room to the side. One look at the maid's glittering eyes and smug expression convinced Cynara that Briggs had wasted no time in telling her mistress about the scene in the corridor, and Cynara was surprised that Cornelia had not immediately accused her. But if Cornelia thought to make her feel guilty by her silence, she was mistaken, Cynara thought angrily. It was Myles who had attacked her, and if there were any accusations to be made, she would make them.

But there was no opportunity either to accuse or defend, for the next hour was exhausting. Cornelia was by turns petulant and demanding; nothing satisfied her, not even the elaborate coiffure that Briggs created for her. By the time Mrs. Ward was at last ready for the evening, Cynara was so tense that she thought she would scream if the woman demanded one more item from her vast wardrobe. The apartment was a shambles, articles of discarded clothing scattered all around, the dressing table littered with open jars and bottles. As Cynara held Cornelia's evening cloak, she thought resentfully that she would be expected to return everything to its proper place before she could escape to the dubious comfort of her own room. She was so weary that the thought brought tears to her eyes, and she did not see John Ward until he was standing beside her, gesturing at the cloak in her hands.

"I'll take that," he said.

He reached for the garment, and as he did so, his hand covered hers for an instant and he squeezed it before she had time to snatch her fingers away. Cynara shuddered, fighting down her fear of him, and looked away. She saw that Cornelia had paused in her self-absorbed inspection before the mirror and was watching them in the glass, and Cynara wanted to scream at her that John Ward's gesture was not her fault; she hated the man and everything about him.

But John had seen his wife's face, for now he moved

quickly to where she was standing. With a murmured "You look enchanting, my dear," he put the cloak around her shoulders.

Cornelia stared at him for a moment before she shrugged out from under his hands. She turned abruptly away to snap an order at the simpering Briggs, and Cynara was horrified when she saw John's eyes meet hers in the mirror; one eyelid dropped in the ghost of a wink at her over Cornelia's head. She looked quickly at Cornelia, but the woman was absorbed in pulling on her long gloves, and hadn't seen the gesture her husband had made. Shivering, Cynara busied herself with the mound of discarded clothing on the bed.

"Briggs, you may wait up for me," Cornelia said as she and her husband went to the door.

Briggs bowed her head in acknowledgment, the picture of the perfect servant, but as soon as the door closed behind them, she turned on Cynara with a hiss. "Don't think I haven't seen what you're up to, girl!"

Cynara stopped folding clothing and turned to the maid. She was still shaken, but she did not want Briggs to suspect the reason why. "I don't know what you mean," she answered as coolly as she could. Briggs had come up to her and was standing so close that Cynara could see the pores in the skin of her long nose. She moved back a step and the tall, lathelike figure moved with her.

"Oh yes, you do. And if I'm not blind, the mistress isn't either, you can be sure of that!"

"I don't know what you're talking about!"

Briggs jerked her head scornfully. "I've seen you, girl, don't think I haven't." She pushed her face even closer to Cynara. "Just remember this—there's been others who thought themselves too clever by far, and lost their place because of it. And where will you go if you're turned out?" Briggs answered her own question with a satisfied nod. "The workhouse. And don't think I would mind seeing you there, miss. Oh yes, indeed I would!"

Cynara took a deep breath, trying to control her temper.

If she became angry and said something she shouldn't, she knew Briggs would report it immediately to her mistress, and it would be one more piece of evidence against her. With a great effort, she kept silent, trying not to see the maid's triumphant expression.

Briggs looked around the disordered room and said, "I want everything set to rights before you retire. And *I* will wait up for the mistress; you won't be needed."

The maid sailed out, and Cynara made a face after her. If Briggs wanted to stay up all hours of the night waiting for Cornelia's return, she was welcome to it, she thought contemptuously; it was certainly no privilege in Cynara's estimation.

By the time Cynara finished restoring order from the chaos Cornelia had left behind, it was late, and she was exhausted. Briggs had not returned, and as Cynara worked alone, she muttered resentfully to herself.

How she hated this room; how she hated this whole house and everyone in it! Angrily, she shoved the stoppers onto the crystal bottles scattered about the top of the dressing table, and wondered how Briggs could possibly think she wanted to usurp her place as Cornelia's maid. The very thought was ludicrous! She snatched up a box of handkerchiefs that Cornelia had gone through peevishly and then discarded, and stuffed them all back haphazardly into the box before shoving it into a drawer. She slammed the drawer shut. Cornelia's maid! She *would* go to the workhouse first, she thought as she savagely jerked the door open again to fold the kerchiefs properly. Turning, she bundled a silk chemise into a ball before pushing it far back into another drawer. Briggs could keep her position, and welcome to it!

She looked around the room, spied a lace-trimmed petticoat on the bed and threw it into the wardrobe, where it fell in an untidy heap on the floor. With an exasperated cry, Cynara reached down to pick it up, but the lace snagged, and with a furious sob, she jerked it free. The lace ripped in her hands, and Cynara burst into tears. Sinking down on the floor in front of the wardrobe, she held the petticoat to her face, trying to hold back the storm building inside her. It was impossible; she couldn't stay here or she would go mad!

The petticoat slipped from her hands as she got to her feet. Leaving it on the floor, Cynara ran out into the corridor, away from the stifling atmosphere of the apartment. The corridor was dark and cold, and Cynara knew her own room would be the same, but she didn't care. She turned left, toward the upper stairs, thinking only that she must find a way to leave Lyrebird Manor. If her only alternative was to put herself into service, she would do so, but she would do it some other place than here.

She was forced to move slowly along the corridor, for the single lamp at the other end did not penetrate the darkness that led to the servants' quarters. Groping with outstretched arms, she found the stair railing. Her foot was on the bottom step when she was grabbed from behind.

The hand clapped over her mouth stifled her scream. An arm around her waist lifted her off the stair and dragged her backwards. Panic stricken, she fought to break away, but could not.

The pressure of the hand over her face forced her head back, and a voice whispered in her ear, "We'll take up where we left off now, won't we?"

The sneering tone belonged to Myles, and Cynara stiffened. She tried to turn her head, but he held her in such an awkward position that she felt the bones in her neck crack in protest. She arched her back, fighting him, but the arm around her waist pinned her own arms to her sides.

"Won't we?" he whispered again. "We have plenty of time," he added, nuzzling his face against her neck. "They won't return for hours."

She felt his lips move wetly down her throat, and she jerked her head. His hand clamped down even harder across her mouth, his nails digging into her cheek, and he laughed again. The oily sound made her skin crawl.

He dragged her backwards until they were almost at the door to his room. Terrified, she tried to claw at him, but he tightened his grip; when she kicked at him, he almost lifted her off the floor. She felt him release the arm around her to reach for the door, and in that instant, she bit down as hard as she could against his hand. His howl of pain could be heard the length of the corridor, and she shoved herself away from him so violently that she crashed against the opposite wall and almost fell.

"You little bitch!" he screamed, lunging for her. "You'll pay for that!"

Cynara twisted out from under his outstretched hands. Her knees buckled, and she staggered, but she was up again before he could reverse his direction. She fled without looking back.

The doors along the corridor flashed by her; she whipped around the curve of the staircase and took the stairs two at a time, not caring that her breakneck speed could cause her to fall the length of the staircase. Behind her she heard Myles's screams of rage as he followed her, and she grabbed the door handle with such force that her fingers slipped off and she fell backwards. She was at the door again in an instant, sobbing aloud when it wouldn't open. At any second she expected Myles to seize her again, and she pulled and jerked at the handle in panic. Miraculously, it turned under her frantic fingers, and she reared back as the door flew open. It crashed against the wall, but before the sound had died, she was through the opening and across the side terrace.

It was pitch black outside, and she couldn't see, but her feet flew over the flagstones and across the expanse that led to the garden. Hunching her shoulders, she put her head down and ran blindly.

Dark shadows leaped out at her as she raced into the garden, and she choked back cries of fear as she ran first in one direction, then in another. She couldn't see the path, and she stumbled blindly, but she kept going. Branches slapped her in the face as she veered too close to the yews, and she put her arms up for protection. Far behind her, she was sure she could hear Myles coming after her. The thought lent speed to her feet and she went on, heedless of safety.

Tears blinded her as she ran, and she heard herself sobbing that she wouldn't let it happen a second time; Myles was not going to catch her as his father had. She rushed forward, and didn't see the object in front of her until it was too late. She careened into it, and went sprawling into the bushes from the impact. Fear forced her to her feet again, and she screamed in pure terror as someone took hold of her.

She fought like someone demented, clawing and scratching, twisting her body desperately to escape.

"Quiet! Quiet! You'll raise the house with all that screaming!"

Strong hands shook her so forcefully that her head whipped back and forth on her neck. The violent motion made her dizzy, and she cried, "Stop! Oh, stop!"

She was released so suddenly that she pitched forward, and now her face was pressed against the rough wool of a shirt that smelled of horses. It was Evan who held her, and she sagged against him, weeping in reaction.

The luxury of tears was denied her. At a slight noise from behind her, she jerked upright. Lifting her head, she listened, her whole body taut.

"It's all right. There's no one here but us."

Cynara turned her head fearfully, her eyes searching the darkness. "He's there. I know he is!"

Evan's face was only a blur against the night shadows. She could not see his expression, but she was suddenly aware that his arms were around her, and that she was pressed against him. She could feel the hard pounding of his heart, matching the chaotic beating of her own, and she was assailed again by the confusion she had felt that night in the stable. What was the matter with her? Only moments before she had run in terror from Myles—now she was fighting a different emotion that she didn't understand at all.

It was as though Evan's embrace had stripped her of her will. If he gave her the least sign that he cared for her, that he wanted her, she knew that she would have no power to resist him. Even now, despite her fear of Myles, she felt her longing for Evan growing inside her, a great wave of heat that began somewhere within, spreading like fire to every nerve, until her whole body seemed to throb. She wanted him to kiss her, she wanted to feel his hands on her flesh, on every part of her body. She longed to be touched, in the most private places of her being; she yearned to feel his mouth on her burning, fiery skin. Trembling, fighting her weakness, she knew that she wanted to give herself to him, to know that the love of a man could be a glorious and passionate act, a surrendering of self and will and pride. All her senses demanded a release of this intolerable pressure, building, building inside her. She reached for him, acknowledging her shuddering need.

And then Evan said impatiently, "What are you talking about? No one is there. You're imagining things."

Her shame was complete. Embarrassed, chagrined, and furious with herself, Cynara drew away from him. What was wrong with her, she wondered despairingly. Why did he arouse all her deep and hidden and utterly abandoned emotions, simply by his presence? She had never known that she could feel this powerful, racking desire for a man, and she was humiliated that she had so completely lost control of herself.

Cringing at the thought that Evan might be aware of her reaction to him, she responded angrily. The tattered shreds of her pride must be gathered together; he must never know her disastrous feelings for him. "What are you doing here?" she snapped.

"I might ask you the same."

His response, delivered in a sarcastic tone, angered her even more. For an instant, she was tempted to shout that she had run into the garden because Myles had attacked her. Would he react to that, she wondered; would anything pierce his indifference? A treacherous part of her prayed that it would, and furious with herself, she flounced away from him and immediately stepped off the path and stumbled. Her temper was not improved when Evan caught her again and steadied her, and this time she did not dare linger in his arms. Jerking her arm from his grasp, she started off without looking back. She stopped. Was Myles waiting for her somewhere, hidden in the shadows?

Cynara turned back to Evan and knew that he was watching her impatiently. Pride battled briefly with her fear of Myles, and lost. "Would you show me the way back to the house?" she asked faintly. "I . . . I can't remember how to get back."

Evan was obviously annoyed at the request. But she couldn't make herself confess that she was afraid to return alone, and she wished that she could see his face more clearly as she waited for his reply. What would she tell him if he demanded an explanation?

To her immense relief, he said finally, "Come along. This way."

He brushed by her without another word, and she fought down the urge to cling to his arm as he strode along. Every shadow seemed menacing, and she was sure that Myles was lurking somewhere, about to leap out at her and attack her again. Would Evan protect her if he did? She wasn't sure, but she crept closer to him all the same.

It wasn't until they had almost reached the terrace and she could see the lighted kitchen window through the screen of the yews that she realized how foolish she had been to go racing into the garden when she could simply have fled to the safety of the kitchen. The stupidity of her actions brought an angry flush to her face, and she looked away from Evan as he stepped onto the terrace beside her.

As if he had read her thoughts, Evan said harshly, "Perhaps next time you should think first. Myles doesn't need much encouragement."

"Encouragement!" she repeated incredulously. "Do you

actually think that I . . . that I . . ." She was so furious that she wanted to strike him.

He shrugged, infuriating her all the more. She couldn't speak; indignation choked her. Whipping around, she stalked off toward the kitchen door, so angry that she almost forgot her fear of Myles. The door banged behind her, the sound loud in the empty yard.

She did not see Evan's eyes following her as she disappeared into the house. Nor did she see his glance move upwards to the window of Myles's room where a lamp burned behind the curtain. The light from the stableyard shone down upon his upturned face, and Cynara would have been surprised at the change in his expression. He stared at the window, his face congested with an anger so great that his eyes narrowed into glittering slits and a muscle leaped and twitched along his jaw. He stood for a long time, unmoving, before he finally lowered his head. Thrusting his hands deep into his pockets, he turned abruptly and disappeared into the stables.

CHAPTER FIVE

THE STABLES WERE dark, but Evan knew his way without the aid of a lamp. He stood in the aisleway between the horse boxes and listened for a minute to make sure that all was well with the animals before he went toward the ladder to the loft.

The loft above the stables had long ago been converted into a series of small rooms where grooms and stableboys slept. There were only two of them now, he and Jimmy, but Oliver had told him that once the loft had been fully occupied, just as the stables below had been filled with horses. That had been a long time ago, when Lyrebird Manor had been famous for the quality of horseflesh it produced. Now things were different, and had been since John Ward had taken command of the Manor.

Evan went to the far end of the loft toward his room. Even from here, he could hear Jacob's loud snores as he slept away his nightly intake of liquor. Jacob had his own private quarters below, as befitted his position as coachman, near the horses in case there was trouble of some kind. Evan's lip curled; Jacob could never be roused in time to help, and Evan remembered the many nights when he had crept alone from the loft to see to a sick horse while Jacob slept on, unaware and uncaring.

Evan took down the heavy coat Oliver had given him and spread it over the blanket on the cot, but he did not immediately climb into bed. Instead, he went to the unshuttered window and stood looking out. From his position, he could see one corner of the house, and as before, his eyes went to a particular window. This was a nightly ritual of his, and although he mocked himself for doing it, he watched that window before he went to bed every night that Myles was home. Sometimes he could see Myles's shadow lurching back and forth behind the curtain, and it was then that his hatred rose like a red tide inside him, blocking every other thought except for the one that consumed him: revenge. One day he would have his revenge on Myles, he was sure.

How he would accomplish this feat—he, the stableboy; Myles, the protected and pampered son—he didn't know; he only knew he would succeed some day. His hatred for Myles was the only thing that gave his life meaning; how else had he endured the countless humiliations Myles had heaped upon him since they were boys?

Shutting his mind to those memories, Evan leaned his arms on the sill and looked in the other direction, toward the dark mass of trees that sheltered Oliver's cottage. He should have gone to see him today, Evan thought, and was immediately annoyed. His annoyance increased as he pictured Oliver waiting patiently for him. Why should he feel so responsible for the old man, he asked himself. Oliver Lindsay should have packed up years ago and left when John Ward dismissed him as steward. Evan had told him so often enough. Was it his fault that Oliver had elected to stay? Yes, yes, it was. Oliver had remained near the Manor for him, and that was why he felt so responsible.

Damn the man! Evan knew that Oliver would welcome him with no sign of reproach. Now he felt guilty, as he had so many times before, for neglecting the old man who for years had been father, teacher, and mentor to him, asking nothing in return except an occasional visit. Evan ground his teeth together; he would go to Oliver's cottage tomorrow, and damn the consequences!

He threw himself on his cot, his hands behind his head, staring into the darkness. The girl, Cynara, entered his thoughts, and he frowned. There was something wrong there, he thought, remembering Myles's lewd comment about her the other day. If Cynara was just another girl seeking to better her position by offering herself, why had he found her running away from the house in such terror?

Shifting impatiently on the cot, he answered his own question contemptuously. Obviously events had moved too quickly for her and she had been frightened of the consequences. Her girlish fancies had probably extended only so far as a chaste kiss or two, and when Myles had responded with far more than that, she had become afraid and run away. It served her right, he thought, to trifle with things she knew nothing about. Perhaps the experience would teach her to be more careful the next time. And there would be a next time, he thought, feeling his anger build; there would be a next time, if he knew Myles.

Evan shrugged, trying to dismiss Cynara, irritated with himself for thinking about her when he should be trying to sleep. But her face was pictured in his mind again, and he remembered her when he had first seen her: he had been struck by her beauty then, and even now, with her hair pulled back unbecomingly from her face into a tight knot at the nape of her neck, wrapped in that hideous dead-black that Cornelia favored for her household servants, that beauty could not be hidden. He laughed to himself, thinking of Cornelia's frustration. The mistress—his lip curled at the word much the same way as Cynara's had done—preferred to be the only swan amongst the drab geese. It must annoy her no end to be confronted daily with the failure of her efforts to turn Cynara into the plain creature she could never be.

Restlessly, he turned over on his side, thumping the flat pillow. Thoughts of Cynara continued to preoccupy him, and he wondered what it was about her that disturbed him so. She even invaded his sleep, he thought angrily. The other night he had awakened drenched with sweat and with an ache in his loins, after dreaming of her.

Flinging himself on his back again, he remembered that night in the stable, seeing again Cynara's sparkling eyes, her parted lips as she gazed in wonderment at the new foal. The lamplight had made a red-gold halo of her hair, and he had tried to fight the urge to touch that hair, to touch her. What impulse had made him put his hand over hers, he didn't know. But that simple gesture had been enough to send a shock wave of desire racing through him. He had wanted to crush her to him, to bury his face in the softness of her throat, to kiss her . . .

No, he had wanted much more than a kiss, he admitted. He had wanted to feel her arms around him, to feel her legs entwined with his as they lay on the straw in the stable. He had wanted to possess her, to know her, to own her.

Tonight in the garden it had taken all his will not to sweep her off her feet and carry her away to some private place where they could be alone, where there was all the time in the world. When he had held her in his arms, the desire that shot like fire through him had shaken him with its intensity. He could hardly stand for the trembling weakness in his legs. He had imagined her, willing and pliant, her soft, smooth body eager for his touch. He would have removed her clothing, button by button, ribbon by ribbon, savoring her, anticipating the sight of her naked body, washed in moonlight. She would be beautiful, he knew; her skin soft and creamy, her breasts firm, her hips gently rounded. He would have gloried in the sight of her, forcing himself to wait, to taste the fullness of that moment when she stood, naked and unafraid, before him. She would help him remove his own clothing, her hands both impatient and caressing. He could almost feel the light touch of her hands on his chest, his thighs; he could feel her delicate fingers on his skin, leaving tingling trails of sensation behind. He would hold her to him, luxuriating in the length of her against his body, and then he would begin to kiss her, covering her body with his lips, tasting every hollow and curve, every swell of breast and line of hip and thigh. They would lie on the grass, and he would caress her, his hands cupping each breast, his mouth moving slowly from nipple to nipple, following the line of her stomach, and down to her legs, where he would rest his head on the mound of her, glorying in the sight and scent and taste of her.

Moving restlessly on the hard cot, Evan rubbed an arm across his face. He could feel the sweat that had gathered on his forehead, but he was more conscious of the throbbing ache in his loins. Uttering a groan, Evan closed his eyes tightly, his fists clenched, exhausted. He would not think of her, dream of her, he told himself fiercely, willing it to be so.

He shifted again, and his hand touched a book he had left by the pillow. It was one of Oliver's precious volumes of Caesar, and he gave a sigh of exasperation. He was too tired tonight to do the translation Oliver had set for him. The book slid to the floor as he fell asleep.

Evan was up early the next morning before either Jacob or Jimmy stirred. This was his favorite time of the day; alone, with only the horses for company, he could almost feel at peace with himself. It would be later, with Jacob shouting orders and Jimmy with his eternal empty snicker, that he would begin to feel that familiar tightening in his stomach, that desire to smash something. For now as he went about the business of feeding the animals, he enjoyed their restless movements as they waited for their hay, or nickered to him as he came up to their boxes.

He was worried about the new foal; it seemed sickly and weak. The mare, too, had lost weight and condition, and for that reason, he had kept them both in the loose box against Jacob's orders. He looked over the partition now, and the foal, who had been resting, lifted its head and stared dully at him before dropping to the straw again. The mare stood over it, nuzzling it anxiously, and Evan frowned as he went to prepare a special mash for her.

He had finished the feeding by the time he heard Jacob shouting at Jimmy to get out of bed. To avoid them, he went out and down to the pasture to check on the horses there. There were only six in the pasture now, counting the old dray horse that was used for pulling the wagon, and as Evan leaned over the fence watching them, he thought of the stories Oliver had told him about Lyrebird Manor.

The Manor had once been a prosperous estate, the garden itself almost as famous for beauty as the estate for the horses it produced. The house had been built some hundred years before Eric Ward came into possession of it. Eric had built the additions to the house with his own fortune and had begun the breeding program that was to make him so well known. After the departure of Eric's eldest son, Sean, for Australia, Eric had designed the lyrebird garden as a memorial, and it was at that time that Oliver Lindsay had been hired as steward. Oliver had told Evan of Eric's two sons who had died in childhood of a fever before he came to the Manor. When Sean and then his son died, the remaining son, Richard, who had later fathered the present John Ward became the heir.

Evan believed he understood Oliver's reluctance to speak of John, for John had dismissed the old man abruptly after some thirty years of service. The dismissal had come soon after Evan's birth, and it was then that he was given the cottage on the edge of the estate, together with a small yearly pittance, which was barely enough to provide Oliver with the necessities.

It was this last thought that caused Evan's anger to flare again. Evan had never considered it right that Oliver had been dismissed so casually, and it angered him even more that the old man accepted his situation so meekly, refusing to talk about it.

But then, Evan reminded himself remorselessly, as he opened the gate to the pasture and let himself through, Oliver was old, in his seventies now, and if Evan, who was so much younger and stronger, could not remove himself from his own situation, how could he expect Oliver to fight?

The dray horse had broken through the bottom rail of the pasture again. Evan collected him from the field beyond, and by the time he had found a rock to use as a hammer and had nailed the board to the fence again, it was late, and he knew that Jacob would be yelling for him.

Vaulting the gate, he was just about to start toward the stables again, when a movement caught his attention. Shading his eyes with one hand, he squinted against the sun toward the cleared field to the right, where a series of jumping obstacles had been set up for Myles's pleasure. He watched the scene for a moment, unable to believe his eyes, his body rigid with anger. Then, swearing, he started up the path at a run.

It was too late by the time he reached the other field. The mare was cowering in terror against the fence, and from a distance, Evan could hear the shrill cries of her foal, locked alone in the horse box. Part of his mind noted the panic of the foal, but his whole attention was taken up by the scene before him, and for an instant he was so enraged that he couldn't move.

Then, as Myles's whip opened up another slash on the mare's flank, Evan leaped forward. He grabbed the whip from Myles's hand and broke it in two. The pieces flew from his hand as he lunged toward Myles, and Myles uttered a strangled sound of fear as he stumbled back.

"Evan!"

The bellow of Jacob's voice penetrated Evan's fury just as his fingers closed around Myles's throat. For an instant, his whole body trembled as part of his mind urged him to ignore Jacob, while another part screamed at him to let go of Myles. He could feel the soft, fat neck under his hands, and the desire to bury his fingers in the doughy flesh of his enemy was too pleasurable to fight. Myles was clawing at him, gagging and sputtering with terror, and Evan gloried in the abject fear in Myles's eyes. His hands tightened.

"Evan! Leave go! What are you doing, boy?"

There was pure panic now in Jacob's voice as the man rushed toward them. Myles was flailing his arms, gasping for breath, twisting his body in a vain attempt to escape the intolerable pressure on his windpipe. Evan looked down into that fat face he had longed to smash so many times, and his vision cleared. Panting, he dropped his hands. He turned away abruptly as Myles fell in a heap on the ground, holding his throat, and he went to the mare. Soothing her with a voice that still shook with the effects of his fury, he took hold of the bridle and began to lead her away.

Jacob was bending over Myles, trying to help him to his feet, and as Evan went by, Jacob struck out at him. Evan staggered slightly with the force of the blow, but he did not look at the coachman or Myles, nor did he pause in leading the trembling mare away from the field.

Behind him, he heard Jacob speaking to Myles in a conciliatory whine. What Myles replied, Evan did not hear, for again the blood was pounding in his head as he ran his hand lightly across the mare's shoulder to calm her. His fingers came away smeared with blood, and he stared at his hand as he walked the horse back to the stable. His hand clenched into a fist, and he recalled that moment of absolute rage when he had reached for Myles.

Whether he would have actually killed him or not, Evan wasn't sure. The urge had been strong in him that for the space of several seconds he had been blinded by the desire to destroy. If Jacob hadn't shouted at him, if the sudden explosive sound of his name hadn't brought him to his senses, he might actually have murdered Myles.

He rubbed his sleeve across his sweating forehead, and suddenly his legs felt weak, and he stopped. Cursing his faintness, he took a firmer grip on the bridle and went on. But the intensity of his desire to destroy Myles had left him more shaken than he wanted to admit, and his steps were slow as he led the mare back to the stable.

Carefully, he unsaddled the horse, easing the head collar on after he had removed the bridle. The animal was nervous, sidestepping back and forth as he worked around her, and no amount of soothing words would calm her. It wasn't until he had smoothed salve over the whip weals on her sides that he remembered the foal and realized the reason for the mare's anxiety. Raising his head, Evan listened, his eyes going to the closed horse box. The silence was ominous, after the foal's frantic cries to its mother before, and Evan became apprehensive.

Leaving the mare tied, Evan approached the box and whistled softly. There was no answering nicker from within, and his feeling of dread increased. Forcing himself, certain now what he would find, Evan pulled back the bolt that held the upper half of the door shut, and looked inside.

The foal was lying on the trampled straw. Evan knew at once from its position that the neck was broken, and he could see that the damage had been done by the foal's repeated lungings at the door as it tried to get out to its mother. At the sight of the blood congealing in the small nostrils, and the grotesque angle of the head, Evan turned away, sickened by the destruction of the young animal he had tried so hard to save.

His hatred for Myles rose in his throat, and he swallowed hard as he shut the door again. Leaning against it, he closed his eyes, remembering the scene he had witnessed earlier: Myles, forcing the mare toward a jump that he knew was too high for her, knowing she was not strong enough to take it successfully. Evan had seen the horse refuse, had seen Myles drive her at it again and again, until at the last, the animal had reared and thrown him.

Evan looked at the mare now, and he went to untie her. He led her into an empty box, ran his hands over her to try to calm both her and himself, and then fed her some hay. He was in the act of shutting the horse inside when he heard someone behind him. He turned. Myles was standing in the aisleway, and he held a pistol in one hand.

Slowly, Evan's glance traveled from the gun up to Myles's face. He reached back and shot the bolt to the box. "I won't let you do it, Myles," he said, as evenly as his anger allowed. "You've done enough harm already today."

The pistol jumped in Myles's hand. "Get out of the way, Evan!"

Evan shook his head. "You won't destroy that mare."

"I will! I will! It tried to kill me!"

"No!" Evan's voice rang out sharply. He recognized the shrill tone in Myles's voice, and his body tensed. "It was your own fault. You knew she couldn't take that fence—you knew it."

"I don't have to listen to this!" Myles shrieked, almost dancing with rage. "Jacob! Come here at once! Jacob!"

The coachman came uneasily into the stable. His eyes went to Evan's set face, and slid away to rest on Myles.

Myles gestured furiously toward Evan. "Take him away!" he screamed. "Take him away!"

Jacob, too, winced at the high whine in Myles's voice. He knew too well what could happen if he disobeyed the young master, and he dreaded the thought of facing John Ward and trying to explain why he had stood by and almost let Evan kill his son. And yet—the mare was valuable; what would the master say if he allowed Myles to shoot her?

"Jacob!"

Jacob looked from one boy to the other, and the sight of Myles's flushed face decided him. He grabbed Evan, hissing as he did so, "Leave be! You can't do nothin' about it now!"

The words were hardly out of his mouth before Myles swung the cane he carried. It came smashing down on Evan's face and shoulder, staggering both Evan and Jacob with the force of the blow. Jacob seized the opportunity to throw the dazed Evan to the ground, pinning him there with the weight of his body.

Evan shook his head, trying to clear it. There was an intolerable weight pressing him down when he tried to get to his feet. When he turned his head to see what it was, his vision was blurred; everything was hazy. And then he heard the high sound of Myles's laugh, and he remembered. "Let go of me, damn you!" he panted, trying to find the strength to fight against Jacob's hands. "Let go, or he'll—"

The report from the gun reverberated through the stable. Evan froze, his body rigid. The moment seemed to stretch on forever, everything held motionless in time until he heard a soft sigh, followed by a heavy, lifeless thud. He closed his eyes, knowing he was too late.

"What is it? What happened?" Quick footsteps entered the stable and stopped. Evan heard a cry and looked up to see Cynara standing in the aisleway, her face white with shock. She was followed closely by Briggs, who put a hand on Cynara's arm as she tried to come forward.

"Stay back!" Briggs hissed.

Jacob heaved himself to his feet, dragging Evan with him. Evan, after that one swift glance at Cynara, did not look at her again. Jerking his arm away from Jacob's grasp, he brushed the dirt from his shirt and ran a trembling hand through his hair. Then, slowly, he turned and looked at Myles, and the look on his face was such that Myles's triumphant expression became viciously defensive.

"I told you not to interfere, Evan!" Myles shouted into the silence. "I told you I would do it. Now what do you say to that? What do you say?" he screamed again when Evan did not answer.

Cynara seemed unable to move as Evan stepped toward her. Bertha reached out and pulled her out of the way and Evan brushed by them without a word. But as he passed her, he felt her eyes on him, and he stiffened when she put her hand out and said chokingly, "Evan—your face . . ."

It wasn't until then that he felt the blood running down his face and inside his collar. He put his hand up and touched the gash Myles's cane had made along his jaw. It was the final indignity, and he closed his eyes briefly as he fought down the urge to turn on Myles and strike him down. To have Cynara see him thus, beaten and defeated, was the last blow. Stepping aside from her, he walked out of the stables without looking back.

"You tried to stop him, Evan," Oliver Lindsay said quietly, as he gently sponged the blood away from Evan's face. "You tried—"

Evan pushed Oliver's hand away and sprang out of the chair. "I should have killed him."

The boy's murderous tone alarmed Oliver. He reached toward Evan again, but Evan pulled away and went to stare unseeingly out the cottage window. Every line of his body was rigid, and Oliver sighed.

Oliver emptied the bowl of water and wrung out the cloth. He watched Evan for a long time before he finally turned to the table and began cutting the bread he had set out. The kettle sang, and he went to the stove to brew the strong tea Evan favored. From time to time he glanced at the tall young man standing by the window and his shoulders slumped dejectedly. Evan was in one of his black moods, and that was always a bad sign.

As he puttered around the kitchen, he thought that it was hard to believe that the small boy he had cared for since his mother died had suddenly matured. Evan was young yet, but almost a man, and Oliver sighed again. His hands shook as he poured the tea, and he thought: I'm getting old. I *am* old. When I die, who will keep Evan safe from himself? The question sent a shiver through him. He thought of the knowledge he had withheld from Evan all these years, and he prayed that the secret would die with him. If Evan ever learned the true story about his birth, murder would be done, and the resulting cataclysm would engulf them all.

"Evan," he called, deliberately shutting his mind from such disturbing throughts. "Come away from there. The tea is ready."

Evan turned from the window, and Oliver saw the naked look of pain in his eyes. His heart moved in response, but he knew from long experience that one sign of sympathy from him would bring back the shuttered look that he hated.

"Come. Sit down," he said softly.

"I can't stay. Chores are waiting."

The bitterness was deep in Evan's voice, and again, Oliver just prevented himself from reaching out to the boy he regarded as his son. He said, instead, "You can spare a few minutes—"

"I'll cut some wood before I go. The nights are cold, and you won't do it yourself."

"I have enough for a few days. Perhaps instead we can have a lesson—"

"I told you, I haven't time!"

Pain flickered again briefly in Evan's dark eyes, and Oliver said quietly, "I'm sorry about the mare and foal, Evan."

"It doesn't matter," Evan answered. But his face was tight as he wrenched open the door and strode outside to the woodpile.

Oliver followed him to the door. When he saw the savagery with which Evan jerked the ax from the stump, he shook his head sadly. There was only one way to relieve Evan's helpless rage and frustration, and Oliver himself held the key. But he was old, and afraid, and the time for heroics was long past. His white head bowed, Oliver quietly shut the door.

Evan did not carry the kindling into the cottage. When he had cut enough to last Oliver for several days, he flung the ax blade into the stump, where it landed, quivering. Without a backward glance at the house, he strode out of the clearing. By the time he reached the path that led back to the Manor, he was running, leaping over fallen logs, dodging branches that swept across the trail, trying vainly to outrace the memory of that horrible scene in the stable.

He ran until he came to a small pool fed by the stream that paralleled the path. Panting, he threw himself down. Blood was drumming in his ears from his exertion, but in his mind he could still hear the noise of the gun and the sound of the falling mare. Bringing up his knees to his chest, he cradled his head in his arms. He had told Oliver that it didn't matter about the mare and foal, but it did. It did. And what mattered most of all was that the animals had suffered because of Myles's stupidity, and . . . his own helplessness.

He clenched his teeth at that last thought, seeing in his

mind the horrified expression on Cynara's face when she had come into the stable. And then, to have her reach out to touch the gash on his face, knowing that Myles had done it . . . He groaned, rocking back and forth, hating the thought of having her witness his humiliation; hating the thought of her seeing him defeated as well.

As if his thoughts had conjured her presence, when he finally raised his head, she was standing there, across the stream, looking at him. He sprang to his feet, furious to be caught in such open misery.

His sudden movement startled her; she took a step back, and he snarled at her, "What are you doing here?"

"I . . . I came to see if you were all right," she stammered.

He glowered at her, wishing that she wouldn't stare at him with those huge eyes. "Why shouldn't I be all right?" he snapped.

"Well, I thought . . . I thought . . ."

She faltered into silence at his fierce expression. Perversely, he took satisfaction in embarrassing her as she had inadvertently embarrassed him. He said harshly, "I don't like to be followed. You have no business coming after me when you should be at the house."

He had made her angry. "I thought you might be upset about what happened," she snapped. "I see I was mistaken, after all."

"Yes," he said coldly, wondering why he had deliberately goaded her. "You were."

She appeared about to say something else, but he turned his back on her. He heard her angry intake of breath at his rudeness, and some part of him wanted to turn back and apologize. He couldn't make himself do it; she had seen him humbled too far as it was. He listened instead to the sharp rustle of her skirt as she whipped around, and then, seconds later, a furious cry.

Evan turned his head. Cynara had caught her foot among some stones on the bank and was trying to jerk it free. Each movement pinned the foot more firmly, and when she looked up and saw him staring at her, her expression dared him to help.

Angry with himself for going to her aid, Evan jumped across the stream and bent to remove the stones. He freed her without comment, and stood again.

"Thank you," she said icily, attempting to move away.

The foot gave way beneath her, and for the seocnd time in two days, she pitched forward into his arms. He reached instinctively for her, and without thinking, conscious only of the firm flesh under his hands, he did what he had wanted to the night before. He drew her closer to him. She struggled furiously, but the more she tried to fight him, the more he wanted to hold her.

"Let go of me!"

He did not feel the blows she aimed at him. He was marveling at the smallness of her waist, the slight swell of her hips, her breasts pushing against his chest.

He had thought about her, dreamed about her, and now she was here. He was shaking, caught up in a passion so strong that, without being aware of it, he held her so tight that she cried out. Desire for her was like an avalanche inside him, runaway, unstoppable, overwhelming with thunderous power. He could not stop himself, anymore than he could have stopped an avalanche. His mouth came down on hers savagely, parting her lips, his tongue thrusting between her teeth, probing her mouth. She fought him, but he held her head in an iron grip, bending over her, forcing her backwards, sheer animal passion blotting out everything but his absolute need for her.

Without volition, his hand went to her breast. He could feel the fullness of it even through her gown, and he gripped her flesh, moving his thumb across the nipple, uttering a wordless sound as he felt it harden and become erect under his touch. His fingers were tearing at the buttons of her dress when he felt the violent trembling of her body, her frantic arching away from him.

A warning shrieked through his mind, penetrating at last

his blind lust for her. He drew back, and in that instant, she freed herself.

"How . . . dare . . . you . . . !" she gasped, her face white.

"What?" He was panting, trying to get control of his raging emotions, staring at her face. Her eyes had darkened to black-green with anger, and tendrils of hair had escaped to frame her face. He thought to himself that he had not really noticed how beautiful she was after all.

"I said, how dare you take advantage of me like that!"

He caught her wrist as she struck at him. The bones felt small and delicate under his fingers, and to his fury, he had the insane desire to pull her to him again. The urge was so strong that his grip tightened, and she cried out with real pain. Cursing himself for hurting her, again he released her so suddenly that she staggered. He could see the red marks of his fingers on her skin, and he was overwhelmed with shame. The thought flashed through his mind that he was no better than Myles, and he muttered thickly, "Get out of here; I won't hurt you again."

Cynara didn't wait to reply; with a whirl of skirts, she whipped around and disappeared up the path.

Evan threw himself down by the stream again, splashing water over his hot face, wondering what had come over him. There had been girls before, but never had one driven him to the point of madness, as Cynara had.

He stopped abruptly, his face dripping, trying vainly to justify behavior that could not be justified. He remembered Myles's coarse assessment of Cynara, that she was not above using her charms to further her interests. He sat back on his heels, staring down at his hands, which had held her minutes before. Was he imagining now the brief yielding of her body against his, before she tried to push him away? Had he really seen a momentary softness in her expression before she struck out at him? He shook his head, trying to clear it. She had been practicing on him, hadn't she? Testing the success of her charms before moving on to more profitable game. And, like a fool, he had almost fallen into her trap.

Leaping to his feet again, he jerked his head angrily. If Cynara thought to ensnare him, she was mistaken. He had no time for such games, and no inclination to be found in an uncompromising position, especially if Myles were to discover it.

The memory he had tried to bury came forcefully into his mind, reminding him of the utter folly of his attraction to Cynara. He had been beaten, and badly, the time several years ago when one of the servant girls had sought him out. He hadn't known, or cared, that Myles had wanted the girl for himself, but when it was discovered that Evan, in a rare gesture of friendliness, had gone walking with her, Myles had been livid. Evan's gesture had been innocent in itself, but by the time Myles was finished, the situation had been blown completely out of proportion. He had accused Evan of any number of misdeeds, of taking advantage of the girl, forcing her to do what he wished, and although both Evan and the girl had denied Myles's accusations, John Ward had been so incensed that he had ordered Evan whipped. Jacob had eagerly complied, and Evan grimaced as he remembered.

He had been only fifteen at the time, not strong enough to fight Jacob when he had tied him to a post. The shirt had been ripped from his back by Myles, who had almost danced with glee at the sight of Evan's helplessness. The whip had descended, crossing his unprotected back with bloody welts until Evan, in spite of his fierce vow not to break under the punishment, had fainted.

He hadn't cried out; at least he had had that little satisfaction. But his back still bore faint scars from the whipping that day, and he still recalled John's warning that if he was every caught with one of the girls again, the punishment would be even more severe.

Evan had never understood John's violent reaction to such a small incident, but the humiliation and the agony of his lacerated back had remained with him. He had not been near, nor even spoken with, the young maids at the Manor until the day Jacob had sent him to fetch Cynara at the station. And Jacob wouldn't have dared send him on such an errand if both John and Myles hadn't been away.

As he walked slowly back to the house, Evan's face was hot at the thought of his behavior with Cynara. He had frightened her, but perhaps it was better this way. If she was afraid of him, she would stay away, and he could not be accused of consorting with one of John's servants. Nor, he thought grimly, would he be tempted to give in to this insane desire for her. He was appalled at his behavior by the stream; it seemed as if some devil had taken hold of him, blocking out everything but the fact that he wanted her.

He still wanted her, he admitted, infuriated by his weakness. The ache in him would not go away. Even now he didn't know what had stopped him; the pure animal passion for her had been more than he could control. In that moment, he had forgotten patience and anticipation; he had wanted to rip the clothes from her, taking her down to the ground, his mouth hot to kiss her, his hands kneading her flesh, his body burning to possess her. The wild surging of his blood had cried for release, *then,* in that instant. It wouldn't have mattered that she fought him; nothing would have mattered except . . . taking her.

He stopped, appalled. He had come near to actually raping her, he thought, more ashamed than he had ever been in his life. He was disgusted with himself, furious that he could have done such a thing.

But even through the overwhelming disgust he felt came the treacherous picture of a naked Cynara, open, waiting for him, reaching for him . . .

He shook his head violently, thrusting the image away fiercely from his mind. He had to stay away from her; he had to suppress his desire for her. He had no intention of inciting John's anger with regard to any girl, even Cynara, for he knew that never again would he submit to another whipping for anyone. The humiliation had been worse than the actual physical pain; both had been burned deep in body and mind, and Evan would never forget.

There had been many times during his youth that he had been cuffed or slapped for real or imagined offenses. Jacob had been given a free hand as far as discipline was concerned, and he had exercised that right so frequently that Evan could not recall a time during his boyhood that he had not suffered numerous bruises. Jacob had also been fond of applying his belt, and Evan remembered many times Oliver had gently smoothed a healing salve over his back and shoulders while a young Evan fought back tears, not because of the pain, but because of the injustice of the attack.

It was strange, he thought, that while he resented and disliked Jacob, he did not hate him with the passion he reserved for Myles. He supposed it was because he knew Jacob was a dull-witted brute of a man, who feared his employer enough to follow orders blindly. No, it was Myles for whom Evan reserved his hatred, for Myles had delighted in tormenting him from the time the two of them were able to talk. It was Myles who was responsible for many of the beatings; Myles, who lied and schemed and whined to put Evan in the wrong and on the defensive from the earliest time that Evan could remember.

And it had been Myles, who, after Evan had fought his way to consciousness again after that savage whipping, had screamed that he would not release him until he begged forgiveness.

Evan's lip curled at the memory, which was still as clear in his mind as if it had happened only the day before. He could still remember the feeling of the rope cutting into his wrists, the stinging sweat running down his face; feel the agony in the torn flesh of his back. He had lifted his head to look at Myles after Myles had shouted at him. The effort had almost caused him to faint again, but he said one word, forcing it out between clenched teeth, fighting pain and weakness to defy his enemy, cementing the pattern that had existed, and always would, between them. He had said, "Never."

CHAPTER SIX

CYNARA WAS HALFWAY back to the house before she realized that her ankle hurt. Annoyed, for now that she had noticed it the pain seemed to become worse, she hobbled on. She was afraid that if she stopped, Evan would find her, and she knew that she could not resist him a second time. It had taken all her strength to break away from him; she could not do it again.

She was confused and frightened and angry. Hadn't she learned anything from that horrible experience with John Ward? Hadn't Myles's attack taught her to be constantly on guard?

Apparently it hadn't, she told herself bitterly. She had been totally unprepared for the surge of emotion that swept through her when Evan put his arms around her. For an incomprehensible moment, she had felt herself yielding to him, and she had been frightened by the intensity of her feelings. Dreaming about him, thinking of him, was one thing; the reality of him was overpowering. She had felt him shaking with the force of his own emotion, and she had been frightened at the response in herself. Even when he had become almost savage, forcing her to kiss him, his hands roaming at will over her body, something within her could not be denied. There had been a fierce exultation in her that she had the power to arouse him to such a pitch, and she had felt that fever of excitement taking control of her until she had actually *wanted* him to force her to the ground.

Closing her eyes at the thought, Cynara admitted with shame that if he had ripped the clothes from her body and thrown her down, she would have abandoned herself to him, gladly and without reservation. Even now her body felt like it was on fire, and she trembled uncontrollably at the memory. Her breasts ached to be caressed, the flame in her loins cried out to be extinguished. She was obsessed with the thought of Evan's hands on her, his mouth devouring her, his hard body demanding a passionate response from her.

She did not know, now, where she had found the strength to break away from him. But something in the recesses of her mind had screamed at her to get away, to escape him, before it was too late. Another shuddering of being in his arms, of feeling his mouth hot on hers, and she would have been lost.

What was the matter with her? Had her experience with John Ward released some wantonness within her that she had never suspected? She shook her head violently, denying the horrible thought. But the idea persisted, and she stumbled back to the house, vowing that she would not seek Evan out again. This powerful, consuming attraction to him must be denied. She could not trust herself with him, and she was frightened.

"Where have you been?" The question was as sharp as Cornelia's expression as she waited for Cynara's answer.

"I went for a walk."

"A walk," Cornelia repeated mockingly. "And who gave you permission to leave the house?"

Cynara's chin lifted at the tone in Cornelia's voice. "No one," she answered boldly, meeting the woman's glance with defiance.

Cornelia closed her eyes for a moment in an expression of long suffering. She reached out and the ever-present Briggs put the bottle of smelling salts in her hand. Cynara was not deceived; this scene had been played too many times for it to be effective in quite the matter Cornelia intended. Instead of feeling guilty, Cynara became impatient with Cornelia's posturing. She waited, daring a sigh. Cornelia's eyes snapped open.

"You went after that—that boy. Didn't you? Oh, don't bother to deny it, girl. You were seen running after him."

"I wasn't going to deny it."

"What!" Cornelia stared at Cynara, outraged.

"I said—"

"I heard what you said, you shameless creature. How dare you stand before me and flaunt your indecent behavior!"

"It wasn't indecent! You—"

"Briggs!" Cornelia snapped. "Where are my salts?"

Briggs hesitated. "You have them in your hand," she offered finally.

Cornelia stared at the bottle as though it had offended her in some way. She waved it agitatedly in the air, and Cynara's nostrils contracted at the strong odor of sal volatile floating toward her. "I want an explanation from you, miss!" Cornelia demanded through the rising cloud of vapor.

Cynara saw the satisfied smirk on Briggs's face. It hadn't taken the maid long to run to her mistress with another tale, she thought furiously. She glared at Briggs, who stared back smugly, infuriating Cynara even more.

"I'm waiting," Cornelia said sharply.

"I don't know what you wish to hear," Cynara answered, her eyes still on Briggs's face. She added, deliberately, "Perhaps Briggs can explain much better than I since she seems to have taken such an interest in affairs that don't concern her."

The maid stiffened. "Really, madam!" she protested, too eagerly. "I don't know what the girl means!"

"Be quiet!" Cornelia snapped.

Briggs subsided, allowing herself an indignant sniff which was carefully inaudible over the drumming of Cornelia's fingers on the arm of her chair. "You have yet to explain yourself," Cornelia said glacially to Cynara.

Cynara had not intention of giving Cornelia an account of her behavior, especially as she was unsure herself why she had gone after Evan. She was silent. The drumming increased in volume.

"Very well, then," Cornelia said at last. "Since you insist upon being stubborn, you will wait in your room until I send for you again. But I warn you—" Cornelia's finger stabbed the air for emphasis "you have defied me once too often. This time your obstinacy will be suitably rewarded, and you have only yourself to blame!"

There was a knock on the door, interrupting her. Cornelia snapped, "What is it?"

"Mama?"

Myles entered. As he came across the room toward his mother, the tyrant of an instant before reverted once again to the pallid semi-invalid. Cronelia drooped in her chair, one hand going to her throat in a helpless gesture. "Myles, my dear . . ."

"Mama, I must talk to you!" Myles shrilled. "Something has to be done about Evan!"

Cynara did not wait to be excused. As she went angrily out the door, she heard Myles say accusingly, "Do you know that he nearly killed me this morning? And all because . . ."

Cynara shut the door. She leaned against it for a moment, her eyes closed. Behind her she could hear the high whine of Myles's voice, the low, comforting tones of Cornelia, and she grimaced with disgust before moving away to her own room. How she despised them, she thought; how she longed to be away from them all.

Cynara was left alone for the remainder of the day. Angry and restless, she paced back and forth, trying not to think of Evan, of Myles and his mother, of John Ward, or of her own future. Throwing herself into the chair, she tried to read the book she had taken from the library, but when she turned page after page without comprehending a word of what was written there, she tossed the volume aside and jumped up again to resume her agitated pacing. What was the matter with her? Why had the incident with Evan assumed such importance in her thoughts? Again and again she tried to tell herself that she had only followed him to offer her sympathy, but she knew she lied to herself. It wasn't only pity that had induced her to follow him and intrude upon his privacy. No, it was something else; something she did not want to admit, even to herself.

She went to the window and looked down upon the stableyard, trying to convince herself that she was not searching for a glimpse of Evan. She saw someone emerge from the stables and her heart leaped in response. But it was only Jimmy, whom she despised, and she laughed harshly to herself for wishing it to be Evan. Turning away abruptly, she sat down on the bed, berating herself for acting like a schoolgirl with a crush. What was Evan to her? He was rude and contemptuous and arrogant. Every time she saw him they quarreled.

Then why was her mind filled with thoughts of him? Closing her eyes tightly, she tried not to remember the strength she had sensed in him—not only the physical power, but the strength of character, the compelling force of his personality that had made her long to seek comfort in his arms.

No, no! It wasn't comfort she sought, she admitted, forcing herself to face the truth of it. It wasn't comfort at all. What she had wanted was the fulfillment a woman needed, demanded, to be whole. She wanted to surrender, body and soul, to Evan, and to have him give the gift of himself to her in return.

For the first time, she began to realize that passion takes many forms: she had dreamed of tender scenes with Evan, where the touch of his hands on her body was gentle, she had imagined an almost savage encounter where his mouth was rough, his fingers almost bruising her flesh. But passion and desire and need had always been there, at the core of every act—the need for expression of yearnings and longings, the desire to be held and touched and loved, the passion that united a man and a woman far beyond her acceptance of his thrusting inside her.

She wanted Evan; she ached for him. The fire that burned within her had been fanned to a white heat that would only be consumed by union with him. She was no schoolgirl, after all, she thought. Her desires and passions were those of a woman, and yet . . . She felt something beyond the crying physical need of her body for fulfillment. Embraced by him, she had not felt so . . . alone.

The thought startled her, and her eyes flew open. Alone. Of course she was alone, she told herself, and nothing would change that. Her fantasies had no bearing on reality, and she forced herself to face the truth. Reality was John Ward having his way with her in this very room; reality was the helplessness of her position with regard to Cornelia Ward. And Evan had no place in her life, just as she had no place in his.

"The mistress wants to see you. Now."

Cynara started. She hadn't heard Briggs enter, but suddenly the maid was standing there, smiling slyly. There was something about the quality of that smile that made Cynara uneasy; it was almost as though Briggs were relishing some triumph that was yet to occur, and which boded ill for Cynara.

"You're to go to the downstairs sitting room," Briggs added, almost gaily.

Surprise was tinged with alarm in Cynara's mind. It was rare that Cornelia ventured from her own apartments, and the fact that she did so now was ominous. Her apprehension increased, but she was determined to remain calm in front of the smirking Briggs. She rose quietly from the chair, but as she went to step by the maid, Briggs reached out and blocked the way.

"I knew it would come to this," Briggs said smugly. "You got too far above yourself, girl, and now you'll pay for it."

"I've no doubt of that," Cynara said coldly. "Especially if you had anything to do with it. Now please let me pass."

The door to the sitting room was partially open when

Cynara stopped in front of it. There was silence within, and she swallowed hard, trying to quell her nervousness. Raising her hand, she knocked once, and then entered.

Cornelia was enthroned on a wing-backed chair by the fireplace. She had dressed for the occasion in a severely elegant gown of dark-blue silk, and her only ornamentation was the brooch at her throat and an enormous sapphire ring. Her glance flicked over Cynara and then dismissed her. She turned to the man standing uneasily at one side.

"This is the girl," she said.

Cynara stared at the man. He was dressed roughly in stained moleskin breeches and collarless wool shirt. On his feet were thick hobnailed boots, and his large, coarse hands had crescents of dirt beneath broken fingernails. An odor of sweat and manure emanated from him, and Cynara's nostrils contracted. He took a step toward her, leaving a trail of dust on the immaculate carpet.

Cynara drew back at the sight of the dark stubble on the man's pocked chin. There was a drop at the end of his bulbous nose and he raised his arm, wiping it away with his sleeve as he came nearer.

His eyes were small, sunk deep into their sockets, and of indeterminate color. When he looked at Cynara, she saw the gleam as his eyes came to rest on her bosom, and she wanted to turn and run from the room. She looked at Cornelia in sudden, awful comprehension. Cornelia ignored her; she was watching the man.

"Well, Smith?"

The man turned. As he did so, he gave the impression of pulling his forelock, though his hands still held his cap. "Well, I don't know, missus . . . ma'am . . . Mrs. Ward," he said doubtfully.

Cornelia winced at the roughness in his voice. "Why not?" she demanded icily.

"Well . . . she be awful young to marry . . ."

"I told you that before and you had no objections."

"Aye . . . aye . . . I did . . ."

With each word the man's head bobbed up and down. It was obvious that he was awed by Cornelia Ward, and more than uncomfortable in her presence. But Cynara was neither awed nor uncomfortable. She had recovered from her first shock, and now she stepped angrily by the man Smith and approached Cornelia Ward.

"This is insane! If you think I will willingly marry—"

"Silence!"

"I will not be silent! And I will *not* marry this man! Nothing can induce me to do so!"

"You will do as you're told," Cornelia snapped.

"I won't!"

Cornelia's fingers tightened into claws on the arms of her chair. Her face was a frozen mask, and when she spoke again, her lips barely moved. "It is not my habit to argue with ignorant young girls who forget their place," she said. "Smith!"

The man was propelled forward by the authoritative note of command. "Yes, ma'am?"

"Do you agree, or do you not?"

Smith, thus cornered, glanced at Cynara, who had turned to glare furiously at him. He swallowed. If he had been awed by the cold Cornelia, he was stricken in a much more elemental manner by Cynara. She was young, yes, and slender—not at all like the sturdy farm girls and women he was accustomed to—and he wondered if she was strong enough to share the numbing burden of endless farm work. His Hettie hadn't been; she had been worn to death in only ten years, and she had been twice the size of this girl. But Hettie hadn't had any looks to speak of, whereas this girl . . . His eyes traveled up and down her body, and unconsciously he licked his lips.

"I'm waiting, Smith!"

The man's head swung back to Cornelia. "Aye, ma'am," he gulped. "She'll do."

"Excellent." Cornelia permitted herself a ghost of a smile. "Now then, I think the marriage will take place—"

"There will be no marriage!"

Both Smith and Cornelia turned to look at Cynara. Her face was white with outrage, and she trembled with anger. "There will be no marriage," she repeated defiantly.

Smith glanced uneasily at Cornelia. "But you said—"

"I know what I said," Cornelia snapped. "The girl will obey, never fear. Now, get out. I will send for you at the proper time."

Smith bobbed his head and backed away, leaving with a rush that clearly indicated his relief at escaping from the room. As soon as he was gone, Cornelia sprang from her chair.

"I warned you, girl, that I have endured the last of your stubbornness. This matter is closed; there is nothing more to discuss." She swept past Cynara and sailed out.

Cynara watched her go. She stood frozen, unable to believe that Cornelia was serious. It must have been an elaborate charade, she thought wildly. Surely, not even Cornelia Ward would insist that she marry that disgusting, horrible, dirty man! She trembled at the thought of him, remembering the avid expression on his face as he leered at her. Marriage! They were both out of their minds!

Shakily, Cynara went to the French doors at the end of the room. It was twilight now, the moon a thin crescent in the dark sky, and suddenly Cynara longed to be outside, away from this room and the memory of that impossible scene. The man's presence still lingered, and she could smell the acrid odor of his sweat. She shuddered again, and unlatched one of the doors, moving outside and down the steps that led to the garden.

The gravel path was a ghostly gray in the dim light, and Cynara followed it for some distance before she came to a gazebo sheltered by the tall yews that curved around it. She went inside and sat down.

Clenching her hands in her lap, she thought that she must leave without delay. No matter that she had no place to go. She would find something. Any place would be preferable to this house; any work infinitely more desirable than marrying that awful man with his cruel, greedy eyes.

But how could she leave? She would have to walk, she thought, trying to remember how far it was to the village. Perhaps someone there would give her a ride to the station. She had a little money; she could pay. She shook her head impatiently. What did such details matter? The important thing was to get away immediately—and secretly. She would leave tonight before she lost courage. She—

"Well, well. Alone at last."

Cynara leaped to her feet at the sound of Myles's voice. She could barely see him, a shadow outlined against the latticework of the gazebo, and for the first time she realized how far she had walked, and how isolated was the position of the summerhouse. Her heart began to race with fear, for Myles was lounging casually against the door, the only avenue of escape.

"What do you want, Myles? Why did you follow me?" To her horror, her voice shook. She made an effort to steady it. "I must get back," she said quickly. "Your mother—"

"My mother is otherwise occupied. She is busy arranging the details of your coming marriage, I believe."

"Nevertheless, she—"

"Oh, come now, This might be our only opportunity to be alone. Or do you already prefer your—farmer?"

"Certainly not!"

"Then—"

She saw him push himself away from the door. Fear leaped inside her again, and she poised to run by him, but he was too quick for her. He raised his cane, and she stepped back warily.

"Surely you don't intend on running away again? That was very rude of you last time, Cynara."

He came toward her and she circled around him, her eyes still on the cane, which was only a thin shadow in the growing darkness. She had no doubt that he would use it if she provoked him, but her fear made her reckless; she tried to dash by him.

The stem of the cane struck her throat. She fell back, gasping.

"That was a stupid thing to do, Cynara. I really didn't want to hurt you."

"Myles—let me go." She heard the sob in her voice with alarm, and knew she must not allow him to realize how afraid she was of him.

"And send you back to that farmer, who is too dull-witted to appreciate your charms? Oh no, I couldn't do that without sampling them myself first."

Tears of desperation gathered behind her eyes. She forced them back, trying to see him in the darkness. To her horror, she saw that he had somehow closed the door of the gazebo without her being aware of it. Her eyes swept the gloom, searching for some kind of weapon to use against him, but the interior was bare of anything but the circular bench around the walls.

Myles laughed suddenly, as though he guessed her intention and was contemptuous. "You won't get away from me this time," he said.

He flung himself toward her. His fingers closed about her arm, and she screamed. "Go ahead," he cried shrilly. "Make all the noise you want. No one will hear you."

He jerked her toward him. She pulled back, unbalancing them both. She fell against one of the benches, Myles on top of her. One of his hands was at the small of her back, the other on her breast. She tried to claw his hand away, and they both crashed to the floor. Myles grunted with pain as she struck out at him. His grasp on her loosened for a second, and she scrambled to her feet. He had a handful of her skirt, dragging her back, and she kicked at him, hearing the solid thud of her foot against his shoulder. She threw herself toward the door, screaming for help.

He flung himself after her. His hands gripped her shoulders, dragging her back again. She whipped around, striking at him with both hands. "Stop it! Let me go!"

Grabbing at her flailing arms, he forced them behind her

back, holding both wrists with one hand. His mouth came down on hers, those horrible thick lips wet with saliva. His fingers fumbled inside her bodice, seeking her breast. He squeezed her flesh, and she uttered a piercing cry of pain and anger. Kicking her legs out from under her, he threw her to the floor as she tried to remove his hand. She rolled away from him, struggling to her feet, but he knocked her down again, straddling her.

He bent his head to kiss her again, and she grabbed a fistful of his hair in each hand. Jerking her hands away, he held them above her head as he covered her face with wet kisses. She whipped her head back and forth, trying to evade him, but now he settled himself on top of her, holding her chin in his hand, forcing her to open her mouth. She gagged as his tongue thrust itself inside.

Somehow, he had pushed her skirt up around her hips. She tried to kick him, but his legs were on either side of hers, holding her. His hand reached down to the tender place between her thighs, and he rammed his fingers inside her. She went rigid with shock, and in the next instant, before she could recover, he had removed his hand and had entered her. The moaning sounds he made filled her ears; the thrust of his body pressed her hard against the floor. Her hair had come loose and was tangled underneath his arm; she couldn't free herself. His pace was faster now, and he gave a sudden thrust inside her that sent a shaft of pain lancing through her entire body. She screamed as the pain ripped through her again and fought violently against his leaden weight.

He had let go of her wrists to fondle her breasts. She pushed vainly against his chest, trying to throw him off. His mouth sought hers again, and she strained her head back. She bit down as hard as she could, and Myles cried out as her teeth sank into his lip.

Rearing back, he shouted, "Damn you!" and slapped her hard across the face.

Her head whipped to the side from the force of the blow,

but she reached up with both hands and clawed at his face. "I hate you!" she shrieked. "You vile—"

He slapped her again. This time she tasted her own blood. The room was spinning; she was too dizzy to see. She felt his mouth against her throat, his teeth on her neck, biting her. He was plunging against her, her hips were ground into the floor with each thrust of his body. She arched her back in a frenzy, writhing under him as she fought to get away. Her movements excited him even more; he pounded against her, uttering animal sounds of pleasure until he gave one last shuddering cry as his final passion surged out from him. Neither of them heard the door to the gazebo crash open.

Myles only had time to register the fact that someone had grabbed him from behind. In the next instant, he was flying through the air, to land with a thud against the bench. He lay there, stunned, unable to breath from the impact against the hard wood.

Cynara looked up, terrified anew at the sight of the dark figure standing over her. In her horror and confusion, she thought that John Ward was standing there, and she tried to scramble back from him. The figure reached for her and she cried out with real fear.

"Don't touch me! Stay away from me!"

"Cynara."

His voice was harsh enough to pierce her hysteria; loud enough for her to recognize that it was not John Ward who spoke. Her voice shook as she said, "Evan?"

"Yes." The single word had a savage inflection, but she was too relieved to notice. Evan reached down and pulled her to her feet.

"Oh, Evan, I—"

The sudden scream of rage from behind her startled her so badly that she clutched Evan's arm in terror. "What—!"

Evan pushed her behind him so quickly that she had to grab at his shirt to stop herself from falling. There was a whistling sound, the shadow of Myles leaping toward them, and an instant later, Evan rocked backward as Myles attacked, swinging his cane like a madman.

"You bastard!" Myles shrieked. "You've interfered for the last time!"

Evan shoved Cynara with one hand, while he raised the other to protect himself. "Get out of here!" he shouted. "Run!" The cane swung a second time, and Cynara heard Evan hiss with pain. He yelled something at her, trying to push her out of the way, but Myles attacked again. The two crashed to the floor, rolling into her, knocking her off her feet. Pulling herself up by the bench where she had fallen, she strained to see. It was impossible in the darkness to distinguish anything other than two grappling shadows, and she hesitated. Should she run for help? But how could she leave? She had to help Evan; she had to stop Myles. The sound of their fighting filled her ears, and she was terrified that Evan would be hurt. What should she do? There wasn't time to think. She was conscious only of the frightening noise of the struggle and her fear for Evan.

Dropping to her hands and knees again, she searched blindly along the floor for the cane. She couldn't find it. A body slammed into her again, sending her slithering along the floor. The air was filled with shouts and curses, the sickening sound of fists meeting flesh, cries of pain and rage.

"Stop it! Stop it!" she screamed. She couldn't see, and her eyes strained against the darkness, searching for Evan. What was happening to him? She had to do something before they killed each other, but what? What?

Floundering to her feet, she ran to the twisting, struggling bodies on the floor. They rolled over and over again, punching and kicking, pummeling each other furiously as each fought for the advantage. They separated suddenly, both leaping to their feet, and in an instant before it happened, Cynara saw that Myles had the cane in his possession again.

"Evan!" she cried. "Look out!"

Myles swung the cane with both hands as Evan turned his head in response to her cry. Her warning was too late. Horrified, she heard the weapon crack against Evan's face.

He staggered, and then fell to his knees. Myles raised the cane again, and without thinking, Cynara leaped toward him.

Her attack surprised him. He faltered back, cursing. Cynara was after him again, fighting to take the cane away from him. Her hands closed around the stem, and for an instant they were engaged in a macabre game of tug-of-war. She was no match for Myles; he jerked the cane with such force that her fingers slipped and she flew backwards. Falling over Evan, who was prostrate on the floor, she put her hand out and happened to touch his face. Her fingers came away wet with blood, and she crouched over his motionless body, staring wildly up at Myles.

"You've killed him!" she shouted. "You've murdered him, you cruel—"

She saw the glitter in his eyes as he lifted the cane again to strike her. There was no fear in her now as she rose to meet him, only a blind rage for what he had done. She rushed toward him, knocking the cane from his hands, flinging him away from her with the force of her attack.

"Murderer!" she shouted, and hit him across the face with her closed fist.

She wanted to strike him again and again, to beat him senseless—to kill him. Myles retreated before her wild fury, his hands raised for protection as she lashed out with both fists. He reached the door. Somehow he found the opening, almost falling down the two shallow steps in his frantic haste to get away from her.

He turned to see her standing on the threshold. Her hair was wild and disheveled; her eyes blazing with anger while tears streamed down her face. "You won't get away with this, Myles! I'll—"

There was a sound behind her. She whirled around to listen. Another sound. A moan. Her heart leaped in response. Rushing back to Evan, she threw herself to her knees beside him, her ear against his chest. She could hear a heartbeat. He was alive.

She was aware of Myles creeping back to the door. Whipping her head around, she shouted, "Get out! Send someone to help, you sniveling little coward!"

"You can't talk to me that way!" Myles shrilled, safe beyond the door.

Her hand grasped the cane lying near her. She raised it, her voice shaking with fury. "If you don't get some help, I'll kill you! I mean it! I will!"

Myles backed away. Weaponless, he was not about to confront her again. He could see the shine of her teeth as her lips drew back. He turned and ran, shouting over his shoulder. "You can't threaten me like that! You can't! You'll pay for that!"

Cynara threw the weapon away from her. Bending over Evan, she whispered his name. He groaned.

"Evan, can you hear me?"

He groaned again. His hand came up to touch his bleeding face, and she drew it away. She did not know how serious the injury was, and when she gently explored it with her own fingers and he moaned, she felt a stab of fear. Was he bleeding to death?

Evan struggled to a sitting position in spite of her restraining hands. When he tried to get to his feet, he fell back with a moan, and she said urgently, "Please don't move, Evan. You're hurt—"

"Go away," he said harshly. "Leave me alone."

"But you—"

"I said, leave me alone."

She moved back, biting her lip as she watched him stumble painfully to his feet. When he swayed unsteadily and she would have helped him, he pushed her away again. "I don't . . . need your help," he muttered.

"Evan—"

"No! Stay away from me!"

He lurched toward the door and barely managed to grab onto the jamb to prevent himself from pitching forward. Breathing heavily even with that little exertion, he leaned against the doorway and rubbed his sleeve over his sweating forehead.

Cynara stepped carefully past him. She was afraid that if he tried to negotiate the steps by himself he would fall. Even in the pale moonlight, his face was tight with pain, and Cynara gasped as she saw the long slash running from his eye to his jaw. Blood glistened darkly in the dim light, dripping onto his shirt, and she was frightened again. How would she get him back to the house without assistance? She had no illusion that Myles would send someone to help, and she wondered desperately if she could manage by herself. She had to; there was no one else.

"Evan, please let me help you back to the house."

"Haven't you . . . done enough?"

His eyes were dark bruises in his face. She couldn't read their expression, but there was no mistaking the harsh accusation in his voice. She was stricken with guilt; it *was* her fault that he had been injured. She said, "I'm sorry, Evan. I didn't—"

He gestured abruptly, staggered, caught his balance again. "You and Myles . . . ." he muttered thickly. "Together. Sorry I . . . interrupted."

"What are you saying?" she cried wildly. "You can't believe—" She stopped. He was staring at her so strangely. He couldn't mean what he said; it was just the pain talking.

Heaving himself away from the doorway, he came stiffly down the steps. She went to help him, for even in the darkness she saw the terrible effort he made to stay on his feet. He jerked away from her again.

"Stay away . . . don't need your help."

This time her temper flared. "Don't be ridiculous!" she snapped. "I can't just leave you here!"

She put one arm around him, forcing him to lean against her as she started forward. He uttered an angry sound of protest, but before they had gone ten paces, she knew that he could never had made it back to the house without her help. She glanced up at him once; his face was wet with sweat, his eyes closed with the effort of putting one foot in front of the other. He was not aware of it, but with each step he leaned more and more heavily against her until it was all she could do to keep them both upright. Staggering under his weight, she forced herself to keep going, praying that they would reach the house before he collapsed.

She looked up at him again. He seemed almost on the point of fainting, and she was alarmed at his pallor. She searched for the house lights, and thought she could see a glimmer only a short distance ahead.

"It isn't much further," she panted. There was a stitch in her side and she wanted to shift position, but didn't dare. She was afraid that Evan would fall if she let go of him even for an instant. Leaning more into his weight, she tried to ease the pain in her side without his being aware of it.

"Stop."

"What is it?" She glanced anxiously at him as he pulled away. The light was less dim here, and she saw for the first time and with horror the condition of his face. The blood was congealing along the deep open slash, and his eye was beginning to swell, the skin around it darkening rapidly into a livid bruise. Uttering a shocked cry, she reached toward him as he swayed, trying to see if the eye itself had been injured. With the blood and the bruising, she couldn't tell, and she came closer, her heart in her throat, afraid of what she would see. But Evan jerked his head away, refusing to allow her to examine him.

"Go on. Leave me alone," he said harshly.

"But, Evan, I can't!" She was almost in tears now, the horror of her experience, the fight between Evan and Myles, the terrible wound he had suffered, all combining to crush her. "Please, Evan," she sobbed, "let me help you. Please!" She was crying openly now, unable to stop.

"Cynara," he said suddenly, his voice rough with emotion. He grabbed her by the shoulders, his fingers digging into her flesh. "Cynara, don't . . . cry . . ."

His hands were shaking as he pulled her close. When she

tried to look up at him, he held her even more tightly. Her cheek was pressed against his chest; she could hear his heart pounding erratically under her ear. She began to tremble; there was desperation in the way he held her, the same nameless despair she felt. Forgetting Myles, forgetting everything, she raised her head. His face was close to hers, his terrible ruin of a face, and her tears began again. She couldn't bear to see him this way; it was as though a knife had pierced her heart.

Reaching up, she laid trembling fingers against his cheek, careful not to touch that gaping slash on his face. Rising on her toes, she kissed him softly.

His response was swift, immediate. Uttering her name with a groan, he clutched at her, his mouth seeking hers, his lips hard and demanding.

The spark that burned within her leaped to flame. At the touch of his lips, she was consumed by her need once more, and this time she had no power to deny it. There was a pounding in her temples, a blaze that raged through her like a forest fire out of control. She had no will to resist; she did not want to oppose her chaotic emotions any more. Her arms went around him, holding him to her; she was oblivious to everything except the pressure of his mouth on hers, her tongue leaping to meet his, his body trembling with a response to the urgent and frantic writhings of her own.

When he pushed her away from him, she almost fell. Stunned, she looked at him and almost cringed when she saw his expression. His eyes were black pits of rage, his mouth drawn into an ugly sneer.

"Small wonder Myles couldn't keep his hands off you," he said, his voice shaking. "What a fool I was to think you needed my help! You knew what you were doing all the time, didn't you?"

His swift change of mood bewildered her. She was confused, fighting the violence of her emotions, her body still throbbing from the passion he had aroused. She gaped at him, too shocked to speak, and when he turned away from her, she couldn't stop him. It wasn't until he had gone several faltering steps that she realized what he had said.

"Evan!" Her voice was a wrenching cry across the darkness, halting him. He did not look around. "Evan, you're wrong!" she cried.

Now he did turn his head. The light from the house shone on his face, and again she was apalled by his expression. "Am I?" he asked cruelly. "I think not. It seems you are well able to take care of yourself after all, doesn't it?"

"I don't understand," she faltered, unable to take her eyes from his ravaged face.

"I mean," he said coldly," that your kind always survives, one way or the other." He paused, swaying unsteadily, holding himself upright by sheer force of will. "I should have known," he finished harshly.

"You should have known—what?" she cried.

But he had turned away again to disappear into the darkness, and this time she was powerless to call him back. Impossible to speak when his words had hit her with the force of an actual physical blow. She staggered, her hand to her mouth, feeling the rush of helpless tears over his deliberate cruelty.

Evan was mistaken, she thought wildly; she was the fool, not he. She had thought him to be different from the rest—and he was, she told herself bitterly, but not in the way she had wanted so desparately to believe. His strength was only the strength of cruelty, after all; she had been foolish to imagine he could offer anything else.

Whirling around, she ran back to the house and up to her room. Safe inside, she threw herself on the bed, clutching the pillow to her face to stifle her sobs. Remembering her instinctive reaching out to him, and the utter contempt and condemnation in Evan's face when she did so, she cried as though she would never stop.

CHAPTER SEVEN

WHEN CYNARA FINALLY pushed away the sodden pillow and dragged herself from the bed to bathe her swollen eyes, the house was quiet. There was a throbbing pain across her temples and her whole body ached; she was exhausted. Only the belatedly remembered need for haste prodded her to pull her portmanteau from under the bed; it had been a pointless extravagance to waste time crying when she should have been gone long ago.

After throwing her few things into the bag, she counted the small pile of sovereigns in her possession. It wasn't enough, but it would have to do. The urge to escape from the house hammered at her, and she grabbed her cloak. She was putting it around her shoulders when the door flew open, and an enraged Cornelia Ward stood on the threshold.

Cynara started violently at Cornelia's sudden appearance. The two stared at each other, and Cynara noticed Briggs standing behind her mistress, her long, thin face twisted with malice.

"So!" Cornelia cried. "It is true!"

She advanced one step into the room, and Cynara was appalled at the vindictiveness in the woman's expression. For a stunned moment, she thought Cornelia would actually attack her physically; never had she seen the woman so openly furious. There was nothing of the invalid about her now; she seemed to vibrate with rage.

"You *were* planning to run away with him, weren't you?" Cornelia demanded shrilly, pointing to the bag Cynara clutched in her hand.

"Him?" echoed Cynara stupidly. "Who?"

"Oh, I suspected it from the first—you with your bold eyes and pert ways! But to run off with that . . . that stableboy!"

"Evan? Do you mean Evan?" Cynara was aghast. "But I never—"

"Don't speak to me, you shameless creature! First you ruin my son, and then you take up with that—"

"Ruin your son? Is that what he told you?" Cynara choked. "He lies. He lies! He was the one—"

"How dare you call my son a liar! Oh, marrying that farmer is too good for you! I will send you away—far away, where you can do no more harm!"

"Listen to me!" Cynara shouted. "Myles—"

"Don't try to explain. I should have listened to my instincts long ago and gotten rid of you before you—seduced my son! Oh, spare me that wide-eyed expression!" Cornelia raged. "I know what you are, and this time I will make sure you never approach my son again!"

Cornelia whipped around. The door slammed behind her, and an instant before it happened, Cynara knew what she intended. Dropping the bag, she rushed over to the door. As her fingers closed around the knob, she heard the harsh rasp of the key in the lock outside. She wrenched at the door, but it didn't move.

"No! You can't do this!" she screamed. She pounded at the door with both fists, grabbed the knob again in a frenzy and kicked at the resisting wood. "Let me out! You must listen to me! Please . . ."

She shouted until she was hoarse, but there was no answer from the other side. Defeated, exhausted, she covered her face with her hands and slid to the floor in a heap. Myles had won after all.

Some time later she heard the sounds of a horse being brought out from the stables, and she rushed to the window. Pulling back the curtain, she saw Watson, the elderly butler, speaking urgently to an obviously annoyed Jacob while Jimmy held the horse. She couldn't hear what was said, but Jacob gestured furiously in the butler's face. Watson stubbornly pointed to the horse, and finally Jacob heaved himself into the saddle. Jerking the reins so savagely that the animal almost reared, the coachman turned the horse and kicked it violently. The animal leaped forward, almost unseating him.

As horse and rider disappeared down the drive that led to the side gate, Cynara saw Jimmy sidle up to Watson and ask him something at which the man shrugged in response. Then both of them turned to stare up at the house. Dismayed, for it seemed to her that they were both looking directly at the window where she was standing, Cynara stepped back quickly. When she peered out again, the yard was deserted.

Her hands trembled as she lit the lamp. Had she imagined the avid curiosity on their faces? She knew she hadn't, and she wondered uneasily where Jacob had been sent in the middle of the night. Had Cornelia ordered her coachman to fetch that horrible man, Smith? Cynara shuddered at the thought, then shook her head. No, it couldn't be that; Cornelia had said something about sending her away. But if that was so, where had Jacob gone?

Long hours later, Cynara heard the first stirrings that meant the servants were up. Rising stiffly from her chair, she passed a weary hand over her eyes. Unable to sleep, her thoughts had forced her back relentlessly to that terrifying episode in the gazebo with Myles. She had relived it again and again in her mind, and each time the horror was no less vivid. Remembering Myles's rough hands fondling her, remembering the savage violation of her body, she wanted to cry. But there were no tears left; she sat dry-eyed, mute, staring at the floor. Now and then her thoughts would turn to Evan, and she would feel a shrinking inside herself. Whether or not it was her fault, Evan had been injured because of her, and as the hours passed she became more and more afraid that he was seriously hurt. He could be lying somewhere, unconscious, with no one to help him, and her fears increased to such a pitch that she sat huddled in the chair, shaking uncontrollably.

When her tension became unbearable, she tried to calm herself by remembering that he had walked away from her under his own power. If he could do that, he would be all right, she assured herself time and again. He would be all right.

But the knot in her stomach refused to go away, and so she sat, fists clenched, trembling, reliving that terrible time in the summerhouse . . . until she thought she would scream with the horror of it all.

No one came to unlock the door until that afternoon. When Cynara finally heard the key in the lock, she turned and faced the door, knowing in advance who was on the other side. The summons might come from Cornelia, but it would be Briggs who begged to deliver it.

It was. Briggs unlocked the door with a satisfied flourish, holding it open with an ill-concealed air of excitement. "Come with me, girl. The master and the mistress want you in the library."

Without waiting for an answer, the maid started off down the corridor. Cynara followed her, marveling at the calm feeling inside her. Her fear had gone; in its place was only a vast emptiness.

They reached the head of the stairs, and Rosie appeared, her eyes wide with distress. Rosie fell into step beside Cynara, darting an anxious glance at Briggs, who had not turned around.

"Oh, miss!" she whispered, almost in tears. "There's trouble—"

It was then that Cynara realized she was not as calm as she believed. Her voice shook when she whispered, "What is it?"

"I don't know, but there's a strange man in the master's study—"

Briggs had turned the corner, and was marching off down the corridor. As Cynara and Rosie trailed after her, Rosie continued in a low voice, "If there's anything I can do—"

Cynara slowed her pace. She had to ask; she must know about Evan. Urgently she whispered, "Rosie, how is Evan?"

Rosie's eyes widened even more. "You didn't know?"

"What?"

"Why, he's—"

"Rosie!" Briggs had stopped at the library door to glare at the little maid. "You have no business here. Go on about your work immediately!"

Rosie's cheeks flushed angrily. She was about to offer a pert reply when Cynara said quickly, "It's all right, Rosie. Really." It was an effort to smile reassuringly, but she did so for Rosie's sake, and with one last worried glance, Rosie moved away reluctantly.

Taking a deep breath, Cynara brushed by the smug Briggs and entered the library.

As before, Cornelia was seated on one of the chairs by the fire. But this time her husband was with her; he stood slightly to one side, his hand resting on the back of the chair. At first glance, they might have been posing for a portrait, and Cynara smiled grimly to herself at the obvious attempt at melodrama. How ridiculous they both were!

There was someone else in the room. As he stepped forward, Cynara drew in a shocked breath as she recognized him. "Mr. Bertram!" she exclaimed.

Bertram inclined his head. "I regret that we meet again in such . . . ah . . . unpleasant circumstances," he said.

"And I regret that we meet at all," Cynara snapped, forgetting all caution as anger surged through her. "How dare you show your face when you have betrayed my father's trust! You charlatan!"

Bertram's face colored at the epithet. He snapped, "I see that your deplorable lack of control is still much in evidence.

It seems obvious that you have brought this contretemps upon yourself, Miss Rosslyn. Perhaps you might reflect on that and apply your conclusions to the situation at hand."

"Which is?" Cynara demanded angrily.

"Simply this," Bertram responded, smiling spitefully. "Mr. and Mrs. Ward have found it necessary to sign a complaint against you. It appears that you were responsible for provoking an attack upon their son, Myles. A nasty business, Miss Rosslyn; but for their compassion, such an act might be construed as attempted murder!"

"That's absurd!"

"Is it? Well, perhaps we should consult the injured party." Bertram glanced at the Wards. "With your permission?"

Cornelia nodded, her expression malignant as her eyes rested on Cynara. "Briggs," she said, "please ask my son to come in."

"Here I am, Mama."

Myles shouldered his way past Briggs, who had been standing, unnoticed by Cynara, at the door. As he passed Cynara, he dared to glance at her triumphantly, and she stiffened furiously. He took up a position beside his mother, and Cynara saw for the first time the cut on his lip, and the swelling under his eye. She wished savagely that Evan had beaten his face to a pulp.

"Tell us the story you told last night, dear," Cornelia said.

"Yes, Myles," Cynara snapped, "Do tell us your story!"

Myles ran his tongue over his lip, winced, and looked away from Cynara. Speaking to Abel Bertram, he began, "Last night, Cynara asked me to accompany her on a walk around the garden—"

"I did no such thing!" Cynara cried, outraged.

"You will be silent, girl," John Ward commanded coldly. "You will have your opportunity to speak when Myles is finished." He looked at his son. "Please continue, Myles."

"Well, I refused at once, of course. You see, she had made similar advances toward me before, and—"

"That's a lie, and you know it!"

"I will not have these constant interruptions!" John Ward took a threatening step toward her, but angrily Cynara held her ground. "Sit down and be still, or I will have you removed. Is that understood?"

There was no mistaking the menace in his tone. If he forced her to leave the room, she would have no opportunity to defend herself. Reluctantly, she sat down in the chair he indicated and tried to calm herself enough to listen to what Myles was saying.

Myles darted a glance at her, then appealed to Bertram. "What else could I do? I'm sure you understand . . . It was very difficult to refuse her . . ."

Bertram nodded solemnly, and it was all Cynara could do to remain sitting in her chair. Gritting her teeth, she waited for Myles to continue.

"We walked some distance, and finally came to the gazebo. Cynara wanted to go in, and at first I refused, but . . ." He shrugged helplessly again.

Bertram said pompously, "Are you trying to tell us that Miss Rosslyn actually made—overtures—toward you?"

"Yes," Myles answered in a low voice.

Cynara could keep silent no longer. Leaping to her feet, she cried, "This is insane! Every word he speaks is a lie!"

"Do you deny that you made advances to my son?"

Cynara whirled around to face Cornelia. "Yes, I deny it. I deny it all!"

Cornelia motioned to Briggs. The maid came forward, and Cornelia ordered, "Briggs, tell us about the incident you yourself witnessed."

Briggs had folded her hands in front of her. Her eyes were meekly downcast, but Cynara saw the smug twitch of her lips, and the surreptitious glance in Cynara's direction before she began to speak. "It was several days after the girl arrived, madam. I believe you had sent her to press one of your gowns. I was on the stairs when she met Master Myles in the corridor, and I saw her draw him to one side. She was whispering and giggling, and then she put her arms around him and—and kissed him!" Briggs looked up, and the malice glittered openly in her eyes. "Poor Master Myles! I could see how embarrassed he was, and I discreetly withdrew before he saw me there."

"And you reported this incident to your mistress immediately?" asked Bertram.

Briggs appeared shocked at the question. "Of course! It was a most disgraceful exhibition, and I thought Mrs. Ward should be informed at once!"

"So," Bertram said to Myles, "Last night does not appear to be the first time Miss Rosslyn tried to force her attentions upon you."

"Oh, no." Myles shook his head. "But last night, there was another reason for her insistence."

"Which was?"

"Mama was going to arrange for Cynara to be married—"

"Married?" Bertram interrupted with surprise. He glanced quickly at Cornelia.

"Yes," Cornelia said, too smoothly. "I thought it best for all concerned. I'm sure you understand?"

They looked at each other. Finally, Bertram said, "Indeed."

"Anyway," Myles said loudly, "Cynara thought I might be persuaded to change Mama's mind. She offered me . . . *anything* . . . if I would speak to Mama about it."

"And what did you say?"

It was Myles turn to appear shocked. "I refused, of course!"

"And then?"

"It was then that she called out to Evan. Apparently, he had been waiting outside. He took me by surprise—" Myles raised his hand to indicate his cut and swollen face "as you can see. I tried to defend myself as best I could, but against the two of them—"

"Do you mean that Miss Rosslyn actually attacked you?"

"Yes. She was furious that I wouldn't help her. It

seems—" Myles glanced again at Cynara, who stood rooted in the center of the room, too stupified to speak. His expression swelled with triumph. "It seems that she and Evan had decided to run away together. And they couldn't very well do that if Cynara was going to be married to someone else, could they?"

For a horrified instant, Cynara thought she was going to faint. Myles had so cleverly piled lie upon lie that she knew it was useless to refute his story. She felt weak with shock; the room seemed to waver dizzily as she fought the blackness bearing down on her.

And then Cornelia said disdainfully, "You see? The girl knows she has no defense."

The faintness vanished abruptly as anger raced through Cynara again. She straightened, staring defiantly at the predatory little group. "It is obvious," she said, and by some miracle her voice held steady, "that whatever I say will be disregarded. Nevertheless—" her eyes fell on one after the other contemptuously "some effort must be made to expose these lies. Last night, Myles followed me to the summerhouse to attack me. If Evan hadn't heard me screaming for help—"

Shrilly, Myles interrupted. "You see! I told you she would try to twist things around! She's only saying what Evan told her to say!"

"That's absurd!" Cynara snapped. "And if you don't believe me, ask Evan!"

"I'm afraid we cannot do that," Cornelia said complacently.

Something in her tone brought Cynara's head up sharply. "Why not?"

"Because"—now there was no mistaking the satisfaction in Cornelia's voice— "the Calder boy is gone."

"Gone! That's impossible!"

"Nevertheless," Cornelia said coldly, "It is true." She paused. "And so there is no one to substantiate your story. A pity, isn't it?"

Cynara hardly heard her. Sinking into a chair, she whispered, "He can't be gone."

John Ward was saying something. They were all looking at her with various expressions of glee and malice, but Cynara did not notice. She was thinking of Evan as he had looked the night before. She saw again the pain in his eyes, the gaping slash across his cheek, the blood dripping from his face. He couldn't have gone anywhere, she thought wildly. They must have done something to him!

The thought brought her out of her chair in a rush. "What did you do to him?" she cried.

"Do to him?" Cornelia repeated contemptuously. "What makes you think we have 'done' anything to him? How ridiculous!"

"It isn't ridiculous! Evan was badly injured—yes, injured!" she shouted into their faces. "Myles had almost killed him! He—"

"Oh, really!" Cornelia sniffed.

"Yes, really!" Cynara was almost weeping with sheer frustration. "Evan was in no condition to leave; he needed my help just to walk back to the house!"

"Then you admit Evan was at the summerhouse?"

Cynara was too angry to notice the oiliness in Bertram's voice as he asked the question.

"Yes, of course he was there!" she snapped.

"And you admit, also, that there was a struggle of some sort in which you took part?"

"Yes," she cried. "I told you—"

"And you threatened, at some point, to kill Myles?" Bertram pressed.

"I wanted to make him go for help! Can't you understand? Evan was injured. I thought he was dying—"

"It appears that he was far from dying, if he had the strength to steal away in the middle of the night." John Ward's voice was cold. He flicked at an imaginary speck of lint on his coat. "It seems to me," he continued casually,

"That when Evan realized your little plan went awry, he thought it best to remove himself. Leaving you—" his bulging eyes rested on her "To explain as best you could. Not the most courageous of champions, wouldn't you agree? But then, I wouldn't expect anything else of him."

"There was no plan!" Cynara shouted.

Suddenly, to her dismay, all the faces seemed to blur before her eyes. Shaking her head, she looked again and saw that they had merged into one fleshy mass. Alarmed, she tried to reach for the chair, but the floor tilted crazily under her feet and she knew she was going to faint. The rug seemed to rise up to meet her, and she only had time to utter a disbelieving cry before everything went black.

". . . then it's all settled. Jacob is waiting outside with the carriage."

Cynara opened her eyes at the sound of Cornelia's voice. Disoriented, she lay quietly where someone had carried her and tried to make sense out of the conversation. There was a buzzing in her ears and she still felt dizzy; the voices drifted in and out of her consciousness without any meaning at all.

"And Abel," Cornelia said sharply, "Remember our agreement."

"Of course, dear cousin," Bertram replied sarcastically. "Would I betray you at this late date?"

"See that you don't. There are ways to insure that you have fulfilled your part of the bargain."

"That won't be necessary."

"Let us hope not."

Cynara struggled to a sitting position. As she did so, her eyes fell on her portmanteau by the doorway. Was it possible, she wondered, that Cornelia was actually going to allow her to leave? Her spirits rose immediately at the thought, and she stood up shakily.

Cornelia saw the movement. "Abel," she said, and gestured toward Cynara.

Bertram approached Cynara. Taking her arm firmly, he said, "Come along, Miss Rosslyn. We must hurry if we are to meet the train."

Cynara pulled back. "Where are you taking me?" she asked sharply, not trusting the peculiar light in his eyes.

"Don't argue with me!" Bertram whispered fiercely.

Cynara saw his glance go nervously to Cornelia, and suddenly she understood. Bertram wanted desperately for Cornelia to believe he was capable of handling this situation. Her first instinct was to refuse to accompany him, but then she realized the alternative was equally repugnant: If she balked at going with Bertram, she would have to remain at the Manor. There was really no choice, after all.

Without further protest, she allowed Bertram to guide her from the room. But before they went out, she paused to look back. She saw the satisfied gleam in Cornelia's eyes, the amused regret on John Ward's face as he turned from where he had been standing by the liquor cabinet. He raised his glass in a mocking salute and something within her rebelled.

"I pity you—all of you," she said clearly, scornfully, her glance resting briefly upon each of them. "You think you have won some kind of victory in sending me away, but nothing could be worse to me than staying here. I find every one of you utterly contemptible."

She would have said more, but Bertram, uttering a groan, almost dragged her from the doorway. Behind her, incredibly, she heard Cornelia laugh shrilly. Bertram obviously heard it too, for he quickened his pace, pulling her after him.

Outside, he handed her unceremoniously into the carriage. Gesturing to Jacob, who glared down at them from his position on the box, Bertram climbed in after her and shut the door.

"Wait!"

The carriage, which had begun to move forward, jerked to a halt as Myles came rushing down the steps toward it. Cynara closed her eyes; she had hoped to get away without being forced to speak to him again. He had proved himself not only to be a cunning enemy, but a formidable one as well; if she was forced to concede victory on his part, at least she would not admit it to his face. Staring straight ahead, she ignored him as he poked his head inside the carriage.

"Well, haven't you anything to say?"

His spiteful tone, and the glee with which the words were delivered, were her undoing. She had vowed that she wouldn't respond to anything he said, but she could not disregard the triumphant malice in his voice. Turning her head, she looked directly into that face she despised. It seemed to her that she would never forget those piglike eyes or the pouting, glistening mouth. His features were singed upon her mind forever, as was the memory of his hands clutching her, and his body violating hers.

"Well?" he demanded, grinning exultantly.

"Yes," she answered clearly, "I do have something to say. I think you are the most disgusting, depraved creature I ever had the misfortune to encounter. And I only wish Evan had killed you when he had the chance."

Myles's face reddened as Cynara's words struck home. Closing his fist, he hit the carriage door so violently that the wood rattled against the frame. His mouth twisted to utter some obscenity, but Jacob, misinterpreting the noise for a signal to move on, raised his whip. The carriage leaped forward, and Myles was forced to jump back to avoid being run over. His shrill screams of abuse followed the carriage down the drive.

Cynara did not look back. Staring straight ahead, oblivious to Bertram beside her (mopping his forehead in relief that they had got away without further incident) Cynara forgot Myles. As the carriage whipped through the tall iron gates with their majestic lyrebird signature, Cynara wanted to forget them all. But it was impossible to forget; whatever memories she carried away with her from Lyrebird Manor, there would always be one face, one memory that lingered treacherously in her heart.

Cynara tried to thrust the thought from her mind. Turning her head, she gazed out at the lush countryside beyond the window. But as the carriage sped on, it wasn't the rich fields she saw, nor the sheep grazing in their green pastures. In spite of her fierce efforts to forget him, she was obsessed with thoughts of Evan. She saw his face, darkly sensual, his eyes that seemed to burn through her, his mouth that could arouse her to fevered response. She saw his hands, strong and long-fingered, and she felt them on her body, touching her, caressing her, making her weak with desire.

He could have done anything with her, she thought dully. When she was near him, she was like clay, to be molded and shaped by him. Her passion for him was beyond her control; she would have offered anything, surrendered everything, just to be in his arms.

Even now, humiliated and shamed by the truth, she could not forget him, could not subdue her torturous longing to have him make love to her. She pictured him, young, strong, hard-muscled, his skin glistening with sweat, his body lean and supple, throbbing with the utter animal maleness of him, and she closed her eyes as a stabbing pain of loss clutched her.

He had gone; he had deserted her, and she had watched him go, knowing what he thought of her, unable to convince him that it wasn't true. It was a terrible irony that her passion for him was the one thing that had driven him away, and she had been helpless, unable to stop him, unable to control the blazing emotion she felt for him.

She should hate him for leaving; she should despise him for what he believed of her. But all she could feel was an aching, agonizing emptiness, as though a part of her had been cut away, leaving her to wither and die. She should hate him, but she could not.

Staring sightlessly out the window, her eyes were hard and bright. She would never see him again; she would never be whole again, and she had no tears left to cry.

CHAPTER EIGHT

"DON'T COME ANY closer!" Cynara said sharply as Bertram approached her again. "You may have imprisoned me in your house, but if you think to do more than that, you're sadly mistaken!"

"You don't understand," Bertram attempted, placatingly.

"I understand perfectly!" Cynara snapped. "Did you actually believe that I would throw myself at you in gratitude for delivering me from Cornelia Ward?" She tossed her head contemptuously as Bertram winced at her choice of words. "Get out!" she ordered. "Leave me alone!"

"Your situation could be worse," Bertram responded spitefully. "And will be, unless you listen to reason."

"Listen to reason!" Cynara mocked. "And what does that mean? Are you trying to threaten me into becoming your mistress?"

Bertram's face reddened. "There is no need to be vulgar," he said stiffly.

"Well, what word would you prefer, Mr. Bertram? Lady-love? Paramour?" Cynara didn't know where the words came from, but she took satisfaction in flinging them into Bertram's now-crimson face. "Whatever you wish to call it, the result is still the same. And if that was your intention, you will have to look elsewhere!"

"Don't play coy with me, Cynara. I know all about you!"

Cynara grabbed the hairbrush on the table behind her. Lifting it, she hurled it straight at Bertram's head as he came toward her. It missed by inches, clattering to the floor behind him, and as she grabbed the lamp, he paled.

"Get out! Did you hear me? Get out!"

The door slammed behind him as he retreated with undignified haste, but safe on the other side, she could hear him shouting dire threats as he locked the door. Finally there was silence, and Cynara was alone again.

Had it only been two days since she had left Lyrebird Manor? Already it seemed like a lifetime, she thought. And now she must not only endure being a prisoner in this house; she must withstand Bertram's advances as well. Grimacing at the thought of the sly oiliness of the man, she went to the windowseat and threw herself down.

Tucking her legs under her, chin resting on her hand, she looked out at the gray, dismal London day. Fog misted the window so heavily that she couldn't see the street below through the thick blankness. The clock ticked loudly on the mantle, and as her eyes went to it, she saw the room in its entirety and she grimaced again.

It wasn't that her surroundings were unpleasant; Bertram had obviously given her the best guest room—in hopes, she thought angrily, of persuading her to alter her opinion of him and allow him to take her to his bed. She laughed shortly; at least she had managed to dissuade him of that. Fortunately, he seemed almost to be afraid of her; his spiteful courage had evaporated rapidly so far from Cornelia's presence, and at the first indication that she would not be subdued willingly, he had been at a loss.

Her expression was bitter as she got up to replenish the fire. She had learned much from her experiences at Lyrebird Manor; she should almost be grateful to Myles and John Ward for opening her eyes. Now it was so much easier to fight back when approached. And fight back she had; the hairbrush was not the first thing she had thrown at Bertram.

As she stared into the cheerfully leaping flames in the grate, Cynara felt tired and depressed. The brief flare of anger at Bertram had faded; she was more discouraged than before. Bertram had refused to explain the reason for her imprisonment; he would not tell her when, or if, he would allow her to leave. And why, she asked herself sourly, was she so anxious to leave here when her future prospects were as dismal as the dreary day beyond the window? The most she could expect was a post as governess, or companion to a dried-up, petulant old woman who might even be worse than Cornelia Ward.

Moving away from the fireplace, Cynara wandered about the room. Inactivity had taken a toll on her nerves. Jumpy and restless, she longed to go outside, even in the chill, just to get away from the confines of this room. Impossible request, she thought irritably; Bertram would not allow her to go out.

Utterly bored, Cynara threw herself across the bed. It wasn't fair that when her spirits were at their lowest point, she should think of Evan. Evan was gone, she told herself; he had deserted her at the very moment she needed him most, and she despised him for that. And yet . . . hadn't she been about to do the same? If Cornelia hadn't locked the door, she would have run away herself. So how could she blame Evan for doing the same?

She did blame him; she did. Squirming inwardly at the injustice of her feelings toward Evan, she turned on to her side, cheek against the pillow. She had to forget him, she told herself angrily. She would never see him again. And she wouldn't even want to see him again, she vowed. She had been stupid and romantic, imagining herself in love with him. Recalling her thoughts as she was driven away from Lyrebird Manor, she squirmed inwardly. How could she have been such a fool? The anger and contempt he had shown her at the last had been his true feelings for her—why had she chosen to believe otherwise? It was clear what Evan Calder thought of her, if he thought of her at all. He had forgotten her, just as she intended to forget him.

But the last thing she pictured in her mind before she fell asleep was Evan's face. She saw him as she wanted to see him, and in her sleep, she sighed.

Cynara struggled to awaken from the grip of a nightmare in which rough hands had grabbed her. A sudden shaft of light stabbed at her closed lids, and with a cry, she woke.

It was no dream. Two dark figures were leaning over her, trying to lift her from the bed. Terrified, she tried to scream as she fought, but a wad of cotton was shoved into her mouth, gagging her, increasing her fear.

Panic gave her strength. Jerking her arms away from one, she kicked at the other man and leaped off the bed.

"Catch her, you fools!"

The voice belonged to Bertram, silhouetted in the doorway. She had no time to wonder at his appearance; the two men were coming after her again. Clawing at the horrible gag in her mouth, she ran past one, ducked under the outstretched arms of the other, and dashed toward Bertram and the open door.

Her rush panicked Bertram. He shouted something, but Cynara's wild dash caught him in midsentence. She collided forcefully with him, and they both crashed to the floor in a tangle.

"Let me go!" Cynara struck at his hands, which had clutched at her during the fall. She kicked at his legs, which were tangled in her skirt, and in desperation, jabbed her elbow into his stomach. He released her with a grunt, and she leaped away from him.

Behind her, she heard Bertram gasp something about a ship, but she didn't look back. The stairs were directly in front of her and she raced toward them. Her hand was on the newel post when an arm caught her around the waist, swinging her off her feet, almost crushing the breath out of her.

"You're hurting me!" she cried.

The arm did not release her. Panic stricken, Cynara fought like someone possessed. Arms and legs flailing, she tried violently to get away. Her frantic movements almost overbalanced her assailant, and he staggered, wrapping both arms about her.

"Give a hand here, Tom! This one's a real hellcat!"

The other man loomed suddenly in front of her. She reached out to claw at his face, her nails leaving a streak of red down one side. He jerked back, one hand going to his cheek in surprise and pain.

"I can't hold her!"

The clawed face came toward her again. "Sorry, little lady . . ."

To her horror, she saw his closed fist. She cried out once as pain burst in her jaw, and bright sparks of light flashed before her eyes as she spun away into darkness.

A long time later, she felt as though someone was rocking her. The undulating motion was soothing, but whatever she was lying on was not. With a great effort, she opened her eyes.

A smoking, grimy lantern was swaying back and forth over her head. There was a face under it, an oval framed in reddish curls with eyes that were wide and knowing.

"You took quite a punch, didn't you? How do you feel now?"

"I . . ." Cynara tried to sit up, then fell back, gasping with dizziness. Her jaw throbbed fiercely, and she felt nauseated and faint. There was a horrible smell of staleness and sweat in the air, and she felt a sickening lurch in her stomach again. What had happened to her? She couldn't remember. "Where am I?" she asked.

The face bent closer. "You're on the *Sea Swan.*"

"What?" She couldn't have heard right. There was a ringing in her ears, and she couldn't think over the pain and that hideous odor and the stifling heat. Slowly, her eyes moved away from the woman bending over her. For the first time, she became aware that they were not alone; women in various stages of undress were scattered about this room which seemed to have no door, only tiny round windows imbedded in curved walls of wood. Twisting her head, wincing from the pain even that small movement caused, Cynara saw other lanterns hanging from hooks, all swaying gently as they cast a sickly yellow glow over the assemblage.

In a sudden panic, she clutched at the hand offered her. "I'm not . . . this can't be . . . we aren't on a *ship!*"

The woman nodded. Patting Cynara's hand matter-of-factly, she replied, "I'm Sarah Janes. You're going to get a bit of a gliff if you didn't know before, but this isn't no ordinary ship . . ."

Cynara had a difficult time focusing on the woman's face. She could feel herself growing faint again in spite of her efforts to resist it. "What do you mean?" she asked shakily.

"This is a transport ship—we're on our way to Australia."

"Australia!"

Cynara's last thought before she fell back into unconsciousness was of Myles. She could see his grinning face, his triumphant eyes, and she knew that while Abel Bertram might have arranged her transportation, and Cornelia Ward might have ordered it, it was Myles who was responsible. As her head fell back against the planking, Cynara vowed that someday, no matter how long it took, Myles would pay, and pay dearly for what he had done to her.

PART II

CHAPTER NINE

" 'ERE, MATE! WHAT'S up with you?"

The man staggered back in astonishment as Evan turned fiercely toward him. In the predawn gloom, the look on Evan's just visible face made the man raise his hand protectively.

"Aw, man, I jus' asked you for a copper or two!" the man muttered defensively as he backed away. As he set off at a shuffling run away from Evan, he cried over his shoulder, "Keep your money! From the looks of that face, you need it more than me, poor bugger!"

Evan watched the drunk until he disappeared in the dark shadows lining the wharf. Only when the man was gone did Evan's hand come up to touch his face. He winced; the gash along his cheek was still tender under his fingers.

Hunching his shoulders against the icy chill that swept across the dock, Evan glanced around. It was still too early for the wharf office to be open, and the dock was deserted. He fingered the few coins in the pocket of his coat and then shrugged. It was senseless to waste his dwindling resources on a room before he knew he could find work; better to find a place here to rest until the offices opened.

A few packing crates stood near the wharf office. Evan moved stiffly toward them and dropped down where they formed an angle. At least here he was sheltered from the wind, and out of sight in case the drunk decided to return with friends.

Resting his head against the hard slats at his back, Evan allowed himself the luxury of giving in to his utter weariness. He had been on the road for almost two weeks and he was exhausted. Perhaps Oliver had been right in telling him to wait until he was strong enough to travel. It seemed ridiculous to Evan that one blow from Myles's cane had weakened him to this extent, and yet he still had spells of dizziness and blurred vision that infuriated him. He had gone on in spite of it, though, because the desire to put as much distance between himself and the Manor had driven him beyond the needs of his body.

The thought of Oliver brought that last night forcefully into his mind. As he had done so many times as a child, Evan had instinctively gone to Oliver that night after the fight with Myles, and while part of him was still ashamed that he had sought out the old man, he was grateful that he had. Oliver had given him so much over the years; it was impossible to think of leaving without at least saying good-bye to the man who had been more than a father to him. It was distressing to remember that last farewell; if he hadn't been so blinded by rage and pain, he doubted that he could have left the old man behind. Remembering now the look on Oliver's face when he had stumbled through the door of the cottage, Evan winced.

"God in heaven!" Oliver, who rarely swore, had been so aghast at the sight of Evan that he stood frozen for several seconds where he had leaped from his chair by the meager fire.

"Oliver . . ."

Evan, dazed and weak, clutched at the door frame, sway-ing unsteadily. "Oliver, I . . ."

"My God!" Oliver dropped the book he held and rushed over to Evan as he started to fall. Staggering under Evan's weight, the old man helped him to the dilapidated sofa just as Evan collapsed.

"What happened?" Sheer horror at the sight of the ugly wound distorting Evan's face thickened Oliver's voice. He stared, transfixed, at the gaping slash whose edges had turned purple with congealed blood. "I must get a doctor—"

Evan reached out and gripped Oliver's wrist so fiercely that he winced. "No. No doctor. There isn't time."

"But—"

"No."

"Evan, listen to me," Oliver pleaded, almost desperately. "That slash must be stitched. I can't do it."

"No," Evan said again. "I didn't come for that." He paused, willing the faintness away so that he could continue. "Oliver, I'm leaving. I can't stay—after tonight . . ."

"Whatever you say," Oliver soothed. He felt his heart pounding with fear as he wondered what had happened. Glancing again at Evan's face, he shuddered, and then went quickly to the tiny kitchen. Returning moments later, he set a tray on the table and took from it a cloth dipped in warm water. This he applied to Evan's cheek, biting his lip when Evan could not hold back a groan.

"Here. Take a sip of this," he ordered, holding a cup of steaming tea to Evan's lips.

Evan drank. The tea was heavily laced with a measure of Oliver's precious brandy, and as the warmth and the alcohol penetrated through his body, Evan felt less weak. He tried to sit up, but Oliver gently pushed him back.

"Let me at least try to clean this wound," Oliver pleaded. "Can you tell me what happened?"

As Oliver sponged and dabbed, Evan related briefly the scene in the summerhouse. The old man remained silent for the most part, exclaiming sharply when Evan told him about Myles's rape of Cynara, and again when Evan told him about the savage attack with the cane.

". . . and that's why I have to leave tonight," Evan finished. "God knows what story Myles has already told his father, and I can't hope to defend myself against his lies." He paused for a moment, his eyes darkening. "And if I go back," he added softly, menacingly, "I'll surely kill him."

"But where will you go?"

Evan started. In the pause that had followed his last words, he had withdrawn into himself, almost relishing the thought of returning to the house and seeking Myles out to kill him. He could feel his hands closing around that fat throat, as they had once before; but this time, he wouldn't stop. He would choke the life out of Myles, as he had wanted to so many times in the past.

Of Cynara, he tried not to think at all. Even now the memory of her sprawled under Myles was enough to madden him. The physical pain he suffered was nothing compared to the mental anguish that picture evoked, and he passed a hand over his eyes, trying to shut out the sight of it.

He could not. His desire for her raged in him, fueled by the thought that Myles had taken what he had dreamed about so many empty nights. Now instead of seeing the summerhouse, his fevered imagination presented another scene, one where Cynara was not afraid, one in which her desire matched his. He could almost feel the warmth of her bare skin, feel the thrust of her breasts against his chest. Her hair would be loose, covering her shoulders like a mantle, and he would grab fistfuls of it, burying his face in the scent of it, in the scent of her. He would lift her in his arms, and she would be feather-light as they kissed, her arms wrapped around his neck, her body straining against his.

The bed he carried her to would have satin sheets, as pale cream as her skin, and there would be a satin curtains he would let down, shutting them inside. It would be dark and warm, and she would pull him down next to her, lips eager, body avid for him. She would be seductive, laughing softly, tempting him one minute with the sweetness of her body, withdrawing the next, exciting him to fever pitch with sinuous movements, offering her breasts for him to kiss before moving playfully away again. She would be the huntress, he the prey, and he would let her play the game until his desire could no longer be contained. Then he would grab her, burying himself in the lushness of her woman's body, driving them both to the madness of pure passion.

"Evan?"

"What?" With an effort, he brought his attention back to the worried Oliver, his dream of Cynara vanishing abruptly at the look on Oliver's face.

"I asked, where will you go?"

Oliver's expression was anxious, and Evan looked away. "I don't know," he muttered. "I haven't thought about it. But wherever it is, it will be far from here—and Myles."

Too distressed for comment, Oliver sat silently, his head bowed. Evan reached across to grasp the old man by the shoulder. "Don't worry," he said quietly. "When I can, I'll send for you."

Oliver glanced up quickly. "No. no. I am an old man. I don't want to be a burden to you."

"Don't be ridiculous!" Evan snapped. "I can't leave you here alone."

Forcing a smile, Oliver said gently, "It's past time for me, Evan. But you have to think of yourself. I know you have stayed all this time because of me. No, don't deny it; I know it's true, and I'm grateful. More grateful than I can say. But you must go—and quickly."

Swiftly, before Evan could object, Oliver got up and went to a cupboard on the other side of the room. When he returned, he carried a small chamois bag which he pressed into Evan's hands. "Here. Take it. I only wish it was more," he added sadly.

Evan felt the weight of the coins inside the bag. He shook his head. "No. I don't need it."

"I want you to have it, Evan," Oliver said softly. Please . . ."

Evan was about to refuse again, but something in the old man's expression made him hesitate. He searched Oliver's face and then nodded abruptly. "You'll get it back," he said harshly, to cover his emotion.

Oliver nodded. "Yes. I know I will." He helped Evan up from the sofa and to the door. "Evan, when you get settled, will you write to me and let me know—" His voice faltered; he could not go on.

"Of course," Evan answered, hearing the break in his own voice. "Of course, I'll write."

Oliver held out his hand. "God go with you, Evan," he said softly.

"And you . . ." Evan grasped the hand Oliver offered.

For a moment they stared at each other, and Evan saw that the faded blue eyes of the old man had filled with tears. Abruptly he pulled Oliver to him in a fierce embrace that acknowledged all the years Oliver had given him, and then he turned swiftly and was gone.

"What's this? Up a little early, aren't you, lad?"

Evan started, cursing himself inwardly for his lack of caution. He had been so absorbed that he hadn't even heard the man approach. As he jumped to his feet, he saw that the sky had lightened without his being aware of it, and that the man in front of him was regarding him curiously.

"Are you the wharf master?" Evan asked. His voice was rough, covering his embarrassment.

The man laughed, exposing a gold front tooth that glinted in the early morning light. He was powerfully built, with broad shoulders under a fur lined greatcoat, his large head capped with a beaver hat. Beneath the hat his round face sported a bristling moustache over a mouth that was full-lipped and smiling. But as Evan faced him, he saw that the jovial expression of a moment before was replaced by a look of pure astonishment as the man's eyes went to Evan's face. Evan shifted uncomfortably, fighting embarrassment over both the scar on his face and the rest of his appearance. He was suddenly too aware of his dirt-stained breeches, heavy boots, and ragged coat.

Trying to hide his discomfort, Evan spoke harshly. "If you're not the wharf master, do you know where I can find him?"

The man waved his hand. "He'll be coming along directly, I suppose," he answered. He paused, glancing keenly at Evan again, and added, "Looking for work?"

Evan nodded shortly. The man's stare was unnerving.

"What kind of work are you good for?"

Again that acute glance. Evan's chin lifted higher. "Anything I can find."

"Do you know anything about ships?"

"I can learn."

"I'll wager you're straight off the farm," the man said.

"And if I am?"

For some reason that he couldn't understand, the man seemed to find his hostility amusing. The gold tooth flashed again, and Evan, sure now that he was being made sport of, went to step by him.

"Hold a minute," the man ordered with such authority that in spite of himself Evan paused. "What's your name, lad?"

Evan glanced over his shoulder. "Who wants to know?" he asked.

"Well, you're a cocky fellow, aren't you?" The man seemed amused again. He stuck out his hand. "Vincent LeCroix, of LeCroix Shipping. And yours?"

Evan hesitated. He had never heard of LeCroix Shipping, but the man's assurance and appearance spoke of wealth, and power. He took the offered hand. "Evan Calder."

"Calder?" LeCroix repeated, frowning. "Did you ever hear of a man named Sean Ward?"

The suddenness of the question caught Evan by surprise. He could not prevent the stiffening of his body at the mention of the Ward name. He saw LeCroix staring quizzically at him and he made a fierce effort to control the muscles of his face.

"No," he answered curtly. "I've never heard of him."

LeCroix fingered his bushy moustache, smoothing it absently as he continued to stare in puzzlement at Evan. "Strange," he mused. "I could have sworn . . ."

Evan sensed danger in that questioning glance. More abruptly than he had intended, he said, "If you will excuse me, Mr. LeCroix—"

LeCroix seemed to have come to some kind of decision; he snapped his fingers as if an idea had suddenly come to him. "You want work?" he asked. "Then come with me. I have a job for you."

Immediately suspicious, Evan asked warily, "What kind of a job?"

LeCroix appeared affronted. "Did I make a mistake?" he asked softly, "Or did you say you wanted work?"

"I did. But I want to know what kind."

They stared at each other, Evan returning the appraising glance in LeCroix's eyes unblinkingly. Finally, the man gave a short bark of a laugh and clapped his arm around Evan's shoulders. He said again, genially, "You're a cocky bastard, aren't you? Come with me and we'll discuss it. But first—" his eyes took in the gauntness of Evan's body "we'll find something to eat. When did you last have a meal? No, don't answer. I suspect you wouldn't tell me the truth anyway."

"Now, then." LeCroix pushed his empty plate away and took out a cigar, trimming it with a gold penknife. Waving away the anxious innkeeper, who had hovered near their table during the huge meal LeCroix had ordered, he lit the cigar, belched, and sat back in satisfaction as he watched Evan finish his second portion of steak-and-kidney pie. "Now, then," he said again as Evan glanced up. "Are you good with figures?"

Evan thought of the long hours spent crouching over the frail light of a single candle in the loft, poring over the bookkeeping problems Oliver set for him. "Fair," he answered.

"Good. There's a position open in one of my offices. I could use you there—as a beginning. After that, well . . . we'll see."

"When do I start?"

"Oh, not so fast, boy, there are other—"

Evan's head had snapped up. "Don't call me that!"

LeCroix stared at him in confusion. "Call you what?"

"Boy."

LeCroix didn't know whether to be more astonished at the fierce expression on Evan's face, or at the utter contempt with which he spat that one word. He watched Evan closely for a long moment, and then nodded to himself, as if he had learned something of value and had filed it away for future reference. "Sorry," he said casually. He bobbed his head and smiled. "Evan," he corrected himself. "Meant no offense," he added, still regarding Evan with that penetrating stare in spite of the smile. "Only a figure of speech, you know."

"Not to me."

LeCroix nodded again. "Well, then. First you can tell me how you managed to get your face in that condition. No," he said calmly as Evan's eyes darkened angrily, "Don't tell me it's none of my business. You're going to be working for me, and I don't want someone who can't hold his temper. It's bad for business."

Evan did not hesitate. With LeCroix's eyes trained steadily on him, he laid down the fork he was holding and reached into his pocket. Withdrawing his last remaining shillings, he put them carefully on the table. He stood up. "It seems I'm not your man after all, Mr. LeCroix," he said evenly. "Sorry to have wasted your time."

Evan had half turned away before LeCroix's voice stopped him. "Sit down, Evan."

Evan looked back. LeCroix was no longer smiling. The eyes that met his own were challenging, the light gray of the pupil altering from gray to cold pewter. "Sit down," he said again, gesturing to the chair Evan had vacated. "We'll drink—to what's past."

LeCroix snapped his fingers. Immediately the hovering innkeeper appeared with two tankards of ale. LeCroix lifted his, waiting calmly for Evan to make his decision. When brown eyes met gray over the raised glasses, the respect in each was not grudging. LeCroix smiled to himself, and the agreement was sealed.

The doctor LeCroix summoned tut-tutted as he examined Evan's face. "There's not much I can do, Mr. LeCroix. It's too late to stitch it. It should have been taken care of long ago." He hesitated. "I'm afraid there will be a scar," he finished apologetically.

"Do the best you can," LeCroix ordered from across the room, where he sat in a comfortable chair by the fire, smoking another cigar.

"Yes, sir." The doctor muttered to himself as he searched the contents of his bag. "This will hurt some, lad," he said, as he pulled a bottle from within and poured some of the contents over a wad of cotton. "Try not to move."

Evan gritted his teeth as the doctor began dabbing at the slash on his face. The stinging of the liquid made his eyes smart in protest as the strong fumes invaded his nostrils, but he did not move, and when the man finished, he patted Evan's shoulder admiringly. "Take this," he said, capping the bottle and pressing it into Evan's hand. "Use it once a day until that gash is healed. Hopefully, there won't be too much of a scar."

"It doesn't matter." Evan accepted the medicine with a muttered thanks as he stood up.

While LeCroix accompanied the doctor to the door, Evan moved toward the window where he stood looking down at the now crowded street below. It was hard to believe that only a few short hours ago he had arrived in Liverpool prepared to take any kind of work that would provide him with food for his stomach and a shelter of sorts over his head. Now he was luxuriously housed in one of the finest hotels in that city, in the company of a man who had only to snap his fingers and people came running.

As he stared down at the smart gigs rolling by on their painted wheels, drawn by high-stepping horses in matched harnesses, at the elegantly dressed men and women who alighted from these carriages and strolled along the street, Evan felt a wild desire to burst into laughter. It was ludicrous to imagine himself down there, walking along in such fine company, but he found himself picturing just that. His hand clenched into a fist on the windowsill, and he surprised himself with the rush of envy for those people below who seemed not to have a care in the world, who looked as though they had never worked a day in their lives. What would it be like, he wondered, and then mocked himself for asking the question. Some day he would know what it was like to wear well-tailored clothing, to eat the best food, to take a moment's pleasure with a beautiful woman. But when he did these things, it would be because he had bought them with his own efforts. Knowing this, he immediately felt superior to those dandies walking below, and then he scoffed again as he caught sight of himself in the window. His reflection brought him back to earth with a thud. His hair was ragged over his ears, the slash across one cheek was an angry red from the doctor's ministrations, his flannel shirt was patched and wearing through at the elbows. The comparison between his own appearance and that of the men on the street below was ridiculous. Angrily he thought that he had a long way to go before he realized his ambition.

Abruptly he turned away from the window and saw LeCroix watching him. He flushed, for it seemed that the man was somehow aware of his thoughts, and he was embarrassed. When LeCroix smiled knowingly, Evan's discomfort increased. He was not accustomed to these searching scrutinies, and it irritated him to know that LeCroix was amused.

"Why are you staring at me like that?" he asked rudely.

LeCroix pursed his mouth. "I was just thinking that we'll have to buy you some new clothes," he answered.

Evan clenched his jaw. He muttered angrily, "I haven't the money to buy new clothes. These will have to do."

LeCroix knew immediately what the muttered admission had cost Evan in pride. Sighing inwardly, wishing that he had been a little more tactful in dealing with the angry young man in front of him, he said, "Oh, don't worry about that. I always supply one new suit of clothing for my employees. Of course," he added hastily as Evan's face expressed his disbelief, "the cost will be taken out of your wages." He laughed uneasily. "Couldn't be more fair than that, could I?"

"And the lodgings?" Evan asked grimly. "I can't sleep here."

LeCroix affected to be surprised at the expected objection. "Why not? I've engaged another room for you directly across the hall."

"To be deducted from my wages, of course."

"Of course," LeCroix answered quickly, although he had had no intention of doing so until now.

"It seems to be an expensive proposition, working for you, Mr. LeCroix."

LeCroix stared at him. Suddenly, he realized that Evan had attempted a small joke, however heavy-handed. He laughed, pleased. "Quite," he agreed heartily. "Come. Let's find a tailor and see what he can do."

It was almost dinnertime before they returned to the hotel. The tailor, an excellent man whom LeCroix had visited before, accepted the pound notes LeCroix unobtrusively pressed against his palm, clapped his hands commandingly to summon his two assistants, and immediately went into a whispered conference with LeCroix while the assistants bore Evan off to a fitting room.

An hour later Evan emerged, and LeCroix was amazed at the transformation. Even though he had at once seen beyond the shabbiness of Evan's clothing to the handsome young man wearing them, he could not have guessed the depth of the change in him. The young man who stood before him, his hair trimmed by an earlier visit to the barber, bore little resemblance to the Evan who had left the hotel a few hours before. Now, instead of patched shirt and stained breeches, Evan was attired in a dark gray coat, white waistcoat, and light gray trousers. He had refused to wear low shoes, preferring Hessian boots, and over his arm he carried a wool greatcoat. But it wasn't only the difference in clothing that LeCroix noticed; it was much more than that.

There was about Evan an aura of dark sexuality, of the male animal at its finest. He wore the new clothing as though he had been born to it, and his handsomeness, the hard, lithe lines of his body, from wide shoulders to lean hips to long, muscled legs proclaimed that he had a right to do so. But there was an inner quality, a power and strength that emanated from him now. Every movement, every gesture proclaimed it. It was as though a fire burned within him, drawing the female moth to his leaping flame, calling a woman to him in answer to a deep primeval urge to mate, to couple, to know the fierce joy of uniting with a man who was, ultimately, the height of maleness. It was a quality that Evan was not conscious of, and therefore it was even more alluring. Women would recognize it at once, and would respond to that unconscious sexuality with the heat and fire that lived in all women, waiting to be awakened by the man who wielded that power over them.

LeCroix sensed this, as he stared at the transformed Evan. He was awed and, without realizing it, envious.

"Well, Evan, what do you think?" he asked, forcing himself to be casual, although he was shaken.

"I think," Evan answered, "that it's time for us to have a talk."

LeCroix was startled at Evan's tone. "Er . . . of course." Turning, he signed the proffered bill with a flourish, barely glancing at the total. At the lift of his hand, one of the assistants leaped forward, signaling to the waiting cab, holding the door open for them.

"Now," LeCroix said when they were settled inside the cab. "What is it?"

"I don't like being made a fool of," Evan said tightly.

LeCroix rarely became angry, but he felt his temper rise now. "What do you mean?"

Evan gestured, the movement taking in the clothing he wore. "I saw the bill; I heard you talking to the tailor about ordering more. Did it amuse you to humiliate me in front of him?"

"Humiliate you!" Now LeCroix was genuinely angry. "Look here, lad! If you want to work for me, you'll have to get rid of some of that pride of yours. A man does a favor for you and you call it humiliating. I can't believe it!"

Evan was silent, studying LeCroix's face, which had turned red with outrage. Was it possible that he had misjudged him? Had he been too quick to find offense where none was intended? He shifted uncomfortably on the seat, unsure of himself for the first time.

"I'm sorry," he said finally, stiffly. "I thought—"

"Well, you thought wrong!" LeCroix glared at him, affronted, and they rode in silence for several blocks. But as the driver pulled to a halt in front of the hotel, LeCroix turned to Evan and said, "I don't know what's happened to you in the past, and I don't want to know. But there's one thing we have to get straight between us from the first. I play fair, and I expect you to do the same. I don't believe in making a fool of any man—God knows we make fools of ourselves too often to need help in that direction from anyone else! But there's one thing I demand, and that's respect. I'll give you your due, and you give me mine, and we should get along just fine. Agreed?"

Evan hesitated, frowning. In all his life, only one other person had spoken to him as someone of worth, and that person was Oliver. Now here was LeCroix, speaking to him as one man to another, and Evan was suddenly ashamed of his accusation. His glance went to LeCroix's face, and he nodded. "Agreed," he answered quietly.

That night, LeCroix ordered dinner sent up to the room. As the waiter entered, trundling a cart laden with covered dishes, Evan looked up from the bills of lading LeCroix had given him to go over. He had insisted on beginning work immediately, and LeCroix, smiling, had handed him a case bulging with paperwork. After several hours poring over receipts, shipping invoices, bills, and other related work, Evan was thankful that Oliver had taught him what he had, or he would have been lost in the maze of figures. He was also hungry, and when he glanced at the table the waiter set, he was surprised to see that there were four plates. He looked inquiringly at LeCroix as the waiter bowed and left the room, carrying a substantial tip for his services.

"Come and sit down, Evan. The ladies should be here any minute."

"Ladies?" Evan was startled.

LeCroix waved expansively. "I thought that since this was our last night ashore, we should—" He stopped. Evan's eyes had darkened dangerously. "What's the matter? There's no harm in—"

Evan stood. "I'll eat in my room," he said harshly.

LeCroix paused. "As you like."

But as Evan turned to leave, there was the sound of smothered laughter from the corridor, and seconds later, the door burst open, revealing two young women, their painted faces bright with excitement.

"Vince!"

One of the two young women came forward immediately, holding out her arms to LeCroix. "Vince! It's been a long time, hasn't it?" Bending over before LeCroix could get up, she kissed him loudly on the mouth.

LeCroix laughed. "You haven't changed at all, Bett—except to become even prettier than last time!"

"Oh, Vince!" Bett, pleased at the compliment, fluttered her lashes. "You always were—" She stopped, catching sight of the silent Evan for the first time. "Why, Vince! You didn't tell us you had company!"

LeCroix lifted his bulk out of the chair. "Ladies, meet Evan Calder. Evan, this is Bett, and that is—"

"Janey," supplied the other girl when LeCroix looked inquiringly at her.

Janey moved slowly into the room, her heavily shadowed eyes on Evan's face. She was small, her head barely reaching Evan's shoulder, but her body was that of a voluptuous woman. Glossy brown curls spilled over rounded shoulders, her arms were bare and smooth, her waist tiny. She had a full, sensuous mouth, a pert nose, and laughing greenish eyes. An aura of animal sexuality emanated from her, and Evan swallowed as she came up to him.

She smiled provocatively, tilting her head up at him, and said softly, "Hello, Evan."

Evan had the absurd desire to run from the room. Helplessly, he looked from Janey to LeCroix and back again. She was so close now he could smell the perfume she wore, so close that he could see the tiny star-shaped patch she wore on one rouged cheek. Her silk gown rustled as she moved, the bodice so low-cut that her full breasts strained against the fabric with every breath.

Evan felt his own breath become short as he looked at her, and when she placed her hand on his arm, his stomach muscles tightened. He saw her eyes go to the scar on his cheek, and when she did not seem repulsed by the sight, he didn't know whether to be relieved or not.

"Evan prefers to dine in his own room," LeCroix said to no one in particular.

Janey turned. "What do you say, Bett?" she asked her giggling companion, whose glance was on Evan's flushed face. "We can't let him eat alone, can we?"

Bett tried to assume a solemn expression, but her eyes danced as she replied, "Oh no, of course not."

"Well, then!" Swiftly, before Evan could object, Janey grabbed three bottles of wine from the table, pushing two of them at Evan, who was forced to take them or have them dropped at his feet. Winking at LeCroix, she took two glasses in one hand, and with the other pulled the unresisting Evan from the room.

Almost desperately, Evan glanced over his shoulder to where LeCroix stood with his arm around the laughing Bett. LeCroix waved, smirked, and shut the door, leaving Evan alone in the corridor with Janey.

"Is this your room?" Janey pointed at the door in front of them.

Inwardly cursing LeCroix, Evan nodded. For some reason, he found it difficult to speak when Janey looked at him.

"Come on, then!"

Laughing, Janey entered the room. Pivoting on one foot,

she turned and held out the glasses to Evan, indicating that he pour the wine. Evan looked blankly down at the bottles he held in each hand, noted thankfully that they had already been opened, and obeyed. Janey's laugh rang out again as he put the bottles down and grabbed one of the glasses, almost spilling wine in the process. She took his hand, leading him over to the sofa in front of the fire.

When she sat down next to him, Evan deliberately avoided looking at her. To his annoyance, he realized he was nervous, and to calm his suddenly pounding heart, he gulped at his wine. Janey, having had the foresight to bring one of the bottles with her to the sofa, poured him another glass.

"What's the matter, Evan?" she asked softly, into the awkward silence. "Don't you like me?"

Evan forced himself to look at her. She was gazing at him over the rim of her glass, her eyes wide and knowing.

"Nothing is the matter," he muttered, looking away again to stare into the fire.

"Do you want me to leave?"

Did he? He wasn't sure. Damn LeCroix for springing this on him, he thought angrily. He had never felt so unsure of himself, so . . . so clumsy. In spite of John's edict at the Manor, he had availed himself of several girls, on rare occasions, but they had been country girls—fresh-faced, plump, earthy girls—not at all like Janey, who confused him with her sophistication and poise. What had seemed natural and simple in the country now seemed to have taken on the proportions of a grand *affaire,* and he was furious with himself for reacting to it like some stumbling school-boy. He jumped when Janey put her hand on his thigh.

"Do you?"

"What?" He seemed to have a difficult time concentrating on what she said; the press of her body against his was distracting.

"Want me to leave?"

Evan tore his eyes away from the hand on his leg. "No."

"Why don't you pour some more wine, then?"

When he looked at the bottle on the table in front of him, he was astonished that it was almost empty. Janey held out her glass expectantly, and he realized that he was supposed to get up and fetch another of the bottles they had left by the door.

"Excuse me . . ." Evan started to get up, but as he did so, Janey's hand moved upward, brushing his strong, lean thigh. Drawing in his breath sharply at the contact, he looked down at her, but she seemed not to notice what she had done, for she was staring absently into the fire. He muttered something and almost tripped as he moved between the sofa and the table toward the other end of the room.

His back to her, Evan closed his eyes as he reached for the bottle. Cursing his shaking hands, he poured a glass for himself and drank it quickly. What was the matter with him? Was he afraid of her? No, no, of course not, he assured himself, swaying unsteadily. It was the damned wine; he shouldn't have drunk so much so quickly, that was all. The room was suddenly too warm, and he loosened his collar, feeling the sweat break out on his forehead. Perhaps he should take off his coat as well.

He turned, the coat in one hand, the bottle in the other, and almost dropped both when he saw Janey calmly stepping out of her gown.

"I hope you don't mind . . . ?" she said, smiling at him.

Evan started, dragging his eyes away from her body. He shook his head, unable to speak.

"It is rather warm in here, don't you think?"

This time he nodded, hoping that was the proper response. Blood had rushed to his head; there was a pounding in his ears. Forcing himself to move, he approached the sofa, still clutching coat and wine, and Janey, not in the least embarrassed, reached out to take both from him. As she leaned forward, Evan saw her rounded breasts beneath the low neckline of her chemise, and he closed his eyes as his body responded instantly to the sight. Janey's gown was on the floor; she stepped over it, and as she came toward him, Evan could see the outline of her rounded thighs under lace-trimmed silk pantaloons. She turned her back toward him, gesturing with one arm. "Please . . . I hate corsets; they're so uncomfortable!"

His hands shook as he reached for the lacings. But at the first touch of his fingers against her bare skin, his nervousness was forgotten. The corset off and flung to the floor, he bent his head, touching his lips to her softly plump shoulder. He heard her murmur of pleasure, and something in him responded to the sound. He felt a tightening in his loins, a swelling throb as his senses reacted to her. She turned to face him, raising her arms, bringing his head down to hers. Her mouth moved against his, her lips parted, and he kissed her, covering her mouth with his own, lost in a rush of passion.

Drawing his head back finally, he looked down at her. He saw then that her eyes were green. Green. Drunkenly, he remembered another pair of green eyes, another face lifted to his, and suddenly he was back by the rushing stream, and the girl he held in his arms was not a practiced harlot, but Cynara. In a daze, his hands clutched at the plump girl he held, but he felt another body, a slender, lithe body that had sent his blood racing with the mere nearness of her.

Swiftly, he lifted Janey from the floor and carried her into the bedroom. In a fever, he reached for her, but she pulled back. Slowly, provocatively, she removed her chemise, tugged at the tie to the lacy pantaloons. Both garments fell to the floor and she turned away from him to climb into the bed. Pulling back the covers, she raised herself on one elbow, beckoning to him.

Never taking his eyes from the sight of her naked body waiting for him, Evan tore at his own clothes. He slid over her, feeling the warmth of her skin touching his. The flame of desire engulfed him, and he grabbed Janey to him fiercely. But the lips he kissed, the breasts he stroked, the legs he felt around him belonged to Cynara.

Evan woke alone the next morning. He groaned as he sat up in bed, clutching his head with both hands. The throbbing behind his eyes was intense; his head felt like it was being split in two. Breathing hard, he sat where he was for several minutes, willing away the pounding in his temples. Finally he managed to summon up enough strength to stagger over to the washbasin to splash cold water over his face. What had happened to him? Everything was fuzzy; he couldn't even think.

And then he saw the empty wine bottles scattered on the floor, and memory returned—somewhat. Whirling around, wincing at the burst of pain inside his aching head at the too-quick movement, he looked for Janey. She wasn't in the room, and he couldn't remember her leaving. He passed a hand over his eyes; he must have been very drunk indeed, to remember only brief snatches of the evening before.

He glanced at the rumpled bed, the bedclothes dragging on the floor, and grimaced. Had she been drunk, too? He couldn't remember which one of them had gotten up to refill the glasses; he only knew that somehow they had finished the wine, and after that . . .

Evan closed his eyes as he recalled the second time, or the third, that they had made love; he had never expected a woman to be so abandoned, so sure of herself. There had been only one awkward moment, and that was when he . . . when he what? He frowned, trying to remember.

The wine had gone to his head too quickly; for an instant, he had thought Janey was someone else. Now the frown deepened into a scowl as he recalled the name he had spoken aloud. Why in hell had he called her Cynara? he asked himself savagely. Why had he even thought of Cynara at all?

Abruptly Evan retrieved his scattered clothing and began to dress. He had promised himself long ago that he wouldn't think of Cynara, and he wasn't going to dwell on her now. Angrily he stepped into his trousers and rammed his feet into his boots. At least Janey was honest, he thought, as he grabbed his shirt from where it had fallen behind a chair; Janey made no pretense of being other than what she was, while Cynara . . .

He paused for an instant, one arm halfway inside the sleeve of his shirt. He wasn't being fair to Cynara; she had been frightened that night with Myles, he knew. But if she had been so terrified, so repulsed, by what had happened to her, why had she practically thrown herself at him?

"Damn!" he muttered. Why was he wasting time thinking of Cynara? He would never see her again, and he had better things to do than to try to understand the motivations of a girl who meant nothing to him.

"Evan?"

LeCroix was in the sitting room. As Evan came in, he held out one of the glasses he carried. "I thought you might need this," he said. "A little hair of the dog, if you know what I mean?"

Evan accepted the glass. His stomach rebelled at the sight of it, but he forced himself to drink the bitter-tasting ale, and after he had finished it, he felt better. At least the throbbing behind his eyes receded, and he was grateful for that.

"Thanks," he said, and avoided looking at LeCroix, who was now smiling openly.

Fortunately, LeCroix did not voice the reason for his amusement. Instead, he said, "We sail tonight, but we must be on the ship long before then, as I want to check my cargo. What do you say we find some breakfast before we board? I imagine you must be hungry, after all that act—" LeCroix saw the glare Evan flashed in his direction, and chuckled. "After missing dinner last night," he amended, his eyes twinkling.

Evan nodded wordlessly; he was not about to provoke more laughter at his expense by trying to explain himself. Ignoring LeCroix's inquiring expression, he said, "You mentioned sailing before, but you never said where we're going."

LeCroix raised an eyebrow. "Didn't I? Hmm. I thought I had. Well, we're going to Australia, lad; that's where my main offices are. I thought you knew."

"Australia!" Some half-forgotten memory flashed into his mind. He remembered Oliver telling him something about Australia long ago. What was it? He shook his head, unable to recall.

"Is something wrong, Evan?"

"What? Oh . . . no, it's nothing," he answered, wondering why it seemed so important to remember what Oliver had said. He shook his head again, looking around for his coat.

He found it neatly folded over the back of a chair. How it had come to be there, he wasn't sure. But as he put it on, something crackled in one of the pockets, and he knew immediately who had put it on the chair. Slowly, aware of LeCroix watching him curiously, Evan took out the folded note. It was from Janey, of course, and he could feel his face flushing as he read it: "Evan—it was the best in a long time. Come and see me again, lover, and whoever Cynara is, I envy her."

His mouth tightening, Evan crumpled the note and jammed it back into his pocket. So he had called her Cynara, after all; he had hoped he dreamed the whole awkward incident. What a fool Janey must think him! But she couldn't think worse of him than he did himself at this moment. How could he have insulted her like that? Damn Cynara! he thought furiously.

"Evan?" LeCroix was standing by the door, waiting for him. He put an arm around Evan's shoulders as they went out and said, "There will be others, lad. Don't you doubt it!"

Evan nodded. But he knew that LeCroix was thinking of Janey, as he was not. There will be others, Evan repeated the words silently in his own mind . . . but would there be? Or would he always think of that one face, that one slender body that made every other woman unattractive in comparison?

He looked across at LeCroix, who was striding along, whistling tunelessly to himself. "Let's go to Australia," he said harshly.

CHAPTER TEN

"Now, REMEMBER WHAT I told you," Sarah hissed into Cynara's ear. "If he looks at you, don't say or do anything. Pretend that you're like that one over there." Sarah pointed toward one of the woman prisoners who sat, hour after hour, huddled into a ball, staring blankly in front of her. Her eyes were unfocused, her mouth slack as she endlessly twisted a strand of hair into a tight corkscrew, first in one direction and then in another.

Cynara shuddered and looked away from the sight of the woman's empty and soulless face. "I can't pretend to be like that, Sarah. If he touches me, I won't be able to—"

"You have to try. You've been lucky so far, but with your looks, he's bound to notice you before long. You don't want him to take you—"

"No!" Cynara said fiercely, repulsed at the thought of being forced to bed by the man who had already taken so many others above deck.

"Well, then?"

"I'll try," Cynara muttered.

Sarah patted her hand for encouragement and moved away a short distance. Cynara watched the first mate, a powerfully built bull of a man with blackened teeth, move slowly among the women in the hold, stopping here and there as one of them caught his eyes.

She forced herself to sit still as he came closer. It wasn't going to work, she thought frantically; if he touched her, she knew she would scream. The two months she had been imprisoned in the hold of the ship had been filled with one horror after another, and it had only been Sarah's calm presence that had prevented her from going mad. And now he had returned, and she knew that if he chose her this time she *would* go insane.

He stopped in front of her and all her instincts screamed at her to get up and run. But where would she run to? There was no escape. Just as there had been no escape for the young girl he had dragged, terrified, from the hold the last time. Later, the women had learned that the girl had thrown herself overboard. Cynara bit the inside of her cheek, trying desperately not to look up.

"Here, you! Get up and let me see what you look like!"

Cynara just managed to prevent herself from crying out as he reached for her. His fingers grabbed a fistful of her hair, jerking her to her feet. With one hand he forced her head back, pushing his face close to hers.

"Well, well. I don't think you're as stupid as you look."

Deliberately, he dropped his hand to her breast and gave it a painful squeeze. Cynara closed her eyes, willing herself not to react, knowing that if she did, she was lost. But when he shoved his face closer to hers, fastening his mouth on hers like a leech, she responded instinctively. She couldn't do it; couldn't maintain this pose with his tongue probing her mouth, almost gagging her. No matter what he did to her later, she had to fight. Rearing back, she shoved him away from her.

"Leave me alone!" she cried, not caring that Sarah had rushed forward to grab her, trying to pull her back.

He had staggered, taken by surprise at the force of her sudden resistance. But now he came toward her again, the heel of one hand sending Sarah sprawling on the floor while he grabbed Cynara with the other. She tried to pull away from him, to go to Sarah, but he jerked her back again so forcefully that she half fell against him before she could recover her balance.

"That's better," he said, holding her fast against his side. "Now we'll see what you're made of."

His arm was around her waist, so tight she couldn't move. He held her chin in his hand, forcing her to look up at him. She saw the black cavern of his mouth as he laughed, saw the sadistic glint of his eyes, and she felt terror rising in her. "Come along, girl. I don't have much time."

He started toward the door at the end of the room, dragging her with him. Panic-stricken, Cynara clawed and kicked, twisting against the arm that held her prisoner. "Let go of me! Let go, you filthy—"

He spun her away from him suddenly, choking off her cry, holding on to her wrist as she staggered. Jerking her upright again, he reached out and delivered a stinging slap across her face that almost blinded her.

"Enough!" he roared, pulling her toward him again. "Enough of that!"

Cynara shook her head, trying to clear it. She could taste the blood from her cut lip, hear the low mutterings of the women who she knew would do nothing to help her. Sarah was dazed on the floor; there was only herself to fight this huge hulk of a man. Without thinking, conscious only of her desire to get away from him, she kicked out as hard as she could, aiming for his groin, catching him in the leg instead.

He fell back, letting her go as he reached for his thigh with a grunt of pain. But in the next instant, he had recovered and lunged for her again. "You bitch! I'll teach you to fight me!"

This time, his closed fist caught her on the side of the head as she was turning away. She fell where she stood.

Painfully, Cynara clawed her way to consciousness. Groaning, she opened her eyes, trying to orient herself. She tried to sit up, but the throbbing in her head immediately became worse, and she sank back again with another moan.

Lying still, she listened. The only sounds she heard were familiar ones: the occasional cough, the snoring of some of the women as they slept, the slap of the waves against the hull. She was still in the hold, she thought with relief; he hadn't taken her away, after all.

Waiting until the pain subsided to a dull ache, Cynara cautiously raised herself on one elbow. She still lay where she had fallen, and slowly she dragged herself to her hands and knees, crawling along in the darkness to where she and Sarah shared a mattress.

"Sarah?" She reached out, blindly feeling her way, trying to find Sarah by touch. She wasn't there. "Sarah, where are you?"

"She's gone."

The whisper came from somewhere to the side of her. Cynara turned her head, fighting a sudden wave of dizziness. "Where is she?" she asked a huddled form she could barely see in the gloom.

"He took her."

"Took her!" Cynara's voice was shrill. "Where?"

"Shhh."

The woman's tone was uneasy, and Cynara dropped her voice. "What happened?" she whispered frantically.

"He took her, that's all." The woman laughed, the sound bordering on the insane, making Cynara shiver. "Better her than us, I say."

"Quiet over there!"

Cynara looked across to where the second voice issued. "I want to know what—"

"Shut your mouth, else I come over and shut it for you! I want to get some sleep."

Cynara tightened her lips; she knew better than to argue with the woman named Maisie. She turned back again, whispering urgently, "Please tell me what happened."

But the huddled form had turned away and Cynara knew she wouldn't speak again. Miserably, Cynara dragged herself up onto the mattress, wrapping the blanket around her for comfort as much as warmth. Trying to tell herself that Sarah knew what she was doing, that she would be all right, Cynara put her head back and closed her eyes wearily. Sarah might be only a few years older than she, but Sarah was far more experienced in the ways and demands of men. She had to be, having been a prostitute for five years or more, Cynara acknowledged. But still . . . Cynara shivered, remembering the man's bull-like strength and cruel eyes.

Sarah would be all right, Cynara told herself again; she was strong in all the ways that counted.

Right now Cynara wished for some of Sarah's strength. She had endured this imprisonment for two months, and already it seemed like a lifetime. Would they ever reach Australia? And when they did, what would happen to her? Her mouth twisted bitterly as she recalled thinking so disparagingly about becoming a governess or a ladies' companion. She would gladly accept such a position now, she thought. Now that it was too late.

Her thoughts turned, as they seemed to do so often lately, to Evan. She wondered where he was, what he was doing, what had happened to him after he left Lyrebird Manor that night. Sometimes when she thought of him she was furious, remembering how he had simply disappeared, leaving her alone to face Myles and his parents. But far too often she thought of him in quite a different way, imagining him suddenly appearing, holding out his hand to take her away from this hideous place. Impossible it might be, but Cynara lived the dream as if it were real, building on it, fiercely willing it to happen.

She uttered a groan that came from deep within her soul. She would never really know Evan, she thought dully. All her dreams and fantasies, all her torturous longings and desires would never be fulfilled. Myles had come between them; Myles with his white fleshy face and thick blond curls that made him look like a malicious, bloated cherub. She could feel her hatred of him surfacing once again. She welcomed the feeling, almost savoring it. It no longer mattered that Abel Bertram and Cornelia Ward had coldly arranged for this hellish voyage; it no longer mattered that John Ward had taken such cruel advantage of her. Her desire for revenge was focused on Myles alone.

Sometimes she was almost afraid of the terrible emotion that shook her when she thought of Myles. She found herself wishing, again and again, that Evan had killed him. Or that she had. And no matter how many times she told herself that such thoughts were wrong, evil, she still could not make herself deny them. She had never believed that she was capable of wishing another human being dead, but she was capable of it; oh yes, she was. And if she ever needed a reminder of how much she owed Myles, she had only to place a hand on the swelling at her waist.

When she first realized that the nausea she suffered from those first weeks was not due solely to the rolling and pitching of the ship, she was stunned. It couldn't happen to her, she told herself in frozen disbelief. *It couldn't happen to her!* She was wrong, mistaken; she had lost count of the days. Terrified, furious, almost demented at the thought, she had waited until there could be no doubt. When she was sure, when she could no longer dismiss the absence of her monthly bleeding as coincidence, her first thought was to throw herself over the rail, as that other unfortunate creature had done. Only Sarah's pleading had prevented her from doing so, and sometimes, in her darker moments, she had almost hated Sarah for interfering.

If she had done what she wanted, she would be free of this intolerable burden that weighed on her mind as heavily as it dragged on her body. She had no feeling for the life growing within her, no feeling except the deep desire to be rid of it. And that was wrong, too, she thought. She should be ashamed of herself for harboring such evil thoughts. But she wasn't ashamed, for she knew that it was far better for the child never to be born, because she would never forget the manner in which it had been conceived.

Sarah did not return until early morning. Carefully stepping over and around the sleeping women, she reached the place where Cynara huddled under the blanket, and sank down with a sigh.

"Sarah . . . ?"

Cynara abandoned all pretense of sleep at the return of her friend, and she sat up. "Sarah—are you all right?"

"Oh, sure. Don't ever worry about me, honey."

"But—what happened? Why did he—"

Instead of answering, Sarah reached across and took Cynara's chin in her hand, turning her head toward the feeble light that filtered in. "He clipped you a good one, didn't he?" she asked, her expression grim as she saw the dark bruise around Cynara's eye and the puffiness of her lip.

Cynara pushed Sarah's hand away. "It doesn't matter. Sarah, why did he take you?"

"He didn't take me, I volunteered."

"You *what?*"

"Shhh. Keep your voice down. I said—"

"I heard what you said! But why? I don't understand."

"Well, the way I figured it, I knew he was going to take someone. I thought it might as well be me."

"But—"

"Look. He's not so bad. I've been with worse before."

Cynara thought of the dirty, hamlike hands, the blackened teeth of the man who had attacked her, and shivered. She looked up, wide-eyed, as a thought struck her. "Sarah, you didn't do it to—to protect me, did you?"

Sarah looked away. "Naw. Of course not. Don't be silly."

"You did!"

"Listen, honey." Sarah's head swung back again, her expression hard. "You wouldn't have known how to handle that bastard. I did. It was as simple as that. Now shut up and let me get some sleep."

Cynara was silent, watching Sarah as she yawned and turned over on her side. Pulling the blanket from around her shoulders, Cynara covered Sarah with it, and then sat back, drawing her knees up under her chin. She stared at the motionless figure beside her for a long time. Finally she whispered, "Sarah?"

Sarah shifted. "What?" she muttered irritably.

"I just wanted to . . . to thank you . . ."

"Not necessary, honey." There was a movement from under the blanket, and Cynara felt something fall at her feet. When she picked it up, she saw that it was a half-crown, and she looked from it to Sarah in surprise. "It was almost worth it," Sarah murmured as she fell asleep again.

CHAPTER ELEVEN

HATCH, THE FIRST mate, seemed satisfied with Sarah. More than satisfied, Cynara thought, for there were occasions when she didn't see Sarah for days at a stretch after that night. But Sarah was noncommittal about the time she spent in the mate's quarters, and Cynara didn't ask. A treacherous part of her was glad it was Sarah and not she who went to his cabin. While Cynara detested herself for feeling this way, she could not change it; even the thought of the first mate made her skin crawl with revulsion.

With Sarah gone so much of the time, Cynara was lonely. Defensively, the other women had formed their own circles of companionship, and the boundaries, drawn the first few weeks at sea, were not to be crossed. In some instances, frustration and boredom caused fights to break out between some of the rougher women, and Cynara always stayed well away from those furious battles.

And so the days slid into weeks, and the weeks into months, and still the ship plowed on, until Cynara thought she would scream. Adding to her own frustration and anger was the continuing swelling of her body. Her condition was noticeable now, and ironically, it seemed to protect her from the overtures the rest of the women were subjected to by the crew when they were allowed their daily hour on deck. Quite a few of the women, like Sarah, had been transported for prostitution, and so were accustomed to leering advances and well able to deal with them. But the rest, petty thieves or pickpockets, or servants who had displeased their masters, were not. Cynara grew to hate the cries and muffled sobs of these women, many of them still in their teens, when they returned to the hold after being dragged into the forecastle to satisfy the demands of the crew. But Cynara was as helpless as the rest, unable to offer comfort or protection. When she heard the weeping and sobbing, she covered her ears, knowing there was nothing she could do to alleviate the pain and misery. It was a nightmare, that voyage; a never-ending hell of dirt and dampness and darkness, of slimy water and rotten food crawling with weevils, of women used and abused, and after five months, all were sure that it would never end.

And then one night Cynara knew that all that had gone before was only a dream; the real nightmare had just begun.

Hatch had left Sarah alone for days. The ship had fought its way through one violent storm after another, and all hands were needed just to keep the vessel afloat while repairs were made.

Sarah and Cynara had huddled with the rest of their companions in the hold, terrified, clutching each other through the long hours as the latest storm battered the ship. All were afraid they were going to die, and the wailing of the women almost rose above the noise of the creaking timbers, the pouring of the sea through cracks in the hull, the yelling of the crew as they desperately followed the shouted orders of the captain. The wind shrieked through the sails, mammoth waves crashed against the ship with a sound that rivaled thunder.

The women protected themselves as best they could, but the towering sea tossed the huge vessel back and forth like a cork, and Cynara and Sarah were thrown from one side to the other with the rest, until all were bruised, wet, and exhausted.

At last, when Cynara knew she could no longer keep at bay the hysteria rising in her, they passed through the worst of the storm into comparative calm. Sarah raised her head. "I think it's over," she whispered.

Her eyes wide and straining, Cynara listened. She could hear the snap of the sails, but the horrible, ear-splitting scream of the wind had died to a low roar. She took a deep breath, letting it out slowly. Thankfully she closed her eyes, allowing her cramped muscles to relax for the first time in hours.

They crawled to where their sodden mattress had been flung against the hull, and Sarah gratefully threw herself down, oblivious to the moaning and sobbing around her as others did the same. She was asleep in seconds.

Cynara, weary as she was, couldn't sleep. Every creak, every slight sound around her caused her eyes to fly open in fear, thinking that the storm was about to begin again. But the strain had taken its toll; her body demanded rest, and finally she fell into an exhausted stupor.

Some time later, she woke with a start. Had the storm begun again? She lay still, eyes and ears straining to identify the sound that had awakened her. And then she saw him, moving slowly among the sleeping women.

Her eyes widened as the figure loomed over her. She recognized him at once as Hatch, but she lost her advantage in the instant she hesitated, wondering if he was trying to find Sarah. His heavy hand clamped down over her mouth, and she was jerked to her feet in the same motion.

Whipping her around so that her back was toward him, he propelled her forward. His hand was still across her mouth, forcing her head back against his shoulder. She couldn't scream, but her hands were free, as she clawed at the suffocating pressure of his fingers, trying violently to get away from him. The struggle was silent—and brief.

His hand never releasing its hold over her mouth, he grabbed her wrist, forcing it behind her back, up toward her shoulder as he pushed her forward. The pain was excruciating; her shoulder felt like it was on fire as he jerked her wrist upward for emphasis.

Panic-stricken, she saw the door coming closer. Despite the agony of her contorted arm, she tried to get away from him again as he reached for the lock. Her head back against his chest, she was in an awkward position to maneuver, but when he put his hand out, she kicked forcefully at the door, praying the noise would rouse the women. But her foot missed by inches, and she heard him grunt as her body slammed back into him.

They were through the door before she could recover her balance, and he was shoving her toward the stairs that led to the upper deck. With one hand on the rail for support, he was forced to release her arm as he propelled her upwards. She grabbed the rail with both hands, bracing her feet against the step.

"Get up there, you bitch!" he snarled, shoving his body forward to make her break her hold.

She held on desperately, and he shoved again, forcing her up two more steps. Her fingers were torn away from the rail as he used his body as a battering ram, but his hand slipped from her mouth as he did so.

"Help! Someone—help!" she screamed the instant she was free.

"Shut up!"

He raised both hands to thrust her forward, and the strength in his arms sent her sprawling on the stairs. Frantically, she grabbed the rail again, but he kicked her hands away. She cried out, moving upwards to get away from him. They were almost at the top of the stairs now, and Cynara saw the door to the outer deck open suddenly.

"Please . . ." she sobbed to the shadowy figure standing in the doorway. "Help me . . ."

But Hatch either had not seen the person standing at the door, or had chosen to ignore him. Reaching down, he grabbed her arm and jerked her to her feet, intending to push her up the last few stairs.

Again Cynara grabbed the rail, holding on desperately. She saw Hatch raise his fist, and she screamed. The fist crashed down across her wrists, ripping her hands away. She lost her precarious balance on the step and crashed into Hatch, who was on the stair below. The impact of her body against his flung him against the rail, and Cynara threw her arms out, trying to grab onto something before she fell. Her fingers slipped and suddenly she was falling backward. She had no time to cry out. She was unconscious when she landed at the foot of the stairs.

The pain lanced through her, bringing Cynara back to consciousness with a rush. It came again, and she doubled over with the force of it, groaning. There was a buzzing in her ear, an insistent noise, but the agony inside her claimed all her attention. What was it? What was wrong with her? She tried to call for help, but now it seemed that a giant hand had her by the throat; she couldn't breathe.

Gasping, she drew her knees up, and whether the sudden cessation of that terrible pain was due to the movement or not, she didn't know—or care. Panting, she dared to open her eyes.

Sarah was bending over her, her face white with shock. "It's going to be all right," she said quickly as Cynara looked up at her. "Everything is going to be fine."

"What . . . what is it? What's wrong?"

Cynara tried to reach for Sarah's hand, but in that instant, she could feel the pain beginning to build again. "Sarah!" she cried in panic as the fiery agony gripped her. "Oh, Sarah, help me . . ."

"I will, honey. I will."

She heard Sarah's response from a distance, was only dimly aware of being lifted from the floor and carried to some other place. Not even the luxury of feeling a bed beneath her was enough to break the grip of the pain that seemed as if it would tear her in two, and between spasms, she tried to call for Sarah again.

"I'm here. I'm here."

She saw a hand reaching for her, and she grasped it tightly. Sweat was running into her eyes and down her face; she was almost blinded by it. "Sarah," she panted, "what . . ."

"Shhh." Sarah turned away to take a glass from someone standing behind her. "Here," she said. "Drink this. It has laudanum for the pain."

Cynara drank quickly, fearing the onslaught of another spasm. She managed to drink half of it before the pain began again, and this time she screamed in pure terror as the torment mounted unbearably. She was going to die; she knew it. But even death would be welcome if it brought an end to this intolerable assault on her body.

"Hold on, honey. It's almost over."

"What?" She couldn't understand what Sarah was trying to tell her. The laudanum was having its effect; she felt like she was drifting now, without a care. There was a rush of something warm between her thighs, and then, sometime later, another surge. She felt drained, empty, and so drowsy that it was an effort to keep her eyes open. There was movement all around her, sharp voices followed by whispered comments as she was moved back and forth, but she didn't care what was done to her.

Cynara fell into an exhausted, drugged sleep, unaware and not caring that she had been delivered of a five month old dead infant, whose birth had been precipitated by her fall down the stairs.

When she woke, Cynara was alone. She lay still, her eyes searching the room, wondering where she was. Her glance took in the tiny room, barely large enough to hold the cot which served as her bed, and she knew that she had never seen it before. Where was she? Her eyes went to the porthole above her head. She could see the sky, a beautiful azure, that she had thought never to see again, and tears filled her eyes at the sight. How long had she been here? She didn't know. She had a confused memory of Hatch, and falling down the stairs, and then the pain. She had never experienced agony such as that, and prayed that she would never have to endure it again. She raised her head suddenly, staring at the length of her body covered by a blanket.

The first thought that sprang into her mind was that she was free. Free of the intolerable burden she had carried for five months. The feeling of elation that accompanied this knowledge made her throw her head back and laugh. Utter relief that the ordeal was over made her laughter rise high and higher, until she was alarmed. What was wrong with her, that she could laugh over such a terrible thing? But she couldn't seem to stop, even when she pressed a hand tight against her mouth.

She turned her face into the flat pillow, afraid that someone would hear her and come to investigate. How could she explain her feelings without sounding demented? But perhaps she *was* mad, she thought; surely no normal woman would laugh so hysterically over the loss of a child.

Suddenly the tears started. And where before she couldn't control her laughter, now she was powerless to halt the storm of weeping that assailed her.

Cynara cried until she was exhausted and there were no more tears left to cry. It was useless, stupid, to weep for what she had lost and would never have again, and yet when she thought of her father and the life she had shared with him, the tears followed even faster. Even Lyrebird Manor had been bearable, at first, because Evan was there. But Evan had gone; he was as dead to her as her father was, and she knew she would never see him again. And she didn't want to see him again, she told herself, for he would always represent the ultimate in betrayal; he had left her when she needed him most.

Now when she cried, it was for the girl she had been. She could feel the door shutting on the desires and emotions that had filled her girlhood, leaving her with a cold emptiness that would enable her to survive at any price. Was this becoming a woman? It would have to be, for her.

When she was able to look up again, she saw that the sky had darkened; it was almost night. Cynara lay in the gathering dusk, staring sightlessly at the scrap of sky visible through the porthole. The emotional storm had drained her, leaving her weak, but it had also cleansed her mind. She was able to think clearly for the first time in months.

Nothing like this would ever happen to her again, she vowed. Sarah had told her some of the ways to prevent conception, and she would use them all, if necessary. Cynara might not be able to save herself from being forced to surrender to a man—that fact had already been demonstrated forcefully, hadn't it, she asked herself bitterly—but she would be damned if she would also be compelled to suffer the consequences, as she had with Myles.

But what would happen to her now? She realized that it was nothing short of a miracle that she hadn't been left to die where she had fallen. While she was grateful that she had been allowed to recover by herself in this room, wherever it was, she was loath to return to the hold. Grimacing at the thought of those dirty and dank quarters shared by women who had been confined too long, Cynara looked at the door, wondering why the captain had allowed her this brief respite from the horrors below.

As if her thoughts had conjured up his presence, the captain chose that moment to open the door. Cynara had seen Captain Baird only at a distance before, but she recognized him instantly. He was of medium height and solid, with enormous side whiskers that emphasized his round, florid face. His eyes, deep blue and penetrating, rested on her face, and she was unable to interpret his expression as he stood in the doorway staring silently at her. Uneasily, she waited for him to speak.

"So," he said at last, his voice a deep rumble, "it seems as if you will recover, after all."

Before Cynara could speak, he tossed a gown upon the cot. She looked at him in surprise as a ghost of a smile flickered across his face.

"Get dressed," he ordered.

The door shut again, leaving Cynara staring blankly after the captain. Did this action of his mean what she thought it did? She closed her eyes as her heart began to pound uncomfortably. Was the captain waiting for her on the other side of that door? Did he expect some kind of payment in return for what he had done for her?

Of course he did, Cynara thought, sneering at herself even for asking the question. But could she do it? She *had* to do it; there was no choice.

Cynara reached for the gown, thinking that there had

never been a choice. Everything must be paid for, she thought bitterly, and where a woman was concerned, there was only one kind of payment that a man demanded. The admission increased her fear, and with hands trembling as much from trepidation as from weakness, Cynara pulled the gown over her head. Her fingers shook as she fumbled with the row of buttons down the front, but at last she was ready and there was no excuse for hesitation.

Willing away the faintness caused by her illness, Cynara ran her fingers through her hair, tossing it back from her face. Then, resolutely, deliberately blanking her mind from what she knew awaited her, she opened the door and entered the captain's cabin.

CHAPTER TWELVE

IT WASN'T UNTIL several weeks after her first night with Captain Baird that Cynara had an opportunity to talk to Sarah. By that time, the seemingly endless voyage was almost at an end, and Cynara, who had spent months longing for just such an occurrence, now found herself wishing that Australia was more than two or three weeks ahead. The time she had spent in the hold now seemed like some horrible dream far in the past, and except for the recurring nightmares that caused her to wake up bathed in perspiration, she had almost succeeded in making herself forget those horrifying months locked in the bowels of the ship. But as the vessel continued inexorably toward Australia, Cynara became more and more apprehensive. What fate awaited her after the ship moored in Sydney Cove?

As she stood at the rail, gazing out at the foaming wake of the ship, the stories and rumors she had heard before from her fellow prisoners surfaced once again to strike real fear in her heart. She was now branded irrevocably as a convict, and convicts had absolutely no rights in Australia. If one was fortunate enough to be assigned to a free settler for the duration of the sentence, the living conditions were carefully regulated—in most cases. But for those unfortunates who were charged, falsely or not, with disobedience, idleness, or some other offense, flogging was the accepted punishment. For more serious offenses, convicts could be confined in a penal settlement, and Cynara shuddered when she recalled that those places, Macquarie Harbour and Port Arthur, in particular, had reputations unparalleled for horror and misery.

Cynara closed her eyes, forcing her thoughts away from the hideous pictures her imagination evoked. It was so unjust, she thought. She had done nothing to merit a convict sentence, but how could she prove it? The captain had told her that the ship carried only a list of the prisoners' names for identification; there were no records of trials, only the length of the sentence was included after each name. In many cases, he admitted, if the original charge was for a lesser crime, such as stealing, there might even be no mention of the offense. Which was certainly to Bertram's advantage, Cynara thought sourly. How simple it must have been for him to arrange for her transportation, if all he had to do was include her name on the manifest. How simple for him, but how difficult for her to prove her innocence. It wasn't fair, she thought angrily.

"Fair?" a voice drawled behind her. "What is?"

Cynara whirled around, embarrassed that she had spoken aloud without realizing it. But when she saw who was there, she forgot her depression, and cried excitedly, "Sarah!"

Sarah smiled, looking her up and down. "Well, well. I can't believe it's you!"

It was true; the transformation in Cynara was startling. No longer ungainly, body distorted with pregnancy, she had regained both her figure and her health. There was color in her cheeks and on her lips, and her hair, held back from her face with a ribbon, shone with its former luster. But the shadow of remembered pain lingered in her eyes, and there was a new hardness about her mouth that told the observant Sarah the depth of the changes in her friend.

Cynara thought of the countless times during the past weeks when she had felt guilty over her improved position while Sarah was still confined in the hold. She had approached Captain Baird about it, but he had waved his hand dismissingly, replying that he had offered Sarah more freedom, but she had insisted that she was happy enough where she was. The subject seemed to annoy him, and Cynara had not pressed him further. There was nothing she could do if Sarah had refused his offer before, but Sarah's position still weighed heavily on her conscience.

As if Sarah had read her mind, she said roughly, "I told you not to worry about me, didn't I?"

"How can I help it? We both know it should be you who—"

"Don't be silly!" Sarah interrupted sharply. "I'm glad the captain prefers you to me. It turned out for the best after all."

"How can you say that? When I think of you in the hold, with those horrible women . . ."

"I've told you before I can take care of myself. Besides, it's not so bad; it's just that you never got used to it, like I have."

Cynara sighed, unsure whether she believed Sarah or not. If their positions were reversed, would she be as complacent? She doubted it.

"Sarah, I never had the chance to thank you—"

"For what? You would have done the same for me, wouldn't you?"

"Of course! But—"

As always, when Cynara tried to express her gratitude, Sarah became embarrassed. "Forget it," she said. "It's over, and I'm just glad you're all right." She glanced sharply at Cynara. "You are, aren't you?"

Cynara hesitated. "Yes," she answered briefly.

They stood together at the rail, pretending sudden absorption with the rush of blue-green water below them, both too aware of the awkward silence that had followed Cynara's response.

"The captain isn't what you thought, is he?"

Startled, Cynara looked quickly at Sarah. She was smiling, her expression amused and knowing.

"How do you know that?" Cynara asked, astonished.

"Well, how do you think?" Sarah drawled. "He tried it on with me long ago."

"He did?" Cynara gaped at her. "Why didn't you tell me?"

"I didn't think it was important," Sarah answered airily. "But I'll tell you this—" she looked at Cynara in mock anger "if you were more successful than I was, I'll never speak to you again. I have my reputation to uphold, you know!"

In spite of herself, Cynara laughed. The sound startled her, for she had thought never to laugh again. "What a relief!" she said, actually giggling as she matched Sarah's mood. "And all this time I thought it was me!"

Sarah shook her head, and they laughed until tears ran down their cheeks, hugging each other as one burst of laughter followed another. At last, hands over their mouths to stifle the sound of their merriment, they heard the first mate calling out to Sarah. Sarah answered, and as she moved away, she turned to wave gaily at Cynara. "Perhaps I'll see you again tomorrow," she called, jerking her head in Hatch's direction as she winked conspiratorially.

Cynara smiled as Sarah disappeared with a pert flick of her skirt. Shaking her head, she turned back to the rail, feeling almost light-hearted as she gazed out across the water. It had been wonderful to talk to Sarah again, even for such a short time; she hadn't realized how much she had missed her.

It was strange, she thought pensively, that she and Sarah had become such friends, for they were so fundamentally different from each other. Sometimes she wondered what Sarah, with all her wordly ways and experience, saw in her. Whatever it was, Cynara was glad that Sarah had offered her her friendship; she suddered to think what this voyage would have been like without her. Sarah was even responsible for the position she was in now with the captain, and while at first Cynara hadn't known whether to be grateful to her or not, now she knew that she had been fortunate indeed. And the captain wasn't so bad, she thought, smiling to herself as she unconsciously adopted one of Sarah's pet phrases; oh no, he wasn't so bad at all.

Cynara thought back to that first night. She had been terrified, she remembered, when she opened the door that led to the captain's cabin, so afraid of who he was and what he could do to her that at first she had thought it impossible to walk into the room. It had taken her several minutes to realize that the cabin was empty and she was alone.

Such was her state of dread that the captain's absence, instead of giving her the opportunity to calm herself, had only increased her fears; she had found herself imagining one horrible scene after the other until she was so frightened that she began to cry. When the captain had entered the room, she had sobbed all the harder at the sight of him, knowing that she was making an utter fool of herself but unable to prevent it.

He was no less astonished at himself than she was when he came forward at once and said gruffly, "Here now. What's all this? There's nothing to be frightened about, girl. Come, sit down." He led her over to a chair, forcing her gently into it, before he turned and bellowed, "Wilson!"

A man wearing a soiled white apron poked his head in. "Aye, sir?"

"Bring me some tea."

"Tea, sir?" The expression on Wilson's face was almost comical as he regarded the captain with disbelief.

"Yes, damn it—tea! Can't you understand a simple order?"

"Aye, sir. Tea." Wilson withdrew, his attitude implying that he had never heard of the beverage.

Cynara had succeeded in composing herself somewhat by the time the tea arrived. The steward, his expression carefully blank, deposited the tray on the table and left, well aware of the glare the captain directed at him, daring him to comment.

"Thank you," Cynara said faintly, accepting the mug from Baird, who poured it himself. It had been a long time since she had tasted anything remotely resembling tea, even the strong, almost black brew that the steward had concocted, and despite her fear, she smiled tremulously at the captain in gratitude.

"Better now?"

Cynara nodded, watching him uneasily as he began to move restlessly about the room. She braced herself for what was sure to come, but to her astonishment, Baird suddenly grabbed his hat from the table. Ramming it onto his head, he muttered something about checking the windlass, then he strode from the room, slamming the door behind him.

Weak with relief that the ordeal had been postponed, however briefly, Cynara sagged in her chair. She had almost finished the remains of the tea when a sudden thought struck her. Was he displeased with her? Had she disappointed him? But of course she had; hadn't he found her weeping like some terrified child? Wincing at the picture she must have made, she wondered why he hadn't thrown her out immediately. Was she glad that he hadn't? She wasn't sure.

Suddenly she was too tired to think any more. She shouldn't have tried to get up from bed so soon, she thought; her illness had weakened her more than she realized. Putting her head back against the chair, she closed her eyes and surrendered to the leaden weariness that crept over her, blotting out all thought.

Cynara woke with a start. She could see a shadowy figure in the darkness of the cabin, fumbling with something on the table. A match flared, illuminating Captain Baird's face as he lit the lamp. At the sight of him, all her earlier fears and indecision rushed back; it was only by a great effort that she prevented herself from shrinking away from him when he held out his hand to her. Swallowing hard, she forced herself to get out of the chair.

With her hand in his, he led her to a curtained alcove which served as sleeping quarters apart from the outer room. Drawing back the curtain so that the light from the lamp dimly illuminated the space where they stood, he took off his jacket and turned to her.

She was thin from her illness, and there were hollows under her cheekbones. She seemed far too delicate and fragile to Captain Baird as he gazed at her, almost like a porcelain figure that would snap at the first touch. Her eyes were enormous in that thin face; she was like a doe, prepared to take flight. He must be gentle, he thought, reaching out to touch her hair.

She started at his touch, her eyes wide and straining, as though she expected him to throw her down. He murmured something soothing, and she subsided as he continued to stroke her hair. He could feel his pulse bounding as his excitement rose, and he cautioned himself to go slowly. This was no ordinary woman, and she must be treated tenderly. How could he convince her that he meant her no harm?

She stood frozen when he put his arms around her and drew her close. The rough wool of his shirt scratched her cheek, but she didn't notice the discomfort. Her body tensed, and he said quietly, "Don't be frightened. I won't hurt you."

Startled at the soft tone of his voice, Cynara lifted her head. He smiled at her. She tried to smile in return, but the muscles of her face felt stiff. Was he mocking her? It was difficult to believe that this man, who shouted obscenities and yelled at his crew, could be so gentle.

"Let me look at you," he murmured, one hand beginning to undo the buttons of her gown.

She closed her eyes as she felt the gown slipping off her shoulders. She wore nothing underneath, and when the garment fell to the floor, she tried vainly to cover her nakedness with her hands. Gently, he took her hands away, his own cupping her breasts while his thumbs brushed softly against her nipples. He bent his head to kiss the pulse beating madly in the hollow of her throat, and then he lifted her from the floor and placed her on the bed.

Conscious of his eyes on her as he removed his clothing, Cynara tried valiantly to stifle her acute embarrassment. The thought flickered through her mind that he was infinitely better than the brutal men who had taken her before, but she could not prevent the sudden stiffening of her body as he lay down beside her. She waited nervously, almost expecting him to change suddenly into the raging maniac she had learned from past experiences to expect.

To her astonishment, she felt his arms tremble as he pulled her to him, and she realized that he was almost as apprehensive as she. Startled, she looked into the eyes that were only inches from her own, and for the first time she saw the chagrin he was unable to hide.

He turned his face away from her, staring up at the ceiling. His hand caressed her back, the curve of her hip as she lay on her side against him, but his touch was almost absentmindedly, as though he were thinking of something else.

Finally he murmured, "Touch me."

Cynara froze. He felt the tensing of her body against him, and he took her hand, guiding it toward the dark triangle of hair between his legs. "Touch me," he said again.

Afraid to refuse, Cynara forced herself to reach for him. Her hand touched his flaccid organ, and even in her inexperience, she knew that something was wrong; terribly wrong, judging from the deep sigh of exasperation and regret that escaped him. Apprehensive, she looked up at him again and saw that his eyes were closed.

What was it? Was there something the matter with him? But he had seemed so sure of himself before, she thought in bewilderment. Had she done something, offended him in some way?

Why did she feel that she was to blame? It was absurd, but her pride was stung at the thought, and she sat up abruptly, confused by her conflicting emotions. Should she have acted differently? Was there something she should have done? No, no, what was she thinking? Only a few hours ago she had been terrified at the thought of being in bed with this man, and now here she was, wondering what she could do to help him.

"It's all right," he said, his voice so low that she could hardly hear him. "You're not . . . to blame."

Startled that he seemed to have read her thoughts, she looked over her shoulder at him. "I'm not?"

He shook his head. "Come here . . ." he said softly. Reaching up, he pulled her back down to lie against him. "It wasn't always like this," he said, his hand stroking her hair. "There was a time . . ." He broke off, uttering a sound that was almost a groan. His arm tightened around her until she could hardly breathe.

Cynara felt the tension in him, the frustration and anger at whatever it was that had rendered him impotent, and again she was afraid that he would blame her.

He said nothing more, and she did not dare speak. Soon she could tell by the change in the rhythm of his breathing that he had fallen asleep. She lay for a long time, staring at the flickering light of the lamp. She was afraid to move, to disturb him, for his arm held her securely against his side, as though he derived some comfort from her presence. But there was no comfort for her, and her mind was a confused jumble of emotions as she thought back to what had happened tonight.

If she continued to fail him, would he send her back to the hold? Of course he would. Shuddering at the thought, she realized that it was inevitable; she had neither the experience nor the knowledge to interest him if he wanted help in curing his affliction, whatever it was, and furthermore, she wasn't sure she wanted to acquire such knowledge.

Still, she found herself wishing desperately that she could talk to Sarah, for she knew that Sarah would be able to tell her what had gone wrong. But she hadn't seen Sarah since her illness, and so she would have to cope with this unnerving situation by herself. If, she amended silently, he allowed her to stay beyond the night.

Closing her eyes, she tried to sleep. But the thought occurred to her that she wasn't interested only in staying free of the dark prison below; she was interested in Captain Baird as well. For the simple reason that he had treated her as a human being, even with kindness, now she actually found herself wishing that she knew of a way to help him. He was a good man, Cynara thought, marveling at this revelation. Or at least, she amended, he had been good to her. He could have blamed her, taken out his frustration on her, become violent when she couldn't arouse him. But he had done none of these things, and she was profoundly grateful to him for that. Was there a way to help him? She didn't know, but she would try.

Feeling the warmth of his body next to hers, Cynara felt herself relaxing. He hadn't taken his arm from around her, and suddenly his embrace was almost comforting. She knew that she had nothing to fear from him, and for the first time in months she was able to drift off to sleep, knowing that she was secure, and safe.

"Cynara?"

Cynara came back to the present with a start. Turning at the sound of her name, she saw that Captain Baird had come up behind her as she stood by the rail. She took the arm he offered her, smiling.

"Hello, Joshua," she said. She was no longer afraid of him, not after that first night. In the beginning she had wondered why he seemed to regard her as someone apart, a woman who must be treated with more gentleness than the hardened prostitutes he was accustomed to. When she had finally discovered the reason, she was almost amused. In simple fact, Joshua Baird was sensitive to class distinctions. He thought of her as a lady, a person of quality who had somehow managed to find herself in a situation from which she was unable to extricate herself. He had said so himself. Thinking as he did, he stood a little in awe of her, as though by the accident of birth she was superior not only in education, but in understanding and sympathy. A lady would never betray by the slightest expression his secret; she would never openly express scorn or disgust when he failed, as had so many other women. Or so he thought.

Cynara was content to allow him this fantasy, which really wasn't a fantasy at all, she thought. Why would she deliberately mock him, if by doing so she was sure to lose his patronage? Sighing, she thought that expediency made liars of everyone, including herself. If someone had told her a year ago that she would compromise herself to this extent, she would have either laughed in their face, or slapped them. And that, she thought wryly, was the kind of lady *she* was.

Once inside the cabin, Baird shrugged off his coat with a sigh. "We'll sight Australia soon, Cynara," he said.

"I know."

Her voice was low when she answered, and he came to her and put his arms around her as she stood with her back to him.

"I'll miss you, Cynara," he said softly.

"Will you?"

He murmured assent, his face buried in her hair. His fingers found the buttons down the front of her gown and, undoing them to the waist, he slipped both hands inside the bodice to caress her breasts.

She stood quietly, no longer embarrassed even when the gown slid off her shoulders. She felt his lips on the nape of her neck, and again, she wondered what it would be like to feel a response to his overtures. Leaning against him, she closed her eyes, trying to imagine how she would feel in any other circumstances. It was impossible. Even with his hands moving over her body, pulling her gown over her hips to the floor so that she was naked to his touch, she felt nothing but a mild impatience to have this interlude over with. Would she ever feel anything again? Or had she already lost the capacity for deep emotion, the ability to feel love?

Her turbulent emotions when Evan had been near her or touched her seemed like a long-ago dream. She could barely recall that wild pounding of her heart, the singing in her blood when Evan held her, and she wondered longingly if she would ever feel such things again.

What did it matter? She was fortunate, and she knew it.

Joshua Baird was a kind man, a good man to her, and even though she yearned to feel passion, and delight, and joy in love, she must be content with what she had.

Baird led her over to the bed. The ritual was familiar to Cynara now, and she helped him off with his clothing. When he was naked also, he pulled her to him for an instant, his arms wrapped tightly around her, as though by the gesture he could make them one.

But as had happened so many times before, his body did not respond to the frantic urgings of his mind. When he pressed her gently down on the bed, she could see that his body had failed him yet again. He lay down beside her, sliding his arm under her shoulders to draw her toward him. His hand cupped her chin as he raised her face to his, and he kissed her passionately. She could feel the désperate desire for release hammering at him, and in that moment she was almost sorry for him. His body shook; his arms trembled around her. "Cynara . . ." he moaned.

This time when she reached for him, she was not the terrified, ignorant young girl she had been that first night. Her touch was sure and steady now, and she gradually increased the rythmn of her hand.

His own hands clutched her convulsively as his pleasure mounted; he kissed her fervently, rolling half on top of her, burying his face in her neck as he pressed his body against hers. He moaned as the tension built to an unbearable level, and then, with a fierce cry of exultation, he stiffened and collapsed on top of her. His breath rasped harshly in her ear as the spasm subsided.

Cynara lay quietly under him. Her face was tight with the bitterness she never allowed him to see, and she wondered what would have happened to her if she hadn't discovered this particular way of satisfying him. Would he have sent her back to the hold with the other prisoners, lady or not? The thought was never far from her mind.

Still, she had to admit that he treated her kindly; not once had he allowed his frustration over his condition to erupt into violence with her, and she was grateful for that. And he had been patient with her, which was a miracle in itself, considering the fact that he could have his choice of any of the more experienced and willing harlots waiting below for the opportunity to ingratiate themselves with the captain, who, after all, could offer so much more than one of his crew.

She realized abruptly that he had propped himself on one elbow and was staring at her bemusedly. As she turned her head to look at him, he raised his hand to trace the curve of her breast. Bending down, he kissed her soundly on the lips before getting out of bed.

"I've been thinking," he said, as he began to dress. "And I might have a solution for this problem of yours . . ."

"What kind of solution?" Cynara asked, immediately alerted. She knew he was referring to the prison sentence she had repeatedly told him was contrived.

Baird sat down, grabbing his boots from where he had carelessly kicked them an hour earlier. "I lose jurisdiction over the prisoners as soon as we drop anchor at Sydney, Cynara. You know that. And since I don't think a magistrate will believe your story without proof, I knew I would have to think of something else."

"And . . . ?" Cynara prodded, when he paused.

She waited silently as he struggled with one of his boots. Finally, when he was completely dressed again, she asked, "What did you mean?"

Baird approached the bed, reaching down to pull the blanket over her. He said, "I don't want to raise your hopes, Cynara."

"You just did," she replied, unable to keep the sharpness from her voice.

Baird laughed. "Let me think on it some more, and then when we arrive at Sydney, maybe I'll have an answer for you."

He left the cabin, carefully shutting the door behind him, leaving Cynara staring after him angrily. Did he really have a solution? If he did, why hadn't he told her outright, instead of teasing her with it?

She threw herself off the bed, snatching her gown from the floor as she did so. He had said that he didn't want to raise her hopes, she thought. Well, the only thing that could do that was the possibility of being released from this absurd prison sentence so that she could go back to England.

She paused abruptly, her arms caught in the folds of the gown as a thought struck her. Suppose Joshua *did* have a plan to free her—what then? She had no money, no friends—except Sarah, who was in the same position as she. She didn't even have any clothes, with the exception of this one crumpled gown. How was she going to get back to England?

Tears of frustration and anger stung her eyes; she brushed them away furiously, trying to think. Even if she managed to find some kind of employment, it would take months —perhaps years—before she was able to save enough to buy a passage back to England. And she had to get back, she thought fiercely. England was where Myles Ward was, and she hadn't endured this hellish voyage and all its conse-quences just to forget that Myles had been responsible; oh, no, she would never forget what he had done to her. She would make him pay for his lies and his cruelty if it took every last ounce of will and energy she possessed.

CHAPTER THIRTEEN

THE LONG VOYAGE was almost over. Joshua Baird had navigated the ship past the mountainlike wall of the rocky coast of New South Wales, Australia, and into a gigantic chasm that in any other circumstances Cynara would have found utterly fascinating. But as she stood on the bridge with the captain, she could not appreciate the beauty of the deep bays, their shores lined with evergreens. She did not see the towering crags above them on either side with their masses of rock jutting out into the inlet. With the captain's arm around her waist, she waited tensely for her first sight of Sydney, several miles further up to the inlet.

Now that they were so close to their destination, Cynara had the absurd desire to burst into useless tears. The past weeks with Joshua Baird had seemed almost like a reprieve; she had found herself wishing that they would never reach Australia, that she could just stay in the captain's cabin, enduring his advances, his hands on her, his mouth over hers—anything that would postpone the inevitable.

It was the not-knowing that she found the most difficult to bear—the awful anticipation of what awaited her when the ship dropped anchor. And now she felt her pulse beginning to race as the ship sailed inexorably on toward Sydney, and her hands felt clammy and cold with apprehension. Beside her, Baird gave her waist a reassuring squeeze, as if she sensed her fear. She tried to smile in response, but it was impossible; she could only stare, her eyes wide and strained, at the space ahead between the high crags.

At last, Joshua gave terse instructions to the helmsman, and the ship hove to in sight of the town. Behind her, Cynara heard the crew utter a simultaneous shout of joy that they had arrived, and Joshua Baird gave a long sigh of relief that he had brought his ship safely to port. He turned away from her, already occupied with the myriad details and decisions that were to claim his attention for the next several days, but Cynara remained alone at the rail.

Twilight darkened into night as she stood there gazing across the water, but finally, when she could see nothing more, she turned quietly away and went to wait in the captain's cabin. He had told her he would go ashore immediately, and would probably be gone for two days, if not more.

Cynara paced restlessly inside the cabin. Wilson, the steward, had set out a meal for her, but she couldn't eat. The sight of the food congealing on the plate nauseated her, but she lifted the glass of wine from the table and drank it quickly, hoping it would calm the fluttering in her stomach. She poured another glass and drank that, and then another.

Was she getting drunk? The thought made her laugh aloud. She had never been drunk in her life, but if that was what made everything seem fuzzy and unimportant, she should have tried it long ago.

The ruby liquid in her glass became more and more alluring. She held the glass up to the light in a mocking salute, and then drank the contents in one swallow, reaching out in the same motion to pour another. Some time later, she noticed blearily that the wine bottle was empty, and she tried to call out to Wilson to bring another. But the cabin floor tilted suddenly under her feet, and she had to grab the back of a chair for support. Staggering, Cynara managed to reach the bed. She fell onto it, gasping, as the room reeled around her. Seconds later, she was fast asleep.

"Cynara? Cynara! Do you hear me? Wake up!"

With an effort, Cynara opened her eyes. Captain Baird was leaning over her anxiously, shaking her shoulder. Each jerk caused the ache behind her eyes to increase, and she muttered, "I hear you. Stop shaking me; you're making it worse."

Baird glanced from the empty wine bottle rolling gently back and forth on the floor to her face. He didn't know whether to laugh at her expression or shake her for getting drunk. And on this morning, of all days! He groaned aloud.

"Cynara, listen to me." He pulled her to a sitting position, propping the pillow behind her. "Damn it, Cynara, are you listening?"

Cynara pulled herself together enough to nod. "What is it?"

"Thomas Hale is coming on board in a few minutes to see you—"

"Hale?" she repeated blankly. Why was it so difficult to think?

"Yes, Thomas Hale. He could be the solution to your problem, if you'll just listen to me for a minute."

The headache had moved to a place in back of her forehead; she winced as she put her legs over the side of the bed and stood up. "Go ahead," she said as she made her way slowly and carefully over to the washstand to splash cold water on her face.

Baird continued eagerly, "I met him last night in one of the public houses. Well, one thing led to another, and when he told me he was looking for a wife—"

"You thought of me?" Suddenly, she didn't need a dash of cold water to wake her; his words had the desired effect, and more.

Hoping she had misunderstood him, she turned toward him. "You thought of me?" she repeated, marveling that her voice could be so steady when inside she was screaming with anger.

Baird nodded, too pleased with himself to notice the sudden flash of bitterness in his eyes. "Hale is rich, Cynara. Besides his own estate, Tamoora, he has interests in half a dozen other businesses, or so I hear. He needs someone not only to be his wife, but also to manage his house, to be mistress of his estate. And he is a gentleman," Baird hurried on when Cynara remained silent. "You could look far and not find half so suitable a catch. It will be the perfect solution for you both."

"Marrying a man I don't even know hardly sounds like the ideal solution, Joshua," Cynara said, her voice steely as she thought back to that other time she had been faced with a similar situation.

"It does when you consider this: by marrying a free man, your convict status is revoked."

He came to where she was standing, her back pressed tightly against the washstand. Despite her preoccupation with what he had just told her, she saw the sadness in his face, and she was moved to ask, "What is it, Joshua? You look so—"

He took her hand and raised it to his lips. "I can't do any more for you than this, Cynara," he said regretfully. "If I could keep you here with me, I would. You—" He hesitated painfully. "You have been very good to me, Cynara, and this is the only way I can express my gratitude."

They were both embarrassed by his emotion. Cynara bit her lip, and Baird dropped her hand and moved away quickly. At the door he paused again, and she could see how difficult it was for him to leave her. A part of her was grateful to him for trying to help her in the only way he knew, but another part was frightened at her helplessness, especially when he said, "Isn't that what you wanted, Cynara—to be rid of the convict charge?"

Or course it was, she admitted silently. More than anything else she wanted that. But freedom at the price of marrying a man she knew nothing about? Exchanging one form of imprisonment for another was not her idea of improving her situation. She said so to Baird.

"You consider it, Cynara. But if I were you, I'd think twice about refusing. Remember, Hale can either marry you or buy your papers. Either way, you'll be his. As his wife, you will have advantages that a convict doesn't dare dream about: free to come and go as you please, to dress well, to entertain . . . You would be a fool to refuse Hale if he offers marriage, Cynara. And remember, too," he added, a strange expression on his face. "A man can't live forever, not at Hale's age, and living as high as he does."

Before she could ask him what he meant, Baird was gone. Cynara stared at the closed door, thinking furiously. Was this Thomas Hale an old man, then? Is that what Joshua meant? Or was he the kind who sated himself with all the comforts and luxuries money could buy, so that he only appeared old and dissipated?

She had known a man just like that, an acquaintance of her father's, who had dropped dead from a seizure after a drunken spree that had scandalized all his neighbors. Was Hale the same kind of man?

Pushing herself away from the washstand, Cynara rubbed her fingers across her aching forehead. No matter what decision she made, the final choice rested with Thomas Hale. It was not a comforting thought.

Cynara wished suddenly that she could talk to Sarah; she had need of her friend's brisk common sense at this point. But then, she knew what Sarah would say: Sarah would jump at the chance Cynara had been given; for her the advantages of marrying a rich man would far outweigh any disadvantages. Cynara could almost hear Sarah's exclamation of surprise and disgust that she would even hesitate over such an opportunity.

Sighing, Cynara began to brush the tangles from her hair. In a sudden mood of defiance, she braided it into a coronet around her head. The style was severe, and as she looked into the tiny square of mirror that the captain used when shaving, she was surprised to see the difference it made in her appearance. She looked more mature, older than her seventeen years, she realized, with abrupt sadness. In fact, she thought, as she examined her face more closely, she didn't only appear older, she also looked—hard. Almost as hard and calculating as Sarah could look. Had she really changed that much?

Cynara laughed harshly to herself. Of course she had changed; she was certainly no longer the wide-eyed inno- cent that Evan . . .

Biting her lip, she turned away from the mirror. Evan would be aghast at the change in her, she thought angrily. She could just imagine what he would say if he knew the things that had happened to her, and she wished fiercely that she could meet him again. Oh yes, she thought, smiling nastily, he would be more than surprised. She could imagine the scene now: Evan with that arrogant expression which infuriated her; she sure of herself, deliberately provocative. She would come up to him, place her hands on his chest and thrust her body against his. Her arms would wind around his neck, pulling his head down to hers, and she would kiss him, her lips covering his, her tongue probing deep inside his mouth. Startled, he would try to push her away, but she would cling to him, swaying her hips, rubbing her breasts across his chest. He would respond, she knew; he would not be able to resist her. As he reached for her, she would move away and slowly unhook her gown, letting it drop negligently to the floor, kicking it away. She would stand before him, clad only in a shift of the finest lace, and she would allow him to see her thus until his passion was fully aroused. Then she would tear the shift off, baring her body, deliberately offering herself—but pulling away when he reached for her again.

She could see herself, walking slowly to a chaise, reclining on it sensuously, lifting one arm casually to loosen her hair. He would rush to her then, and she would refuse him with a laugh, sure of her power over him. He would plead with her, beg her, and she would remain unmoved. Oh, yes, she would teach him to desert her; she would make him squirm at the memory of the things he had said to her that night after Myles had raped her in the summerhouse. For once she would have the upper hand, and she would glory in seeing him humbled.

Humbled. Cynara came out of her reverie with a start. If anyone was to be humbled, it was she, faced with the coming meeting with Thomas Hale. She must be ready for him; she must get control of herself so that she would not be afraid of him when he came.

She did not have long to wait for the captain's return. Minutes later, he ushered in a man who made Cynara forget completely about Evan. She felt an immediate and strong dislike for him, even though he had stopped in the doorway to stare at her in admiration. Standing, she faced him silently, and did not realize that her chin had lifted almost defiantly as she returned his stare.

If this was the man Joshua had told her about, she thought disdainfully, he was certainly no gentleman, no matter how correct his clothing, nor how easily he wore an aura of wealth and power. Everything about him was rough and coarse, from his heavily jowled face with wide mouth and small eyes sunk deep into their sockets, to his broad, round shoulders with the muscles bulging along his arms. Even his hands were those of a common workman, with stubby fingers and square nails, and his legs, encased as they were in expensive black broadcloth, were heavy and short, almost bowed.

The man spoke for the first time, his eyes on Cynara, but addressing Captain Baird, who stood slightly behind him, nodding encouragement at Cynara. "Is this the girl, then, Baird?"

Cynara winced inwardly at the sound of his voice. It was rough and harsh, like his appearance. But there was an underlying note of cruel arrogance as well, and Cynara stiffened in response as his glance raked her insolently.

Despite her said situation, Cynara was not about to let Baird speak for her. Before the captain could answer, she clearly, "My name is Cynara Rosslyn, Mr. Hale."

"You know my name?" Hale affected to be surprised.

Cynara inclined her head briefly. "Captain Baird has mentioned you, yes."

"And what did the captain say?"

Cynara met his narrowed eyes unflinchingly. Deciding that it was useless to pretend ignorance, she answered, "Only that you were looking for a wife."

"You seem to know a great deal about my affairs, Miss Rosslyn."

There was no mistaking the sarcasm with which he used her surname, and Cynara stiffened even more, regarding him with a hauteur that made Captain Baird wince. "Not at all, Mr. Hale," she replied, her tone indicating that his affairs were of no consequence to her whatsoever. As indeed, she thought contemptuously, they were not. How dare the man stare at her in that disgusting manner! Who was he after all, but an ignorant boor posing as a gentleman!

Hale seemed amused by her show of defiance. "What a proud creature you are!" he exclaimed. "Do I sense a bit of the aristocrat about you, Miss Rosslyn? Ah well," he said, before she could answer, "It doesn't matter does it? You have the look of one, and that makes all the difference."

He turned to Captain Baird. "I think you were right about her, Captain. This is no ordinary woman." He waved his hand dismissively. "Leave us. I want to talk to her alone."

Baird seemed about to object, but at the frown Hale directed at him, he moved toward the door. With one last glance and a reassuring nod at Cynara, he went out.

As soon as the door closed behind him, Hale sat heavily in a chair. Cynara watched him warily as he took out a cigar and proceeded with the business of lighting it. Blue smoke curled upward around his head as he sat back and stared at her in silence.

"Turn around," he ordered finally.

"I beg your pardon?"

Hale gestured with his hand, inscribing a circle in the air with one finger. "Turn around and let me look at you," he ordered again.

Her lips tight, Cynara obeyed. When she faced him again, he motioned toward the chair opposite him. "Sit down."

"Thank you."

There was no mistaking the icy sarcasm in her voice, and Hale flushed, his expression becoming ugly. Leaning forward, his face so close to hers that she could see the dark flecks in the merciless gray of his eyes, he said, "Don't tempt me too far, my girl. I can offer you a great deal—if I choose to do so." He paused to make sure that his words had the proper chastising effect, and then he added, "And what I choose depends upon you."

"In what way?"

Hale glared at her angrily. "In what way?" he repeated unbelievingly. "Look here, girl. As a convict, I can make your life miserable—"

"I am not a convict."

"What?"

"I said, I am not a convict. I committed no crime."

Hale burst into raucous laughter. "I've heard that before!" he said scornfully.

"Nevertheless, it is true."

"Well, true or not, it doesn't make much difference, does it?" He glanced at her slyly. "Unless, of course, you can prove you were unjustly accused?"

Cynara was silent, and Hale laughed again. Then he slapped his knee as though he had come to a decision. "Get your things together. You're coming with me."

"You've decided, then, to buy my papers?" she asked, trying not to reveal her complete dismay.

"Buy your papers?" Hale regarded her in surprise. "Hell, no. I think I'll marry you instead!"

"Marry me! You would have a convict for your wife?"

Hale smirked. "I thought you said you weren't a convict?"

"I'm not! I only meant—"

"Enough! I told Baird I wanted a wife, and I meant just that." He paused. "You can manage a home?"

"Yes, but—"

"And you know how to entertain?"

"Well, I—"

He rose suddenly from his chair, grabbing and lifting her in the same motion. His eyes swiftly traveled the length of her body, and he pulled her close, his hands roaming over her as she tried to struggle away. Laughing at her efforts to free herself, he said coarsely, "You have the look and feel of a good breeder, too. I want a son, to inherit what I've built. With your looks and blood, and my own background, he'll inherit everything he needs to go far in this world. If you give me a son, there's no telling what I will do to reward you!"

He held her away from him for an instant, taking her face in his hand, forcing her to meet his eyes, which had suddenly turned a cold pewter color. "And if you don't give me a son, you'll curse the day I boarded this ship and saw you. Understand?"

Cynara understood too well. But as she nodded, her expression carefully guarded against betraying her private thoughts, she offered a silent thanks to Sarah and the knowledge she had shared so freely. If she was forced to marry this man, and it seemed that she would be compelled to do so, then she would marry him. But not even he, with all the power and strength at his command, could force her to give him the son he so arrogantly demanded—not if she could help it.

Hale left to make arrangements about taking her off the ship with him. Cynara took the opportunity to slip away to find Sarah, who was standing at the rail, gazing out at the town of Sydney shimmering in the heat of the noonday sun.

"You're going to be married! That's wonderful!" Sarah exclaimed when Cynara told her what had happened.

"I'm not so sure," Cynara replied glumly.

Predictably, Sarah focused on the one thing that was most important to her. "But you said this man is rich—"

"There are more important things than wealth, Sarah!" Cynara said sharply.

"Are there?" Sarah was in no way intimidated by Cynara's sour expression. "Name one," she challenged teasingly.

"I don't like him, Sarah. He's—"

"Listen, honey. If it was me, I wouldn't care what he was like. Just think—when you marry him, you won't be a convict any more. Isn't that worth something to you?" She waited for Cynara's reluctant nod, and then she continued eagerly, "And you'll have fine clothes, carriages, a beautiful home, servants—what more could you want?"

Yes, what more could she want? Cynara asked herself gloomily. Hale was offering her much more than freedom from a prison sentence; he was giving her all the advantages that wealth could bring. But at what price?

"He wants a son, Sarah," she said.

"Ah . . ."

Cynara looked away from Sarah's knowing expression.

"And you don't want to give him one—is that it?" Sarah asked quietly.

Cynara shook her head.

"Well, there's ways to get around that," Sarah said complacently. "I'd count my blessings, honey, if I were you."

Suddenly deeply ashamed of her preoccupation with herself and her own problems, Cynara grasped Sarah's hand and held it tightly. "I wish you were coming with me!" she said, trying not to cry at the thought of being parted from Sarah.

"So do I!" Sarah tried to grin, and failed. "Don't worry," she said roughly. "I'll get along; I always have."

"If there was only some way I could be sure to see you again—"

"Oh, you'll be seein' me," Sarah said, pushing Cynara's shoulder jokingly, averting her face so that Cynara wouldn't see the quick tears that sprang into her eyes. "I know where you'll be, my fine lady. But if I come to visit, I'll be sure to come in the back door. I don't imagine your fancy new husband will take to a convict whore traipsin' in by the front way, do you?"

"I don't care what he thinks!" Cynara replied fiercely.

"Aw, maybe you will, someday."

"Oh, Sarah!" Cynara was in tears, despite her efforts not to cry.

"Now, don't go blubbering, else you'll have me doing it, too. That would be a pretty sight, wouldn't it? Two grown women falling on each other's necks!"

They looked at each other, and then suddenly, they were in each other's arms. "I'll miss you, Sarah," Cynara sobbed.

"And I'll miss you, too, honey." Sarah dashed a hand across her eyes, pushing Cynara away at the same time. "Go on, now. Go on, before I make a bigger fool of myself than I already have."

"Goodbye, Sarah . . ."

"Goodbye, Cynara—and good luck."

"To both of us—"

Cynara raised her hand in farewell as Sarah abruptly turned and fled down the ladder to the hold. Trying desperately to hold back her tears, Cynara closed her eyes tightly for a moment. Then, wiping her face with both hands, she turned toward the door that led to the captain's quarters.

". . . now pronounce you man and . . . er . . . . wife."

It was over. Cynara couldn't believe it, even when the magistrate smirked and called her Mrs. Hale. To her astonishment, he actually giggled when he asked her to affix her signature to the marriage papers, and she looked at him curiously when she took the pen, wondering why he seemed so furtive one minute, so amused the next. He had been extremely nervous during the entire brief ceremony, stumbling over the words as if they were unfamiliar to him, and she thought that maybe he had been drinking. He certainly seemed confused, she thought.

When she straightened from signing the name she couldn't regard as hers, she happened to catch the broad wink that Hale directed over her head to the magistrate. There was something sly about that wink, and something definitely secretive about the answering expression on the man's face. Cynara wondered uneasily what the reason could be.

But there was no time to question it, for Hale had stuffed the papers into his pocket, and was hurrying her out the door. His carriage was waiting, his coachman standing at attention by the open door. To her gratification, he smiled at her, and she smiled back. Gathering up the skirt of her gown, the wedding dress of beige muslin with chocolate-brown braid trim that Hale had ordered finished in two days, she prepared to mount the steps into the carriage. But as she put her foot on the step, another carriage went by, and she happened to glance up. The street was hot and dusty, the sky above a harsh blue that glared in her eyes, so that she saw his face only for an instant. But the shock was so great that her foot slipped on the step, and she would have fallen had not the coachman leaped forward to catch her. She sagged against the man, suddenly unable to catch her breath.

"What the hell . . . !" Hale was looking at her in angry consternation, and she tried to speak, to offer some excuse for her clumsiness, but she could do nothing more than shake her head weakly.

"It must be the heat, sir," the coachman offered tentatively.

"Well, let's get her inside the carriage then!" Hale snapped.

Somehow, with their assistance, Cynara managed to climb inside. Gasping, she leaned against the upholstery, and thought: It couldn't have been. It had to be my imagination. It had to be!

"Some water, Thompkins!" Hale ordered the hovering coachman.

"Yes, sir!" Thompkins sped away.

"What is it?" Hale demanded. "What happened?"

With an effort, Cynara focused her attention on Thomas Hale, bending over her in the close confines of the carriage. "I'm sorry," she said weakly. "I . . . felt faint for a moment."

"Is it the heat—or is it something else?" he asked harshly.

"Something else?" Cynara repeated blankly. Now that she was sitting down, out of the sun, she felt her composure returning. How could she have thought, even for an instant, that she had seen Evan?

She felt like a fool. What would Evan be doing here, in

Sydney? It was impossible; she had imagined the entire episode. The past few days had been exhausting, hectic, what with the dress fittings Hale had ordered, the shopping she had been forced to do in such a hurry, everything a rush because Hale insisted on having the wedding ceremony at once. She was tired, that was all; she was tired and hot and nervous, and she had simply seen a man who happened to resemble Evan Calder. It would have been a shock to anyone, she comforted herself, trying to ignore that part of her that asked why she reacted so intensely to the sight of the man she had vowed earlier to forget completely.

"Did Baird lie? Are you—pregnant?"

The coarse question brought her attention angrily back to Hale. "No," she answered icily. "I am not."

He stared at her intently. "All right, then," he said finally, clearly not convinced that she spoke the truth. "But if you're lying to me . . ."

The unspoken threat hung in the air between them. Cynara straightened, carefully adjusting her skirts, ignoring him as he settled himself heavily opposite her. Thompkins came running up with the water, and Cynara accepted the cup with a stiff smile of gratitude.

Thompkins climbed up onto the box, and the carriage started off at Hale's terse command. Aware that he was watching her carefully, Cynara averted her head, staring out the window, pretending absorption with the strange scenery beyond. But she saw nothing of the countryside they were passing through; she was reliving that moment of utter shock when she happened to glance into that passing carriage.

It couldn't have been Evan, she repeated to herself, almost desperately. Certainly there were thousands of other men with black curling hair and dark eyes.

But as the carriage rattled on, Cynara asked herself again and again: And how many of those black-haired, dark-eyed men would have a long, thin scar that ran from temple to jaw? Thousands? In her heart, she knew there was only one . . .

CHAPTER FOURTEEN

"EVAN? EVAN! WHAT IS IT, MAN? You look like you've seen a ghost!"

Evan forced himself to sit back against the carriage cushions. Distractedly, he ran a hand through his hair, reached inside his coat pocket for a cheroot, changed his mind and withdrew his handkerchief instead. Mopping his face, he muttered, "It couldn't have been Cynara . . ."

"What? I didn't hear you, Evan."

Evan pulled at his collar, which suddenly seemed too tight, almost choking him. He mopped his face again, and realized suddenly that LeCroix was watching him anxiously.

"I'm sorry, Vincent," he said. "I didn't hear what you said."

"Evan, are you all right?"

LeCroix's expression of anxiety had altered to one of puzzlement as he stared at Evan. "Of course I'm all right," Evan said curtly. "What makes you think I'm not?"

"Well . . . You looked so strange, for a minute, back there. As if you had been startled by something. What is it? Can I help?"

Now that Evan thought about it, he was sure that he hadn't seen Cynara at all. What would she be doing here, in Sydney? He scoffed at himself. Surely there were other women with that proud tilt of the head, that tall, slender figure! He had simply imagined the resemblance, that was all.

"Evan?"

Evan turned to LeCroix. "It was nothing," he said with a tight smile. "I thought I recognized . . . someone. I was mistaken."

But had he been mistaken? Other women might carry

themselves in that proud manner, but could another woman possess that vibrant shade of auburn hair, or eyes so green that the deepest jade paled in comparison? Evan shook his head, mocking himself for that flight of fantasy. It hadn't been Cynara, he told himself once more, and wondered why his heart still beat so rapidly.

"I was mistaken," he said again, and told himself that he believed it.

If LeCroix was dissatisfied with Evan's answer, he did not show it. He knew little more about Evan than he had seven months or so ago on the dock at Liverpool, but he knew enough now to realize that Evan never explained himself if he chose not to do so. Sighing, LeCroix absently stroked his moustache as he settled back against the seat. What was it about this young man that intrigued him so, he wondered. It was true that Evan had proved himself invaluable, even in the short time he had been in LeCroix's employ. His grasp of business matters was astounding in one so young and inexperienced, and yet LeCroix knew that this was not his sole interest in Evan. Perhaps it was the fact that while Evan performed each task required of him with admirable efficiency, he continued to withdraw from all gestures of friendship with cool detachment. It was almost as though he were afraid to commit himself to any relationship, however casual, and that was disturbing to a man of LeCroix's open and friendly nature. Was Evan hiding something—LeCroix had long suspected that he was, but that made the mystery about Evan all the more intriguing.

Vincent LeCroix suddenly resolved to pursue the idea he had been privately contemplating for weeks now. But he would go about his investigation without letting Evan know. He didn't have to imagine what Evan's reaction would be if he discovered that LeCroix was poking about, trying to discover if and how Evan Calder was related to the Wards of Australia.

But as LeCroix though about it, he wondered whether he

might be stirring up something that was better left alone. If Evan was related to Sean Ward, and it seemed certain that he must be, for the resemblance between the two men could not be coincidental, what difference could it make to Evan now? Sean Ward was dead, and so, presumably, was the rest of his family, killed after Sean had died, by one of those damnable bush fires that sprang up so suddenly and devastated everything in their path.

LeCroix stared out the window as the carriage moved rapidly down the street, wondering why it was so important to him to learn what he could. Was it because he had come to regard Evan as the son he never had? He glanced covertly at the tall young man beside him. Ah, if only his Mary had lived, he thought sadly, he might have a son Evan's age now.

Forcing his mind away from memories of the bride who had died too young and too soon after their marriage, LeCroix once again addressed himself to the mystery about Evan. Suddenly he remembered a scrap of conversation he and Evan had had one night when both of them had reached too often for the brandy. Recalling that conversation, and the pain and disillusionment on Evan's face that night, he knew that he had to pursue his investigation. If he could discover Evan's connection with Sean Ward and his family, it could take Evan away from him. Even knowing that, he had to try.

Evan had been sprawled in his chair, one leg negligently over the arm of it. He and LeCroix had retired to the library to discuss business, had drunk too much wine with dinner and brandy after. LeCroix was just on the point of heaving himself out of his own chair for bed, when Evan had muttered something about a lyrebird.

LeCroix had stared blearily at Evan. "What was that?"

"Lyrebird," Evan had repeated drunkenly. "Oliver told me they were real, but I didn't believe him. 'S funny one would show up in England, isn't it?"

LeCroix had a difficult time focusing on the conversation. "But there aren't any lyrebirds in England," he answered sagely, shaking his head and almost falling out of the chair.

Evan jerked his head angrily. "There's one," he corrected. "The garden . . . and . . . " He rubbed his hand across his forehead, trying to remember something else. "The ring," he muttered finally. "There was a ring with a lyrebird on it. The model for the garden . . . I saw it once, but Oliver took it away . . . "

LeCroix had narrowed his eyes, trying to focus on a memory of his own. He had seen a ring before with a lyrebird insignia, he thought confusedly. Or had he? He had decided that it was all his imagination, and standing, he had patted Evan's shoulder and tottered off to bed.

Until now, LeCroix had forgotten that incident, but as he sat in the carriage, he remembered it suddenly, and knew that he had been given a clue to the mystery about Evan Calder. Closing his eyes, he tried to recall if he had ever actually seen a lyrebird ring. It seemed that he had—but where? And when?

"Vincent, there is something I want to talk to you about," Evan said abruptly, disrupting LeCroix's thoughts.

LeCroix looked at Evan. "Well, what is it?" he asked, when Evan hesitated. The lad seems uncomfortable, LeCroix thought to himself; it was so unlike Evan that LeCroix immediately became alerted. Good God, he thought in complete dismay, is Evan planning to leave for greener pastures? The thought was so upsetting to him that his expression became grim as he tried to hide his feelings. "Well?" he asked again.

"I need a loan, Vincent," Evan answered calmly, trying not to notice the harsh note in LeCroix's voice. "One thousand pounds."

Whatever LeCroix had expected Evan to say, it was not this. He stared blankly at the tense young man opposite him for a full minute before he was able to pull himself together enough to repeat, "A loan?"

"Yes." Unflinchingly, Evan met LeCroix's startled eyes. "One thousand pounds. I will give you a fair rate of interest, Vincent, and I will repay you the note plus interest within one year."

"A thousand pounds is a lot of money," LeCroix said forbiddingly. He lowered his brows and pulled on his moustache, staring at Evan as if debating the question. Inside, he was grinning widely. What had the young upstart got himself into now? A woman? Mentally, LeCroix shook his head. Evan would never get himself into a scrape with a woman; he was too clever for that. What could it be, then? Gambling debts? Again, he shook his head. Evan would gamble on some things, he knew, but only those with an almost certain return of success; dice and cards were not for him. What then? It had to be a business venture of some kind, Vincent decided.

Swiftly, he went down a mental list of business opportunities he had heard about in the last few weeks. There was none that Evan could be interested in, not for an initial investment of a thousand dollars. What then?

His curiosity aroused, LeCroix glanced sharply at Evan. He wanted to ask what the loan was for, just as a matter of interest, but he knew that Evan would have told him if he wanted him to know. Damn it all, he thought in sudden annoyance; if Evan doesn't trust anyone, how can he expect others to trust him? LeCroix shifted irritably against the cushions; the fact of the matter, and he might as well admit it, he thought in frustration, was that he did trust Evan. If Evan said he needed a loan, then he needed a loan; it was as simple as that.

"What do you offer as collateral?" he asked finally, knowing that Evan would expect the question, be suspicious if he didn't ask. LeCoirx had no intention of demanding collateral; Evan's word was as good or better than any bond, but there was that damnable pride of Evan's to contend with. He would be insulted and outraged, thinking that LeCroix was patronizing him, if he didn't ask for proof of repayment.

This was the question that Evan had both expected and dreaded. In point of fact, he had nothing of value to offer LeCroix, and LeCroix knew it. But the loan was a necessity. Evan hated asking LeCroix for the money, but he knew that without it he could not buy the mill he wanted for the eventual production of his own woolen goods. This was his first step in making money of his own, and Evan was determined not to lose the mill, even though it stood derelict at present and would cost a handy sum to refurbish. It was a gamble, but Evan knew he could make it into a producing business if only he had the chance.

"The only thing I have to offer as collateral is myself," Evan said finally.

"That's rather an unusual arrangement," LeCroix countered, trying not to smile at the stiff embarrassment on Evan's face.

"I have nothing else. If I default on the loan, I will work for you for two pounds a week." Evan was now receiving ten pounds a week, an unprecedented sum, even for a chief clerk, but he insisted upon paying two of that for his room and board to LeCroix—"The other eight you can apply to the debt until it is cleared. Is that satisfactory?"

LeCroix hesitated. "And the two pounds you pay for your board . . . ?"

"I will continue to pay it," Evan said briefly.

"But that means—"

"I know what it means, Vincent."

LeCroix frowned, trying to calculate the sum in his head, but Evan anticipated him. "If I default, it will take three years to repay, including interest."

"Three years is a long time to be indebted to a man, Evan. Are you sure?"

"If everything goes the way I planned it, you"ll have the money before the note comes due. If not—" Evan shrugged. He had calculated the risk; in his mind he was prepared to take the consequences of failure. But the chances were remote; Evan did not intend to fail.

"All right, Evan," LeCroix said. He hesitated a moment, then sighed. "I suppose you want to stop at the office and draw up a note right now?"

Evan nodded, and LeCroix sighed again. Had he ever been that stiff-necked with pride? Somehow, he doubted it.

That afternoon, the money in his pocket, Evan went to see Harry Bisbee, the owner of the mill. He found the man sitting on the sagging front porch of his dilapidated shack, a half-empty bottle of rum on the floor beside him. Sunken eyes in an unshaven face looked up at Evan as he mounted the creaking steps to the porch.

"How'd you get my name?" Bisbee asked belligerently when Evan had stated what he wanted.

"I asked around."

"Don't know what you want that mill for anyway," Bisbee said, shaking his head. "It won't do you no good."

Evan's reply was cool. "That's my affair, isn't it?"

The man took a swallow from the bottle and coughed. He offered it to Evan, who declined, and then he said, "If you buy that mill, son, you'll end up like me—sittin' here, wonderin' what happened."

"My offer is three hundred pounds—for the mill and the land with it. It's a fair offer, Mr. Bisbee."

Bisbee squinted up at him. "Fair?" He scratched his head. "Do you know what I put into that mill, son? Ten years of my life. And for what? So that whorin' Mr. Thomas god-almightly Hale, could run me out. That's what'll happen to you, if you buy that mill, son. Mark my words!"

Agitated, the man heaved himself out of the chair, grabbing on to Evan for balance. "He'll ruin you too, lad, if you try. He don't want no one else involved in the wool business but him. No one!"

Calmly, Evan disengaged himself from Bisbee's grasp. "I thank you for your advice," he said, hiding his distaste as Bisbee breathed alcoholic breath into his face. "Will you accept my offer?"

Bisbee stared blearily at Evan for a long moment. At last

he rubbed his shirt sleeve across his mouth, wiped his hand on his trouser leg, and held out the hand to Evan. "You just might do it, lad," he said. "You just might do it, if you've got the grit to fight back."

He turned away, staggering toward the open door of the shack. "Come on in, Mr.—?"

"Calder," Evan supplied again, almost amused at the sudden respect the man gave him. "Evan Calder."

"Come in, Mr. Calder. I got the deed around here some-where."

Several minutes later, deed in hand and three hundred and fifty pounds poorer—Bisbee had proved to be a haggler—Evan walked out of the ramshackle house. As he mounted his horse Bisbee called out, "Good luck to you, son! And remember, that bastard Hale don't play by no rules!"

Evan raised his hand in farewell, turning his horse toward town. As he rode, he thought that if Thomas Hale thought to run him out of business, he was going to be surprised. When it came to fighting without rules, hadn't he learned from one of the masters himself? Evan's lips twisted bitterly as he thought of John Ward, who had cheated more than one farmer out of his property during his tenure at Lyrebird Manor. Oh yes, Evan thought, he had learned much from John Ward. And what knowledge he hadn't gained could be bought with the rest of the money he had in his pocket. There were plenty of men around who could be persuaded to protect his property from "intruders," as long as they were properly reimbursed for their trouble.

Evan put his horse into a canter, a tight smile on his lips and a ruthless determination in his heart to succeed where Bisbee had failed. He was pleased with this day's work, he thought—no, more than pleased; he was exultant. He had given himself five years to reach his goal, and if everything went the way he had planned, at the end of that time he would be in a position to buy Lyrebird Manor. Not that the Manor itself meant anything to him, he thought as he entered the road that led to LeCroix's home; it was the acquisition of it that was important to him. He had learned long ago from a chance remark of Oliver's that John Ward had mismanaged the estate so badly that there was danger of his losing it. Evan hoped savagely that John could keep himself out of the bankruptcy courts long enough for Evan to buy the mortgage. It would be worth all the years of humiliation and hardship he had endured to see John's— and Myles's—face when he foreclosed. He longed for that day ruthlessly, and suddenly he laughed aloud, startling the occupants of the gig he was passing.

Absently, Evan touched the brim of his hat in salute to the woman in the carriage. As he did, he noticed that her dress was a light beige in color, and he was immediately and forcefully reminded of the woman he had glimpsed so briefly that morning. Had it been Cynara? Even though reason told him no, his muscles tightened at the thought. Then he jeered at himself. What would Cynara be doing in Sydney? He must have been mistaken.

Cursing, for now that he thought of her he couldn't get her out of his mind, he rode on, wondering how he would react if Cynara was here in Australia. Would he act the besotted suitor, courting her, coming to tea, or taking her for long drives? He mocked the idea, knowing how impossible it would be to follow such a chaste ritual. As soon as he was alone with her, he would act out his dreams of her; the only reality would be Cynara in his arms.

Evan shouldered his way through the crowd that massed together inside a tiny grog shop. It was dark inside, the guttering candles stuck into empty bottles along the bar giving off little light, which was precisely the way the occupants preferred it. The shop was located in one of the low-life sections of Sydney; a burly lookout was posted at the barred door to give warning should the constables suddenly appear, as they did with regularity. Inside, conversation was conducted in low tones; sometimes money passed from hand to furtive hand under a table. Men did not

glance at their neighbor unless they had business with him
or unless a newcomer arrived.

Evan gave little notice to the secretive and glowering
stares turned in his direction as he entered. LeCroix had
given him a name and a description of the man he was
looking for; the search occupied all his attention. Vincent
had assured him the man would be here, and Evan finally
saw him, sitting at a table in a dark corner, a very large man
with his cap pulled low over his eyes.

"Are you Jerry Hauser?" Evan asked as he made his way
to the table.

The man squinted up at him. "And if I am?"

Evan was not intimidated by the dark glare the man
directed at him. "If you are," he replied coolly, "I have work
for you."

"You're a trifle young to be seekin' out the likes of me,
aren't you?"

"Age has nothing to do with the quality of a man's
money," Evan replied evenly. "However, if you prefer to
wait for a better offer . . . " He turned to leave.

"Hold your hand a minute," the man said quickly. "I
didn't say nothin' about waitin' for a better offer." He
gestured to the chair opposite him. "Sit down," he offered
roughly. When Evan complied, the man leaned forward
and demanded, "Who gave you my name?"

"Vincent LeCroix."

"Vince?" The man raised an eyebrow. "How do you
know him?"

"Let's just say that I know him," Evan replied. He had no
intention of revealing at this point that he was employed by
LeCroix; he wanted to make sure that this man understood
that he was to work for him and not Vincent.

"All right. So you know him," Jerry said sullenly.
"What's that got to do with me?"

He listened intently as Evan proceeded to outline what he
wanted from him. At the end of the terse recital, Jerry's eyes
gleamed in anticipation. "All you want is for me to guard

that mill? No questions asked?"

Evan nodded, noting again the size and strength of the man.

Jerry leaned back in his chair, his glance going pointedly to the empty glass in front of him. Evan gestured for two drams of the ubiquitous rum from the proprietor. When the rum was placed in front of them and Jerry had downed his, the man spoke. "I'll need a partner."

"That's up to you."

"There's a good man—Bill Cummins—that I know. He's out somewhere in the bush right now, but I could find him. We've worked together before."

Evan did not hesitate. "Get him."

"Don't you want to meet him?"

"If you say he's a good man, I believe you," Evan replied. He bent forward suddenly, his eyes hard. "But if I learn that either of you are taking good money to do a poor job, neither of you will ever be heard from again. Understood?"

Jerry had expected this threat; he would have been disappointed if it hadn't been made. There was no doubting the ruthlessness underlying Evan's manner, young as he was. Hauser respected that as much as he would have in an older man. He stood abruptly, offering his hand.

"Give me three days to find Bill," he said. "We'll be back."

The big man turned away from the table, threading his way through the crowd to the bar. Evan saw him speak to the proprietor, then with a lift of his hand in Evan's direction, Jerry Hauser disappeared out the back door. Seconds later, another dram of rum was brought to the table, and as Evan lifted the glass and drank, the smile on his lips was grimly triumphant.

CHAPTER FIFTEEN

"WELL, EVAN," LeCroix said one night six months later. "You load the first of your own wool on the *Augusta Mary* tomorrow. How does it feel to be a successful businessman?"

"It feels a lot better knowing that the wool is on the ship right now," Evan replied as he accepted the glass of brandy that LeCroix offered him.

Surprised, LeCroix looked up. "But I thought—"

"I know. It wasn't supposed to be loaded until morning. I had Jerry and Bill take it to the ship tonight. I thought it would be—safer that way."

"Ah, yes," LeCroix nodded. "I see."

Evan sat down, swirling the contents of his glass absently. He thought of the reports he had received from Jerry this past week, and he frowned. Once or twice Jerry and Bill had heard noises during the night, but when they had gone outside to investigate, all they had been able to see were fleeting forms racing away under cover of darkness. The guards had yet to be attacked, but Jerry felt it was only a matter of time. Not that he was worried, he had assured Evan as he patted the stock of the rifle he held; it was just that he thought Evan should know in case there was trouble.

Evan had heeded the warning; he had ordered the precious wool removed to the ship ahead of schedule, and now he was glad he had.

"I think I'll take a ride out there and see if everything is all right," Evan said suddenly.

"But, Evan, it's after eleven!"

Evan put down his untouched glass. "I know. It's just that I have a feeling—"

But before LeCroix could ask Evan to explain, they were both startled by a heavy pounding on the front door.

"Evan! Evan, are you there? It's me, Jerry. For God's sake, open the door!"

LeCroix's butler, Biggs, hurried to open the door just as Evan and LeCroix rushed out into the hall. Biggs looked quickly at them, and when Vincent nodded, he opened the door.

The man who stumbled through the doorway and almost fell at their feet was unrecognizable at first. His face and hands were black with soot, his shirt hung in singed tatters. He grabbed onto the newel post and stood there gasping as the three men stared in stupefaction. Evan was the first to move, exclaiming, "Jerry!"

LeCroix, taking command as Evan started forward, snapped an order at the butler. "Fetch the doctor, Biggs. This man is injured!"

"It was two of Hale's men," Jerry panted. "Recognized them. Two of the sheds are on fire. Bill stayed to fight it, but I came to tell you . . . " Jerry sagged suddenly, his eyes rolling back into his head as he started to topple over.

LeCroix and Evan grabbed him before he could fall. "Go on, Evan," LeCroix said quickly. "I'll take care of things here and follow."

Evan was out the door and dashing toward the stables before LeCroix finished speaking. There was no time to light the lantern hanging by the door; Evan rushed inside and grabbed a bridle from one of the hooks by a box, stumbling against something in the darkness. Ignoring the saddle on the rack, he bridled the horse and led it outside in a matter of seconds, swinging up onto the animal's back as he urged it forward. He left the yard at a gallop, and tore down the road at a full run.

Long before Evan arrived at the mill he could see the glow of the fire in the darkness. Cursing, he pulled the heaving horse up in the yard, throwing himself off the animal before it had come to a stop. A quick glance told him that the fire had been confined to several of the outlying buildings; miraculously, the larger mill had escaped destruction.

Pushing his way through the small crowd of people who

had come to help or to stand back and gawk, Evan searched frantically for Bill, the other guard. He found him lying on the ground, surrounded by a knot of people. Shouldering his way through, he knelt by the prostrate man, glanced up at the faces bending over them, and shouted, "Someone get a doctor!"

"I'm a doctor—"

A short, elderly man appeared, his black bag in one hand. "Stand back, everyone," he ordered. "Give this man some air!"

"Is he alive?" Evan asked after the doctor had bent to put his ear against Bill's chest.

"Yes," the man said briefly, "but we have to get him back to town." He looked up. "Does anyone have a wagon?"

"I do."

Willing hands reached for the fallen man, and he was lifted and carried off to the waiting wagon. As the doctor climbed in after him, Evan put out a hand and asked quietly, "Will he live?"

The doctor glanced at him in sympathy. "Is he related to you, son?"

Evan shook his head. "His name is Bill Cummins. He works for me."

"I think he'll be all right. We won't know for several days, but I believe he just took too much smoke. How did the fire start, anyway?"

Evan looked away from the man's kindly face. "I . . . don't know," he answered, his voice hard. "I wasn't here."

"Ah, well. It's a good thing no one was seriously hurt, isn't it?"

"Yes."

The doctor looked at him strangely for a moment, wondering at the violence behind that single response. Then, signaling to the driver of the wagon, he settled himself beside his patient, and the wagon rumbled away from the mill.

The excitement was over; the fire had been contained,

and people were leaving for home. Evan stood in the yard, calling out his thanks to the men who had helped put out the blaze, and they nodded back at him, replying that they were glad to have helped. Everyone in Australia understood about fires; the huge brush fires that began almost spontaneously could rage for days out of control, devastating everything in their wake. All were relieved that this one had been stopped so quickly. All except Evan, who knew that this fire should never have started.

LeCroix rode in just as the yard emptied. It was a measure of his concern that he had not taken time to order his carriage, but had come by horse instead. Heaving himself out of the saddle, which he detested, LeCroix glanced around, his expression grim.

"Well, thank God the mill itself wasn't destroyed," he said finally.

"He won't get away with this," Evan said, his voice harsh.

"You had best leave it, Evan," he advised. "You can't prove it was Hale—or whoever he hired."

Evan kicked at a smoking timber. "I don't have to prove it. We both know it was he."

LeCroix nodded; he could not deny the statement. Still, he was worried about what Evan might do, and he said, "Maybe you should forget this wool business—" He fell silent. The glare Evan directed at him made him realize the futility of the suggestion. He finished lamely, "After all, you have more than enough to do as my assistant—"

"Are you suggesting that I can't do both?"

The ominous tone in Evan's voice was not lost on Le-Croix. "No, of course not," he replied hastily. And it was true. Despite Evan's interest in the mill, he had never skimped on his services to LeCroix, and Vincent, even if he had not been as fond of Evan as he was, would have hated to lose such an able assistant. It was an indication of Evan's competence that while some of LeCroix's employees privately grumbled about such a young man holding a position they would have liked themselves, they could not fault him for taking advantage of LeCroix's obvious favor. Evan Calder worked as hard—or harder than they did themselves.

LeCroix grimaced at the acrid smoke rising from the still smouldering ruins. "There's nothing you can do tonight, Evan. Why don't we stop at Mollie's on the way home? It might do both of us some good."

It was Evan's turn to grimace. "Like this?" He gestured toward his soot-dusted face and clothing. "Mollie wouldn't let me in the door!"

LeCroix laughed. He put an arm around Evan's shoulders and led him toward the horses, saying, "You don't know women very well, lad, if you can say that. Why, one look at you and the girls'll be falling all over themselves trying to comfort you. Nothing brings out a woman's mothering instincts more than the sight of a man who's had a bit of trouble!"

"Somehow I can't imagine our Mollie being motherly," Evan said wryly. "More likely, she'll bring out the brandy bottle instead."

"Just wait, lad," LeCroix chuckled. "You'll be surprised, I'll warrant."

"Jesus Christ! What happened to you?"

Mollie Gentry had answered the door herself. The hour was late and all the girls were occupied upstairs. She had been about to retire to her own apartments to review the account books when she had heard the door knocker. Frowning, for very few patrons came to the house without appointments, she had opened the door and stared, nonplussed, at the two men standing on the doorstep.

But Mollie was never at a loss for words for long. She took one look at Evan's face and reached out to pull him inside. "Good lord! Have you been in a fight?" Mollie's glance went to LeCroix, and she raised an inquiring eyebrow in his direction.

LeCroix shook his head. "It wasn't exactly a fight," he began. Then, noting the frown Evan turned on him, he shook his head again and fell silent.

"What happened?" Mollie demanded, her eyes still on LeCroix, trying to interpret the expression on his face.

"I'm not a child, Mollie," Evan said mildly. "I can speak for myself."

"Well, then?"

"First, I'd like to clean up, if you don't mind—"

Mollie hadn't been successful in her particular line of work for so many years without learning when to press for answers and when to wait for a more opportune time. She studied Evan for a moment in silence, and then with a sudden gleam in her eye, she clapped her hands once, and said, "I know just the thing. Why don't you both wait in the drawing room until I can make some . . . arrangements?" She gestured toward the door opposite which led to the drawing room, and added as she moved swiftly away toward the stairs, "Vince, there's some excellent brandy on the sideboard. Help yourself. You both look like you need it."

Seconds later, drinks in hand, Evan and LeCroix sat down to wait for Mollie's return. The drawing room was one of LeCroix's favorites; the red velvet and heavy, ponderous furniture suited him, and he usually felt comfortable and relaxed here. Tonight, he was neither; Evan had jumped up again and was pacing the floor, every movement revealing the rage that had been building in him from the moment Jerry had first staggered in with the news of the fire. LeCroix watched him in silence, knowing there was nothing he could say to make Evan any less furious. He gulped at the fine brandy, hardly tasting it, and prayed that his instincts had been right in bringing Evan here. He just hoped that Mollie would return before Evan exploded with fury. If anyone could alleviate Evan's anger and frustration, he thought, it would be Mollie or one of her girls.

Mollie's was an exclusive brothel, far removed from the

seamy establishments above King's Wharf, and her girls were all selected carefully, not only for physical beauty, but for other attributes as well. The girls might be hard in some ways, and certainly experienced, but because Millie did not allow perversions or cruel practices in her house, there was a certain gaiety and ease that was transferred to the patrons when they came here.

The house itself was set back on a side street, and Mollie had taken pains to assure that from the outside it appeared correct and circumspect. There were even lace curtains at the front, imported at great expense, and carefully tended flower beds lining the walk to the door lent an air of respectability to the white-painted wood frame house.

It was surrounded by a picket fenct, also white, and the hitching rail at the entrance was assiduously blacked every day by the handyman and gardner, who also served as Mollie's attendant guard, if necessary. Behind the house was a small stable which housed Mollie's two horses and smart landau, and the trap she often drove herself.

The outside of the house might be eminently respectable and almost austere, but the inside was as luxurious as money could buy. To the left of the entryway was the drawing room, and to the right of that was the parlor, decorated in a delicate French design, with spindly tables and striped silk-covered sofas and chairs. Throughout were plush carpets and carefully arranged gilt-framed paintings, illuminated by expensive rose-quartz lamps. The massive crystal chandelier was the focal point of the parqueted entryway. Upstairs the apartments were decorated in individual colors, blue, green, gold, and mauve, with Mollie's private suite in shades of rose and ivory. Mollie had chosen all the furnishings for the house, and LeCroix considered it one of the most elegant residences he had ever entered.

Mollie herself was unique. For one thing, she was the only women in all of Sydney with hair so blond that it appeared the palest of spun gold. The effect was startling, as well it should be, for Mollie spent a great deal of time and trouble and expense dyeing it that shade, and she deliberately enhanced its effect by designing the elaborate coiffures that had become her trademark. No one knew Mollie's age; many had guessed it to be somewhere in the late thirties, but all would have been surprised to know that Mollie Gentry was approaching fifty. By face and figure she appeared much younger than she actually was, and if this was due to a strict regimen of diet and facial treatments, Mollie considered it no one's business but her own.

Rumor also had it that Mollie had once been married to a European count, an item that Mollie neither admitted nor denied. But it wasn't difficult to believe that the speculation was true; except for her colorful language and her choice of profession, Mollie Gentry appeared every inch the lady when she wanted to. More than one gentleman had been impressed by the haughty imperiousness she could summon when displeased, and in those moments her expression and manner rivaled those of the most blue-blooded aristocrat. But she could also be fun loving and witty, laughing gaily at a cleverly lewd jest, or flirting outrageously with the men who came to call. It was part of her fascination and charm that she could be as changeable as a chameleon. No one ever knew what to expect from Mollie Gentry, and she had carefully cultivated this all her life. She and Vincent LeCroix had been lovers for years, and he was as entranced by her now as he had been when they had first met.

Mollie appeared in the doorway, beckoning to Evan. "Come with me," she ordered, tossing over her shoulder as she turned toward the stairs, "Vince, make me a drink, will you? I'll be back directly."

Evan followed Mollie, his eyes going to the hourglass figure in front of him as she mounted the stairs. Mollie always wore bold colors; tonight she was wearing a sapphire velvet gown, cleverly fashioned to hug her figure in all the right places. The contrast between her gilt hair and the vibrant blue of the velvet, as well as the swaying of her hips as they went up the stairs, all combined to dull some of the helpless rage Evan felt at what had happened tonight. As he walked behind her, he found himself wondering suddenly what she would be like in bed.

So preoccupied was he with his thoughts, he almost collided with her when she stopped in front of a door Evan had not noticed before. Fortunately she seemed unaware of his lapse, and opened the door with a flourish, revealing the most elegant and luxurious bathroom Evan had ever seen.

A huge copper tub resting on carved wooden legs stood in the center of a tiled floor scattered here and there with rugs. Steam rose from the hot, fragrant water filling the tub, and on a stand nearby were thick towels heated by means of felt-covered bricks inserted between the folds. A stove, easily accessible from the side of the tub, kept additional copper cans of water ready for use when needed. A fire blazed in the black marble fireplace at the end of the room, heating the air to an almost tropical temperature.

"Now," Mollie said, glancing around quickly to make sure everything was in order, "Just leave those clothes on the chair here, and I'll send one of the maids to clean them before you leave." She smiled at Evan, gave him a quick kiss on the cheek, and added, "It's all yours, love. Hope you enjoy it."

Minutes later, Evan was submerged to his shoulders in the huge tub which allowed him to stretch almost full-length. Propping his feet on the rim, he leaned against the back rest, sipping at the wine Mollie had thoughtfully left close at hand. The steaming water, the warm air, and the wine had combined to relax him in spite of himself, and he closed his eyes, listening to the crackling of the fire, the only sound in the room.

For a time the memories of that night, the sight of his property on fire and two of his men injured trying to defend it, faded into the background of his mind. Tomorrow, he thought drowsily, tomorrow he would take care of it. Right now he was enjoying the luxury of feeling the tension leave him as the herb-scented water soothed his tight muscles. He was almost asleep when he realized that he was not alone.

When he heard the slight rustle behind him, he thought sleepily that it was only the maid, come to take his clothes away to be cleaned, and he paid little attention until he felt a hand at his shoulder. Startled into instant alertness, he stiffened and half rose out of the water. Blue eyes in an oval face topped by reddish curls laughed at him as he sputtered and reached for a towel.

"Mollie thought you might be lonely," the young woman said, her eyes traveling over his wet and dripping body as he stood there, indecisive, his hand arrested in the act of grabbing for the towel.

Evan stared at her. "Lonely?" he repeated, unable to take his eyes away from the figure outlined under a black silk wrapper.

"My name is Sarah," she said, smiling at Evan's obvious physical response to her presence. She was wearing nothing under the wrapper.

Since that night when Evan had met his first prostitute through Vincent LeCroix there had been other women; brief, casual encounters that ended in a romp in bed with a willing and practiced partner. Evan was no longer the inexperienced, callow youth he had been that first night, and there was a look in Sarah's eyes that promised much in the hours ahead. He smiled and made a motion to get out of the tub, but Sarah shook her head, stopping him.

"I didn't want to disturb you, honey. I just came to help."

Gently, she pushed him back into the water, her hands lingering on the muscles of his shoulders a moment longer than was necessary. Taking a bar of soap, she began lathering his back, working her way toward his chest, which suddenly felt constricted. Her hands moved down to his stomach and back again, massaging, and Evan closed his eyes. Resting his head against the back of the tub, he could feel her breasts against him as she leaned slightly forward. Her fingers continued to knead his flesh, and he felt the rising tension of desire. When her hands moved still lower to massage the muscles of his thighs, he heard her utter a sigh, and he raised one arm, turning her head toward his. Her eyes, close to his own, were half closed; he could see the tip of her tongue between red parted lips. He kissed her, casually at first, and then with passion as her hands moved again toward him, now erect with desire. They broke apart, breathing heavily, both startled by the intensity of their reaction.

She moved away as Evan reached for her again, and she murmured, "Wait . . ."

Evan watched as she came around to the side of the tub, untying the sash of her wrapper and letting it fall to the floor. She stood, posed provocatively with one hand on her hip, looking down at him as he savored the sight of her naked body. Then, with a quick movement, she stepped into the tub with him.

Evan was so surprised that for an instant he couldn't move. But then the sensation of her wet body, her back against his chest, rubbing against him, sent such a rush of pleasure through him that he pulled her closer. Her full breasts swayed slightly in the water, and Evan was fascinated by the sight until she began to move sensuously against him. He closed his eyes, abandoning himself to the desire she had aroused in him.

She had found the bar of soap from somewhere, and turning around so that she faced him, she offered it to him with a laugh. Catching her mood, he took it from her and began soaping her body. Suddenly she had her hands on him and they were washing each other. She laughed gaily as the water splashed on them and over the side of the tub, dripping to the floor in soapy bubbles. Her hair had become wet; it clung to her face in tendrils, making her look like a voluptuous water sprite as she dipped her hand in the water and sent a spray of drops into his face. Sputtering, he reached for her just as she threw herself against him.

The sudden contact of flesh against soapy flesh made them both gasp; the physical sensation of wet and slippery bodies pressed together ignited a response that was overwhelming, and Sarah wrapped her arms around his neck at the same time he pulled her closer to him. Lifting her face, she brought his head down to kiss him.

The touch of her lips on his, the probing of her tongue as she kissed him, released the flood of desire Evan had held at bay from the moment she stepped into the tub with him. Suddenly, he was caught up in a rush of passion so violent that he heard her gasp in surprise as he crushed her to him. His mouth came down fiercely on hers, and she answered his kiss with a passion he knew was not assumed. Her hands moved over him, seeking, exploring, touching him in ways that wrenched a moan from him as the pressure in his loins increased to an unbearable pitch.

Her thighs parted, she guided him inside her. He felt her muscles expanding and contracting, her movements almost frenzied as she thrust against him. His hands found the smooth flesh of her buttocks, and he gripped her tightly, holding her against him as they began to move in unison, their mouths locked in mutual desire and demand. The climax was swift, sudden, and fulfilling to both. When it was over, Sarah lay against him, uttering soft sounds of contentment while Evan held her, his hands moving gently over her body as he closed his eyes.

The water in the tub cooled, but neither made a move to get out. Almost asleep, they luxuriated in the langour of passion well spent.

"Aw, honey, you aren't going to leave so soon, are you?"

Evan stopped dressing to look down at Sarah's sleep-touched face. Hours before, they had moved from bathtub to bedroom, and after another storm of lovemaking, they had fallen reluctantly asleep, sated and exhausted. When Evan had awakened, he was rested and refreshed, and he smiled to himself in the darkness. LeCroix had been right, he thought; an interlude at Mollie's had been exactly what he needed to enable him to think clearly again. His rage of the night before had cooled to an icy calm, and he was able to make his plans.

"So soon? It's nearly six, Sarah," he answered, smiling at her pouting expression.

She sat up in bed, the sheet falling away to display a body arranged provocatively. Again, Evan paused, this time to watch her stretch luxuriously as she deliberately tried to entice him back into bed. He laughed and shook his head, and Sarah pulled him close to the edge of the bed, getting up on her knees to press her body against his as she wound her arms around his neck.

"You can't leave without saying goodbye," she murmured, her lips brushing his chin.

He dropped a kiss on the top of her head, disengaging himself from her grasp before he was tempted to stay. He had work to do today, he reminded himself; the shipping invoices for both LeCroix's cargo and his own on the *Augusta Mary* needed to be attended to, and he had to find out how Jerry and Bill had fared after last night. He felt a twinge of guilt at the thought that he had completely forgotten his men after Sarah's appearance, and he resolved to make it up to them in the form of a bonus. After that, he thought grimly, he had to see a man about a fire. If necessary, he would ride the twenty-five miles to Tamoora and have it out with Hale himself.

Leaving Sarah with effort, he saw LeCroix at the foot of the stairs as he came out of the bedroom. Vincent, looking refreshed himself, coffee cup in hand, stood talking to a remarkably vibrant, clear-eyed Mollie. They both turned as Evan descended, and Mollie offered to have some coffee brought to him.

Evan shook his head. "Thanks anyway, Mollie, but there isn't time. I shouldn't have stayed this long as it is."

"I hope everything was satisfactory?"

The question was rhetorical; Mollie knew that she had chosen well, and she made a mental note to reward the new girl, Sarah. From the look on Evan's face, Sarah had done her work well, and Mollie was always generous when pleased. Besides, she had a special affection for Evan Calder;

she had often been tempted to take him upstairs to her own private quarters to introduce him to the pleasures a more mature woman could provide. She had no doubt that Evan could take it all in stride, possibly offering a few embellishments of his own, if she ever decided to issue the invitation.

She saw now that Evan was smiling in response to her question.

"Everything was perfect—as usual, Mollie," he answered. He reached inside his coat pocket for his money clip, but Mollie shook her head.

"This one is on me, Evan. Vince told me what happened last night. I'm sorry."

Evan's smile disappeared. "Not as sorry as Hale is going to be," he said softly.

He saw the worried glance that LeCroix and Mollie exchanged, and he said now, in an attempt at lightness, "Sarah is . . . quite a girl."

Mollie nodded. "She came in one of those hideous transport ships about six months ago. I happened to see her as she came off the ship, and I bought her papers. She's proved herself . . . very adept. Don't you think so?"

Evan did indeed think so; to Mollie's delight, he was smiling again as the horses were brought from the stables. Evan and LeCroix rode off in the early morning light.

Evan waited until they had almost reached the office before he spoke of his intention to visit Thomas Hale. Vincent was appalled.

"You can't simply arrive on the man's doorstep and accuse him of firing the mill!"

"Why not? He was responsible, wasn't he? It's time he learned that not everyone is frightened of him and his tactics."

Evan's tone was dangerously ominous, and LeCroix realized he would have to tread lightly if he wished to convince Evan that a more subtle approach would be advantageous, especially when dealing with a man like Thomas Hale. Pausing to marshal his words carefully, he said casually, "Mollie mentioned last night that Hale is giving a ball next month—"

"So?"

LeCroix raised his eyes heavenward, as if seeking patience from above. "I've always thought it better to confront the enemy on neutral ground before—"

"And Tamoora is neutral ground?" Evan interrupted sarcastically.

"Well, it would be on such an occasion," LeCroix pointed out. "Hale can hardly cause trouble during his own party, can he? It would be the perfect opportunity to let him know that you're prepared to fight him, if necessary."

Evan was silent, considering what LeCroix had said. "And how would I manage to get invited to this ball?" he asked finally. "Hale would hardly issue an invitation after last night."

"Oh, Mollie can manage that," LeCroix answered nonchalantly. "A word or two in the right ear—"

"All right," Evan said abruptly. "I'll try it your way first, but if that doesn't work . . . " The threat of violence hung in the air.

"Fair enough," LeCroix said, trying not to show his relief as they turned into the street that led to his offices. "I can't ask more than that."

They separated, LeCroix stopping at the office, Evan going on to the hospital to inquire about Bill and Jerry. To his relief, neither had suffered any lasting ill effects from the fire the night before. Both had been released before Evan arrived, leaving a message for Evan to tell that they would both be at the mill in case they were needed.

That afternoon, when Evan had completed his work at the office, he rode out to the mill. As the three of them stood looking over the destroyed outbuildings, Jerry tried to offer Evan a muttered apology for not having prevented the fire.

"Forget it," Evan said brusquely. "At least the mill wasn't burned, and the wool was already safely on the ship. It could have been worse."

Indeed, he thought, it definitely could have been worse. He could have been ruined before he started. At the thought, he felt a surge of anger at Hale and his hirelings. If he hadn't recognized the logic of LeCroix's suggestion to wait before confronting the man, he would have turned his horse in the direction of Tamoora at that instant. Reason prevailed, and the only outward sign of Evan's rage was the tightening of his hand on the reins of his horse.

"Can you take care of things here?" he asked the two men.

Both nodded, and as Evan wheeled his horse in the direction of the town, he said warningly, "I'll take care of this in my own way. I don't want anyone rushing off to make things worse than they are. Understand?"

Jerry nodded sheepishly, embarrassed that Evan had seemed to read his mind. Bill turned away, muttering an oath, but signaling with a jerk of his head that he would comply with Evan's order. Sighing, they started on the work of clearing away the debris from the fire.

Evan rode away, dismissing the mill from his mind. He had intended to wait until his next shipment of wool was completed before he took up the option on the timber land he was interested in, but after the destruction of the night before, he decided to sign now. If something happened to the mill after all, at least he would not be left empty-handed. With the money he had earned from this shipment, he could take the option, provided he budgeted himself very carefully over the next few months.

He would also take time to have a look at the wheat land Bill Cummins had told him about a short time ago. During Bill's travels, he had come across a farmer who was interested in selling his acreage, all prime land near the Hawksbury River. If the man named a fair price, Evan thought he might approach LeCroix for another loan. Now that he had repaid his first loan, with interest, LeCroix would not refuse him another, especially if Evan offered him a percentage of the crop as collateral.

All in all, Evan supposed he should be grateful to Thomas Hale. With the near destruction of his mill, he had learned a valuable lesson. Never again would he have all his money invested in one venture. Even the most certain of businesses could fail or be destroyed with one blow, he realized now with a touch of impatience at his lack of foresight. He would expand—on a limited scale at first, but investing every cent of profit, every ounce of energy into other ventures until he surpassed even Vincent LeCroix or Thomas Hale in the amount of money at his disposal. Only then would he be invulnerable.

Absently, his hand came up to touch the scar on his face. The scar might be faded now, but the memory of Myles's attack would never fade; the humiliation of losing that fight with his enemy had been burned indelibly into his mind. He needed no tangible evidence to remind him of that night; he would never forget it until he had revenged himself for all the years of humiliation that had culminated in that one last savage swing of the cane. The day he became owner of Lyrebird Manor would be the day he had succeeded in his revenge; until then, there was no other objective in his life. Everything else, he assured himself, was meaningless.

The harsh glare of the afternoon sun shone in his eyes as he spurred his horse into a canter. But Evan noticed neither the hard light nor the reddish dust rising in clouds from the animal's hoofs as he rode on. In his mind, he was standing on the hill overlooking the lyrebird garden, and thinking that only his possession of it would free him from this terrible drive for revenge.

CHAPTER SIXTEEN

CYNARA TURNED AWAY FROM THE WINDOW, allowing the curtain to drop from her hand to shut out the harsh glare of the sun. The room dimmed slightly as the drapery fell back into place, and Cynara closed her eyes wearily. How she hated the sun here; how she hated the seemingly endless blue sky that stretched over the thousands of acres that comprised Tamoora.

Not that she had seen much of Tamoora, she thought bitterly. Thomas Hale kept her a virtual prisoner; she was allowed to leave the house and wander on the grounds, but apart from the small oasis of flowers and shrubbery, there was only the empty red-tinged land, dotted here and there with scrub, or the trees that were called ghost gums because of their whitish-gray bark. Far away, almost invisible to her eye, were the Blue Mountains, a faint line along the horizon, lost in the shimmering heat. Even the small lake at the back of the house that Thomas Hale was so proud of was not a lake at all; it was more a shallow pond, a tiny body of water dependent for existence upon the whims of nature, where drought seemed to be the norm.

Even for all that, she longed to take a horse and ride into that emptiness; anything, any activity, would be welcome after so long a time of imprisonment. But Hale guarded her movements with a close eye, as he had apparently instructed his servants to do. If she walked too far, approaching the boundary he had set for her, someone would unobtrusively appear behind her, reminding her that the master wouldn't want her to get lost. Lost! Sometimes she wished she could simply keep going, disappearing into the huge emptiness of the Australian "outback," where only the roaming bands of aborigines seemed able to survive. Such thoughts frightened her, and invariably she would turn back toward the house. She was not ready, yet, to risk her life for a whim. But oh! If she could only take a horse and ride! There were times when she thought she would scream with frustration and boredom.

And she would never become accustomed to the harsh, shrill laughter of the birds the natives called kookaburras, or the sight of the kangaroos racing across the open land, springing powerfully into the air on hind legs that could kill a man with one blow. She found the reptiles repulsive as well; she had heard tales of lizards that grew ten feet long, and snakes that were so poisonous that the venom from one alone could kill a hundred or more sheep. No, she was not ready to venture out by herself.

It was a hard land, a country that seemed to Cynara to be too vast and too empty. She longed for the lush greens and soft shadows of the English countryside with an intensity that almost made her ill at times, and yet she knew that this yearning for her home was only an excuse. In other circumstances, she would have found it challenging, a demanding exercise of her own strength and determination, an opportunity to prove that she could accommodate herself to the strangeness of a country so alien to everything she had ever known. But not now; oh, no, not now, married to Thomas Hale, who sometimes seemed to be the reincarnation of the devil himself.

She had been married to Hale for almost seven months, and every day brought with it a new humiliation, another subtle cruelty she must endure. Sometimes she was so angry and frustrated at his treatment of her that she longed to break things, to smash the precious knickknacks of which he was so proud. The house was filled with evidence of his wealth; his opal collection alone, displayed in locked glass cases in the drawing room, was worth a small fortune. She had been intrigued at first by the shimmering, multicolored stones set onto a background of black velvet, but now she hated them because they were so Australian, so much a symbol of everything she despised. Sometimes she had the urge to break the glass and hurl the opals across the room, or throw them out the window into the everlasting dust that she hated as much as she hated the hard glare of the sun.

"Ah, there you are, dear wife."

Cynara had not heard him enter her apartments. For all his bulk, Thomas Hale could move as softly as a cat when he wished to. It was another of his habits that irritated her; she never knew when he would come up behind her, mocking her with that superior smile she had come to detest.

"Yes, Thomas?"

Cynara had adopted a cool manner of speaking to him simply because she knew that it annoyed him. He would have preferred her to cower in his presence, but that she would never do. If she had nothing else, she had her pride, and she raised her chin now and stared across the room at him as he lounged in the doorway.

"You're not dressed."

Cynara looked down at the simple sprigged cotton she had chosen that morning because of the heat. She said nothing, irritating him even more.

"Have you forgotten that the Whitleys are coming to tea?" There was a steely edge to his voice as he glanced pointedly toward the clock on the mantle. The hands read three o'clock. Tea hour at Tamoora was four.

Cynara had forgotten. What was more, his reminder of the arriving guests increased the headache that had been hovering since noon. She detested Gerald and Millicent Whitley, just as she disliked all of Hale's acquaintances. But was it really their fault that they seemed to regard her as a curiosity? Thomas Hale had taken pains to inform all and sundry that his wife had been imprisoned on a transport ship, and now the Whitleys, especially Millicent, stared at her as if they expected her to run suddenly amok and attack them. This attitude of Hale's guests would have amused Cynara, if she hadn't known that this was yet another of his cruel jests. She often wondered what pleasure he could derive from branding her in such a way; it seemed that this would reflect badly upon him. To her anger and disgust, he had managed to turn the situation to his advantage; she suspected now that he was admired for his honesty. Worse still, he was applauded for his rescue of such a poor unfortunate as herself.

"You have a wardrobe of gowns suitable for every occasion," Hale reminded her as he sauntered across the room to where she stood. "I suggest you choose one that will not disgrace us both in front of our guests."

Cynara ignored the hand he put out to touch her cheek; she knew he was only taunting her with the gesture. "I suppose they will be staying for supper?" she asked.

"Of course. And the night as well. Please see that a room is prepared, my dear, and—" Hale turned away "Ask Eva to send the menu to me so I can choose the appropriate wines."

Cynara inclined her head, not trusting herself to speak. He really was insufferable, talking to her as if she were a child, and a dim-witted one at that. Her fingers itched to slap the patronizing expression off his face, and she clenched her hands as he left the room, closing the door softly behind him.

When he was gone Cynara threw herself into a chair. Grimacing, she pictured the afternoon and evening ahead, enduring Millicent Whitley's shrill, nervous chatter, the quiet appraisal of Millicent's husband. And what of her own husband, Cynara asked herself grimly; which personality would he assume tonight?

Cynara sighed in exasperation. Now she would have to make the effort to change her gown, an unappetizing prospect in this heat. Why was it always so hideously hot?

But as she forced herself out of the chair again, Cynara knew it wasn't the temperature alone that caused her irritation; it was Hale himself. She had seen that look in his eyes just now—the look that meant he would come to her room tonight. Once again she would have to endure the touch of his hands on her, the act that she still considered a violation of her body, regardless of the fact that he was her husband, and entitled by law to claim the rights that were his.

He had left her alone the first months of their marriage, a situation that suited her admirably; she was not anxious to submit to conjugal relations with the man who mocked and derided her. She had known he was waiting to make sure she hadn't been carrying a child at the time he married her, but whatever his reasons, Cynara had been relieved that he had avoided her. Now, of course, the situation was changed; when it became obvious that she was not pregnant, he came far too often to her apartments.

How she hated the way he looked at her, his leering appraisal of her body! For some reason, her aloofness seemed to excite him. In forcing her to do the things he demanded, it was as though he was demonstrating his mastery over her. He didn't make love to her; he compelled her to submit, enjoying her helplessness, proving that he was the stronger.

At times Cynara couldn't help comparing her husband to Joshua Baird. To her surprise, she found herself actually missing the captain, for while she had been unhappy on the ship, he had provided companionship, and he had always treated her with tenderness and concern. Despite his physical disability, he had been solicitous and kind—something Thomas Hale had never been. She shuddered, imagining what Hale would be like in the same circumstances.

And then she smiled. So far, she had been successful in denying Hale the heir he coveted. It had been her own revenge, small as it was the only satisfaction she derived from this empty marriage. But she knew she could not continue to be so fortunate in avoiding pregnancy forever. What would she do then?

Thrusting the unwelcome thought from her mind, Cynara went to the wardrobe to select another gown. Perversely, while Thomas Hale seemed to delight in taunting her, he had insisted that she be dressed in a style that suited her position as the wife of one of Australia's wealthiest men.

Her wardrobe was extensive; for several weeks after her
arrival at Tamoora, there had been a seamstress in residence
to complete what Hale had mockingly referred to as her
trousseau. Cynara had the best of everything money could
buy, from lace-trimmed silk chemises to elegant heavy satin
evening gowns. She had everything she could want, and she
hated it all.

"We haven't had a real party around here for ages,
Thomas! I think it's so exciting!"

Millicent Whitley's shrill voice grated on Cynara's
nerves. How she had endured the woman's vapid and pointless conversation during tea, let alone throughout this interminable meal was beyond her. Thankfully, dessert was
being served and this endless evening would soon be over.
The smile she had forced since the Whitley's arrival was
slipping; her jaw was sore from clenching her teeth.

"Don't you think so, Cynara?"

Cynara replied that it was exciting, and offered Millicent
another portion of trifle in the hope that it would occupy the
woman's attention long enough for a blessed silence to fall.
The ploy failed as Millicent shook her head, refusing her
third helping of dessert.

"Oh, no, I simply can't. I have to watch my weight
constantly, else I become too plump! How *do* you keep such
a slender figure, my dear? I declare, I quite envy you!"

Millicent bridled and waited coyly for someone to reassure her. To Cynara's grim amusement, Thomas Hale
leaped in gallantly. "Nonsense, Millie. Why, there's something infinitely attractive about a voluptuous woman, I
always say." He leered suggestively at Millie's full bosom
straining at the confines of her low-cut bodice. "A man
needs a place to rest his head, and where better than what
nature and a good appetite have provided?"

Millicent simpered, glancing at Hale from under sparse
lashes. "I declare, Thomas," she giggled.

Hale grinned at her and raised his glass in salute. Gerald

Whitley said nothing, pretending to be absorbed in arranging his silverware on his plate, and Cynara glanced down at her clenched hands in her lap. From the corner of her eye, she observed Millicent reaching eagerly for the trifle again, her hands with the too tight rings cutting herself another lavish portion. Cynara raised her napkin to her mouth to hide the derisive curl of her lips as Mrs. Whitley attacked the dessert with the air of a starving woman.

Hale looked down the table at Cynara as she glanced up again. "My wife has not much of an appetite, I fear," he said. "Her health suffered greatly from conditions on the transport ship."

Millicent paused, her fork part way to her mouth. Across from her, Gerald Whitley cleared his throat and grabbed at his wine, his face reddening at the reference to Cynara's imprisonment. Hale, as if oblivious to the awkward silence at the table, continued, "But we hope soon to have her healthy as a horse. The doctor has prescribed a tonic—you have taken your medicine today, haven't you, my dear?" he inquired solicitously, his eyes gleaming with malice.

"Yes, Thomas," Cynara replied evenly. "But my health cannot possibly be of interest to our guests. I'm sure you and Mr. Whitley can discover a more suitable topic of conversation if we leave you to your port." She rose swiftly. "Millicent?"

There was a scraping of chairs as the two men stood. Cynara smiled blandly at them both, observing with satisfaction the tightening of Hale's mouth, the flash of anger in his eyes. She sailed from the room, Millicent in tow.

Once in the drawing room, Cynara did not give her guest an opportunity to speak. With another headache pounding at her temples, she thought that music would be infinitely preferable to conversation, and she said quickly, "Do play the pianoforte, Millicent. You have such a deft touch."

Millicent made a deprecating gesture with one hand, saying coyly, "How kind of you to say so, Cynara. But I'm afraid you exaggerate . . ."

She paused, and Cynara ground her teeth together in exasperation. Did the woman really expect to be fussed over and reassured at every juncture? But it seemed she did; she was looking at Cynara expectantly.

Cynara forced herself to answer effusively; anything, she thought, to avoid further conversation with this impossible woman. "Exaggerate? How modest you are, Millicent!"

Millicent blushed with pleasure. It was true, she thought; she did pride herself on her modesty. How clever of Cynara to notice that! "Well . . . " she said hesitantly, "if you insist . . . "

"I do," Cynara answered firmly, resisting the urge to take the woman's fat arm and lead her forcibly over to the piano.

Millicent relented. If Cynara insisted, what else could she do but comply? She sat down immediately, her hands poised above the keys. "What would you like, my dear?" she asked, almost fondly.

"Oh, whatever you wish . . ."

Mrs. Whitley nodded, her face twisted with concentration. Seconds later, a faltering series of notes rose limply from the keys, and Cynara closed her eyes. But the music at least kept the woman occupied, and with a murmured excuse about the closeness of the air, Cynara went to the French doors at the other end of the room and opened them to the cooler night air. For an instant, she had the desire to dash across the broad veranda and disappear into the night, leaving all these hateful people behind. How exhilarating it would be to pick up her skirts and run! She hadn't done that since the day she had rushed into the woods after Evan . . .

Her urge to flee vanished abruptly at the thought of Evan. With a fierce effort, Cynara forced back the tears that sprang into her eyes at the memory, and she turned back to the room just as Thomas Hale entered with Gerald.

The crashing at the piano ceased with the entrance of the two men, and Cynara breathed a sigh of relief. Now that the men had returned, she would excuse herself with the plea of a headache and escape to her room.

But Hale, as if sensing her intention, caught her eye and frowned heavily. "Aren't you feeling well, my dear?"

Cynara was not about to suffer another of his pointed remarks about her health. Reversing her decision immediately, she answered airily, "A slight headache, Thomas. It is nothing."

"Perhaps a little sherry . . . ?"

His concern was solely for the benefit of his guests and Cynara gritted her teeth at the obviousness of it all. She shook her head.

Hale turned to the puzzled Millicent. She had heard the edge in Cynara's voice, and the slight sharpness in Hale's response, and for the first time she realized that there were undercurrents here that she did not understand. She looked to her husband for clarification, but he was staring at Cynara with a fatuous expression that immediately irritated her.

"Gerald—" she began warningly.

Thomas Hale diverted her attention at once. "Sherry, Millicent?" he asked as he went to the cupboard.

"Oh, no, thank you, Thomas," Millie giggled. "Spirits of any kind always make me silly. I just can't seem to tolerate them!"

"I think I will have a glass after all," Cynara said abruptly.

"Very well, my dear."

Oh, the absolute inanity of it all! Cynara thought she would scream if she had to endure one more simper from Millicent Whitley, who was saying now, "Well, if Cynara has a glass of sherry, I will, too. Then we can both be silly together!"

Cynara accepted the glass from Hale, fighting the urge to swallow it in one gulp and then hurl the glass across the room. Instead, with Millie already giggling beside her, she sipped it slowly, only half listening as Gerald began talking about a fire at someone's mill.

"It still is a mystery how it got started, "Gerald said musingly. "I hear that the owner had guards posted, who maintain that the fire was deliberately set."

"Oh?"

Hale's elaborate pose of unconcern immediately caught Cynara's attention. She tried to listen to what they were saying over the shrill conversation Millicent directed at her about the high price of silk or lace or some other ridiculously unimportant commodity. Suddenly it seemed very important to understand what Gerald and Hale were saying. Nodding at Millicent now and then to indicate that she was listening, Cynara strained to hear what Gerald said, and more significantly, how Thomas Hale answered.

". . . why someone would want to fire that mill is anyone's guess. It's not even worth the trouble, since the mill itself isn't even fully operable yet." Gerald shrugged, glancing keenly at Hale. "I suppose it was some troublemaker, out for mischief."

"Yes," Hale replied carelessly, "I suppose it was."

"Still," Gerald pressed, "the owner is determined to learn who caused the destruction; the last I heard he offered a reward for any information."

"And what does this young man intend to do if he receives the information he desires?"

"Young man? I don't believe I said he was a young man, Thomas," Gerald said in affected surprise. "Do you know him, perhaps?"

"I make it a point to learn who my competition is, however small," Hale replied smoothly. "I have an investment of my own to protect, don't I?"

Gerald laughed loudly. "I can't imagine your being hurt by this young upstart, Thomas. Why, you own half the land and sheep in this area! Not to mention most of the mills in operation. I don't think you have any reason to worry—not you!"

"Oh, I'm not worried, Gerald—"

"Still," Gerald said with a touch of malice, "I've also heard that this young man is someone to watch. He started as a clerk with Vince LeCroix, and is now his assistant— quite a jump in prospects for a young man, don't you think?

You might keep your eye on him, Thomas—" Gerald poked Hale in the ribs and winked "if you haven't already, eh?"

Hale took a deep breath, glancing around the room. When he saw Cynara watching him, he flushed and said, "I think that's enough business talk for tonight, Gerald. We mustn't forget the ladies . . . "

Millicent, who had run tirelessly on from silks and laces to lazy and incompetent household servants, leaped into the silence with a gay, "Anyone for cards? I do love a game or two of whist, and we have just the right number of players! Oh, do say yes, gentlemen!"

Thankfully, the evening had ended at last. The game or two of whist had extended to three or four games, and by the time Cynara managed to regain the quiet of her apartments, there was a ringing in her ears, and she was exhausted. Whatever Thomas saw in those two people was beyond her; she found them utterly enervating. Gerald was perhaps a little better than his wife; at least he managed to interject an intelligent remark occasionally into the conversation, but Millicent! Was there ever a more vapid, silly woman than Millicent Whitley? Cynara doubted it. But the Whitleys, unfortunately, were Tamoora's nearest neighbors. In a country where farms could comprise thousands of acres, their land so vast that it was often counted in square miles instead of acreage, Cynara supposed it behooved one to remain on friendly terms with those who might be the only other souls for miles around. Besides, Gerald Whitley was Thomas's legal advisor, so there was a dual purpose for Hale's hospitality to the Whitleys. Cynara just wished that there were some way Gerald could leave Millicent behind when he came to visit.

What a relief to retire to her room! Cynara, clothed in a fawn nightdress, a robe belted loosely at the waist, sat at her dressing table, brushing her hair. She was so tired that was an effort to draw the brush through the long strands, but this was a nightly ritual she had become accustomed to since her arrival at Tamoora. It seemed that she lived in a constant state of tension, and this simple chore was relaxing at the end of a long day. The two hundred strokes she had set herself was an act that required no thought, and she was free to think of other things. Although why she needed time to think, she didn't know. What was there to think about, other than the empty futility of maintaining this fiction of a marriage to a man she despised.

If only she had something to occupy her time! The housekeeper, Eva Cole, managed the household admirably with little assistance from Cynara; the cook, a remarkable woman named Hertha, held sway in the kitchen. There were upstairs maids, parlor maids, and kitchen maids for the house, as well as the butler and Hale's valet; outside were grooms, gardeners and stableboys, not to mention the platoon of men who tended Tamoora's sheep and cattle.

She had wondered at first why Hale, a bachelor for so many years, had wanted a wife when he had surrounded himself with these paragons of efficiency who managed his life and his household so well. But she had soon discovered that while he wanted a woman who was coincidentally his wife sitting demurely and elegantly at the foot of his table when he entertained, what he desired above all was a receptacle for the seed that would produce the heir to this empire he was in the process of building.

Cynara's expression was bitter as she acknowledged the crudity of her thoughts, but the coarseness did not alter the fact that he had selected her for that purpose and she resented it.

Putting down the hairbrush, she moved away from the dressing table to the doors that led to the balcony. Leaving the doors open, she stepped outside, hugging her arms around her body, wondering how much longer she could endure this empty existence that had promised so much and had given her nothing but heartache. Many times she had thought of leaving, but there was nowhere for her to go. A woman did not simply walk out on her husband, no matter how great the provocation. And what reason did she have for leaving, after all? Any other woman in her position would be ecstatic at her good fortune. Why, then, was she so unhappy?

Cynara leaned against the balcony rail, hands over her face. Had she forgotten so quickly all those months on the ship when she had longed for such simple things as wearing clean clothes, or washing her hair when she wanted to? Had she forgotten that she had come to this country as a convict, wrongly accused or not, and that she should be grateful that she had escaped the harsh life that most prisoners were subjected to? How dared she claim to be unhappy when she had been so fortunate!

Ashamed of herself, Cynara dropped her hands and stared out past the balcony rail into the darkness. She could see the glimmer of the lake in the moonlight, the dark shadows of the willows surrounding it on one side. From the trees at the end of the balcony came the soft sound of the galahs, those gray birds with the beautiful rose-colored breast feathers. From far away in one of the home paddocks, she heard the bleat of a lamb seeking its mother.

The night was peaceful with these sights and sounds, and Cynara felt some of the tension leave her as she came to a decision. She would force herself to accept her situation—oh, not to the extent of giving Hale the child he wanted, not if she could help it—but she would ignore his pointed and sarcastic remarks, submit to the demands of his body, try to find something to occupy her time. She would try to be a wife to him, if that was what he wanted . . .

There was a noise behind her, and she turned to see him standing there, a glass of brandy in his hand. He closed the door behind him and Cynara forgot all her resolutions of an instant before as he stared at her with that expression she had grown to detest.

His approach tonight was the same as it had been that first night he had come to her; the same as it had been on all the nights after that. He simply stared at her for a long moment, sipping at his drink, his expression condescending, as though she had failed him in some way and he was displeased with her for being so stupid.

At first this silent scrutiny had made her nervous, and then later it had annoyed her to the point of making her cry: "Why do you stare at me like that?"

He had been quick to reply. "You're my wife, aren't you? Doesn't a husband have a right to look at his wife?"

But he was not looking at her, she thought wrathfully. He was *leering,* staring at her with an expression that reduced her to an object, as though she were a horse, or a cow, or a sheep that he was examining at the fair, debating a purchase, wondering if the blood lines were sufficiently good to improve his stock. It had made her furious at one time, but now she forced herself not to react to it. Waiting silently, she watched him walk across the room to join her on the balcony.

"Ah," he said, turning his face upwards to view the immense star-spattered black sky, "It's a beautiful night, isn't it?"

Cynara had turned away the moment he approached. Now he reached out and grasped her wrist, holding her prisoner beside him as he continued to stare fatuously at the stars. Cynara glanced at his profile, and then away again, saying nothing, wondering why he had made the unusual effort at conversation.

Suddenly she realized that the Whitley's had been assigned the only other room on this side of the house that opened onto this balcony. Cynara could picture Millicent Whitley listening avidly, her ear pressed against the wooden shutters of the guest room. She had a sudden impulse to laugh, thinking of Millicent crouched there, as Hale deliberately postured for her benefit. The impulse did not last long.

"Shall we go inside, my dear?" he asked tenderly, holding her wrist tightly so that she could not escape.

Cynara had no intention of trying to fight him; she had

learned long ago that his strength was no illusion, and that he would use it against her if she balked. But she also had no desire to join in this game of pretense for Millicent Whitley's benefit.

"You're hurting me, Thomas!" she hissed.

"Am I?"

She glared at him as he smiled malevolently. This was a side of him that he never allowed others to see, and it infuriated her that she alone was the beneficiary of his artful deceit. Angered, she tried to free herself.

He pulled her sharply against him, his hand at the sash of her robe. Laughing softly, he untied it, knowing that she did not dare make any sound that his guests might overhear. There was a row of tiny buttons down the front of her nightdress; he slowly unbuttoned each one while his arm held her closely to his side.

When his hand slipped inside the opening down the front of her nightgown, she stiffened. Surely he did not intend to take her here, on the balcony! She glanced over her shoulder at the closed shutters of the guest room in a panic; if either of the Whitleys chanced to come out now, she would die of shame.

Hale asked again, his tone amused, "Shall we go inside?"

She could have struck him for taunting her this way; if one of her arms had been free, she actually might have done so. As it was, imprisoned in his grasp, she could only nod, thinking how much she despised him. He was mocking her now, but she knew that if she did not acede to his wishes he was fully capable of forcing her to the balcony floor. Repulsed at the thought, she realized that he would probably be excited by the possibility of discovery.

But he was not satisfied by her silent aquiescence. His hand found her breast again and squeezed. She almost cried out, but the look on his face stopped her. Swallowing hard against the anger that threatened to choke her, she willed her voice to steadiness, and answered, "Yes, Thomas. It is getting late . . . "

To her relief, he moved toward the door, pulling her with him. Once safely inside, she could endure anything; it was the thought of anyone else witnessing her humiliation that had stilled her tongue on the balcony. How she hated him for forcing her to be a participant in this mockery of a marriage!

Hale made an elaborate business of closing the balcony doors. He turned to her once more, smiling maliciously as he removed her robe with solicitous care. He folded it over a chair, and then held out his hand for her nightdress.

The ritual was the same as it had been ever since the first time. Closing her eyes, Cynara forced herself to take off the nightdress, knowing that he would tear it from her body if she did not obey. She had never become accustomed to his leering appraisal of her as she was compelled to stand naked before him, but he seemed to delight in staring at her in this way. She stood defiantly now, as she had that first night. He would never know the fierce effort of will it took for her not to cringe away from him; she refused to give him that advantage over her, for she knew that if she once indicated how repugnant this scene was to her, he would devise yet another little game to debase her further.

He came to her, grasping either side of her face. Lowering his head, he kissed her on the mouth, and then took a step back. She knew that he was excited; his fingers trembled as he traced the line of her jaw to her throat, and then between her breasts to the flatness of her stomach.

"Soon, my dear, eh?" he said, his hands spanning the distance between her hip bones. "You have disappointed me thus far, but you won't continue to do so, will you? You will give me the son I want before long, or . . . "

He had no need to voice the threat; he had made it clear long before now what he would do to her if she did not become pregnant. Once, he had even brought her transport papers to her apartments, taunting her with the fact that he had not destroyed them. If she failed to produce the heir he desired, he was fully capable of divorcing her and turning her over to the authorities to complete the prison term.

Her fear of what could happen to her as a convict held her silent now, as it had over the past months. On more than one occasion when he had practiced his subtle cruelties here in this very room, she had wanted to scream at him that she had deliberately avoided conceiving, that she would continue to do so as long as she was able. But her fear was stronger than her hatred; she had heard stories of convict women who were forced into a life of prostitution, available to any man who desired their services. At least, Cynara reasoned in her saner moments, she was forced to submit only to this one man. How could she endure it if there were a stream of faceless others who demanded what Hale demanded of her, or worse?

He turned down the lamp now, and walked unsteadily to the bed. She was compelled to follow, to take her place alongside him after he had thrown off his clothing. His huge body, white and hairy, repulsed her, and she closed her eyes as he rolled on top of her, forcing her legs apart to make room for his own.

It was always the same; until this moment, he was controlled. But at the instant his flesh touched hers, he became a madman. It was as if the contact between their bodies had released something inside him, allowing his passion to rage free.

"Ah, Cynara!" he cried, his hands clutching at her convulsively. "You are so beautiful . . . "

Slobbering kisses over her face, her throat, her breasts, he began thrashing against her, his desire mounting with each thrust. The sounds he uttered became moans; his hands were everywhere. He fastened his mouth over hers, his tongue probing deeply as he began to reach the climax.

Cynara suffered it all passively. She had offered no resistance after that first night when he had literally choked her into submission. He had been savage then, and she had been terrified, sure that he would kill her if she did not do as he wished. She was no longer afraid; as long as she did not fight him, she was safe. He wanted no response from her other than complete surrender, and though she despised herself for giving in to him, she had learned to control her anger and disgust, forcing herself to lie still until he had finished this rutting assault on her body.

It was her revenge against him; this passive resistance that showed her refusal to participate in something that was so demeaning to her. If he had shown the least bit of gentleness or consideration, she might have reacted differently. As it was, she felt nothing but utter contempt for him, and complete revulsion for this act that should be an expression of love and affection and mutual desire.

At last, with his shuddering groan, it was over. He lay where he had collapsed at her side, breathing heavily, one arm fallen across her waist. Soon, she knew, he would rise and go to his own apartments. To her relief, he had never elected to spend the entire night with her, and she prayed he would not do so now. As soon as he left, she must perform the chore that had kept her safe all these months.

Cynara smiled bitterly to herself in the darkness as she waited for the rich and powerful Thomas Hale to leave her. If she had her way, not all his money or influence or strength would produce the son he so coveted.

Cynara laughed at the thought, but the sound that she uttered was almost a sob. Where had all her dreams gone? She remembered her fantasies of loving and being loved by a man, and all those dreams seemed so empty, so long ago and far away. Where was the passion and the excitement and the desire? Would she ever feel these things, or was she doomed to endure the caresses of a man she despised? There had to be more than this, she thought despondently. She needed more, so much more.

She needed . . . a man like Evan. A man who could excite her by a gesture, a look in his eyes. With Evan she would feel that wild singing of the blood, the almost savage abandonment of mind to body. She ached to feel his hands on her, those wonderful hands that evoked such passion in her; she longed to feel his lips on her, teasing, tantalizing, carrying her to dizzying heights of passionate love. Oh God! How she yearned for him! In this moment, she wanted him only for what he could do for her—no romantic dreams of tenderness—for the fierce coming together of man and woman, acknowledging physical need, surrendering to it, demanding release from the passion that drove the body to seek its own fulfillment. Her body cried out for that release, and there was only . . . Thomas Hale.

CHAPTER SEVENTEEN

"ARE YOU READY, MY DEAR? The guests will be arriving soon."

Hale entered the room as Cynara stood in front of the mirror watching the maid, Jessie, fuss with the hem of her skirt. Through the reflection, she saw the quick glance and secretive smile Hale and the girl exchanged behind her back, and her lip curled at her husband's use of an endearment to her when at the same time he was in the process of flirting with the maid. When Jessie flushed in return, Cynara was irritated to the point of speaking sharply to her.

"That's enough, Jessie; the skirt hangs properly now. Please fetch my fan."

"Yes, Mrs. Hale."

The girl's tone was a shade too servile, and Cynara looked at her with displeasure as the maid curtseyed and went to the dresser. Did Jessie really think she cared that Hale had chosen her for his latest bed partner, or that Cynara was unaware of what went on under her own roof? No, it was their sneering at her that made her angry. Even now, as she pretended to examine her appearance in the mirror, Hale leered at the maid again, and this time Jessie shot a triumphant glance in Cynara's direction. To her disappointment, Cynara chose to ignore her and turned instead to her husband.

"Yes, Thomas," she answered. "I am ready."

There was a challenge in her tone, daring him to voice a complaint about her appearance. She knew that she looked well tonight, but she was aware that Thomas Hale could, and would, fault her for the slightest flaw. Not that there was anything for him to criticize, she thought proudly; her gown, ordered especially for this occasion, had been selected by Hale himself, but even so, Cynara had to admit that the color and style flattered her. The green silk shot through with silver threads shimmered as she moved, the

voluminous skirt floated elegantly to the floor to cover
matching silk slippers tied with silver ribbon. The extremely low neckline that he had insisted upon displayed a
great deal of her shoulders and breasts, and the tight bodice
emphasized a waist that had no need of tight lacing to
produce its slimness. The diamond necklace that Hale had
produced from his safe glittered around her throat, and
there were diamond ear drops in her ears.

She had refused Jessie's sullen offer of assistance for her
hair, deciding to arrange it herself. Disdaining the ringlets
that were the fashion, she had chosen instead another style:
deep waves on either side of her face swept up and back into
a mass of curls high on her head. She had no need of false
switches to achieve its effect; her own hair was thick and
long enough to make this artifice unnecessary. Nor had she
used the rouge and powder on her dressing table; nervous
excitement, or apprehension, she wasn't sure which, had
heightened her color without the aid of cosmetics. With a
last glance in the mirror, Cynara accepted her fan serenely
from the smirking maid, and waited for Hale to speak.

Always correct when in the presence of others, even the
maid with whom the night before he had enjoyed a romp,
Hale said now, "You look enchanting, my dear. Shall we go
down?"

As they went toward the stairs, Cynara could hear the
musicians Hale had hired for the evening tuning their instruments. Days before, the huge ballroom, usually closed
off from the rest of the house, had been opened, aired, and
cleaned under the eagle eye of Eva Cole. There was not a
speck of dust to be found, a miracle in itself, considering the
constant daily battle Mrs. Cole waged with the grit that
settled even before the maids could leave the room with
their dusters. But tonight, all was shining and immaculate,
from the crystal chandeliers and gilded wall sconces to the
waxed and buffed parquet floor. Gleaming silver punch
bowls reposed at each end of the huge buffet tables that had
been set up in the drawing room; the pristine white table-

cloths waited to receive the mammoth amounts of food Hertha and the kitchen help had spent days preparing.

Cynara felt far removed from the entire scene. Thomas Hale had ordered his staff to make arrangements for a ball, and they had done so without assistance from her; he had given special instructions to the servants, and those orders had been followed to the letter without her advice. Cynara had not even seen the guest list; all invitations had been issued by Hale himself. And now, at the appropriate time, when everything else had been made ready, he had brought her out for inspection, dressed in a gown he had chosen himself, wearing diamonds around her throat and in her ears that he had presented to her for this night alone. If she had ever needed a lesson to convince her that Tamoora and everything on it, including herself, belonged to Thomas Hale, this had been the occasion.

She dreaded the evening to come. She knew she would be paraded before this collection of Hale's friends and acquaintances, most of whom she had never met. Cynara had overheard some of the servants speculating that the master was giving this ball to introduce his new bride, and she had laughed aloud at this, knowing that he intended no such thing. Or perhaps he did, she thought suddenly, as they began to descend the stairs; perhaps he had designed this grand occasion to humiliate her publicly, so that all of Sydney would know, if they hadn't been made aware of it already, that the great Thomas Hale, humanitarian that he claimed to be, had taken a former convict as his wife.

The thought startled her so badly that she almost stumbled on the stairs. Recovering quickly, she glanced covertly at Hale. Was that his intention? Could even Thomas Hale be so cruel? No, whatever his reason for giving this ball, it certainly had nothing to do with her. Or had it? She had a sudden desire to break from him and run back up the stairs to lock herself in her room. Only her pride forced her to remain at his side; pride, and the tightening of his hand on her arm. With his uncanny ability to read her thoughts at times, he held her tightly. His fingers dug into her flesh, and she winced with pain.

"Come, my dear," he said softly. "Surely you do not wish to engage in a scene before our guests?"

"I have no intention of doing so," she replied with a lift of her head and a challenging glance in his direction. "Do you?"

"Would I be so rude?" he asked, mockingly.

She did not reply to this, and Hale, seeing the flash of anger in her eyes, laughed softly as they crossed the entryway to take their place by the ballroom door. He bent toward her, his eyes cold, as the butler, Roberts, opened the front door to admit the first arrivals. "Smile, love. If you disgrace me tonight, you will regret it."

Cynara refused to be cowed by this threat. "And why would I wish to disgrace you, Thomas?" she asked haughtily. "Haven't you given me everything I could want?"

The icy contempt in her voice made him flush angrily. But there was no time for him to reply; already the entryway had filled with people, and through the open door, Cynara could see other carriages driving up. She watched with satisfaction as Hale was forced to swallow his anger to greet the first of his guests.

Millicent Whitley, Gerald in tow, was elbowing her way to the front of the reception line. As they approached, Millicent exclaimed enviously, "Why, Cynara! What a beautiful gown!"

Cynara inclined her head graciously at the ringleted, bejeweled, and beflounced Millicent. "Thank you. I—"

Hale interrupted, his eyes glittering maliciously. "Nothing is too good for my wife, Millicent," he said. "When I think of what she was forced to suffer, I try to do all I can to make it up to her . . . "

Millicent stared at him. "Why, what do you mean, Thomas?"

Gerald grabbed at his wife's arm. "Come along, Millie," he said, uncomfortably avoiding Cynara's eyes. "We're holding up the line—"

Millicent was not to be swayed. "What did you mean, Thomas?" she asked again, guilelessly.

Hale waved his hand, as though the subject distressed him. He glanced significantly at Cynara, and then arranged his heavy features into an expression of pity.

Beside him, Cynara felt the color rising to her cheeks. She was furious at his deliberate reference to her imprisonment, and now she saw the avid expressions of the guests crowding behind the Whitleys as they waited intently for a response. With a burst of defiance, Cynara raised her voice so that all could hear what she said.

"My husband refers to the matter of my transportation, Mrs. Whitley," she said clearly. "The fact that I was wrongly accused and never received a trial before being deported distresses him even more an it does me. Surely, you understand now why the subject should be avoided?"

Millicent was clearly confused. Hadn't Thomas introduced the matter himself? But Cynara did not give her the opportunity to ask questions; she drew the woman to one side immediately.

Lowering her voice, Cynara said confidentially, "Millicent, I know you would never stoop to gossip—"

Mrs. Whitley bridled righteously. "Certainly not!"

Wincing inwardly, Cynara forced herself to continue smoothly, "Thomas and I would consider it a great favor if you would use your influence to stop any speculation before—"

Bristling with importance, Millicent held up her hand. "Say no more, my dear," she replied solemnly, "I understand perfectly. You can depend on me."

Patting Cynara's arm sympathetically, Millicent sailed off with the air of one about to do battle. Cynara, watching her go, smiled to herself before she turned to receive the next guests. At least one hurdle had been successfully overcome, she thought with satisfaction. Now all she had to do was get through the rest of the evening.

If Hale was angry at Cynara's performance, he did not

show it. He was an excellent actor himself, and he realized that she had neatly turned the situation to her advantage, leaving him with no option but to abandon the subject of her imprisonment. Still, he was not about to allow her to have the last word; turning dramatically to his guests, he said, "My wife is quite right; let us have no discussion of this abominable practice of transportation. As you know, many of us, including myself" he smiled modestly "have worked diligently to end the transportation of convicts to New South Wales. So let us use this occasion for what is intended, my friends. We will have nothing but gaiety tonight!"

He smiled again, and Cynara thought wrathfully that his impromptu speech would have been far more effective if he hadn't continued to use convicts on his own estate. It was only by a fierce effort of will that she prevented herself from glaring at him in utter contempt for his hypocrisy.

But the awkward moment had passed, and Hale was satisfied. The guests, taking their cue from their host, began to laugh and talk with animation, and the formal reception line moved quickly past them and into the ballroom, where the musicians quickly took up their instruments.

As Hale led Cynara onto the floor to begin the dancing, he smiled down at her and hissed, "Cleverly done, my dear. But don't expect to get away with such a maneuver again!"

He bowed elaborately over her hand, and Cynara, curtseying in response, replied with a brilliant smile that hid her disdain, "Why, I don't know what you mean, Thomas. You said yourself that the subject of convict transportation distresses you. Perhaps I only thought to spare your feelings."

"Did you now? That seems to be a consideration conspiculously lacking in your attitude up until now, my dear."

"That could be because you have not extended the same courtesy yourself," she replied.

Before Hale could answer, they were separated in the intricate steps of the dance. Cynara smiled to herself, knowing that, for the moment at least, Hale was held in check. He did not dare humiliate her now in front of his guests or he would look like a fool. She was safe—for the moment.

Two hours later, Cynara managed to escape from the warm, crowded ballroom to the veranda outside. It was a relief to get away from the press of people, and she stood in the darkness, fanning her flushed face. She had not lacked for partners; since she and Hale had begun the dancing, she had not left the floor. But now she needed to get away, even for a few minutes, to be by herself; it had been an effort to smile and converse with the men who had come up to her one after the other. She had been successful in ignoring the open curiosity in their expressions; she had even managed to extricate herself gracefully from the leading questions some had asked. But the faint condescension she had detected in one or two had made her angry. Were they secretly laughing at the pose she had maintained throughout the evening? Did they really think that as a former convict she had no right to intrude on their company?

Cynara tossed her head. What did she care what they thought? It was enough that she had managed to get through the evening thus far without worrying about Thomas Hale and what he might say to humiliate her.

The small garden off the veranda beckoned to her; it seemed quiet and peaceful in the moonlight, and she moved toward the steps that led to it, thinking to snatch a few minutes of privacy before she was forced to return to the ballroom. Suddenly she realized that she was not alone.

She turned, and in that moment, her heart seemed to falter and then stop altogether. He was standing there, so close that she could have reached out and touched him. In the light from the open doors behind him, she could see him clearly, and from somewhere in the chaos of emotion that assailed her she noticed that he was taller, almost towering over her, and that he had matured from a boy into a man.

She couldn't speak; she could only stare at him breathlessly. He was even more handsome than she remembered, his face lean and chiseled with maturity, his shoulders broad under his evening coat, his legs long and muscled. His hand rested lightly on the rail, and she closed her eyes, remembering how many times she had imagined those hands on her.

She was shaking, trembling so badly that she thought she would swoon, here, at his feet. She must say something, anything. If she waited much longer, he would see the terrible longing that shook her, making her want to throw herself at him just to know the blissful embrace of his arms again.

And then she noticed the arrogant expression she hated, and her pride came to her rescue. Although her hand shook slightly when she extended it to him, she was able to say, foolishly, "Evan. What a surprise."

"Is it?" he asked, bowing over her hand. "Then I must apologize for startling you."

How could he be so calm? Didn't he feel any of the emotions she was experiencing? She almost hated him for his control, and the anger that surged through her enabled her to say, "I meant that it was a surprise to find that you knew . . . my husband."

"Then you were not aware that I was included in your guest list?"

She would not tell him that she had not seen the guest list. Instead, she lifted her chin and answered haughtily, "Your name must have been added at the last by Thomas."

"Indeed."

Why were they sparring in this cold-blooded manner? She had dreamed of this meeting ever since that last terrible night in the summerhouse, and now that the moment had come, she could only stare furiously at him, angry that he had chosen to ruin everything by mocking her, angry with herself for being such a fool.

Thinking now about her dreams of him, she felt her face flame with humiliation, even as she fought her desire for him. She had imagined him reaching blindly for her, unable to conquer his towering need, his hands moving feverishly over her body, his mouth searing hers with a thousand kisses. She would cling to him, thrilling to his touch, and then would run away to some other place, tearing at their clothes, unable to delay an instant longer to hold each other, their naked bodies straining, sweating, uniting with the power that drove them together.

Oh yes, she had imagined it all, and now he was standing here, staring at her with an infuriatingly bland expression, and instead of wanting to throw herself at him, she longed to scratch his eyes out.

Turning away abruptly, she looked out blindly across the darkness, praying that if she ignored him, he would leave her alone.

But it seemed he had no intention of leaving her alone. To her horror, she saw him take a step toward her.

"If my being here disturbs you—" he began.

"How absurd! Your presence affects me not at all, Mr. Calder."

"I see."

He paused, and Cynara closed her eyes, willing him to go away. If he came any closer, she thought frantically, she would not be able to maintain this haughty pose her pride demanded. She would have no pride at all, no dignity. She *would* throw herself at him.

"Cynara . . ."

She heard the strangled sound of his voice with amazement. Only moments before he had been so remote, so aloof, while she had been forced to suppress her own feelings by sheer force of will. Slowly, she turned to face him again, unsure whether she had only imagined the longing she had heard in that one word, afraid to betray herself in case he was only mocking her again. But there was no mistaking the expression in his eyes, and without being aware of it, she took a step toward him, no longer able to fight her need to be close to him. Their hands touched, and she noticed, with wonder, that he was trembling, as was she.

"You two know each other?"

They sprang apart at the sound of Hale's voice. He had come up behind them noiselessly, appearing suddenly at Cynara's side to put a proprietary arm around her waist. She stiffened at the contact, hearing at the same time the hostility in his voice. Unable to answer, she regarded him silently, wondering how much he had seen.

"We met once—in England," Evan said, too smoothly.

"Well, well," Hale replied. "So you're from England, too, Mr. Calder."

"Yes."

Evan's tone was curt; it was obvious that he did not intend to elaborate.

Thomas Hale affected not to notice Evan's abruptness. He stared quizically at him for a long moment, and then said, "It's strange, but I believe I've seen you somewhere before, Mr. Calder."

"That could be. I have lived in Sydney now for eight months," Evan answered coolly. He paused, and then added deliberately, "It's possible that you have paused by my mill and seen me there."

Cynara was surprised at the current of animosity that leaped suddenly between the two men. Puzzled, she looked at Hale and then at Evan again, wondering why, if Hale had never met Evan, he had invited him to the ball. Some sort of challenge had been issued that she was at a loss to understand, but there was no doubt that Evan was waiting tensely for Hale's answer.

"Oh?" Hale said casually. "You are in the wool business, too?"

"Among other things. I decided to expand after the mill suffered a—slight set back some time ago."

The animosity was stronger now; it was almost palpable as Evan stared evenly at Hale. But Hale was not to be drawn. He murmured, "How unfortunate for you."

"Yes, it was. But it will not happen again."

"Oh? How can you be so sure?"

"A friend of mine tells me that if all else fails, one fights fire with fire—or whatever is appropriate at the time. Don't you think that is an excellent maxim to follow, Mr. Hale?"

"Ah, yes. But only if one believes in violence." Hale waved his hand in the air deprecatingly. "I myself do not believe in such extreme measures."

"Very wise of you."

"Not at all. Simply an instinct for self-preservation."

"Which we all have, in various degrees," Evan said, his voice hard. "Some more than others," he added dangerously.

"Hmm. Yes, quite. I see your point, Mr. Calder."

"I had no doubt that you would, Mr. Hale."

Evan bowed, prepared to take his leave after this strange conversation, but Hale's next words stopped him. "You say you are from England, Mr. Calder," Hale said in an abrupt change of subject.

"Yes. I believe we discussed that already."

Again, Hale ignored Evan's abruptness; he seemed intent on pursuing the point, and Cynara began to wonder why it was so important to him when he said, a shade too casually, "Strange. I would have sworn you were Australian . . . "

"Why is that?" Evan's tone was disinterested.

Hale shrugged. "It's just that you resemble a man I met once," he answered. "His name was Sean Ward."

Both Cynara and Evan stiffened at the mention of the Ward name. Only by a fierce effort of will did she prevent herself from glancing quickly at Evan to determine his reaction. But she should have known that Evan was adept at concealing his surprise; his answer, when it came, was steady.

"I don't know anyone named Sean Ward," Evan replied, in a voice that indicated only boredom for this conversation.

Cynara, who had learned to read the nuances in Hale's expression, was surprised to see that he seemed relieved by Evan's answer. Her suspicions aroused without knowing why, she looked at him closely as he waved a casual hand.

"Well, that was twenty years ago; you couldn't have known him, could you?"

Now Evan seemed impatient to end the conversation. "No, I couldn't have known him," he replied shortly. Again, he made a move to leave, and once more Hale stopped him.

Watching carefully to determine Evan's reaction, he said, "I believe Sean had a son. His name was Aron, but of course—"

"Aron!"

Cynara jumped as the word almost exploded from Evan. His face paled, and she saw that the iron control he had exerted moments before had deserted him.

Thomas Hale saw it, too. But before he could pursue this astonishing—and ominous—reaction on Evan's part, Cynara had put her hand on Evan's arm.

"Evan, are you all right? What is it?"

Evan's response to this gesture was even more intriguing to Thomas Hale. He narrowed his eyes speculatively as Evan jerked away from her touch. "It was nothing, Cynara," he muttered.

"But—"

Well, well. This was interesting indeed, Hale thought to himself. He glanced at the white-faced Cynara, and then back to Evan again. It seemed that these two were more than casual acquaintances after all. Without being aware of it, they had betrayed themselves, and he thought that perhaps Cynara could be . . . persuaded . . . to reveal some information that would help him get rid of this young upstart who seemed not to be intimidated by threats of violence. Maybe the subtle touch was needed, after all, Hale mused. He had to do something—and quickly—because if what he suspected about Evan Calder were true, then it would be dangerous for him if Calder discovered what had happened so many years ago regarding Sean Ward's estate. If this young man ever discovered that Sean's death was no accident, he could raise quite a fuss—especially if it was brought out that before Sean died, he had signed over most of his land to a man name Thomas Hale.

Hale smiled to himself in the darkness. He would speak to Cynara tonight after the guests had departed. And she would tell him what she knew about this mysterious Evan Calder, or live to regret it.

CHAPTER EIGHTEEN

"I'VE TOLD YOU AGAIN AND AGAIN, I know nothing about Evan Calder!"

"My patience is wearing thin, my dear. I'll ask you once more—"

"You can ask all you wish," Cynara snapped, out of patience herself. "I have nothing to tell you!"

Angrily, she threw herself into a chair, ignoring Hale's heavy frown as she did so. It was late, the ball had concluded several hours before, and those guests who had been invited to stay the night because of the long trip to their own homes had been conducted long ago to the chambers that had been prepared for them.

Cynara had returned to her own apartment with relief that her duties as hostess had been fulfilled; the evening had been a strain, and she was exhausted. To her annoyance, Hale had followed her, and this inquisition—there was no other word for it, she thought irritably—had begun. But her aggravation had swiftly turned to alarm at his interrogation about Evan, and now she was frightened by the tenor of his questions. Why was he so interested in Evan? She knew Hale well enough to realize that jealousy was not his reason for questioning her about Evan, although at first he had tried to make her believe that it was. Intuition told her that whatever his motive was, the result would be harmful, if not dangerous, for Evan. Consequently, she had evaded Hale's persistent demands, hoping that he would eventually tire of questioning her and be forced to believe her assertion that her acquaintance with Evan was only casual.

Glancing covertly at him now, she knew that he was not convinced. She wondered again how much he had observed of that scene between them on the veranda. Tiredly, she tried to review what she had said to Evan, and he to her, but her thoughts were a jumble, and she could only hope that nothing of significance had been said. But how could it have been, she asked herself bitterly; they had spent what little time they had together sparring like two ill-mannered children, when everything of importance had been left unuttered.

Passing a weary hand over her eyes, she tried to think why Evan might present a threat to a man like Thomas Hale. It couldn't be anything financial, because she knew that Hale was one of the richest men in Sydney, if not all Australia. Nor could it be business; Hale had his fingers on the pulse of too many concerns to feel threatened by a young man like Evan. No, it had to be something else—but what? And then she recalled the conversation about the man named Sean Ward, and her eyes narrowed. Hale's interest must be connected in some manner with that man, or he wouldn't have pressed the point, trying to make it seem unimportant, when Cynara had known at once that it had been, at least to Thomas Hale.

She sat up straight in the chair as a sudden thought struck her. Twenty years ago Sean Ward had had a son named Aron. Was it possible that Evan was that son? No, what was she thinking of? Evan was too young. But even if he had been Sean's son, why should it matter to Hale?

She looked up abruptly, and asked, "Who was Sean Ward?"

"We're not speaking of Sean Ward," Hale answered sharply. "We're talking about Evan Calder."

"I have nothing to say about Evan Calder," she replied stubbornly.

Hale advanced upon her so suddenly that she had no time to protect herself. Whipping her out of the chair, he grabbed her chin, forcing her head up to look at him. "I want you to tell me—now!"

Cynara tried to jerk away from him. "I don't know anything!" she cried. "How many times do I have to tell you?"

He threw her away from him so abruptly that she

staggered and almost fell against the chair. Furious, she glared at him as he went to the table and poured himself a glass of brandy. Downing it in one swallow, he turned back to her and said menacingly, "Perhaps a few days of contemplation locked alone in this room will help you to remember, my dear. If your memory fortuitously returns, you have only to let me know, and you will be released. I will be most interested in hearing what you have to say."

"Why is this so important to you?" she demanded as he went to the door.

"Perhaps it is because I prefer to know who my adversaries are, love," he replied mockingly.

"What threat could Ev—Mr. Calder be to you?"

Hale laughed. "He is no threat to me at all—at least, not in quite the way you mean."

"What then?"

Hale ignored the challenge in her voice. Opening the door, he said, "I hope a night's rest will jog your memory. If not, I'm afraid we will have to resort to . . . ah . . . more drastic measures. Oh, and don't worry about our guests; I will contrive some suitable excuse, I'm sure."

The door closed behind him before she could reply. She heard the click of the lock and tossed her head defiantly. What a ridiculously melodramatic exit, she thought contemptuously. If he thought to shame her in front of his guests, he was going to be mistaken. Let him tell them what he wished; it made no difference to her.

Cynara unhooked the elegant ballgown she still wore and threw it into the corner, where it fell crumpled to the floor. Sitting down at dressing table, she stared at herself in the mirror. Why did she feel she must protect Evan?

The entire scene had been ludicrous. Even if she had been willing to tell him what he demanded, what could she reveal, after all? The only thing she knew was that Evan was illegitimate, and that he had spent almost eighteen years of his life at Lyrebird Manor. Beyond that, he was as much a mystery to her as he was to Thomas.

Then why hadn't she told him that? It was little enough to disclose, and the only harm done would have been to Evan's pride. But she hadn't told him anything; she had said, over and over again, that she knew nothing about him, that they had only met once. She hadn't even mentioned where or in what circumstances this brief acquaintance had taken place. Why?

Impatiently, she unclasped the diamond necklace from around her throat and pulled the ear-drops from her ears, tossing both to the tabletop as contemptuously as she had discarded the gown. Avoiding her reflection, she jerked the pins from her hair and began brushing it almost savagely. Would Evan thank her for this quixotic defense? No, he would not. In fact, she could just imagine his fury if he ever discovered that she had tried to protect him.

Flinging the hairbrush down, Cynara flounced away from the dressing table and snatched her robe from the foot of the bed as she went toward the veranda doors. To her immediate outrage, she discovered that they were locked from the outside. The realization that Hale had planned to imprison her all along made her furious.

Tears of frustration gathered in her eyes; she brushed them away angrily, resisting the temptation to kick at the door in a fury. What was she going to do now?

If only there was a way to send a message to Evan; at least then she could warn him. But that was impossible; there was no one here she could trust enough to take a message, even if she knew where to find him. And what could she say to him, after all? That there was some sinister meaning behind Hale's interest in him? He would probably laugh in her face; from the conversation tonight on the veranda, he was fully aware that Thomas Hale was capable of anything.

Then, Cynara remembered the conversation that night with Gerald Whitley. Gerald had mentioned something about a fire at a mill, and Hale had dismissed it, too casually. And then tonight, Evan had spoken of fighting fire with fire because his mill had been damaged.

Sinking into a chair, Cynara realized that Thomas Hale had already taken steps to harm Evan. That he had done so could only mean that he had been sufficiently alarmed by Evan's presence to do something as drastic as setting a fire. But why? What did Hale know about Evan that she did not?

She was too tired to think about it any more. There was nothing she could accomplish at this moment, even if she had known what to do. Wearily, she went to the chest of drawers and withdrew a nightgown. As she undressed and pulled it over her head, the only thing she was sure of was that Thomas Hale would never learn from her about John and Cornelia Ward and Evan's connection with them. It might only be coincidence that Sean Ward shared John's surname, but surely it was stretching credibility to assume that an English family with the name of Ward merely chanced on the idea of using the Australian lyrebird as both the name of their estate and the design for their garden.

Hale himself had said that Sean Ward was Australian. Cynara knew for a certainty that John Ward and his family had never traveled out of England, for she had heard John say so on one occasion. So there had to be a connection between the two, and if there was, Cynara would not be the one to mention it to Hale. Instinctively she knew that such knowledge in Thomas Hale's hands would be dangerous to Evan. She would not give her husband any more weapons than he already had.

With that determined promise to herself, Cynara climbed into bed and turned out the lamp. But as soon as she put her head back against the pillow, the thoughts of Evan that she had successfully held back all evening crowded in on her, and despite her fierce efforts not to think of him, she saw him in her mind as he had been that night. Little things that she had not really noticed at the time came back to her now; she remembered the excellent cut of his evening clothes, the way he had allowed his hair to grow, so that it almost covered his ears. But now she recalled, too, that he seemed even more self-assured than he had before; that in addition to his natural arrogance, he had acquired a new poise and sophistication that made him seem even more formidable. No one who did not know him would guess his true age; he seemed years older. But with this new maturity, he was also more aloof, more controlled, as if there was a violence inside him that must be held under tight rein. Thinking about it now, Cynara shivered; if he ever allowed the rage she sensed in him to go unchecked, the results would be appalling. The scar on his face might have faded to a thin line, but Cynara knew that the internal scars he carried would never disappear.

Turning her face into the pillow, Cynara willed herself not to cry. She had known the instant she had seen him that the memory of that night in the summerhouse and what followed afterwards would always stand between them; she had seen it in his face, and in every gesture he had made. He would never forget the humiliation he had suffered that night; he would never forget that she had witnessed it.

The tears she had tried to hold back came now. Sobbing, she cursed Myles and the destruction he had brought through his evil passions. All was lost between her and Evan; she would never know the thrill of loving and being loved by him. Her dreams vanished in the mist of tears, even as her body burned for him. She wanted him—God! How she wanted him! Her breasts ached to be caressed by him, her arms longed to hold him close, to feel his skin against her own flesh.

Clutching the pillow, she doubled over with an almost physical pain as Evan's face floated before her eyes. She was obsessed with him, haunted by him, and she writhed on the bed, wondering desperately if she would ever be free of him.

But as she wept for Evan and whatever chance they might have had and lost, she vowed that Myles would pay for what he had done. Thomas Hale could not live forever; one day she would be free of him and Tamoora, or part of it, would be hers. The house and the land meant nothing to her; she would sell it at once and return to England to confront Myles. But this time, she thought fiercely, she would no longer be helpless. She would be in a position to pay, and handsomely, to see Myles and his family brought to justice.

Even through her tears, Cynara smiled fiercely to herself. If it took every last farthing she owned, she would have her revenge. No matter the cost, the money would be well spent. She might have lost Evan, but she would exact the utmost in retribution from Myles Ward.

It had to be enough, she told herself as she fell into an uneasy sleep, that she would avenge herself on the one person who had earned all the hatred and contempt of which she was capable. She lived for the moment of her triumph over him because now she had nothing else.

"Mrs. Hale! Mrs. Hale! Please open the door! Something awful has happened! Mrs. Hale—can you hear me?"

Cynara struggled to awaken from the grip of a nightmare in which she was trapped in some dark menacing place with a ranging storm outside. The wind shrieked through the trees, banging a loose shutter against the window. And then she knew it was no shutter; someone was outside with an ax, trying to get in to attack her. Terrified, she opened her mouth to scream, but she couldn't make a sound. To her horror, she watched the blade of the ax break through the wall, and then she saw Myles's grinning face beyond the opening he had made. She knew he was going to kill her . . .

She woke with a start. Disoriented, she listened to the banging on the door for several seconds before she realized that the noise was real, and not part of her nightmare.

"Mrs. Hale! Can you hear me?"

The hysterical voice belong to the housekeeper, and Cynara leaped out of bed, fumbling for her robe. "Yes, yes, I'm coming!" she called.

Brushing the hair from her eyes, Cynara went quickly to the door. "What is it?"

"Please let me in, Mrs. Hale—"

Cynara reached for the doorknob, forgetting that it was locked in her complete astonishment at hearing the shrill note in the housekeeper's usually reserved voice. The door refused to yield, and Cynara said, as calmly as she could, "You will have to unlock the door from your side, Mrs. Cole—"

"What? What?"

"Unlock the door, Mrs. Cole!" Cynara said sharply.

She heard the jingling of keys from the housekeepr's belt, and then a muffled exclamation as the woman struggled with the lock. When the door finally burst open, Cynara stared in surprise as the housekeeper rushed in and actually grabbed her.

"Oh, Mrs. Hale—" the woman gasped as she hung on to Cynara. "Something terrible has happened—"

"What is it?" Cynara's tone was curt. "Mrs. Cole, please control yourself and tell me!"

"It's . . . it's . . . "

To Cynara's utter stupifaction, the housekeeper burst into tears.

"Mrs. Cole! If you don't tell me at once—"

"It's the master, Mrs. Hale. He's . . . he's dead."

"Dead!"

Mrs. Cole made an effort to control her tears. "They're bringing him in now—"

"Bringing him in? What do you mean?"

But the housekeeper burst into renewed weeping, and Cynara was forced to lead her to a chair. "Mrs. Cole," she said, gritting her teeth with impatience, "I must know what happened."

"They . . . they went out this morning—"

"Who is they?"

"The master and some of the guests. They were going hunting—"

"And?" Cynara resisted the urge to take the housekeeper

by the shoulders and shake her.

"And the master's horse stepped into a hole and went down. Mr. Hale struck his head on a rock, and . . ."

Cynara sank into a chair, ignoring the weeping Mrs. Cole. So Thomas was dead, she thought blankly. And only last night she had told herself that he couldn't live forever. She didn't know whether to burst into tears or laugh hysterically at the thought that she was free. Free! It seemed impossible. She couldn't believe it; she could only stare at her hands clasped tightly in her lap, thinking that she felt no sorrow, no grief that he was gone. She felt nothing; she was numb.

"Oh, Mrs. Hale! Whatever am I thinking of? I'm so sorry; I shouldn't have told you so abruptly . . ."

The housekeeper was bending contritely over her, patting her arm awkwardly. "It's quite all right," Cynara forced herself to say, faintly. "It's just that it was such a shock—"

The woman's eyes filled with tears again. "Yes, it was that," she replied, dabbing at her face with her handkerchief. "He was such a good man . . ."

A good man! Was the housekeeper out of her mind? But of course she wasn't; hadn't Thomas always taken pains to present himself in the best possible light to everyone but his own wife? Suddenly Cynara realized that she should endeavor to show a little grief over the loss of her husband, or the housekeeper would think it strange. But no matter how she tried, she could not force herself to cry. The tears that she had shed so readily last night refused to arrive on command now, and she had to be content with a sorrowful expression that she hoped would deceive Mrs. Cole.

Apparently she was successful, for the housekeeper straightened and said quietly, "I've already taken the liberty of sending for Mr. Whitley. I'm sure that he will make all the . . . er . . . arrangements."

"Thank you, Mrs. Cole," Cynara replied in the same

hushed voice. "Oh, and one more thing, if you please. I do not wish to be disturbed for a while. I'm sure you understand."

The housekeeper inclined her head. "Of course."

The door closed softly behind her, and Cynara jumped to her feet, knowing that such elation was wrong, but unable to contain it. She twirled around the room, and then paused, ashamed of her action. The man was dead; even he deserved a little respect, she told herself severely.

More soberly now, she went to the wardrobe to select a gown of dark gray silk. It was the most somber color she owned, and she supposed she would have to order mourning black before the funeral.

But there was no need after all of a black gown. Hours later, in an interview with Gerald Whitley, who had been appointed executor of Thomas Hale's estate, she discovered the extent of Hale's treachery, and she recalled with horror his words to her at the time of their first meeting: "If you don't give me a son, you'll curse the day I boarded this ship . . ."

CHAPTER NINETEEN

"I'M VERY SORRY, Cynara," Gerald Whitley said, avoiding her eyes. "The will is valid. I tried to dissuade Thomas from this course, but I could not." He hesitated, and then said again, awkwardly, "I'm truly sorry . . . "

Cynara knew that if she were forced to stay a moment longer in the library with Gerald after this appalling disclosure of Thomas Hale's perfidy, she would burst into tears of anger and disbelief. Lifting her chin, she looked away from Gerald's pitying face. Once again she had been betrayed. It wasn't fair, she thought angrily, and then realized that things were seldom fair for those who were helpless.

"You have told me everything, then, Gerald?" she asked quietly.

Gerald inclined his head. "Yes."

She managed to rise gracefully from her chair, willing herself not to give in to the chaos of emotion that raged inside her until she could be by herself. "You will excuse me, Mr. Whitley? I must be alone for a while."

Gerald had risen with her. "Of course. I understand," he replied solemnly.

He made a motion to come around the desk to accompany her to the door, but Cynara shook her head. "Please. I'm quite all right. I know you have a great many things to attend to."

She paused, forcing him to meet her eyes. "I assume the funeral service will be tomorrow . . . ?" When he nodded, she said evenly, "You will understand if I decline to attend?"

Gerald nodded again. "I will offer some suitable excuse. No one need know . . . " He stopped, his face flushing.

"Thank you, Mr. Whitley. You are very kind. I want you to know that I appreciate your efforts on my behalf."

Somehow she managed to make her way to the door and

up the stairs to her room. Safely inside, she carefully shut the door and leaned against it for support. Now that she was alone, she did not cry. If she had been numb upon hearing of Hale's death, now she was frozen. How could he have done this to her? He must have been mad, insane!

But of course he was, she told herself as she pushed herself away from the door and fumbled her way to a chair. She had known that from the very beginning, hadn't she? But what was she going to do now?

One thing was certain: She would not remain here, waiting submissively for the authorities to come and take her away. She had not suffered Hale's cruelty and mocking taunts these past months to surrender so meekly now: She would go away. *Run* away, if she had to, and it appeared now that she did. But where would she go?

What did it matter where she went? she asked herself bitterly. The important thing was to escape from Tamoora before she was made prisoner again. She would go where she had to, she would do whatever she must to support herself, but she would *not* give herself up to the authorities, no matter what the law was. They had no right to hold her, to force her to complete a prison term that had not been earned in the first place. She would leave Tamoora as soon as possible—this very night.

But the decision was easier than the actual implementation of it, and she sat where she was for a long time, thinking of what Gerald Whitley had revealed to her in that disastrous interview in the library. She had been unprepared for it then, and she could not believe it now. In one stroke, all her grandiose plans for returning to England had been smashed, and she was far worse off than before.

Eyes burning with unshed tears, Cynara stared sightlessly at the floor, remembering her horror and disbelief when Gerald had spoken of Thomas Hale's treachery.

"This is somewhat irregular, Cynara," he had said when she seated herself and looked at him expectantly. She saw that he held a sheaf of papers, and that his hand trembled as he took his own chair behind the desk. At that moment, she had a sudden and inexplicable premonition of disaster, but she repressed it firmly; she would wait until she heard what Gerald had to say.

"Properly, Thomas's will should not be heard until after the service," Gerald had continued, his voice strained. "But since it concerns you to such an extent, I thought it would be best for us to speak privately before the others hear . . . "

He had hesitated awkwardly, and she said, trying to be calm, "Please go on, Mr. Whitley."

Gerald laid the papers before him on the desk, straightening and aligning them, smoothing the crumpled corner of one as though he were trying to give himself time to think.

"Mr. Whitley?"

"I'm afraid there is no painless way to tell you this, Cynara," he said finally, "other than to speak out plainly . . . "

But now he paused to clear his throat, and Cynara thought that if he kept her in suspense much longer, she would reach across the desk and shake it out of him. Her heart had begun to beat wildly with apprehension at Gerald's manner, and it was only by a fierce effort of will that she remained quietly in her chair.

"I was not aware of this until a month or so ago," Gerald continued finally, glancing away from Cynara's white face, "When Thomas came to my office. At that time, he told me . . . "

Again, he paused, and Cynara wanted to scream with impatience. "Told you what, Mr. Whitley?" she prompted, as calmly as she could. Without being aware of it, she clutched the arms of her chair until the knuckles showed white.

"I'm afraid, Cynara, that Thomas never married you—"

"*What!*" Cynara heard the shrill note in her voice and steadied herself forcibly. "That's impossible," she said flatly. "He lied to you, Mr. Whitley. We were married by a magistrate in Sydney."

Gerald shook his head. "No. It was all a sham. Thomas told me that he wanted you to believe you were married, because he thought that would make you"—his face reddened—"more amenable. If you had given him a son, he would have married you in truth to legitimize the child. But until then . . ."

Cynara sat back in her chair, no longer listening. She was remembering that day in the magistrate's office. The man had stumbled over the words to the ceremony as if he were unfamiliar with them, she recalled now, wondering bitterly why she hadn't been suspicious at the time; he had also smirked when he called her Mrs. Hale. Was it true what Gerald was saying? She wouldn't believe it!

"But I signed the marriage papers," she said insistently.

Gerald shook his head again. "Those papers weren't legal, Cynara," he said gently. "Thomas hired that man to pretend to be a magistrate. Actually, he was only a junior clerk in the office."

He paused once more, and Cynara closed her eyes in dread. "I'm afraid that isn't the worst," he said finally. "Thomas added a codicil that day in my office to his will . . ."

"And what does this codicil say?" Cynara asked, unable to conceal her bitterness.

"It says that if you have not given him a male child at the time of his death, you are to receive nothing from the estate. And further," he said in a rush, as though to get it over with as quickly as possible, "That you are to be given over to the authorities to complete the remainder of your prison sentence, if any . . ."

For a horrible instant, Cynara thought she would faint. The room seemed to darken, and from far away she heard Gerald Whitley's exclamation of surprise and concern. With a great effort, she willed the blackness away to see that he had half risen from his chair. She waved her hand weakly, indicating that she was all right, and he sat back again reluctantly.

"I'm very sorry, Cynara," he said.

Sorry! Cynara thought now, alone in her room. If he was so apologetic, why hadn't he done anything to change Thomas's mind? No, she wasn't being fair; she should know better than anyone that the man she thought her husband would not be swayed once he had made up his mind.

Her husband! Cynara's lip curled derisively. All these months she had endured him and his cruelties—and for what? Enraged, she sprang out of the chair to pace up and down the room.

What a fool she had been, telling herself all this time that because he was her husband, she must stay to suffer at his hands! How he must have laughed at her puny attempts at defiance, her haughty posturings, knowing that at any time he could deliver this blow to her pride and integrity. She had even been forced, because he was her husband, to allow him her bed, and it was this thought that infuriated her the most. He had known—he had *known!*—that she would have fought his violation of her body, so he had deceived her in this monstrous way, making her believe that it was his right as her husband.

Cynara ground her teeth together in a fury. If she had despised him before, she loathed him now. She was glad he was dead, she thought savagely, because if he had been alive, she surely would have killed him herself at this moment. Her hands actually clenched into fists at the thought, and if by some miracle he had suddenly appeared before her, she would have bludgeoned him to death on the spot.

Suddenly appalled at the violence of her emotions, Cynara forced herself to take a deep breath. She looked down at her hands, willing herself to relax. She was wasting time, and there was no time to spare. She must make plans to get away from Tamoora tonight, before Gerald Whitley overcame whatever pangs of conscience he might have and called the authorities.

Moving quickly to the window, Cynara looked out.

There was no one to be seen; all except the most necessary work had been suspended for the day out of respect for the master's death, and Hale's servants had retired early to their own quarters. The ground would be clear for her escape, if she could only manage to get out of the house without detection.

Cynara crossed the room again to open the door a crack. A hushed silence greeted her, and she thought that the household servants had probably gathered in the kitchen to console each other and to speculate about what would happen to them now that Hale was gone. So much the better, she thought, as she carefully closed the door again; she wanted to meet no one on the way out.

Turning away from the door, Cynara moved swiftly now to the wardrobe. She took a shawl and spread it on the bed, returning once more to the wardrobe to select two plain cotton gowns. She didn't take more than these, plus a few underthings and a nightgown; a bulky package would attract attention and be difficult to carry.

The clothing wrapped into as small a bundle as she could make, Cynara stepped out of the gray silk she wore and donned one of the cotton dresses. With a last look around the room, she decided she was ready.

But as she went to the door again, something caught her eye. The diamonds she had discarded so carelessly the night before glittered on the dressing table, and she stopped. She took a step toward them and stopped again, resisting the temptation to take them with her. She would need money of some sort, she thought, but surely there was something else she could take; how could she explain having diamonds in her possession?

Frowning, she tried to think. She knew Hale kept money in the house, but she had no idea where. She would have to think of something else. The opals! The glass cases that displayed them were kept locked, but she knew where Hale kept the key. She would take only a few of the smallest ones, and hope that if she ever needed to exchange them for money, she could do so without arousing suspicion.

Cynara met no one as she crept downstairs. Only two lamps had been left burning in the entryway; the rest of the house was in shadow as she tiptoed across the hall toward the drawing room where the opals were located. She paused at the entrance to the drawing room and glanced quickly down the corridor. A thin ribbon of light shone beneath the closed library door, and she wondered if Gerald was still there. If he was, she must hurry; she had no wish to try to explain what she was doing if he suddenly appeared.

Noiselessly she opened the door and slipped inside. The gloom was even more intense here, and she stood with her back to the door for several moments, allowing her eyes to adjust to the darkness. She did not dare light a lamp in case someone should see the light and come to investigate. Now she could see the shadows of sofas and chairs, and she threaded her way cautiously around them toward the fireplace, pausing every few steps to listen intently for the sound of any approach.

The key to the cases was in a concealed niche to the right of the fireplace. She found the panel and slid it sideways, reaching in for the key. Her fingers closed around it, and she drew it out, stopping to listen again.

But the house was quiet, and now she moved swiftly to the nearest case, fitting the key to the lock by feel, hearing the tiny click as the mechanism was released. The glass door opened, and the opals were there, waiting to be taken.

She remembered the location of each stone—hadn't she stared at them often enough, wanting to rip them from their cases in childish retaliation against Thomas Hale?—and her hand went unerringly to the bottom row where the smallest of the opals were displayed. She took three from their beds of black velvet and closed the case again. The sense of urgency heightened as soon as she had the opals in her hand, and she locked the case quickly, glancing nervously over her shoulder at the door. Seconds later she had replaced the key, fumbling at the panel in the darkness, and was halfway to the door, when she stopped.

She looked down at the stones she held, and even in the gloom she could see a slight shimmer from the opals against her palm. With every passing second increasing the chance of discovery, she hesitated, arguing with herself.

Did she have the right to take the opals? Of course she did. She had earned these and many more the past months posing as Hale's wife. She should receive something for all the humiliation she had suffered, shouldn't she?

She took another step toward the door. No. She wouldn't take them. She wanted nothing of his, after all.

Quickly, she retraced her steps, and when the opals had been replaced and the key hidden once more, she breathed a sigh of relief. She might be caught for escaping Tamoora, but no one could accuse her of taking something that wasn't hers. It was a small comfort, she thought bitterly, as she turned toward the door again.

She froze at a sound from the corridor outside. Footsteps were approaching the drawing room door, and Cynara closed her eyes in a panic. If she was caught here, there would be no way to explain away the bundle of clothing in her hand; it would be obvious that she was trying to escape. All the stories she had heard about what happened to convicts who tried to run away raced through her mind, and she glanced frantically around, trying to find a place to hide the incriminating bundle. Without it, she could perhaps brazen her way through any questions; with it, she was lost.

But just as she had decided to toss it behind one of the sofas in the hope that it wouldn't be noticed, the footsteps passed the door without pausing. Her relief was so great that she was forced to lean against a chair until her legs could support her again. She let out the breath she had been holding and strained to listen. The terrible thought occurred to her that whoever it had been had stopped to wait for her to emerge.

Every sense screamed at her to take her chances and run, and yet she forced herself to stand there motionless, while the seconds ticked by. Was someone really there, or was her imagination running wild?

There was only one thing to do: she must make herself move toward that door and open it. Any action would be better than simply waiting for discovery; already the strain was making her feel lightheaded and faint with apprehension. If she waited much longer, she knew she would never be able to do it.

She wasn't sure how she managed to make her way across the room, but suddenly she was pressed against the door, the doorknob gripped tightly in her hand. There was no time to hesitate; she had delayed too long as it was. With only a quick glance up and down the blessedly empty corridor outside, she dashed toward the front door.

Thankfully, the big doors were unlocked. They swung wide as Cynara let herself out, and she forced herself to stop long enough to close them behind her. The wide drive to the house was in front of her, and without a backward glance, Cynara leaped down the steps and fled into the night.

CHAPTER TWENTY

NO ONE WAS MORE SURPRISED than Mollie when the maid, Betsy, hesitantly entered the drawing room late the night of the ball at Tamoora. Mollie was entertaining a few friends, and she looked up, startled, when Betsy beckoned nervously to her. Excusing herself gracefully, Mollie went to where Betsy stood just inside the doorway, and asked curtly, "What is it? You know I don't like to be interrupted at this hour."

Betsy dropped a small curtsy. "I'm sorry, Mrs. Gentry," she answered, looking apprehensively over her shoulder, "but Mr. Calder is at the door. He wants to see you."

"Show him in," Mollie said impatiently. "What is the matter with you?"

"Well, I thought . . . " The girl swallowed. "I thought it would be best if you saw him alone."

Mollie glanced sharply at her. "What do you mean? Is something wrong?"

"I'm not sure, Mrs. Gentry. He looks—strange . . . "

Alarmed, Mollie did not question the maid further. She brushed past the girl into the entryway, and stopped at the sight of Evan standing in the open doorway, a thunderous expression on his face. Startled, she waved away the maid, who had followed her, thinking quickly that it would indeed be best to deal with him herself. Betsy slipped away gratefully; she had always admired Evan's tall handsomeness from afar, but tonight when she had answered the door, she had been almost afraid of him, and she was glad Mollie was there to take charge.

Mollie stood where she was for a moment, staring at Evan. He was still dressed in evening clothes, but covered with dust, as though he had ridden long and hard—as indeed he must have, he thought rapidly, if he had been to

Tamoora and back again by this hour. Surreptitiously she glanced at the clock in the hall, and saw that it was after three. It was obvious that he had been drinking heavily before coming here, and she looked at him closely; she had had experience with angry men and alcohol, and she knew that the combination could be dangerous. Mollie had no intention of allowing him inside if he was going to wreck the place.

"Is Sarah free?" he muttered, grabbing onto the door-jamb for balance.

"It depends," Mollie replied evenly. "She isn't if you want to use her as an outlet for your temper."

The significance of her statement was not lost on Evan, drunk as he was. He flushed. "I've never hit a woman, Mollie," he said with as much dignity as he was able under the circumstances. "I don't intend to begin now."

Mollie looked at him steadily for a moment longer, weighing her decision. At last, she stepped aside and motioned him in. "She's upstairs."

Evan nodded his thanks and went to pass by her, but Mollie put her hand on his arm, detaining him. "It will be her decision, Evan," she said quietly. "If she tells you to go—"

"I understand," Evan replied roughly.

"Be sure you do."

Mollie watched as he made his way up the stairs, holding onto the bannister for balance. She heard Sarah's voice, high with surprise, inviting him into her room, but still Mollie did not move from her position at the foot of the staircase. Tapping her fingers thoughtfully on the newel post, she stared absently at the closed door of Sarah's room, and wondered what had happened to put Evan in such a state. She had never seen him drunk before, and she was worried. What was wrong? Had something happened at Tamoora between Evan and Thomas Hale? Or was it something else? Reflectively, she moved away from the staircase and back to the drawing room and her guests. She would ask Vincent

when she saw him again, she thought. Evan was one of her
favorites; if she could help in some way, she would.

Upstairs, Sarah was helping Evan out of his coat. He had
not spoken a word to her since he had entered, and wisely,
she waited. Like Mollie, she was surprised at his appearance,
for usually he was faultlessly dressed. Nor had she ever seen
him drunk; he had told her once that liquor clouded a man's
mind, rendering him incapable of judgment, a state he
despised. Intuition kept Sarah silent, but she had never
known Evan to lose control, and she was concerned. She
glanced at him anxiously, but he ignored her, alarming her
further by making straight for the table where she kept a
decanter of whiskey and several glasses.

Pouring one glass, he raised it in her direction and
downed it in one swallow. She watched him repeat the
performance with a second and begin on a third before she
moved toward him nervously.

Ignoring his frown, she went to him and took the glass
from his hand. "If you're going to drink all my whiskey,
love, don't you think we should get more comfortable?"
she asked softly.

As she spoke, she was busy with his silk cravat, untying it
to toss over the bed post. She pressed herself against him,
running her hand inside his shirt, hoping to take his attention away from the whiskey before he became completely
unmanageable.

Evan took a deep breath. Since leaving Tamoora he had
ridden hard, stopping only once at an inn along the way to
refresh himself and to rest his horse. But the more he had
drunk, the more obvious it had become to him that he was
not going to forget Cynara. He saw her in every glass he
raised and emptied, he felt her presence beside him and in
him, until the ache in his loins became an unbearable pressure. Vowing again and again to forget her, he had ordered
dram after dram of rum, trying to drown the memory of
her in alcoholic stupor, until even the innkeeper, a rough
customer who was accustomed to hard and heavy drinkers,

had offered him a room in which to sleep it off. Evan had refused, lurching out the door to his horse, his rage and frustration driving him to Mollie's at this ungodly hour when he should properly have been home—alone—in his bed. It had taken him three hours to make his way back here, and every mile had increased his fury, until even the vast amounts of liquor he had consumed seemed to have little effect on him. He looked blearily at Sarah, who somehow managed to lead him to the sofa.

She was standing with her back to the lamp, and through the thin silk wrapper she wore he could see the lush outline of her body. The sight aroused him, and he reached for her, pulling her down beside him. She raised her face to his, her lips parted in anticipation, and suddenly he wanted her. His mouth came down hard on hers, his hands going for the sash at her waist. The wrapper parted under his impatient fingers, and he slid his hand inside, fondling her breasts. Her moan of pleasure excited him even more, and his mouth left hers to kiss the full breasts she offered him. She moaned again, her hands fumbling at his trousers.

"Evan, let's—"

But his mouth on hers stopped whatever she had been about to say, and he forced her back against the sofa to lie on top of her. Her legs parted willingly, and he thrust himself against her. He was beyond all thought now, existing in a world of the senses where nothing mattered except the feel of her woman's body rising to meet his. He kissed her fiercely, driving from his mind the thought of another face, another body, and then suddenly he was swept along by the demand for release. The moment of climax raced toward him, and he crushed her to him. They writhed together, their hands caressing at first, and then, as need claimed them, frenzied.

From somewhere he heard her moan of ecstasy, but the sounds she made as she pulled his mouth down fiercely to hers were lost in his own savage cry of release. He was far away in that instant, in a sheltered place by a crystal stream, and he laughed exultantly. He had wanted her from the first time he had seen her standing on the train platform; he had wanted her, and desired her, he had needed and loved her. And in that final instant when time shuddered and stood still for him, he had finally possessed her. He laughed again, a deep sound that was a cry of triumph.

Evan felt a cool hand on his forehead. Groaning, he opened his eyes to see Sarah bending over him. The room was dim, the draperies closed against the sun, but even the little light that entered hurt his eyes, and he groaned again.

"What time is it?" he muttered.

"Going on noon," Sarah answered with a laugh. "How do you feel, love?"

How did he feel? Like his head was about to be split open. With a great effort, he managed to sit up and swing his feet over the edge of the bed. But even that small movement increased the thunderous pounding behind his eyes, and he brought his hands up to cover his face, wincing.

"Here—"

Sarah pushed a cup of strong black coffee at him, guiding it to his lips when he seemed incapable of doing so himself. The coffee was heavily laced with whiskey, and Evan turned his head away, grimacing at the sharp smell of the liquor.

"Drink," Sarah ordered. "It will make you feel better."

Evan complied; it was easier to obey than to resist, especially when he looked up and saw that Sarah was grinning at him. What had got into him last night? The only thing he remembered was coming here in a drunken stupor. Looking around the room now, he couldn't even recall coming upstairs; he couldn't remember anything after leaving the ball at Tamoora.

Evan stood up so abruptly that he staggered. His head was spinning, and the room seemed tilted to one side, but he forced himself to reach for his clothes. Thinking about Cynara was what had gotten him into this condition; he would forget her if it took every ounce of will he possessed.

But as he dressed, he found himself thinking of Cynara after all, and he was enraged all over again. He had seen her at once when he arrived. So great was his astonishment at seeing her again that he had stopped in the doorway, stunned into immobility. She was dancing with a fat, balding man who seemed unable to keep his eyes away from the deep cleavage of her gown, and her head was tilted to hear something the man said to her as he lurched around the floor. She had never seemed so desirable to him as in that moment when she tossed her head and said something in reply, and Evan felt a stirring of excitement that infuriated him.

He had watched her, wondering why she had been invited to the ball, seething inwardly at the idea that she was well enough acquainted with Thomas Hale to garner an invitation. It *had* been she on the street that day, he thought suddenly; how could he ever have convinced himself that he had been mistaken?

Seeing her now, managing to appear graceful in spite of the awkwardness of her partner, Evan thought cynically that she hadn't changed at all. And yet, as he continued to stare at her, despite his efforts to tear his eyes away, he saw that she had changed a great deal.

In the fourteen months since he had last seen her, she had completed the metamorphosis from young girl to full womanhood, and the result was devastating to Evan. She was easily the most beautiful woman in the room, and yet she seemed unaware of it—or pretended to be, he told himself angrily. He accepted a glass of champagne from a passing footman and continued to gaze at her, unable to believe that she was the same girl he had known at Lyrebird Manor.

She seemed even more sure of herself now, but in a different way. She had acquired the poise and assurance that enabled her to ignore the ogling of her dance partner, or the sly glances of the envious women watching her as she floated around the floor, and without realizing it, Evan nodded to himself, admiring her proud carriage, the almost defiant lift of her head. When he saw her companion tighten his hold around her slim waist, he was stricken with a pang of jealousy so strong that it staggered him; he wanted to stride across the floor and fling the man away from her, sweeping her into his own arms. So fierce was his desire to hold her, to dance with her, that he drank his glass in one swallow and reached for another. He had not come here to make a fool of himself over a woman, he reminded himself forcibly; there was more important things to attend to.

Forcing himself to look away from Cynara, he glanced around the crowded room, searching for Thomas Hale. But again and again, without his being aware of it, his eyes came back to Cynara, and he knew that before the evening was over, he had to speak to her alone.

"Beautiful woman, what?" a voice said in his ear. "It's a pity, though, isn't it?"

Evan turned. A foppish young man was standing beside him, and Evan grimaced at the strong, sweet scent of cologne that drifted toward him. The man postured, one hand on his hip, staring insolently at Cynara, and Evan disliked him at once. He was about to move away without answering, when the significance of the young man's remark struck him. "A pity?" Evan repeated coldly. "What do you mean?"

The man gestured haughtily in Cynara's direction, increasing Evan's dislike even more. "I refer, of course, to the fact that she is a convict." He sniffed disdainfully. "I never thought to see the day when felons would be allowed to mix in polite society, no matter how beautiful they were."

Evan had a sudden urge to take this sneering young man and fling him up against the wall. "You're mistaken," he said, as coolly as he was able.

The man shook his head. "Oh, no," he replied, affecting a yawn. "Thomas has certainly made every effort to inform one and all that he rescued his wife from a transportation ship. Rather a coy way of proving to us what a great humanitarian he is, is it not?"

The young man sauntered away, leaving a white-faced Evan staring blindly after him. Was it possible that that insolent fop was telling the truth? No, he would not believe it. Cynara a convict? Even the idea was absurd. And yet, why would the man lie?

Evan recalled suddenly the rumor that Hale had married, and that the bride had arrived on a transport ship. He had heard the tale some months ago, but he had discredited both stories, the first because Hale had never brought his bride to Sydney, the latter because he could not imagine Hale taking a convict as a wife. He had dismissed the rumors, eventually forgetting them completely—until tonight.

Now, observing Cynara, seeing the elegant gown she wore, the diamonds around her throat and in her ears, he knew that one part of the story had been true. He ignored utterly the convict tale; it was too ridiculous to believe. But the other. . .

Evan followed Cynara with narrowed eyes, enraged at the thought that she was married to the man he considered his enemy. It certainly hadn't taken her long to find a rich husband, he thought contemptuously. But then, hadn't he always known that Cynara could take care of herself? Having failed with Myles, she had moved on to bigger game, and had found herself one of the richest prizes of all in Thomas Hale.

Disgusted, infuriated with himself for the blind rage he felt toward Cynara, Evan put his empty glass on the table and made his way abruptly to a side door. As much as he wanted to leave right now, he could not. He had not come all this way to go without confronting Thomas Hale, but he knew that if he spoke to him now he would lose his temper and accomplish nothing but to make himself appear a fool.

The side door led to a veranda that extended down one wall of the house. Evan walked to the rail that looked out over a shadowed garden, fighting the urge to walk down the steps and claim his horse to ride away from here and never return. Instead, he took a cheroot from the silver case LeCroix had given him, and proceeded to light it. When he realized that his hands were shaking as he struck the match, he flung it angrily away from him over the rail and took a deep breath, trying to steady himself. Just seeing Cynara again had revived memories that he had thought buried, and he was furious that she had caused him to lose control of himself in this appalling manner.

Shifting his weight, Evan wondered angrily why no other woman had ever affected him in this way; with all the others, he could walk away, unmoved; but not with Cynara. It was almost as if she were a part of him that could not be cut away; a part of himself that he needed to be complete, whole.

Muttering an oath at the absurdity of his thoughts, Evan glanced to one side, and froze. As if he had conjured up her presence, Cynara had stepped out onto the veranda, some distance away from him. He stood motionless in the shadows as she walked to the rail and looked out across the darkness, unaware of him.

He watched her, telling himself that he was not affected by her at all. But even the way she stood there, her head lifted defiantly though she thought herself alone, set his pulse racing, as it had when he had seen her dancing, and he took a few steps toward her. The light from the doorway behind her shone on her profile, and he saw that her face was strained and white. The gown she wore shimmered as she moved, and when his eyes dropped to the rapid rise and fall of her breasts against the low bodice, his hand tightened involuntarily on the rail.

And then she turned and saw him standing there, and the deep green eyes that he remembered so well widened. Her lips parted slightly with surprise, and he had the fleeting thought that he had never seen her look as beautiful as she appeared in that moment. He was so close now that he could see the burgundy highlights in her hair; so close that he could have touched the dark fringe of her lashes as she lowered her eyes.

Staring at her, Evan felt weak, his breath was short, as though he had run for miles. She was so beautiful, so desirable. There was a frenzied pounding in his head, and a swelling of blood in his loins. He wanted to crush his mouth down her lips, savoring the sweet taste of her; he wanted to run his hands over her slender body that aroused him to the point of madness. He wanted to make love to her, here, on the veranda, with the music swelling triumphantly in the background, and the caress of the night breeze on their writhing bodies. Both of them would be oblivious to everything but the sight and taste and scent of each other; oblivious to anything but their passion and joy in being together at last. He was about to reach blindly for her when she looked up again.

Extending her hand, she said only, "Evan. What a surprise."

The coolness of her voice was like a slap in the face. Enraged, he stared at her; his hands, which had wanted to caress her, now desiring instead to shake her senseless. He could feel himself stiffening, every muscle in his body tightening, as he fought to control both anger and desire. Bowing over her hand, he muttered something in reply; he didn't know what. The moment was gone, and when he straightened again, he had a tight rein on his emotions. Two could play the game, he thought furiously, agonizingly. He would not let her know how close he had come to surrender.

Thinking about it now, as he dressed, he could not remember the rest of the conversation. He only knew that her remoteness had angered him, that he had wanted to shake her and embrace her at the same time. They had spoken reservedly to each other, when all the time he had wanted to shout at her and demand to know why she had married Thomas Hale. There had been so many questions he had wanted to ask, so many answers he would have demanded from her, and yet in the end they had said nothing to each other, acting like strangers meeting for the first time and detesting one another at first sight.

There had been only one moment when his control had broken. From the depths of some nameless emotion, he had spoken her name. He had heard the longing in his voice with dismay; he had not meant to betray himself so openly, and yet he could not call back the sound. He could only stand there, watching with amazement as her expression became open and vulnerable. He had reached out for her, and to his surprise, her hand trembled as it touched his.

But then Thomas Hale had suddenly appeared, and the moment was gone, as if it had never been. If indeed it ever had existed, Evan thought now, wondering if it had all been his imagination.

"Evan?"

Evan looked up from pulling on his coat. Preoccupied with his thoughts, he had forgotten Sarah completely. She was standing in front of him, her expression betraying her anxiety.

"Evan, what is it? You look so angry."

"Angry?" He forced himself to laugh shortly as he swung her off her feet and kissed her soundly. "How could I be angry with you, Sarah? Didn't you rescue me from myself last night?"

But Sarah had seen the quick flash of pain in his eyes, and she wondered. Evan's lovemaking the night before, despite all the liquor he had consumed, had surprised her with its savagery. She had never known him to be so fierce, so . . . so driven. It was almost as though he had been trying to exorcise a demon—or a woman.

Sarah was surprised at the thought, and she looked quickly away from Evan in case he should see her sudden distress. Dismayed, she rejected the idea that she was jealous; it had never happened to her before with one of her customers, and she would not admit the possibility now. It was just that she liked Evan, she told herself—and why shouldn't she? He was an excellent lover, considerate and exciting at the same time. He had never made her feel, as had so many other men, that she was just a body to be used and then forgotten until physical need drove him to her again.

But all the same, to her intense chagrin, she heard herself asking, without being able to stop the words, "Who is she, Evan?"

She knew at once that the question had been a grave error. Evan turned to her so angrily that she backed away from him, appalled at his savage expression.

"Who is she?" Evan repeated fiercely. "Perhaps you had better explain what you mean."

Sarah faltered before the hard gaze of his eyes. "Forget it," she said, forcing lightness when she had the absurd desire to burst into tears. Glancing down, away from his angry glare, she brushed a spot of lint from his coat. When she looked up again, it was with a determined smile. "Come back and see me soon, all right?" she asked.

Evan stared at her for a moment longer, the crimson color gradually leaving his face as he controlled his anger. Was his damnable preoccupation with Cynara so obvious, he asked himself, or had he betrayed himself in some way last night? Cursing inwardly, he couldn't remember.

He saw that Sarah's face was strained, her eyes troubled despite her effort to smile. He bent down and kissed her gently, suddenly ashamed of his outburst. When he straightened, he said softly, "I'd like to come back, Sarah— if you want me to."

"Oh, Evan! Of course I do."

He took his hat and gloves from the table, turning to look at her from the door. "Thank you, Sarah," he said, and was gone.

Thoughtfully, Sarah went to the window and pulled back the curtain. In a few minutes, she saw Evan's horse being brought around, and then Evan himself coming out to claim the animal. His black hair glistened in the sun as he mounted, and Sarah felt a stir of excitement at the way he sat his horse. Even the fact that he wore last night's formal evening clothes in the middle of the day did not detract from his handsome appearance; somehow, on Evan, it seemed perfectly natural, where anyone else would have looked ridiculous.

Sarah waited at the window, wondering if he would look up before he rode away. But he did not. Without a backward glance, he sat his tall hat at a casual angle on his head, and touched his horse lightly with his heels. The animal sprang forward, carrying him away from the house, and Sarah stood at the window until she could see him no longer. Who was she, Sarah wondered, the woman who had captured Evan's heart? He had not admitted it, but she had struck a nerve with her question. Whoever she was, Sarah thought, the woman was in his blood. She had to be, if he had tried so savagely to drive her away last night— and failed.

Smiling sadly to herself, Sarah let the curtain fall back into place.

CHAPTER TWENTY-ONE

"I THINK IT'S TIME FOR US to have a talk," Evan said abruptly to Vincent LeCroix the night after the ball at Tamoora. He had waited all day before approaching Vincent, preferring to begin this discussion away from the office and interested ears, but now, with the two of them alone in the library, he could wait no longer. He was sure that LeCroix knew something about Sean Ward, and he intended to find out what it was.

"A talk?" LeCroix was startled. Glancing quickly at Evan's set face, he gave him one of the whiskeys he had just poured, and motioned Evan to a chair. Faintly alarmed at Evan's manner, he sat down in the one opposite, and said, more calmly than he felt, "What about?"

Evan ignored the offer of a seat. He strode to the fireplace instead, setting the untouched glass on the mantle. He turned back to LeCroix. "About Sean Ward," he said evenly.

LeCroix was in the act of taking a swallow from his own glass. He sputtered and choked, his face reddening. "Who?" he managed to say as he grabbed for his handkerchief.

"Don't be coy, Vincent. It doesn't become you."

"I wasn't—"

"I remember your asking the first time we met if I knew a man named Sean Ward," Evan continued, overriding him. "And last night Thomas Hale asked me the same question. Now I want to know who Sean Ward is, and why I should have known him."

LeCroix cleared his throat. He looked up at Evan, standing obdurately by the fireplace, and thought quickly. In the months since he and Evan had returned to Australia, Le-Croix had sent out discreet inquiries into the fate of Sean Ward and his family, and had been rewarded with some very interesting information. But how much to tell Evan?

He decided that at this point it would be wise to proceed cautiously, and judge from Evan's reaction exactly what to reveal.

"Evan," he said carefully, "You must promise to be truthful with me if I tell you what I know. Will you do that much, at least?"

It was Evan's turn to heistate. During the course of their association, he had come to respect LeCroix: he had also learned to trust him, as much as he would ever allow himself to trust anyone. But to be completely truthful? It was too much to ask, even for Vincent, and Evan equivocated.

"As much as I can," he answered finally.

LeCroix sighed. It would have to do, he thought; at least he hadn't received a flat no.

Taking a deep breath, Vincent said, "This is very important, Evan. Had you ever heard of a family named Ward before I asked you about Sean?" He watched Evan carefully as he waited for the response.

"And if I have?"

LeCroix sighed again. This was going to be more difficult than he thought. "If you have," he replied with some asperity, "There might be some connection between them and Sean Ward."

"What connection?"

"Damn it, Evan! Why all this evasiveness? Do you actually think I'm trying to trap you in some way? Me? After all this time?"

Evan had the grace to flush. He shook his head, but didn't answer.

"Well, then?" LeCroix demanded.

"I don't understand how there could possibly be a connection between a Ward family in England and the Wards in Australia," he said stubbornly. "After all, it isn't an uncommon name."

"If you could be honest with me, perhaps we might be able to discover a relationship after all!" LeCroix said sharply, losing patience.

Evan stared at Vincent's reddened face for a long moment. It was obvious that LeCroix was angry, and perhaps he had every reason to be, Evan admitted to himself. Abruptly, he took his glass from the mantle and drained it, making a sudden decision.

"All right, Vincent," he said, throwing himself into the chair LeCroix had indicated earlier. "But this matter is strictly between us."

LeCroix nodded solemnly. "Of course."

Evan took a deep breath. "There was a family named Ward—John and Cornelia Ward, and . . . their son, Myles. I was born on the estate, Lyrebird Manor—"

"Lyrebird Manor?" LeCroix interrupted, startled. He had seen the flash of hatred in Evan's eyes when he had mentioned Myles, but he forgot that now in his agitation. "You did say Lyrebird Manor?"

"Yes. I never thought about the significance of the name until I came here—"

"Lad, you don't know!"

Evan stared at Vincent, nonplussed, as the man heaved his bulk out of the chair and began pacing back and forth in front of him with excitement.

"I knew there had to be some connection!" LeCroix crowed triumphantly. "Your resemblance couldn't have been mere coincidence—why, you're the image of old Sean himself, and this proves it!"

"What are you talking about?"

LeCroix stabbed his finger in the air toward Evan. "Do you know what the name of Sean's estate was?" he asked excitedly. Without waiting for an answer, he continued dramatically, "It was Lyrebird Hill! Lyrebird Hill! Do you know what that means?"

"It doesn't mean anything, Vincent. You're just grasping at straws—"

"Like hell I am! Listen, from what I've been able to piece together"— he didn't tell Evan that this piecing together had taken many months and a great deal of money— "Sean

Ward was originally from England. He came here to make
his fortune, and believe me, he did! Lyrebird Hill was one of
the finest wheat and cattle ranches in this part of the country
during Sean's time, and that's saying a great deal for those
days, when the colony was just beginning! But what's even
more important—"

"What happened to it? Lyrebird Hill. I've never heard of
it."

For the first time, LeCroix seemed uncomfortable.
Should he tell Evan that Sean's estate had been annexed to
Tamoora after Sean's death? No; he decided not to mention
that. Evan was no fool; he would wonder why. Still, he had
to say something; Evan was staring at him, curious over his
hesitation.

He said finally, hoping that Evan would accept his explanation without further question, "It was sold. But—"

"To whom?"

LeCroix winced inwardly. He waved his hand dismissively, answering, "It doesn't matter, does it?"

"I don't know—does it?"

Evan was watching him intently. Damn it all, LeCroix
thought irritably; does nothing go by him? Aloud, he replied firmly, "No, it doesn't matter, Evan. The important
thing is that right before his death, Sean sent his son to
England. Apparently, he wanted the boy, Aron, to meet
his—"

To LeCroix's surprise, Evan's voice held a strangled
sound as he interrupted, "Aron was Sean's son? Are you
absolutely sure?"

"Yes," LeCroix answered, staring in amazement at
Evan's suddenly pale face. "Why—did you know him?"

Evan shook his head, glancing away from the puzzlement
on LeCroix's face. "No, I didn't know him," he replied in a
low voice. "But he was at the Manor, a long time ago—
before I was born . . . "

"Are you sure?"

"I . . . remember a friend of mine speaking of him."

"Then—" Excitement rekindled in LeCroix's eyes. He started to speak excitedly, but at the bitterness in Evan's expression, he paused. "Did you know you father, Evan?" he asked quietly. "Or your mother?"

"No," Evan replied flatly. "According to John Ward, my mother was a slut who was working as one of the maids at the manor. My father—" he shrugged. "John never told me. Not that it matters. Whoever he was—" he looked up at LeCroix "and there's no proof that it was Aron, Vincent—he didn't marry my mother. I'm sure of that."

"How do you know?"

How did he know? Evan felt a sharp stab of hope, then suppressed it firmly. Surely Oliver would have known, he thought. And if he had, Evan felt that the old man would never have kept the information from him deliberately, especially when there had been so many instances during his childhood and youth when Evan had expressed bitterness about his illegitimacy. "I know," Evan said, with finality.

"Well, before we eliminate the possibility," LeCroix insisted, "Perhaps we can talk to someone who might know more than you do."

"Who?"

LeCroix sighed regretfully. "I only know her name—Hester Cord," he said. "She was Sean's sister-in-law—his wife Emily's sister. Hester lived with the family here for a time, before Sean died, and before the fire—"

"Fire? What fire?"

"Apparently, directly after Sean died, there was a fire out that way. Everyone except this Hester Cord perished. Supposedly Aron was in England at the time, and he was sent for, but no one ever heard from him again. It seems that Hester, if she is still living, is the only surviving member of Sean's family."

"And you don't know how to trace her."

Evan's voice was flat, and LeCroix patted his arm awkwardly. "I'm sorry, Evan. But I haven't given up hope yet; I have a man working on it right now."

Suddenly realizing the magnitude of what LeCroix had tried to do for him, Evan stood and offered his hand. "Vincent, I don't know how to—"

"Forget it," LeCroix said gruffly, embarrassed. He grasped Evan's hand tightly. "Maybe if we both put our heads together we can find her . . . "

Evan nodded, obviously suppressing disbelief. He collected their glasses and went to the cabinet to pour fresh drinks. "Do you think this Hester Cord might still be in Australia?" he asked quietly.

"It's possible," LeCroix replied. He accepted the drink from Evan, and added tentatively, "But she would be an old woman now, Evan. And what's even worse, the rumor is that she went a little mad after the fire. Even if you found her, she might not be able to tell you anything. Oh, damn it all! I shouldn't have gotten your hopes up!" he burst out. "I'm sorry, Evan."

"There's nothing to be sorry about, Vincent," Evan said reassuringly. "I wouldn't have gotten this far without you, and I'm grateful.

And he was grateful, he thought, as his mind leaped ahead to the possibilities. If he could find Hester Cord, if she could remember anything that might be a help to him—if, if . . . Irritated at the absurd leap of hope he felt over what could easily be a lost cause, Evan said good night to LeCroix, and went slowly to his room, wondering if it would even be worth the effort to initiate a search for the missing Hester Cord.

Restlessly he undressed and fell wearily into bed. The events of the night before were catching up with him. Did he really want to find Hester Cord? He asked himself as he pounded the pillow impatiently, trying to find a comfortable position. Or was it all just a pointless chase?

Hands behind his head, he stared unseeingly up at the ceiling. Forcing himself to be honest, he had to admit that he had wanted to know who his father was from the very first time a young Myles had taunted him with his illegitimacy.

It had been so important to him as a child, he remembered, this ignorance of who his father had been. And when Myles had taunted him, he had been forced to resort to the only defense he had: his fists. Again and again he had been punished for fighting Myles, but no threat on John's part had ever been effective enough to restrain Evan when he heard Myles shrilling: "Bastard! Bastard!"

LeCroix was so sure that his resemblance to Sean Ward was no coincidence. Perhaps that was a beginning, Evan thought. He would prove to himself who he was. He would find this Hester Cord; he would find her and demand that she tell him what she knew about Aron. At least then he would know if the cry that had resounded throughout his youth had been true or not. And if it turned out that he was no bastard after all, Evan thought savagely, then he had one more score to settle with John Ward.

Evan was morosely silent the next morning at the breakfast table, and LeCroix, after one look at his face, decided to retreat behind yesterday's copy of the *Sydney Gazette*. He hadn't had time to read the paper the day before, a fact that disgruntled him, for he preferred to keep his finger on the pulse of things, no matter how insignificant. But today as he read, he was unable to concentrate on the printed lines before him. With one eye on Evan, he barely scanned the articles within until a name fairly leaped off the page at him.

"My God!" he exclaimed sharply. "Evan, did you hear about this?"

His hand shaking with excitement, LeCroix spread the paper on the table, pointing to the item. Evan frowned when he saw the name Thomas Hale, and he made a dismissive motion with his hand. But LeCroix was insistent, stabbing his finger at the page. "Read it!"

More to please LeCroix than for his own interest, Evan took the page and began reading. His eyes widened slightly as he scanned the obituary on Thomas Hale, and when he finished, he put the paper down with a slight smile. "So," he said softly. "Hale is dead."

"The old bastard killed himself!" LeCroix said with some relish as he reclaimed the paper and folded it carefully so that the article was on top. From time to time, as he sipped at his coffee, he glanced at it almost fondly.

"Not exactly," Evan pointed out absently in response to LeCroix's remark, "It does say that there was a hunting accident—"

"Hmm. Yes. So it does." Vincent patted the paper lightly with his hand, his expression thoughtful. "I wonder what will happen to Tamoora now?" he mused. "Didn't I hear somewhere that Hale had taken a young wife . . . ?"

Evan's reaction to this was so startling that LeCroix gaped at him in astonishment as he threw back his chair and stood up. "Excuse me, Vincent," Evan said hurriedly. "There's something I have to do—"

Without waiting for a response, Evan went swiftly from the room, leaving LeCroix staring after him in bewilderment. What had he said? Just an innocuous remark about Hale's new wife. Frowning, LeCroix poured more coffee for himself and sat there, sipping it, wondering if he had correctly interpreted the expression on Evan's face. For a moment, he had thought that Evan seemed excited— hopeful—but of course that was absurd. Did Evan really think that Hale's widow would give him any information regarding her own husband?

Alarmed at the thought, LeCroix half rose from his own chair. Should he follow Evan? No, that was ridiculous. And yet, LeCroix cringed at the thought of Evan's losing his temper in front of the man's recently bereaved wife, and he stood up again indecisively, staring at the door Evan had rushed through moments before. He heard the stamp of hoofs in the stable area as Evan ordered his horse brought out, and he was about to follow him when he saw that he was too late. The girth had scarcely been buckled before Evan was in the saddle, and horse and rider were cantering toward the street before LeCroix could move from the dining table.

Irritated with himself for not acting sooner, LeCroix called for his carriage to be readied, and he settled back for another cup of coffee. He would go to the office as was his custom, he thought, and mind his own business. Evan was a man grown; he would not take kindly to being followed, even by a well-intentioned old man like himself, he thought wryly.

But in spite of his efforts not to worry about what Evan might do, LeCroix's expression betrayed his anxiety as he climbed into his carriage thirty minutes later. It was only by exercising the greatest restraint that he stopped himself from ordering the coachman to take the road to Tamoora after all. It was so unlike Evan to act impulsively that he was worried.

Evan was halfway to Tamoora before he pulled his horse to a walk from the fast trot he had demanded from the animal most of the way. What was he doing, dashing out to Tamoora like some hot-headed young fool? Did he think Cynara would swoon and fall into his arms, thanking him for coming to her? As annoyed as he was for giving in to impulse, Evan had to smile in grim amusement at the thought of Cynara throwing herself at him in gratitude for his sudden appearance. She might throw herself at him, all right, but it would probably be in a fit of temper over his conceit than out of gratitude. So why was he going?

He had known from the instant he had finished reading the announcement of Hale's death that he had to go to her; nothing else had mattered but that. As soon as he knew Cynara was free, he had rushed off, and to hell with the consequences. She might spurn him—she certainly would try—but this one time in his life he would declare his true feelings.

And what were his feelings? Was he even sure he knew himself? It had been agony for him, knowing that she was Hale's wife; the knowledge had eaten away him like a festering wound, until he was obsessed with it. But now Hale was dead, and he wasn't about to lose his opportunity.

He had lost her once; he wouldn't let her go again. He wanted to have Cynara with him, to protect her.

Protect her! Evan grimaced at the thought, thinking how Cynara would disdain the idea that she needed his protection. But she did need it, he assured himself, whether she admitted it or not. And he wanted to be the one to give her things, to care for her, to . . . He stopped, pulling back on the reins so abruptly that his horse tossed its head in surprise as he came to a halt.

Evan was surprised as well. He had been about to admit that he loved Cynara. Loved her. He examined the thought almost gingerly. What did he know of love? he asked himself scornfully.

What matter the definition? He wanted her, yes. Sometimes his physical desire for her was enough to shake him as he pictured her in his arms, in his bed. They would be good together, he knew. He had long ago sensed the fire in her, and he wanted to be the man who fanned the blaze in her with his own passion. Once aroused, she would be all woman, surrendering and demanding at the same time, seductive, tempting, wanton. She would be all women to him, all he would ever want or need. They would know each other in the fever of passion, and in the tenderness of love.

But even more than his physical need for her, he wanted her with him . . . because she was Cynara. He needed her to be complete, whole. It was as though she was his other half, the part of himself that could be gentle, tender, loving. Closing his eyes, he realized that all his life he had been searching for someone with whom he could be himself, someone who would understand the terrible things that drove him, and would somehow forgive him for them. He wanted someone who would be encouraging, supportive... loving. He didn't know why he felt Cynara was the woman he sought; she had certainly never offered him encouragement, or even the smallest indication that she loved him. But there was something between them, some

powerful attraction that transcended passion. He had recognized this from some deep private place inside himself,
and he knew that he and Cynara were meant to be.

But then another thought struck him, and he sat there, in
the middle of the road, his face suddenly grim. The hot sun
beat down on his head—in his haste, he had forgotten his
hat—but he did not feel the perspiration beading his
forehead. A kookaburra laughed at him from a gum tree, a
flock of galahs took flight ahead of him, but he heard and
saw neither. He was thinking of Myles, and he knew that as
much as he wanted Cynara, he desired his revenge against
those at Lyrebird Manor even more. He couldn't give that
up, even for her.

Evan spurred his horse forward. Would Cynara wait for
him while he bolted off to England to complete his little
chore? He laughed aloud at the thought, jerking his head
derisively at himself. Surely he knew her better than that!
By the time he returned, she would have found someone
else; Cynara was not a woman to be set aside or left behind;
she was too vital, too beautiful. If he left her here, she would
marry again, if only to spite him, he thought angrily. No, he
would have to take her with him if he wanted her at all.

And how would he do that? he asked himself curtly.
Impossible to think of asking her to become his mistress; she
would never stand for it. And to be honest, he wouldn't
want her to. No, he didn't want her as his mistress, he
wanted her as his . . . wife.

His wife! God, what was he thinking of? Thrusting the
idea from his mind, Evan rode on, only to pull the confused
animal to a halt again. Damn it all, he thought angrily, if that
was the only way to have her, he would have to ask her to
marry him.

His abrupt decision both elated and dismayed him. But
his mind was made up; now that he had come to this
momentous conclusion he was anxious to carry it through.
He urged the horse forward again, never once thinking of
the possibility that Cynara would refuse. She would go

back to England with him whether she wished to or not. Once they were married, she would have to follow him. Once he was in possession of Lyrebird Manor, nothing else mattered; he would have accomplished everything he had set out to do and more. After that, he would even return to Australia, if that was what she wished. He was quite a land-owner himself now, he thought; he would build a house for her, a home they would both be proud of, if she would only do this one thing for him.

He thought of Tamoora not at all. With Hale's death, it had ceased to exist for him, except for the remote thought that if Cynara inherited any part of it, she could do as she wished with it. He smiled, almost tenderly, at the thought of Cynara toying with the management of Tamoora. How she would enjoy that independence, he thought; it would be good for her to have something all her own—but not too much, he thought wryly; he wanted her to depend upon him, as well. He smiled again, ruefully, admitting to himself for the first time that Cynara, if she put her mind to it, could probably manage both him and anything else she chose to with ease. Amused and alarmed at this admission, Evan thought that he would have to see to it that she never discovered the extent of her power over him, or he would be lost.

He touched his horse again, lightly, and after a slight hesitation, the animal broke into a canter. Suddenly, Evan was very eager to arrive at Tamoora.

It wasn't until he had passed through the great gates that opened the drive to the house that Evan had his first doubt. What if she had actually loved Thomas Hale? What would he do if she was prostrate with grief and refused to see him? The thought was so repugnant that he grimaced. It wasn't possible that she had loved him, he thought; there had been no evidence of tenderness or affection between Hale and Cynara the night of the ball, he remembered. On the contrary, Cynara had seemed almost repulsed when Hale had put his arm around her. And as for Hale himself, he had treated her distantly, as if she were no more than an ornament he had acquired for his house. Evan recalled too well his own outrage at Hale's disdainful treatment of Cynara, and he was sure now that there had been no love between them. Whatever it was that had drawn them together, he hoped that it had disappeared with Hale's death. If it hadn't, Evan thought grimly as he came up to the house, he had ridden a long way for nothing.

Tying his horse to the rail, Evan bounded up the front steps, oblivious to the convention requiring a more sedate approach in the presence of death. His hand was at the ornate door knocker before he noticed the almost deserted aspect of the place. Glancing around, he saw that there were no servants, no workers, in sight—surely an unusual circumstance in the middle of the day. Then he thought that everyone might all be at the service—in his hurry he had forgotten to ascertain the time of the funeral—in which case he would have to wait.

Damn it all! he thought irritably. He had no desire to speak to Cynara while she was still swathed in those detestable widow's weeds! He should have forced himself to wait a decent interval before racing out here like some besotted fool. It was too late now; he could hardly get back on his horse and leave without at least offering his condolences, hypocritical as it would be. He allowed the door knocker to fall from his hand.

To his surprise, the door was answered seconds later by a woman who was presumably the housekeeper, for she had a ring of keys at her waist. She regarded him suspiciously, in silence, until he was forced to introduce himself.

"My name is Evan Calder," he said. "I would like to speak to Cy . . . to Mrs. Hale, if I may."

The tight-lipped answer, when it came, astonished him. "There is no Mrs. Hale."

Evan stared at her, nonplussed. "I beg your pardon?"

"I said, there is no Mrs. Hale."

Evan felt his temper rising. "Don't be ridiculous!" he said

curtly, wondering if he should brush past her into the entryway and search for Cynara himself. "Please send for her at once."

The woman shook her head. "I'm sorry—"

To Evan's immediate outrage, she began to shut the door in his face. He put his booted foot inside, forcing it open again. "Look here!" he said sharply. "I don't know what your game is, but I demand to speak to Mrs. Hale—now!"

The woman was forced to yield to Evan's superior strength. Ungraciously, she said, "I told you before, there is no Mrs. Hale. They were never married. There! Now I've said what the whole countryside will know before long. They were never married!"

"I find that difficult to believe," Evan said, holding his temper with an effort. "Especially when I was introduced to Mrs. Hale at the ball just the other night."

"I don't care what you believe, Mister. It's true. Mr. Whitley told us all this morning after the mis—after that woman disappeared."

"Disappeared! What do you mean?"

"Well, what do you think I mean? She's gone. She must have skipped last night, when she found out about—"

"Where did she go?"

"That's what all of us would like to know," the woman said darkly. "It's a good thing for her that she didn't take anything—at least, nothing we've been able to find yet. It's going to be bad enough for her as it is—there's still penalties, you know, for escaped convicts . . . Say, mister, are you all right?"

Evan had stepped back, his face paling. There it was again, that reference to Cynara as a convict. He looked at the woman's set face, and managed to say, "You said something about a convict. Surely you must be mistaken."

The woman jerked her head. "A convict I said, and a convict I meant. The master took her off one of those transport ships, and made her into a lady. He was a good man, a kind—"

"I'm sure he was everything you say"—and more, Evan thought grimly—"but there has to be an error here. I would like to speak to—who did you say?"

"Mr. Whitley? He's the master's lawyer—"

"Mr. Whitley, then," Evan cut in impatiently. "I must see him at once."

The woman shook her head, and Evan ground his teeth together in rage. One second more, he vowed, and he would throw her aside and go looking for the man himself.

"He isn't here now," the housekeeper answered quickly, seeing Evan's face darken. "There were things he had to attend to—namely, notifying that cousin of the master's— the one who inherited all this." The woman swept her arm out, indicating Tamoora. She added, sniffing disdainfully, "I just hope the man knows what he's doing—else I pack my bags and leave at once. I never did like the idea of a stranger here, at Tamoora."

"Yes, yes," Evan said irritably. "Where can I find Mr. Whitley? Tell me that much at least."

"He has an office in Parramatta," the woman offered reluctantly. "But it won't do any good!" she called out as Evan leaped down the steps toward his horse. "He doesn't know where she is, either!"

"Mr. Whitley, I have to find her!"

"I'm sorry, young man, but I can't help you. I don't know where she is."

They stared at each other across the polished expanse of desk in Gerald Whitley's office. Evan, drumming his fingers steadily on the desk top, tried to control his temper. A drop of sweat rolled from his forehead into his eyes, and he brushed at it impatiently. He had ridden as fast as the horse could take him to Parramatta, never once thinking that Gerald Whitley would not be able to help him find Cynara. He sat now in the office, staring at the man with the pudgy white face and soft hands, and the only thing that prevented Evan from reaching across the desk to shake any information out of him was the concerned expression in the lawyer's eyes.

"I really wish I could help," Gerald sighed. "I admired Cynara . . . "

"Admired? Why do you speak of her in the past tense?" Evan demanded.

Gerald passed a hand in front of his eyes. "Perhaps it would be best to let her go," he suggested gently. "According to the terms of the will—"

"Yes," Evan said harshly. "What exactly were the terms of this will?"

Gerald debated to himself. It was really none of this rash young man's business what Thomas Hale had done with his estate, and yet . . . Gerald *had* liked Cynara; he had always thought she had spirit and character, along with that incredible beauty she seemed so unaware of. What was more, he hadn't liked what Thomas had done at the time he made his will, and he didn't like it now. It wasn't fair, certainly not for Cynara, and not for him, either. Had Thomas really expected him to go along whole heartedly with his treacherous scheme? He felt a stirring of disgust at his own complicity, and suddenly, his decision made, he glanced up at Evan. "You know, of course, that Cynara was a convict—"

"I had heard rumors to that effect," Evan replied coldly. "But I did not believe them."

"Well, there's evidence, whether we choose to believe it or not."

"We?"

Gerald appeared uncomfortable under Evan's close scrutiny. He flushed, but said firmly, "Yes. We. I didn't believe it myself . . . until I saw the papers."

"Do you have them?"

"Oh, yes. They were part of the estate."

"Let me see them." Sure of compliance, Evan held out his hand.

Reluctant, but realizing that since he had gone this far, he might as well continue, Gerald searched through the papers on his desk, and extracted one from the bottom of the pile.

He passed it across to Evan. "It's somewhat . . . irregular," he said. "But then, convict records sometimes are."

Evan paid no attention; he was busy reading. When he finished, he threw the papers contemptuously on the desk and said flatly, "It has to be a forgery."

"I'd like to agree. Unfortunately, there is no way of proving it, is there?"

"The sentence says seven years—for what? No charges have been listed. Nor," he added darkly, "any mention of a trial."

"Still—"

Evan slammed his hand down on the desk, causing Gerald to jump. "I want to buy them," he said harshly.

Gerald considered this for a moment, his lawyer's mind working out the possibilities. Finally, after a long look at Evan's set face, he nodded and smiled. "That could be arranged, I think." He hesitated, then added softly, "Are we of the same mind?"

For the first time a ghost of a smile appeared on Evan's lips. He inclined his head. "Once I own the papers, I intend to free her. The record will have to be attended to later. I will be returning to England in the near future, and can start proceedings there. But for the time being, this will have to do."

He stood. "How long will it take? The arrangements about the papers?"

"No time at all," Gerald replied happily, "If you will come with me to the magistrate's office . . . "

The papers were in Evan's pocket. Standing outside the magistrate's office in the hot, dusty street, Evan extended his hand to Gerald Whitley. "Thank you," he said quietly. "And if you hear anything . . . "

Gerald nodded. "I will let you know immediately." He paused. "I hope you find her," he added softly.

Evan's face was grim. "So do I, Mr. Whitley. So do I."

But where to look, he asked himself as he walked away from Whitley toward his tired horse. Where to look? The lawyer had told him that Cynara had disappeared the night before; no one had seen her leave, no one had seen her since. The servants had been sent out searching, but to no avail. She could be anywhere by now, Evan thought. Where would she go?

Taking the rein, Evan led his horse across to the livery. He would have to leave the animal here for the time being and arrange for another to take him back to Sydney; even in his hurry, he could not ask his horse to make the return trip that day; he had pushed it too far as it was.

The transaction complete, Evan transferred his saddle to a fresh horse. He swung up, pushing the animal into a fast trot, heading once again toward Sydney. He would have to ask Vincent's help, he thought. LeCroix had proved once before that he knew the right people; he might be able to come up with more information than Evan could garner by himself.

Without realizing it, Evan had urged the horse into a brisk canter, anxious to get back to Sydney and begin the search. He had to find Cynara, he thought distractedly; he had to find her before something happened to her.

Evan was halfway home when he passed the road leading to Michael's Inn. Wincing inwardly at the memory of his sojourn there after the ball, he rode past the turn-off. Thirsty as he was, he could not take time to stop; he had to get back before nightfall. A feeling of urgency was upon him. He admitted to the fear that Cynara could be lost, or injured, or—worst of all—taken by the homeless and often wanted men who were called bushrangers. Anything could happen to a woman on her own, and for the first time in his life, Evan found himself actually praying—that he would find Cynara, and before anyone else did.

He rode by the signpost stuck into the dirt at the side of the road. The wooden sign advertising the name of the Inn hung by one corner, the paint faded and peeling. Evan barely gave it a glance in passing. After his behavior there two nights before, he never wanted to enter the place again.

CHAPTER TWENTY-TWO

WHEN CYNARA WOKE THE MORNING after her flight from Tamoora, she lay for a moment in the bed, wondering where she was. The room was small and contained no furniture except the bed and a battered chest of drawers, and she looked around, trying to get her bearings. A pair of boots, the leather scuffed and cracked, stood by the door, and suddenly it all became clear. She sat up, her hands going to her mouth, and she winced as she touched her swollen lip.

She looked quickly at the door, almost expecting Ben Knowles to appear there. Instinctively, she clutched the sheet closer to her, and in that moment, she realized that she was naked. The horror of the night before flooded her mind, and she closed her eyes, uttering a groan. She hadn't dreamed it after all, she thought, and tears sprang into her eyes at the memory.

Angrily she brushed away the tears and sprang out of bed, running to the door. As she had half expected, it was locked, and she turned away, snatching up her shift and torn gown from the floor. Dressing quickly, she went to the window and looked down on the deserted yard. She must get away from this madman, she thought, wrapping her arms around her body. She had to get away—but how?

There was no escape at present; she knew only too well. Hadn't Knowles told her so the night before? Her hand came up to her face again, gingerly touching the cut at the corner of her mouth. He had made it clear last night that he would prevent any escape, and she reflected bitterly that it was her fault she was in the position she was in now. If she hadn't been both frightened of pursuit from Tamoora and weary, from stumbling around in the darkness in search of a place to stay the night, she would never have approached this disreputable place called Michael's Inn. Cursing the fate that had turned her footsteps in this direction, she relived in her mind the scene from the night before.

Knowles himself had answered her tentative knock at the back door. He had stood there, shining the lamp into her face so that she was unable to see him, and he had asked roughly, "Are you the girl from Sydney? You took your time getting here, didn't you?"

Cynara had tried to explain, but he had cut her off, almost dragging her inside. Fortunately she had had the sense to come around to the back door. He had pulled her with him into what appeared to be a kitchen, and beyond a thick, scarred door at the opposite end, she could hear the sound of drunken revelry. She shuddered to think what the reaction would have been from those drunken men if she had chanced to step into the main taproom.

Before she could collect herself enough to speak, Knowles had said, "You can start in here. Drue will take the bar for the rest of the night, since you're so late, but you can take her place tomorrow. The stupid slut—she can't even pour a dram without spilling it! I hope you know what you're about, else you'll go, too!"

Knowles had started to push a dirty apron at her, and then he had stopped, actually seeing her face for the first time, "You're not the one I sent for," he growled accusingly. "What happened to Sadie?"

"I don't know any Sadie," Cynara had answered, backing a step away from him as he pushed his face close to hers "I... I saw your light, and..." Cynara stopped, glancing quickly around the kitchen, listening to the raucous shouting in the room beyond. She couldn't stay here, she thought, no matter how tired she was. "Please, I've made a mistake," she said faintly, edging toward the door. "I have to leave now."

"Oh, you do, do you?"

He had placed himself between her and the doorway, blocking escape. He was a big man, barrel chested and broad shouldered, with greasy black hair and small, pale blue eyes. A thick stubble of beard covered the lower part of his face, making him appear even more menacing, and Cynara felt a sharp stab of fear at the way he stood there, hands on his hips, leering at her.

"Yes," she forced herself to say, "I must. If you would please get out of the way—"

"Oh, I don't think you'll be leaving just yet. I could use you around here. Yes," he added, licking his lips. "I certainly could do that."

"I don't think so," Cynara said sharply. "Now please get out of the way."

"Please, is it?" he mimicked, swaying slightly in the doorway. "Since you're so fine on manners, let me introduce myself." He bowed mockingly. "The name is Knowles. Ben Knowles. You can call me Ben. If you play your cards right, we'll get along fine."

"Listen to me, Mr. Knowles," she said swiftly, trying desperately not to show her fear of him. "If you don't permit me to leave at once, I'll—"

"You'll what?" He grinned. "To my mind, a pretty little lady like you doesn't wander into a place like this unless you're on the run from somethin'. Now what could it be?"

Did he know something? Was it possible that he had already been warned to be on the watch for her? Cynara felt the blood drain from her face as she put a hand on the table to steady herself. "I don't know what you mean," she said faintly.

"Oh, I think you do. And as long as we have an understandin' between us, there shouldn't be any trouble, should there?"

He dropped his hands to the table and leaned over it. She backed away again, unable to take her eyes from his face. "How about this?" he continued. "I won't say anythin' and you'll stay and work for me."

"Work for you!"

He nodded, staring deliberately at her breasts. "Yes. I think you'll work out much better than Sadie, when all's said and done. Oh, I do, indeed."

Cynara had the impression that he was stripping her naked with his eyes. The image was so repugnant to her that she stiffened, answering haughtily, "That is out of the question, Mr. Knowles."

"Is it? I don't think so."

He reached out so suddenly that she had no time to move away. Imprisoning her arm in a hard grip, he said softly, "And don't think to run away from me, girl. Terrible things can happen to a woman on her own out in the bush . . ."

Despite her fear, Cynara managed to free herself from him. "You can't force me to stay here!"

"Can't I?" His expression turned even uglier. "We'll see about that."

He stared after her. Seeing the door clear, Cynara leaped for it. Her hand was on the latch when he spun her around, pinning her against the wall, massive arms on either side of her shoulders. A blast of rum-laden breath hit her in the face as he bent close to her, and she turned her head away.

"You'll stay," he threatened. "If you know what's good for you."

"You can't do this!" she cried. "I—"

To her horror, he clamped one hand over her mouth, stopping her cry of protest. In the next instant, he had twisted one arm behind her back, pulling her away from the wall and toward the center of the room.

Her fear of a moment before was nothing compared to the terror she felt now as he propelled her toward a dark hole at one side of the kitchen. She struggled fiercely to break his grip, but he jerked her arm upwards behind her back so sharply that she thought it had been wrenched from its socket. She cried out, but the sound was muffled under his hand, and she heard him laugh. Tears of pain sprang into her eyes as he jerked her arm again, and she thought she would faint at the shaft of pain that lanced through her twisted arm.

She stumbled as he pushed her forward, and with an oath, he pulled her to her feet once more. Sagging under his grip,

Cynara tried to throw him off balance, but he was too strong for her. Cursing, he shoved her again.

The dark hole was a staircase. Her eyes widened as she realized that he intended to take her upstairs, and without thinking, knowing only that she must get away from him, she shoved her feet out as he pushed her onto the stairs. Locking her legs, she braced herself, leaning backwards into him. The scene was so similar to the one on the ship that she felt terror spreading through her. With a great effort she held onto consciousness, flailing at him with her free arm, trying to block the excruciating pain the movement caused in the arm still imprisoned behind her.

Somehow, she managed to hit him in the face, and he swore again, twisting her around to face him. His heavy arm lifted, and a split second before it happened, she raised her own arms, trying to defend herself. Her forearm deflected the blow he aimed at her face, and his fist slid to one side, striking her cheekbone instead. Dazed, she staggered back, and he swept her off her feet, throwing her over his shoulder like a sack of meal, carrying her up into the blackness of the floor above.

She heard a door crash open as he shoved one foot against it, and in the next instant he had thrown her down on a bed. She sprang up again, dashing toward the open door. In the darkness, she couldn't see, could only guess where the open doorway was, but she put her head down and ran. As she tried to rush past him, he reached out and caught her again. "Not so fast," he spat. "I'm not finished with you yet!"

He flung her down again. This time her head hit something solid, and great pinwheels of light flashed before her eyes, blinding her with pain. Before she could recover, he had gone to the door. She heard it slam, and following that, the harsh grate of the key in the lock. "I'll be back after a while," he called out. "Just you be awaitin' for me!"

His heavy footsteps sounded on the stairs as Cynara threw herself at the door. Fumbling in the darkness, she managed to find the latch, but as she had known, it would not yield to her frantic efforts to open it. God! How had this happened? Screaming, she beat her fists against the door until she was exhausted. No one heard her; no one came to help.

Sobbing, she turned away from the door and stumbled toward the dark shape of a dresser, where she could dimly perceive the outline of a lamp. Her hands shaking, she felt along the top of the dresser until her fingers came in contact with a box of matches. She took one and struck it, only to have it go out again when she was unable to hold it. Biting her lip, she willed her hands to be steady, and succeeded in lighting the lamp on her second attempt. Turning up the wick, she glanced around, praying that there was some way to escape.

The room was extremely small. Beside the chest of drawers, with the drawers hanging lopsidedly, articles of clothing half in and half out, the only other article of furniture was the bed, and from this she looked quickly away. A small window was set into the opposite wall, and Cynara ran toward it at once. Using all her strength, she managed to open the window and leaned out. Her heart sank.

The back wall of the inn swept away from her straight to the ground below. Even if she jumped, she would surely injure herself trying to escape this way, for the ground below seemed far away, and there was nothing to break her fall. A sob of frustration escaped her, and she tightened her lips, telling herself that she must be calm and try to think. She had no doubt what Knowles intended to do with her; she had no doubt that she would not be able to fight him off. He was too strong. But if she could surprise him in some way . . .

At the thought, she glanced quickly around the room again, searching for some kind of weapon to use against him. If she waited by the door for his return, she could attack him as he came in. If luck was with her, she could stun him long enough for her to escape. It was a desperate chance at best, but the only thing she could think of in this terrified state.

The room yielded nothing in the way of a weapon. The only thing she found was a pair of heavy hob-nailed boots, surely not sturdy enough to stun him, she thought, panicked. And yet, if she were desperate enough—if she hit him hard enough the first time—she just might daze him long enough to flee.

She waited behind the door for an hour or more. By the time she heard him coming up the stairs, her arms were stiff from holding the boots, and she was not sure she would be able to raise them, let alone hit him with enough force to stun him.

The key was in the lock. She was able to lift the boots after all when she heard that sound, and she waited, for what seemed an eternity, for the door to open. As soon as she saw the shape of his head pass through the open door, she brought the boots down with all the strength she was able to summon.

He gave a grunt of surprise, and staggered, his hand to his head. She did not wait to see the effect of her attack; without looking back, she leaped by him and out the door.

"Come back here, you slut! Come back here!"

The shouting behind her gave speed to her feet; she ran down the dark corridor, praying that she would see the stairs before she raced headlong into them and fell to the bottom. But she had no chance to find the staircase; a hand caught her in mid-stride, jerking her off her feet and flinging her against the wall.

She hit with enough force to knock the breath from her. Gasping, she tried to find her feet again, only to be shoved backwards. There was the flash of a hand through the air, and the strength behind the blow whipped her head back onto her shoulders. Before she could recover, he had grabbed her again, and was dragging her back along the corridor.

"Let . . . go of me!" she panted, clawing at his arm.

"Shut up!"

He pulled her along so rapidly that her feet went out from

under her again, and she fell. "Get up, you slut! Get up, I say!"

The hand descended again, cracking against the side of her head. Cynara screamed. The sound echoed through the corridor, and she screamed again, calling desperately for help.

A small dark shape appeared suddenly on the stairs to the attic. Cynara saw the form at the same time Knowles did, and she cried, "Help me! Help me—please!"

The shape did not move. Knowles had raised his fist, shaking it threateningly. "Get back to your place!" he shouted. "This is no affair of yours!"

To Cynara's horror, the form, which she could now see well enough to discern was a young girl, or woman, turned obediently and made her way back up the stairs. Cynara screamed after her, "Don't go! Get someone—"

Knowles laughed, and Cynara lunged backwards, trying frantically to get away from him. "Let go of me, you filthy monster!"

The girl was gone and Cynara knew that she was alone to fight him. Renewing her struggles, she kicked at him as he pulled her toward him again. Rewarded with a grunt of pain as her foot contacted his shin, she kicked out again, heaving her body away, trying to break his hold on her. He was too strong. With one last shove, he pushed her inside the room again and slammed the door behind him. Cynara faced him, her expression wild as he stood against the door, panting from exertion.

"Stay away from me!" she cried.

"Regular little hellcat, aren't you?" he gasped. "We'll see how much fight you have after I get through with you."

He took a step toward her and she backed away. When she felt something press into her spine, she dared a look behind her and saw to her horror that she had backed herself into a corner. There was no escape. Her hands formed into claws, she waited for him to come closer. She was beyond fear now; only the primitive urge to defend herself possessed her. So fierce was her expression that Knowles actually hesitated when he saw her face. Then, giving a short laugh, he lunged for her again.

She clawed at his face, his arms, his chest, as he grabbed her. Whipping her head back and forth as he struggled to kiss her, she beat at him with her fists. She did not scream again; she needed all her strength to fight this mountain of a man whose hands held her in a grip she couldn't break, no matter how hard she fought.

"Enough of this!" he panted.

He flung her away from him so abruptly that she staggered and fell. She was springing to her feet again when he put his foot against her shoulder, sending her sprawling backwards. Before she could recover, he had reached down, grabbing the neckline of her gown.

Cynara cried out as he ripped her bodice to the waist, and she scrambled backwards, trying to hold the torn edges together. He reached for her again, and this time she bit him, her teeth sinking deep into the fleshy part of his hand.

"You little bitch!" he howled, drawing back his hand. "By God! You won't do that again!"

He took her by the shoulders, lifting her from the floor in the same motion to throw her on the bed. Outraged she felt his hands on her breasts, and she tried to push him away. Suddenly, he was on top of her, ripping at his own clothing in a frenzy. Tears of rage and pain coursed down her face, she was covered with sweat from her struggles, but she could not hold him off any longer. Exhausted, she lay under him as he pounded away against her; she had no strength left to fight his assault on her body. Even when he entered her, thrusting against her so savagely that she thought she would be torn in two, she did not move. His hands were in her hair, holding her head as his mouth fastened wetly on hers, his tongue probed inside her mouth so deeply that she gagged. Her struggle before had excited him to fever pitch; he reached his climax in seconds, stiffening against her as he bellowed with ecstasy.

It was over. Cynara turned her face away from him, staring blankly at the wall beside the bed. His body was heavy, almost suffocating her, and yet she made no move to get away from him. What did it matter, she thought dully. He had proved that he was stronger than she, that her struggles against him were useless. She didn't care anymore what he did to her; she was too tired to care.

But as she lay there in the darkness, listening to his breathing evolve into loud snores, she knew that it did matter. She had lost this battle against him, but she was not going to give up. She had never completely surrendered herself to any man who forced himself upon her; she would not start now.

Suddenly she thought of Evan, and she choked back a sob. How she wished now that she had surrendered to her first impulse when she had seen him at Tamoora! She thought about it now with longing, wishing that they had run off into the darkness to make love in the moonlight. It wouldn't have mattered that there were guests filling the house, that Thomas might be searching for her, that anyone could have found them. Remembering Evan, so tall and strong and handsome in his evening clothes, nothing would have mattered but him. She would have slipped out of that shimmering gown and run naked into his arms, pulling at his clothing so that she could feel him against her. She would have reached desperately for him, crying out to him to hold her, to kiss her. He would have obeyed, his desire matching hers, his mouth seeking, his hands hot on her body. They would have lain in the grass, surrounded by night air and moonlight, and it would have been glorious to feel the strength of his arms, the weight of his body over hers. Her frantic need to be loved would have been answered, and she would have been at peace.

But she had been too proud to let him know her feelings, and she was paying a high price for that pride. If she had given in to that wild urge to run away with him, at least she would have the memory to sustain her; if Evan had made love to her, she would always have that precious moment to recall. If she only had that, she could somehow endure the attentions of the man beside her until she could think of a way to escape him.

Forcing herself to lie quietly under the weight of Knowles's arm, Cynara prepared herself to wait until he was deeply asleep before she tried to ease away from him. Her face throbbed where he had struck her; she felt stiff and sore from her struggles against him. But even the physical discomforts she suffered did not compare to the anguish of her thoughts. Even at that moment she hated Thomas Hale far more than she despised the man beside her, and she knew that her feelings for Hale were trivial compared to her hatred of Myles Ward. He was the root of her troubles; because of him, she had been reduced to this state.

Staring at the dim outline of the window, through which pale moonlight was just visible, Cynara was consumed by self-loathing. How easily she had assumed that upon Hale's death she would be free! What a fool she had been not to realize that he would triumph over her even after his death. She remembered with disdain that only last night she had sat in her room at Tamoora coolly making her plans to return to England and confront Myles.

Closing her eyes, Cynara felt bitterness wash over her. Well, her plans for Myles would be postponed, she told herself acidly, and she had only herself to blame. How infuriatingly smug she had been, and how she was paying for it now!

The snoring beside her ceased for a moment, and Cynara held her breath. If he woke and came after her again . . .

But no, he was just changing position in his sleep. She waited tensely until he settled again, praying that he would move far enough away from her so that she could climb over him and off the bed.

Grunting, he rolled over onto his stomach, and her hopes for escape were dashed when her hair became entangled under the arm he flung over his head. Hardly daring to

breathe in case she should wake him, Cynara tried to free
her hair. But at that moment, his hand closed around a long
tress, his fingers twining themselves among the strands, and
she knew that she could not free herself without disturbing
him. A sob of frustration broke from her lips, and she
covered her mouth quickly to prevent another. Far better to
wait out the hours of the night ahead of her, she thought,
than to risk waking him and enduring a repetition of what
she had just been through.

Gritting her teeth, Cynara moved as far away from him
as possible, drawing the sheet over her as best she could. She
lay back, every muscle taut until his snoring became steady
again, but still she could not relax.

She lay in the darkness, her thoughts racing. Did he only
suspect that she was running away from something, or did
he know for certain? No, it was impossible for him to be
sure, she told herself. If he had discovered that she was a
convict, he would have taunted her with the information at
once. But even as she told herself that, she felt a nagging
doubt that made her doubly cautious. She would have to
plan her escape carefully. Ben Knowles had made it clear
exactly what kind of man he was; if she tried to flee and he
caught her, she had no doubt of the outcome. And if he ever
discovered her convict status, she knew that he would not
hesitate to use it as a threat over her, forcing her to do as he
wished. Groaning inwardly at the thought, Cynara wondered how she was going to get away from him.

Her thoughts racing back and forth like a trapped animal
in a cage, Cynara waited tensely for daylight. How long
could she fight Ben Knowles before she was forced to
surrender out of sheer hopelessness? Pressing a hand tightly
to her mouth to stifle the cry that hovered too close to her
lips, Cynara stared blindly into the darkness, praying that
daylight would not be long in coming.

Finally, exhausted, she fell into a weary sleep, and had not
awakened even when he had left her side sometime in the
early morning. Now, dressed and waiting nervously for his

return, she realized that she was no closer to solving the problem of her escape than she had been the night before.

The key scraped in the lock, and Cynara, who had been sitting on the extreme edge of the bed for lack of anywhere else to sit, sprang up and faced the door. No matter what Ben Knowles had done, or would do, to her, she would not grovel before him. She would face him proudly, even if her legs had begun to shake. Grasping the edge of the dresser for comfort as much as support, Cynara lifted her head and waited for him to enter.

But her preparations had been for naught. Instead of the burly form Ben Knowles that she had expected, the slight figure of the girl she had glimpsed the night before in the corridor came in.

Cynara stared at her as she hesitated on the threshold, balancing a small tray in one hand while she pocketed the key to the door with the other. As yet the girl had not looked at her. Her head was down, her face hidden by light brown hair that hung limply over her shoulders. The urge to push this slight form to one side and dash to freedom was overwhelming; Cynara knew that the girl was not strong enough to stop her. But the knowledge that Ben Knowles might be waiting below, expecting her to try that very thing, held Cynara back. Biting her lip, Cynara forced herself to stand where she was while the girl closed the door behind her.

Still with her head down, the girl crossed the room and deposited the tray, which held a pot of tea and a cup, on the dresser. As she came closer, Cynara saw that while she was young, she was not as youthful as she had appeared from a distance. She realized, with surprise, that the girl might even be a year or so older than she herself was. True, her figure was immature, but this was due to her extreme slenderness rather than lack of years. The faded and patched dress she wore was more suited to a young girl, and this added to the illusion of youth. Cynara noticed also, with a pang, that the hands which had carefully set down the tray were red and rough to the wrists, the skin cracked and sore-looking from hard work. But it was the girl's face that held her interest, for her expression was blank, the brown eyes empty and dull. Was she stupid? Cynara wondered despairingly. Her hopes had lifted at the sight of the girl; she thought it possible to enlist her help in getting away. But as Cynara continued to look at her, she realized that she could not expect any assistance from this wretched creature who hardly seemed aware of her.

"My name is Cynara," she said gently, touching the girl on the arm when she gave no indication of having heard her.

The brown eyes lifted to hers. "Cy . . . na . . . ra?"

Cynara nodded, suppressing another wave of pity. She forced herself to smile. "What is yours?"

"Mine?"

The chapped hands clasped each other convulsively, and for the first time Cynara wondered if the girl was really stupid, or just terribly frightened. She nodded encouragingly. "Yes, your name. What is it?"

"Drue."

The answer was so low that Cynara had to bend forward to hear it. The girl, as if startled by the sound of her own voice, glanced nervously over her shoulder at the door. Her slight body tensed to flee.

"Don't be afraid," Cynara said quickly. She noticed with dismay that her own voice had lowered to match Drue's, and now she found herself glancing toward the door as the girl had done. Whatever else Ben Knowles had done, he had managed to reduce the two of them to abject terror, and Cynara felt herself rebelling at the thought. She stiffened, forcing herself to get a grip on her fear. What could he do to her that he hadn't already done? But the answer came back forcibly to her mind, and she closed her eyes for a moment of her imagination raced ahead, providing vivid descriptions of what he could do if he wished.

Trying to be calm, Cynara said, "Thank you for the tea, Drue." She indicated the tray with a motion of her hand when the girl looked blankly at her.

"He . . . he doesn't know," Drue whispered. She seemed to have trouble speaking, for she swallowed with difficulty before she was able to continue. "If he . . . found out . . . "

The implication was clear, and Cynara replied hastily, "I won't say anything. Drue—" She put out her hand as the girl began to edge toward the door. "Drue, why are you here?" she asked urgently. "Why do you stay with him?"

The girl's eyes widened with fear as she looked toward the door again. "I have to stay," she whispered. "He is . . . my husband."

"Your husband!" Cynara voice was shrill with surprise, and Drue's face blanched. She put a hand over her mouth as she backed away, and Cynara lowered her voice with an effort. "But surely you can—"

Drue shook her head wildly. She turned and ran to the door, her slight body trembling from head to foot. Her hand on the latch, she stiffened, and then she turned to look over her shoulder at Cynara. "I'll help you if I can," she whispered. "But you must wait . . . until it is safe . . . "

"Drue—"

But the girl was gone, leaving Cynara staring after her with mingled feelings of astonishment and admiration. The girl was obviously terrified out of her wits by Ben Knowles, and yet she had offered to help her. There was hope after all, she thought eagerly, her spirits rising at the thought. But her elation vanished as quickly as it had come. How could she accept Drue's offer of help, knowing the danger the girl would be in if Knowles ever discovered that his own wife had helped her to escape? His wife. Cynara realized that it had taken courage to come to this room to bring her the tea, and that was the act of one woman offering what little comfort she could to another, despite the danger to herself. She knew suddenly that if she managed to get away from here, she could not leave without offering to take Drue with her; she would never forgive herself if she left her behind now.

Pouring a cup of the tepid, weak tea, Cynara drank it quickly. She must have all evidence of Drue's visit out of sight before Knowles came back, as she was sure he would. She had just finished the cup when she heard his footsteps on the stairs, and glancing around swiftly for a hiding place, she just managed to hide the tray under the bed before he came in. They stared at each other, Cynara fighting down her fear of him as he filled the doorway with his bulk. The memory of his rough hands last night and the savage way he had taken her increased that fear, but she was determined not to show it. Raising her chin defiantly, she waited for him to speak.

If Knowles was aware of the effort she made not to appear afraid of him, he did not seem impressed. Hooking his thumbs into his belt, he gazed at her in silence, until she wanted to scream at him to say something—anything would be better than seeing that triumphant smile hovering at his lips.

In the end, it was Cynara who broke the silence first. "You are mistaken if you think to keep me here against my will," she said haughtily. "I have no doubt that there are people out looking for me at this moment. When they find—"

To her dismay, Knowles laughed, a great guffaw that filled the room. "Oh, I've no doubt," he said, mimicking her tone, "That there are people looking for you. The question is: who are they? Could it be the constables?"

He looked at her narrowly, and she forced herself to respond calmly, "I cannot imagine why you persist in believing that I am running away from something. I assure you—"

"Don't take the high tone with me!" he threatened, suddenly tired of the game. "I've been around long enough to know when something is amiss—and there's something here that needs to be looked into!"

"I haven't the faintest idea what you mean!"

"Don't you, now?"

He actually swaggered as he moved away from the door.

"Perhaps I should send a message to the constable," he said, smiling slyly. "I could tell him that I found you wandering around, carrying nothing but a small bundle of clothes. Surely not the way a lady travels, don't you agree? Don't you think he might be interested?"

Cynara bit her lip. She didn't know whether to believe him or not.

Knowles laughed again. "I thought so!"

He was so close now that she could see the pupils of his eyes expanding and contracting as he gazed at her. "Why don't you and I make a little deal of our own?" he asked, grabbing her chin, forcing her to look up at him. "You tend bar for me, and I won't say anything that could get us both in trouble. Can't be more fair than that, now, can I?"

She tried to jerk her head away, but he held her fast, his fingers tightening around her jaw. "If anyone asks," he continued, "We can always say that you're my wife's cousin—or sister. How about that? We could keep it in the family, so to speak."

The man was detestable—and frightening. She tried to shake her head, but his grip tightened even more. "And perhaps we can have a little business on the side," he leered. "Some of the men who come in haven't had a woman for a long time—their business taking them into the bush for one reason or another, if you get my drift . . . "

Cynara's outrage at his suggestion gave her the strength to break away from him. Her reply was fierce as she backed away. "If you think that I will...will prostitute myself—"

"Oh, I think you'll come around to it, sooner or later," he said confidently. His hand went to the heavy leather belt around his waist, a gesture that was not on Cynara. Her face paled and she backed away again, bumping against the edge of the bed, her eyes riveted on the thick brass buckle of the belt.

"Well, what do you say?"

Cynara's lips were so stiff that she could hardly get the words out. "If you dare—"

"Oh, I dare, all right," Knowles sneered. "Don't doubt that for a minute."

Cynara didn't doubt it at all. She looked past him, trying to assess the distance to the door from where she stood, wondering frantically if she could leap by him on legs that seemed suddenly too weak even to hold her upright.

"Why don't I give you a little time to think about it?" Knowles said softly. "Maybe by tonight you'll see it my way. If not—" His hand strayed to the belt again.

"I don't need time to think about it!" Cynara cried recklessly as he moved to the door. "I'll never—"

"We'll see," Knowles said with assurance as he closed the door behind him. "We'll see."

Yes, Cynara thought defiantly, we will. But her bravado was only a front, and she knew it. Inside she was terrified. The fact that she had reason to be was small comfort, and she was aware that Knowles could, by his superior strength, make her do almost anything. He had succeeded in reducing poor Drue to a frightened shadow; couldn't he do the same to her? No, no! She wouldn't let that happen. She would get away from here before tonight—before Knowles returned. But how?

Wildly she glanced around the room, almost as if she expected a route of escape to open up before her. But nothing had changed; there was only the locked door in front of her and the window that was too far above the ground to the side of her. And then her eyes fell on the bed. Where the idea came from, she didn't know, but she seized it eagerly, thrusting the consequences from her mind. Running to the bed, she jerked the sheets from it. If she could tear them into strips and knot them together, tying the end to the bed, she could use them as a makeshift rope and lower herself down from the window! There was the satisfactory sound of the material ripping lengthwise, and she was so relieved at her success that she actually laughed aloud. The sound died in her throat as she looked fearfully at the door.

She sat back on her heels, stiff with tension, listening for

the noise of his footsteps on the stairs. But when there was
no sound from below, she bent to her task again, taking care
this time to pull the sheet slowly toward her, trying to make
as little noise as possible.

When both sheets were in strips, she began knotting them
together as rapidly as possible, conscious of the passing
time. What if he came back and discovered what she was
doing? Thrusting the horrible thought from her mind, she
finished the last of the knots, testing them each time to make
sure that they would hold. They seemed strong enough, but
there was no way she could be certain that they would hold
her when she entrusted her entire weight to them. She
would just have to take her chances; there was no time to
think of another plan.

Bundling the sheets under the bed and out of sight,
Cynara drew the stained coverlet up over the mattress,
looking critically at the result. If Knowles came in, he must
not be suspicious.

Trying not to think what she would do if he returned for
a repetition of the night before, Cynara forced herself to sit
calmly on the edge of the bed, waiting for nightfall. As soon
as it was dark, she would make her escape. But what about
Drue? Biting on the fingernail she had broken in her hurry,
she thought about her. Impossible to take the girl with her
now, she thought. But once she had reached safety, she
would somehow manage to send someone to help her.

The long hours passed so slowly that Cynara thought she
would scream with tension. Every sound she heard from
below caused her to start nervously, but throughout the
long afternoon Knowles did not come upstairs again. Nor
did she hear Drue. It was almost as if she were alone at the
inn. Her heart leaped at the thought, but she repressed the
urge to try her escape before dark. Knowles was somewhere about, she was sure; if she tried to flee now and he
caught her, she would not get another chance.

She tried to pass the time thinking of pleasant things,
recalling bits and pieces of conversations with Sarah, the

fantasies they had woven during the long voyage to Australia. Sarah had maintained that if she could have anything she wanted, it would be her own house—a big house, she had said, stuffed with servants anxious to wait on her, filled with beautiful furniture, her wardrobe bursting with wonderful creations made especially for her. She would have several lovers dancing attendance on her, each of them more fascinated than the last by her beauty. Sarah had painted a picture of luxurious comfort, a life of charm and laughter, with herself at the center, enjoying it all immensely. They had laughed together, and each time Sarah told the story, the house became larger, her gowns more gorgeous, her lovers more numerous.

Cynara thought about that now, and was even able to smile at the memory of Sarah's sparkling eyes, her quick gestures, her merry laughter at the outrageousness of it all.

And what did she want? she asked herself wistfully, trying to fall into the game again even though she was alone. What did she really want?

She thought of the home she had grown up in—a lovely small manor house of mellowed brick with ivy and wisteria climbing the walls. Besides her own room, which she had been allowed to decorate herself, she loved her father's study the best. It had three walls of books, doors opening to the garden, and a deep leather chair she was allowed to use for her lessons. How often had she sat there quietly studying when she was young, her father working solemnly near by at his huge desk!

But she remembered then how dissatisfied she had been at times with her father's plans for her. She had wanted excitement, she recalled ruefully; she had wanted to reach out beyond the confines of the sleepy village, to experience new things. She had even dreamed about being swept off her feet by some dashing young man. Silly, childish dreams, she realized now, wincing at how young and romantic she had been.

But still, it had been a peaceful time, and she had been

happy then despite her occasional rebellion at the quiet and prim life her father wanted for her.

And now—now she was in Australia, in love with a man she didn't understand, possessed by thoughts of him that were far removed from the naive dreams of her girlhood. Now she knew what it was to suffer the passions and longings of a woman. Now she knew what it was to love a man with all her being to *want* to give herself to him, to become such a part of him that they had to become one. Her body was an instrument of torture, tormented by need, impaled by desire. Even the thought of Evan could start up the clamoring inside her, limbs trembling, her skin on fire. The dashing young man she had dreamed about when she was young was a difficult, volatile, secretive man driven by needs of his own, but able to reduce her to quivering, pulsating surrender, with no will of her own. The unrequited love she had read about in novels was not a selfless, sacrificing, and beautiful emotion—it was a searing of the heart and body, a soundless cry of despair that such towering need would remain ever unfulfilled.

The light had faded as she sat there lost in reverie, and she went to the window to look down at the yard below. Glancing away from the sight of the ground so far below her, she looked instead across the landscape, imagining she could see the lights at Tamoora.

Had they begun searching for her, there? Of course they had, and long before this. Gerald Whitley would have no choice once he discovered she had gone.

Staring in the other direction, toward Sydney, Cynara wondered if she could make it there before getting caught. It was a long way, almost fifteen miles, she judged, and she would have to stay away from the main road. What if she got lost? What if . . .

But she refused to think about the terrible things that could happen to her alone in the bush, as Knowles had said; she had enough on her mind to worry about right now. Resolutely, she turned away from the window. It was dark enough now to begin.

Hands trembling as much with nervous excitement as with fear over what she was going to do, Cynara pulled the knotted sheets from under the bed. Looping one end of the rope around the bedstead, she leaned back against it with all her weight, testing to make sure it was securely tied. Then, tiptoeing to the window, she raised it, inch by inch, wincing when it screeched protestingly. The window open at last, Cynara dared to put her head out, squinting in the darkness, trying to probe the shadows in case Knowles had come outside. All seemed quiet.

With one last glance around the room, Cynara threw the rope out the window. Looking down, she saw the end of it dangling far above the ground, and she realized that she would have to jump the last few feet. But it was too late to turn back, and she must make her move at this moment; time was speeding by, and she was sure Knowles would come for her soon.

Her heart pounding, Cynara lifted herself onto the window sill. Taking a deep breath, she grasped the twisted sheet with both hands and prepared to lower herself to the ground.

Her whole attention was taken up with moving her body around so that she could face the wall of the inn, bracing herself with her feet as she went down. She did not see the figure looming behind her until it was too late.

Knowles grabbed her at the instant she happened to look up. She uttered a terrified cry, losing her grip on the sill. Her body seemed to hang for a moment in empty space, and she grabbed frantically for the rope, closing her eyes when she felt the rough wood under her hands.

But her relief at not being dashed to the ground below was short-lived. Knowles had her by the shoulders, and with a mighty heave, he hauled her back inside the room. In the next minute she was flying through the air as he threw her away from him.

"You treacherous little slut, you! I'll teach you not to try that again!"

From where she lay sprawled on the floor, gasping for breath, she saw him lunge toward her. He picked her up as easily as if she had been a rag doll, and slapped her viciously across the face. Her piercing scream rent the air as he hit her again, and she raised her arms, trying to ward off the blows that seemed to be coming from everywhere at once.

His curses mingled with her cries as she fought to get away from him, but he seemed to fill the room; no matter which direction she rushed, he was there. Her hair was in her eyes, blinding her as she lunged away from him again. She fell against the bed, put her arms out to shove herself away, and dashed toward the door. She was almost there when he grabbed her again.

Frantically she pulled away from him, hearing the material of her skirt rip as it tore away from his hands, and then she was leaping for the door again and freedom.

"I'll teach you a lesson you won't soon forget!" he roared from somewhere behind her. "When I'm through with you—"

She was thrown to the floor a second time. But this time she turned on him, screaming, "Stop it, you bastard! Stop it!"

His arm was drawn back again. He reached down to haul her to her feet, but she surged up, surprising him by shooting her arm out and raking his face with her nails. Shouting with pain, he put his hand up to his cheek, feeling the wetness of the blood trickling down his face. Her attack enraged him further; his own hand shot out and she was thrown against the wall.

There was no escape; he was like a madman, his fists weapons that could kill her. Sobbing, she raised her arms over her head and sank to the floor, huddling in a tight ball as blow after blow descended. He was going to kill her; she knew it, and she couldn't stop him. With each blow, her body jerked convulsively; she could not even scream any more. The pain was like a tide surging over her, calling her away into hell. Helplessly she went with it, and did not even feel the last of the blows as he stood over her, panting.

There was a cool hand on her forehead. Moaning, Cynara reeled back into consciousness, wondering if he had blinded her. The darkness was absolute; she thought then that she had died. But the hand was real; she could feel it trembling as it stroked her face.

A voice close to her ear whispered, "Lie still, lie still, he's gone . . . "

Lie still. Even the movement caused by her tortured breathing sent fresh waves of pain raging through her. She took a shuddering breath, peering into the darkness.

"Drue?" Her voice was a cracked whisper, and she felt the hand tremble again before it was removed. Something was pressed against her parched lips.

"Drink. It's only water . . . the best I could do . . . "

Cynara tried to obey. But it was an effort to raise her head and she sank back again, trying to close her mind to the agony that seemed to penetrate every pore of her body.

"Oh, Drue . . . " The sound was a moan; she felt tears spring into her eyes.

"I have to leave now . . . "

Cynara clutched at the hand. "Don't go!" she choked, panicked. "What if he comes back?"

Drue gently removed her hand. "I have to," she whispered urgently. "He won't return until everyone is gone. And then . . . "

Even through her pain, Cynara sensed the fear in Drue's voice. "What?" she cried. "What then?"

The sound of the girl's swallowing was audible. "I'll . . . try to keep him away from you . . . for tonight . . . "

Cynara closed her eyes. Oh God, she thought. She couldn't allow Drue to do this for her. "No," she forced herself to say. "I'll be all right . . . "

She had the impression of Drue shaking her head. "I'll try . . . " she whispered again, and was gone.

Where she found the strength to move, Cynara didn't

know. Inch by inch, she forced herself to sit up, tightening her lips to prevent the cry of pain that hammered at the back of her throat. She would make no sound that would send back here, she vowed.

Dragging herself over to the dresser, she pulled herself to a standing position. Clutching the dresser edge, she swayed, fighting the nausea that attacked her. Finally she managed to slide her hand along the dresser top toward the box of matches. Fumbling, she dropped the box and took a deep breath, willing herself to reach for it again. The wick defied her feeble attempts to light it, and she wasted several matches and a great deal of her fading strength before she finally got it lit. Somehow, the light was comforting, less terrifying than the darkness, and she braced both hands on the dresser, holding herself upright only by force of will. As yet, she did not dare look down at herself; she was afraid of what she would see.

She was too weak to stand; she must get over to the bed before she fell. But the distance from the chest to the bed seemed impossible; she could only stare at it, feeling weak tears filling her eyes again.

At last she forced herself to put one foot slowly in front of the other. In this manner, walking stiffly and with as little movement, as possible, she reached the bed. Sitting gingerly on the edge, she waited to lie down until the second attack of nausea passed. Then, inching sideways, she winced and bit back another moan as she lay down.

Was she going to die? She felt hysterical laughter rising in her throat at the thought of Knowles being forced to explain how he had bludgeoned a woman to death for the simple reason that she had tried to defy him. But the laughter stopped as suddenly as it had begun and she started to sob instead. She wouldn't die, she thought; she would live, compelled to stay here, enduring Knowles's cruelty because she knew what would happen to her if she tried to leave. There was no escape . . . no escape. She knew she would not survive another beating such as this, and now the seed of dread had been planted in her, blossoming like a choking weed, growing until her fear of him seemed to shadow her entire being. For the first time she understood the blank emptiness in Drue's eyes. It was called hopelessness.

CHAPTER TWENTY-THREE

THE TAPROOM WAS CROWDED, and too warm from the presence of the men gathered there. A thick haze of smoke hung in the still air from the dudeens, or pipes, every man seemed to have in his mouth. There were raucous cries as Cynara tried to edge her way through the tables, carrying a heavy tray filled with empty glasses.

It had been over a week since that terrible night Knowles had beaten her for trying to escape, and he had allowed her two days locked in that room, to recover. After that, he had dragged her down the stairs, pushed a tray into her hands, and told her that in addition to the work he expected from her during the day, she was also going to help out in the bar at night. The beating had weakened her more than physically; she had been unable to defy even when she knew that Knowles wanted her in the bar so that his customers would be able to see her. So far there had been no mention of her being forced to accompany any man upstairs, but she knew it was only a matter of time. Knowles was protecting himself thus far; he didn't want anyone to see the marks he had left on her body until he was sure they had faded completely. What she would do when that time came, she didn't know. She had defied him once, and the memory of his savage response was too fresh in her mind to make her want to repeat the action.

The thought of having to give herself to any of the men here who wanted her, and who had enough money to pay for the pleasure, was so utterly repulsive that she knew she would have to find the strength somewhere in her to resist. If only she didn't feel that her situation was so hopeless, she thought despondently, as she shifted the tray to a more comfortable position on her hip.

Looking up, she saw that a man was blocking her way, grinning down at her as she tried to pass by him.

"Let me by!" she said sharply.

"Aw, come and have a drink with me!"

Cynara had been up at dawn, working steadily the day. It was now almost ten o'clock in the evening, and she was simply too tired to humor him. Brushing a tendril of hair from her perspiring forehead, Cynara glared at him. "It's not allowed!" she snapped.

"If it was, would you have one with me?" he wheedled.

"No! Now, let me—"

He grabbed her suddenly around the waist, pulling her toward him to kiss her drunkenly on the mouth. Cynara reared back, revolted, and the tray she held tilted alarmingly. "Let go of me!" she cried, trying to push him away and hold onto the heavy tray at the same time.

"One little kiss—"

The heat, the noise of the crowd as the men shouted to one another across the room, her exhaustion, and the effrontery of the grinning man clutching her all combined to provoke her unthinking response. He pulled her toward him again, pushing his whiskered face close to hers, his lips puckered for a kiss. Without hesitation, she raised the tray and brought it down on his head.

Fortunately, he was a big man; the tray did little damage except to stagger him. But as glasses rained down on all sides, he bellowed with anger and surprise, staring at her with an expression of disbelief. Then, conscious of the laughter of his companions at the ridiculous sight he made standing in the middle of the mess around him, he bawled at the top of his lungs for Knowles.

"Begod! I'll have it out of your hide, Knowles, for what this serving wench just did to me!" he roared as Knowles came rushing out from the kitchen.

At any other time, Knowles's expression would have been almost comical as he stood there, gaping at the sight before him. The kitchen door he had burst through swung back, hitting him with a slap, but he did not notice it. Staring blankly at the furious man, the broken and splintered glass on the floor, the rest of the room rocking with laughter, he could not for an instant take in what had happened. But then his glance met Cynara's white and angry face, and his own became dark with fury.

"What have you done, girl?" he shouted as he started forward.

"It's a fine man who can't control his serving maids!" someone called from across the room to another round of laughter.

"If I was you, I'd step careful, Ben—this one has a temper!" called another.

"She seems a bit more than you can handle, Ben," shouted a third. "And expensive on the glassware, to boot!"

Cynara wanted to scream at them to be silent; she could see that every laughing comment only increased Knowles's rage, and in spite of her own anger, she was frightened at the expression on his face. He stood there, his head swinging back and forth like an enraged bull prepared to charge, and suddenly Cynara could not look at him anymore. Swiftly she bent to retrieve the broken glass, wondering what had possessed her. The man who had tried to kiss her was only feeling the effects of too much rum; she had had no need to react so strongly. The brief moment of satisfaction she felt when the tray came crashing down on the man's head had vanished as quickly as it had come; now all she wanted to do was to clean up the mess and escape to the kitchen, praying that Knowles would be distracted enough by his customers to forget about her.

It was a vain hope. She looked up to see him pushing his way through the crowd, his heavy arms shoving the laughing men out of his way. When he neared her, he reached down and jerked her to her feet, bringing his hand back to slap her across the face.

The sharp sound of his open palm meeting her cheek rang out in the suddenly still room. Cynara staggered back, her hand to her face, eyes blazing with anger. Someone caught hold of her, setting her back on her feet again, but she did not notice.

"You filthy—" she began, outraged.

Knowles had drawn his arm back again, preparing to strike her once more. "Here! Hold your hand, man!" a voice from behind Cynara cried angrily. "It wasn't nothing but a bit of fun!"

"Fun!" Knowles spat, still holding Cynara's arm. He turned furiously on the speaker. "I'll thank you to stay out of my business!" he snarled.

He turned back, his hand lifted again.

"Say somethin', Crowlee," the speaker shouted. "Tell him you put her up to it!"

Crowlee, the man whom Cynara had hit with the tray, lumbered forward, his expression no longer angry. "T'was my fault, Ben," he admitted, abashed. "I asked for it."

"The hell you say!"

The expression of discomfort changed to one of belligerence. Crowlee's hand shot out, covering the innkeeper's wrist, tightening to make him let go of Cynara's arm. "I said it was my fault, Ben," he repeated quietly. "Leave it be."

"Aye—leave it be," someone said soothingly. "It was just a little sport that got out of hand. No need to bash the girl for it."

Knowles swung his head, his glance taking in the room full of glaring spectators. A few of the men had risen from their chairs, their attitude indicating their willingness to fight. Cynara followed Knowles's glance in amazement. A few minutes ago these men had been tossing lewd comments in her direction; now they all seemed banded together to protect her. She felt a rush of gratitude toward them, and when she looked back at Knowles, she was no longer so frightened at what he would do.

"What do you say, Knowles? Let's let it rest," a man called.

There was a murmur of agreement from the crowd, and Knowles was forced to admit defeat unless he wished to take them on one by one. Several seemed eager for the opportunity; their hands clenched into fists, they stared at him aggressively.

"Get yourself upstairs," Knowles growled to Cynara. "I'll take care of you later."

Angrily, Cynara began to object, but she stopped, unwilling to inflame him further. Tight-lipped she turned away, but another hand on her arm halted her. The man, Crowlee was at her side, glaring at Knowles.

"I don't think so, Ben," Crowlee said.

Knowles seemed about to explode with rage; his voice was a snarl as he said, "What do you mean, Crowlee?"

Crowlee ignored him. Turning to the room in general, his hand still on Cynara's arm, he called out, "What do you say, men? I think she needs our protection."

"You have no right—" Knowles began viciously.

"Don't we?" Crowlee left Cynara and walked over to Knowles. Ben Knowles was a big man, but Crowlee topped him by a head, forcing Knowles to look up at him. "I'll be back, man," he said, "and if this girl has a mark on her, you'll answer to me—"

"And me—"

"And me!"

The cries resounded throughout the room. Ben Knowles's face was a study in crimson as he struggled to control his anger. He looked around at the nodding heads. "You can't tell me what to do!" he choked.

"I think we can." Crowlee jerked his head. "What do you say, men?"

There was a chorus of assent, and Cynara felt like bursting into tears at the sudden and unexpected championing of these men. She looked around dazedly, trying to take in the grinning faces. Then, holding her head high, she smiled tremulously at them.

"Thank you," she said quietly. Before she could burst into tears, she ran from the room.

Struggling up the stairs, she stumbled twice, unable to see because of the tears in her eyes. Whether their threats were enough to stay Knowles's hand after they left, Cynara didn't know. It was enough that they had tried, and she was grateful to them.

In the room she had shared with Knowles, Cynara shut the door and leaned against it, trembling. There was no doubt in her mind that he would manage to punish her in some way for the humiliation he had suffered just now, but she was safe for a while. He would not dare follow her so soon, with the men downstairs watching him.

What had caused those men to come to her defense? Was it the fact that Knowles had actually struck her in front of them? She put her hand to her cheek; it throbbed under her fingers, and she thought that it was curious for the men to have reacted so strongly to his hitting her, when only moments before they had been offering lewd suggestions as she moved among them clearing tables. Most of them were rough and common; a good many were thieves, bushrangers—those men who preyed on the unwary to make their own dishonest living. Now a few were felons, who after serving their sentences had found themselves with no direction but to wander aimlessly about, earning a few pennies where they could, spending it as fast as they made it on liquor or women. Why should they have reacted so strongly to an action they had undoubtedly performed themselves on other helpless women?

It had to be Crowlee's leadership, she thought; they had followed where he led, joining in a new game they didn't quite understand. She wondered why Crowlee himself had been moved to defend her. Suddenly she was sorry she had hit him with that tray. If she hadn't been so tired, her nerves stretched to the breaking point, she would never have done such a thing.

Cynara knew that Knowles would make her pay for her actions. Glancing at the dresser, she considered pushing it against the door to bar his way, but she rejected the idea at once. If Knowles came to this room tonight and found the door blocked, he would be furious enough to break through any barrier. She had no wish to fuel his anger by a gesture that would be futile in the end.

Willing herself not to fall asleep, Cynara waited until she

could hear the heavy bolts being shot on the front door. Her whole body tense, she listened for the sound of his footsteps on the stairs, wondering if she would be able to defend herself against him when he came.

His heavy tread came down the corridor and she stiffened, waiting for his entrance. To her astonishment she heard him pass by the door with only a slight hesitation and then continue down the corridor. Springing up, she put her ear to the door. If she heard him start up the steps to the attic, where Drue slept, she would open the door and face him. She would not allow Drue to take any punishment brought on by her own stupid actions.

But a door to a room down the corridor opened and closed, and Cynara breathed a sigh of relief. At least for tonight, Knowles had been sufficiently cowed to leave them both alone.

Stumbling back to the bed, Cynara fell into it and was immediately fast asleep.

To Cynara's surprise, Knowles did not come near her for a week or more after the incident in the bar. In fact, he made a studied effort to ignore her, and if it hadn't been that Drue would bear the brunt of it, Cynara would have dared to slack on some of the never ending chores she had been forced to do over the past weeks. As it was, she made sure to do as much as before, giving Knowles no opportunity to find fault with her.

She knew that he was seething inside; it was obvious from his glowering expression and the tightness of his jaw. She and Drue trod carefully, only too aware that the slightest thing could set him off, like a powder keg exploding when the fuse was lit.

Cynara admitted to herself that she had never been as afraid of anyone as she was of Ben Knowles. The fact that he had beaten her senseless had much to do with that fear, but it went deeper than that. She knew that his rage over the humiliation he had suffered that night made him even more dangerous than before. He was not a man who would easily accept defeat and she knew that when the time came, she would be the target for his fury. That he blamed her she was only too aware, and she knew that he had completely forgotten that it was his temper that had contributed a great deal to his being made a fool of.

But Cynara had learned in the past weeks that anyone could be made to do anything if enough force was applied, and the knowledge was like a great festering sore inside her. Would she be strong enough to resist him when he could no longer be restrained by Crowlee's threat? She didn't know. The evil in Knowles ran deep; she suspected that once aroused he might even kill her.

If only she could think of a way to escape him, she thought desperately as the days dragged by. She knew that he watched her as closely as before, and she did not dare try again until she was sure she would be successful.

Besides, there was Drue to think of. The two women had formed a closeness, based more on silence than on words. Often, their eyes would meet in mutual relief when Knowles stomped through the kitchen and out. Cynara had vowed that she would not leave until she could take Drue with her; she would not abandon her to Knowles, no matter how frantic she was to get away.

Knowles had not dared to ban Cynara from the taproom; he knew that the men would ask for her. So she continued to serve at night, and strangely, now that the customers had declared their protection of her so openly, there were no more lewd remarks tossed in her direction. Instead of leering at her and grabbing for her as she passed by, many of them now touched their caps and grinned companionably at her when she served their rum or collected the empty glasses.

Several times after a friendly gesture from one or the other of them, she was tempted to ask for help. But each time she bit back the words; she did not want to exchange one form of imprisonment for another, and she knew too well how such a request would be viewed. These were rough men after all; her plea was certain to be seen as an invitation, and she shuddered to think of being forced to repay a debt to any one of them in the only terms he would understand. So she was compelled to wait for the right time, knowing that Knowles would not be restrained much longer.

And then one night she heard the devastating news that Crowlee had been killed in a skirmish with a tribe of aborigines. The influence that had kept Knowles at bay was gone. She saw him staring at her from across the room when the men had finished their story, and the smile that curved his lips sent a shiver of fear through her. She knew as well as Knowles did that Crowlee had been a self-appointed leader; where he had led, the other men had followed. Now that he was gone, there would be no help for her. Direction-less, the men would not protect her.

Only a fierce effort of will kept Cynara there, carrying the heavy tray around the room collecting glasses. Her imagina-tion took hold of her as she worked, and she could picture one horrible scene after another with Knowles until she had frightened herself so badly that she knew she had to get away tonight, before the inn closed.

Escape was much easier to imagine than to accomplish. She must not make Knowles suspicious, no matter how desperate she was. If she and Drue could get out the back way without his being aware of it, they might gain enough time to disappear before he realized they were gone.

Every nerve screaming with tension, Cynara made her-self move slowly about the room, watching Knowles con-stantly from the corner of her eye. When she saw that he had begun a conversation with someone at the opposite end of the bar, his back to her, she slipped past him, moving swiftly toward the swinging door into the kitchen. She turned urgently to Drue, who stood at the sink, her arms plunged to the elbow in water, washing the glasses that were piled on the sideboard.

"Drue—"

Drue turned toward her questioningly. "Drue, listen to me," Cynara whispered. "Crowlee is dead—"

"Dead!" Her small face paled. "How did it happen?"

Cynara shook her head; there was no time to explain now. "Drue, I'm going to leave tonight—right now. I want you to come with me."

Drue's face, if possible, paled even more. She shook her head. "I . . . can't."

"Yes, you can," Cynara insisted. "I won't leave here without you."

Drue shook her head again. "No," she answered with unexpected firmness. "I won't leave. I . . . I want to stay."

"You don't mean that!"

"Yes, yes I do." Drue cast a quick glance at the door. Reaching out, she grasped Cynara's hand holding it tightly. "You go ahead."

"Don't you see?" It was Drue who spoke urgently now. "Once you're gone, things will be like they were before. There won't be any woman here but me. He'll have to turn to me then . . . "

Cynara couldn't believe her ears. She stared at the young woman, stupified. "But Drue! You know what he's like. How can you possibly want to stay?"

"He's my husband, Cynara," Drue answered simply.

Again Cynara seemed unable to speak, and Drue continued, "You don't know what he's like, Cynara . . . you don't know," she repeated.

Cynara put a hand to her head. This couldn't be happening, she told herself; she hadn't heard right. "Drue," she said again, "I can't believe you want to stay. He . . . he has some hold over you, doesn't he?"

"Yes, but not the way you think. I . . . I love him, Cynara."

"Love him!" Cynara thought of the silent wraith Drue had been when she first came to this horrible place. It was impossible; she would not believe what Drue was saying to her. "Drue, you're coming with me. I know we can find help—somewhere—once we—"

"No. Go on, now." Drue looked at the door again, cocking her head to listen. The muffled sound of Knowles's laughter came to them through the battered door. "Now," she said. "He won't come in here for a while."

Cynara looked helplessly at the young woman, who seemed to have grown in stature in the past minutes. "Please come with me," she pleaded.

Drue gave her a light push with her hand. "Hurry. You don't want him to catch you. If he comes in, I'll tell him that—"

"You'll tell him what?"

They both jumped as if shot. Neither of them had heard the door open to the kitchen, and when Cynara turned and saw him standing there, hands on his hips, his face almost black with anger, she felt her heart stop. Without thinking, she leaped for the back door, but he sprang across the space that divided them and grabbed her before she reached it. From somewhere, she thought she heard Drue's cry of protest, but there was no time to answer. Knowles had his hands around her throat, and she raised her own, trying to break his hold. The blood was pounding in her ears; she couldn't breathe. Panicked, she jerked her knee up, catching him high on the thigh. He broke away, uttering a strangled sound as he bent double, clutching himself.

Cynara saw the bread knife on the table. In a flash she had grabbed it, her hand tightening around the handle until the knuckles showed as white as her face above it.

"If you come near me again, I'll use this!" she hissed, aiming the blade toward him. "I swear it!"

Knowles hesitated, but only for a second. Straightening, he lunged toward her, and drew back in almost the same motion, a red streak of blood appearing on the hand he had flung toward her.

"You bitch!"

"I mean it, Knowles! One step more and I'll—"

He had regained confidence. Almost swaggering in front of her, moving slightly closer to her with each movement, he said assuredly, "You won't use it. You're not the type. Give it to me . . . " He held out his hand.

Cynara shook her head, her eyes never leaving his face. She gripped the handle of the knife tighter. "One step more," she threatened.

He took the step and again the knife flashed in the air, sliding down his arm, leaving a trail of blood that mingled with that she had drawn on his hand.

"Give that to me!" he shouted, lunging suddenly for her, both arms outthrust.

He hit her with the full force of his weight, sending her crashing against the table. By some miracle she had retained possession of the knife, but now he grabbed her arm, trying to wrest it from her. She cried out as his fingers dug into hers, but he could not make her let go. She knew that if he took the knife he would use it on her, and her fear gave her a strength she didn't normally possess. Rearing back, she overbalanced him, and now it was he who floundered against the table.

He looked up to see the blade flashing toward him; he tried to scramble frantically away. At the back of her mind, Cynara heard Drue scream again as she plunged the knife down, but she was beyond thought. Blindly she struck, hardly aware of what she was doing as she drove the knife at Knowles.

Knowles roared with anger and fear; the blade quivered as it embedded itself in the table top, narrowly missing the flesh of his arm, pinning his sleeve to the table instead.

Panic-stricken, Cynara watched Knowles free himself, the huge muscles in his arm knotting as he jerked his arm up and away, leaving his shirt sleeve behind like a grotesque dismembered arm pinned to the table. His fist swung in an arc, catching Cynara across the chest; she reeled backward with the force of the blow. He came after her as she screamed, and a second blow across the side of her face knocked her to the floor. Straddling her, he reached down and jerked her to her feet again, his face so distorted with rage that he was unrecognizable.

"You slut! I'll teach you to come after me with a knife!"

She reeled again as he hit her. There was a ringing in her ears, and sparks of light shot before her eyes. She gave a weak cry of protest before falling to the floor again. She lay there, too dazed to move.

Then there was pandemonium in the kitchen. Dimly Cynara was aware of people all around, of Drue sobbing, of another feminine voice she almost recognized, rising shrilly above the rest. But she couldn't see; there was a warm trickle of something running down her face, and she realized that it was her own blood. Knowles had opened a cut along one checkbone.

"Let me through! Did you hear me? Let me through!"

Again that voice sounded familiar to Cynara. She looked up, trying to see, panicked because everything was blurred. Shaking her head, she blinked and saw the shadowy figure of a woman bending over her, and behind her, another form, pushing Knowles out of the way.

"My God! I don't believe it!" the figure cried. "Cynara? Is that you?"

Rubbing her sleeve across her face, Cynara tried to see. "Sarah?" she said unbelievingly. "Sarah?"

"Yes, it's me honey." Anxiously, Sarah pushed the tangled hair from Cynara's face, grimacing when she saw what Knowles had done. She turned quickly to her companion. "William, help me!"

The young man stood looking helplessly down at the two of them. He hesitated, and Sarah said sharply, "William! We've got to get her out of here!" Pulling out a handkerchief, Sarah began dabbing gently at Cynara's face, trying to wipe away some of the blood without touching the wound itself. Drue appeared beside her, holding a bowl of water, and Sarah muttered a gruff thanks as she dipped the cloth into it and wrung it out. "Cynara, this is William

Delmore. He'll help you—won't you William?"

Delmore's hesitation vanished when he took a closer look at Cynara. With sudden authority, he turned to the crowd surrounding them and ordered, "Move back, please. And some of you men—you, and you—" he pointed to two of the spectators "help me carry this woman to my carriage."

"Just a minute!" Knowles's voice rose angrily. "You can't do this!"

"Why not?" There was an edge to William's voice as he turned contemptuously to Knowles. "I should inform you, sir, that I am a solicitor. And from what I've seen here tonight, this young woman is well within her rights if she decides to bring charges against you." He glanced deliberately around the kitchen, and then back at Knowles's darkly flushed face. "I think," he said coldly, "that it would be to your advantage not to appear in a court of law."

Knowles swallowed, his eyes going from Cynara to Sarah and back to William Delmore again. "There's no need to bring the law into this," he muttered at last.

"Very well." Delmore had the situation well in hand. Dismissing Knowles, who had backed away, his face almost purple with suppressed rage, Delmore turned once again to the men he had commandeered. "If you please," he said, indicating Cynara.

Cynara was lifted gently from the floor. Sarah was beside her, holding her hand. Cynara raised her head, seeking Drue. "Drue—" she whispered.

The slight figure came toward her hesitantly. When she was close, Cynara said pleadingly, "Drue, please come with us."

Drue shook her head. Patting Cynara's shoulder, she answered simply, "I can't. Don't worry, Cynara. I'll be all right." She leaned close to Cynara, whispering, "God go with you."

"And you . . . " Cynara answered faintly.

Cynara was carried from the kitchen, through the silent taproom, and outside. It seemed a miracle to her when she saw the carriage waiting, Delmore's coachman scrambling down from his box to open the door. Could it really be happening, she wondered dazedly. She had dreamed so often of running away from this accursed place and Ben Knowles. Now she was leaving in style, complete with carriage, and she felt hysterical laughter rising in her at the thought. Weak tears coursed down her face instead when she was set gently against the cushioned upholstery, and she put a hand to her mouth to stifle the sobs that wanted to burst from her when she realized that the nightmare was over at last.

Sarah climbed inside after her, and taking a folded rug from under the seat, she draped it around Cynara. They heard Delmore give an order to his coachman, and then the carriage started slowly off, away from the inn and Ben Knowles and the silent crowd that had gathered outside.

They rode in silence for a while, Sarah fussing over Cynara, trying to make her more comfortable, holding the kerchief to her face until the bleeding stopped.

At last Sarah turned to the silent Delmore and said in hushed voice, "We have to take her to a doctor."

"No, no!" Despite the faintness that seemed to increase with every jolt of the carriage, Cynara tried to sit up. She fell back, reaching for Sarah's hand. "No doctor," she said weakly. "I'll . . . I'll explain later."

"But Cynara—"

"No."

"Well—" Clearly, Sarah was doubtful. She looked to Delmore for assistance. "William—say something!" she ordered.

Delmore cleared his throat. It was obvious that he wished himself removed from the entire episode, but now that he had committed himself, he was determined to carry it through. Leaning forward, he said, somewhat awkwardly, "If you think that man Knowles will give you any more . . . trouble . . . please don't worry. I know his sort; he won't dare come after you with the threat of the law in front of him. In fact, I think you should bring charges against him—"

"Oh, no!" The thought of facing Ben Knowles in court, having to explain her own position, made Cynara react with horror. "No," she said again, shuddering.

Sarah put in quickly, "All right, honey—no court. But you should see a doctor."

Cynara shook her head, wincing at the increased throbbing the movement caused. "I'll be all right," she said. "If I can just find some place to spend the night."

Sarah sat back. "I know just the place," she said, smiling at Cynara in the darkness. "You can stay with me at Mollie's."

"Mollie's."

Delmore interrupted, clearing his throat again. "Sarah, do you think—"Oh, Mollie won't mind," Sarah said confidently.

Mollie didn't mind at all. As soon as Delmore's carriage pulled up to her front door and Delmore and his coachman, carrying Cynara between them, mounted the steps and entered the house, Mollie was there taking charge.

After one look at Cynara, she asked no questions of Sarah; instead she led the way past the sitting room and down the corridor.

"She can stay with me for the night," Sarah ventured as Mollie paused before a door.

"Nonsense. The guest room will be much better," Mollie answered. Her hand on the doorknob, she turned to look at Sarah. "Send Betsy to me. Tell her to bring some hot water bottles and more wood for the fire. Oh," she added when Sarah began to move away, "Tell her to send a message to Doctor—"

Cynara, who had not spoken a word until now, roused herself. "No doctor," she muttered.

"Nonsense!" Mollie said again, gesturing to the men to bring Cynara inside. "You must have someone to look at that cut." Seeing Cynara's distress she added quietly,

"Don't worry. Doctor Engel is discreet. Otherwise I wouldn't have him."

Sarah went off, after a whispered word to Delmore to wait for her upstairs, and Cynara was deposited gently on the sofa. Mollie soon had a fire going, and then she bustled around the bed, turning down the coverlet, plumping the pillows, sliding the hot water bottles between the sheets.

Cynara had watched these preparations dazedly. Her head throbbed, she felt like bursting into tears of weakness and relief at this unexpected kindness. Wordlessly she looked up at Mollie as the woman bent over her, gently examining her face. Shaking her head, Mollie took the chair opposite the sofa and said, "I think it's best to wait for Doctor Engel; that's a nasty cut, but you'll feel better soon."

"I don't know how to thank you—and Sarah." Shuddering in spite of the fire, Cynara added, almost to herself, "If she hadn't come when she did . . . "

Mollie said nothing to this, busying herself tactfully with the tea she had had brought in. Cynara accepted the cup Mollie passed across to her, trying to stop her hands from shaking long enough to drink.

She had just managed a sip or two, using both hands to hold the delicate china, when the door opened and the doctor was admitted.

Doctor Engel was tall and thin, with piercing eyes and a no-nonsense manner. He came forward at once, acknowledging Mollie with a brief nod of his head, but his attention was focused on his patient. Those sharp eyes took in the situation immediately, and he asked no questions.

Silently and competently, he examined the cut, shaking his head at the bruise already forming on her cheekbone and at her jaw. His hands were gentle as he turned her face toward the light, his fingers tender when he explored her injuries. Finally he grunted with satisfaction, and said, "It looks worse than it is. But I'm afraid you'll have quite a headache for a few days, and that cut will take some time to heal. I doubt that you'll have a scar—you were very lucky, young woman."

Cynara thought of the moment when she had plunged the knife toward Knowles; she had wanted to kill him in that instant, and she would have driven the knife into his heart if she had been able to. She shuddered. Yes, she had been lucky, she thought. What would have happened to her if she had killed him?

"Several days' rest, I think," Doctor Engel said, turning to Mollie, "And she'll be as good as new."

He removed a bottle from his bag which he gave to Mollie. "A few drops tonight should make her sleep. A few more tomorrow, if she needs them, but none after that."

Mollie inclined her head as she accepted the small bottle. "I'll set to it," she answered quietly.

"I'll look in tomorrow, if you like." He rose, retrieving his bag from the floor. Looking down at Cynara, he said, "I don't want you up and about for two days, at least."

"But doctor, I can't—"

Doctor Engel was not a man to accept protest from his patients. He said severely, "A blow to the head, such as the one you've sustained, can have serious consequences if you aren't careful. A few days' rest is better than a relapse later."

Cynara subsided. "Thank you, doctor," she said, forcing a thin smile.

Doctor Engel reached down to pat her shoulder. "That's better. I'll see you tomorrow—until then, it's bed for you!"

Mollie went to see the doctor out. When she returned, she said briskly, "Doctor Engel is a good man—a good doctor—but if we don't obey his orders, he'll wash his hands of us both. Come along now; we'll put you to bed, and then perhaps we can talk in the morning."

She helped Cynara get up from the sofa, and despite her effort to manage alone, Cynara was forced to lean heavily on Mollie as they went toward the bed. The maid appeared and between them they undressed Cynara and helped her slide between lavender-scented sheets. Cynara sank back gratefully against the pillows, accepting the cup of tea that Mollie had already laced with the laudanum. She drank, feeling a luxurious sense of relaxation seeping through her, and she looked up sleepily at Mollie.

"I'll have Betsy sleep on a shakedown, in case you need someone during the night," Mollie said, gesturing toward the maid who hovered anxiously at the foot of the bed.

"You don't have to—"

"Oh, I don't mind, miss," Betsy said shyly. She adjusted the coverlet, adding, "If you want me, just call out. I sleep light, so I'll hear you."

Cynara looked from one to the other, hardly able to keep her eyes open now that the drug was taking its effect. "Thank you . . . thank you both. And Sarah . . ."

"I'll tell Sarah," Mollie said. "Go to sleep now."

Cynara was asleep before Mollie reached the door.

Cynara didn't know whether it was the medicine the doctor had given her, or the fact that for the first time in weeks she had had a quiet night; whichever it was, when she woke the next morning, she felt refreshed, except for the faint throbbing that persisted in back of her eyes.

Catching sight of herself in the mirror over the dresser as she pulled herself to a sitting position in the bed, she winced. The bruises on her face were dark purple and her cheek was swollen, giving her a lopsided appearance, but she surprised herself by not really caring how she looked. It was enough that she had escaped Knowles at last.

The maid, was gone, as was the cot Cynara dimly remembered being brought in the night before. She saw that someone had put a pot of hot chocolate on the bedside table, and she reached for it, removing the knitted cover that had kept it warm. The chocolate was hot and rich, and Cynara was sipping it gratefully when Mollie quietly opened the door and looked in. She came forward when she saw that Cynara was awake.

"How do you feel this morning?"

"Much better," Cynara acknowledged. "I don't know how to thank you, Mrs.—"

"Mollie, please. And don't thank me; it was all Sarah's doing."

Cynara looked down at the cup she held. "Yes," she said quietly. "If Sarah hadn't come when she did, I don't know what would have happened to me."

"Sarah's a good girl. She's been with me for some months now." Mollie saw the tears gathering in Cynara's eyes, and she added softly, "Do you want to tell me about it?"

Cynara's first impulse was to shake her head. She didn't want anyone to know what she had been through these past weeks. Not only did she still fear the consequences of her running away from Tamoora; she was ashamed to admit what Knowles had done to her, her terror of him. But when she looked up to see Mollie's sympathetic eyes on her, she knew she had to say something.

"It's not a pretty story," she muttered finally.

"I didn't think it would be," Mollie replied calmly.

Cynara glanced away again. She didn't even know Mollie, and yet there was something about her that she trusted, something in her knowing expression that told Cynara she would not judge or condemn. She opened her mouth to speak, but the words refused to come; she could only stare helplessly at her hands, clutching the cup tightly, praying that she wouldn't break down completely.

Mollie was aware of Cynara's distress. She said briskly, changing the subject, "Sarah tells me that the two of you are old friends—" she saw the guarded look come into Cynara's eyes, and continued smoothly "but I want you to know that I'm not interested in what's past, my dear. In my opinion, I think the practice of transportation is an abominable one, especially where young girls are concerned. The poor things have absolutely no way of protecting themselves—but you know that already, don't you?" Mollie's eyes were again sympathetic as a flash of pain came and went quickly in Cynara's face. "So as far as I'm concerned," she finished, "you are simply a young woman who needed my help."

"I don't want to cause you any trouble," Cynara said, carefully replacing the cup of chocolate on the table. She clasped her hands together tightly and stared down at them, continuing in a low voice, "If the authorities should find out that you—"

Mollie interrupted with a laugh. "Oh, don't worry about the authorities," she said casually. "I never do. Several very highly placed men are good friends of mine—they wouldn't allow any unpleasantness here, I assure you."

Cynara looked up, suddenly aware of the power behind Mollie's statement. Her face mirrored her surprise, and Mollie laughed again, rising from the chair she had taken. "But now, I think it's time to let Sarah in—she's been waiting outside to see you, rather impatiently, I might add."

Mollie opened the door, and Sarah rushed in. She was wearing a rose-colored silk wrapper, her curls held back from her face by a ribbon of the same color, and Cynara marveled that she was the same woman she had known on the ship. Last night she had been too exhausted and too frightened to notice Sarah's appearance, but now she saw that Sarah seemed young and vibrant. She also noticed, as Sarah plopped down on the bed and reached for her hands, that while her own were rough and red from the work she had been forced to do at the inn, Sarah's were soft and well cared for, the nails long and carefully buffed. She had gained weight as well, just enough to make her lush body even more rounded and appealing, and Cynara thought sadly that these things pointed up more than anything else the difference between them now.

But what did appearances matter, she thought suddenly. She was reunited with Sarah, even for a short time, and that was all that counted.

Cynara said with a determined effort at cheerfulness, "You look so well, Sarah. I'm glad that things have worked out for you. They have, haven't they?"

Sarah hesitated for an instant, then, taking up the cue, she exclaimed, "Yes, it was the luckiest day of my life when

Mollie saw me coming off the ship—" Again there was that fractional pause, both remembering the horrors of the voyage they had shared, and then Sarah plunged ahead gaily. "I love it here. Mollie is so good to all of us, you know. And—" she winked at Cynara "I'm doing what I do best. What more could I ask?"

"So you're happy then?"

"Oh, yes." The determined gaiety faded abruptly from Sarah's face. She grasped Cynara's hand more tightly. "But what about you, honey? There's no sense beating about the bush, is there? It's obvious that you've had a rough time of it. Do you want to tell me about it?"

"Yes," Cynara answered quietly. "But first I want to know how you found me. It . . . it seems like a miracle . . . "

Sarah laughed softly. "It wasn't that—more like an accident. If I hadn't persuaded Willima to take me for a ride, and if we hadn't decided to stop for something to drink . . . " Shaking her head, Sarah compressed her lips, remembering the scene in the kitchen. "When we came into that horrible place, William was all for leaving immediately. But then we heard all the noise. I heard someone scream. I didn't know it was you, of course, but I knew we had to do something to stop it. It sounded like someone was being murdered."

"He would have killed me, Sarah. I know he would have .

"Who was he, Cynara? How did you ever get mixed up with someone like him? I thought you were married to that man—what was his name?—Thomas Hale."

Suddenly, with Sarah's silent encouragement, Cynara found herself relating the events that had occurred to her since leaving the ship. The words tumbled out: the tale of her bogus marriage to Hale, the terms of his will that had forced her to flee from Tamoora, the meeting with Ben Knowles and her imprisonment at the inn. When she had finished, the two women sat quietly for a moment, and while there were tears in Sarah's eyes, Cynara's own were dry. It seemed like such an endless nightmare that she had little emotion left to express. When she saw that Sarah was on the verge of weeping, she squeezed Sarah's hand. "It's all right," she said. "If one of us was to be more fortunate than the other, I'm glad it was you. You deserved it."

"But I'm more used to hard times," Sarah said at last, wiping her eyes. She added quietly, "Who would have thought it?"

Cynara shook her head. "I was a fool to have believed Hale. I knew from the first what kind of man he was—" she waved her hand, not wanting to pursue that subject. "As for the rest, I suppose it was my fault." Looking at Sarah, she added, "The strange thing, the one that bothers me the most, is Drue. She refused to come with me when I told her I was going to leave. She was afraid of him, Sarah, I know it! Why wouldn't she come?"

"She said she loved him, honey—"

"Yes, but—"

Sarah shrugged. "People are strange—God, who should know that better than we?" She laughed shortly. "If she wanted to stay, there was nothing you could do about it."

"I don't understand it!" Cynara said fiercely. "How could she choose to stay with him, after all he had done!"

"Maybe she had nothing better," Sarah said quietly.

Cynara was silent, wondering if it was true. But it wasn't right, she thought sadly, remembering the times Drue had braved Knowles's wrath to offer what little comfort she could to her. Though she had not wept for herself, she felt tears coming into her eyes over Drue.

"Now," Sarah said briskly, trying to break the depression that had settled on both of them. "We have to decide what to do about you." She glanced sideways at Cynara. "Mollie told me that she would be glad to have you here—in an official capacity, of course. What do you think?"

Cynara didn't need time to think. Stunned, she stared at Sarah. "Sarah, I couldn't! Oh, it's not that I'm ungrateful for Mollie's kindness—you know I am. But I . . . I couldn't! Oh, Sarah!" she cried, panicked.

The thought of unknown men claiming the right to use

her as they wished made her ill. She couldn't do it; she wouldn't do it! All those dirty, lecherous hands on her, those wet mouths, those ugly pale bodies with flabby stomachs and hairy legs! She could imagine it now, herself at the mercy of a parade of nameless, faceless men, forced by necessity to bow to their demands. Oh no—she wouldn't be used again, not by any man. She would starve first!

Closing her eyes tightly, Cynara clung to her dreams of Evan. How could she endure any man not he? He was the one who excited her, who made her weak even being near him. He had only to look at her to arouse her to passion; he had only to gesture, and she would be his. If any man's hands sought the secret places of her body, if any man's lips brought a willing response of her own, they would be Evan's. She would submit to no one else, for no other man had ever evoked this throbbing desire in her, this need to surrender completely, giving up everything her body and soul could offer.

"Cynara?"

She opened her eyes. Sarah was looking at her anxiously. "I'm sorry, Cynara—I didn't mean to upset you," Sarah said quickly. "Mollie would never force you into anything—truly!"

Sarah was crimson, embarrassed that she had made the offer to her friend. It was such an unusual occurrence to see Sarah actually blushing that Cynara laughed, and the awkward moment passed.

"I knew you wouldn't want to stay," Sarah muttered, still uncomfortable. "Mollie knew it too, I think. But we thought we should ask. You understand, don't you?" She waited for Cynara's nod, and then continued, more eagerly, "After we got you settled last night, I talked to William. Together, I think we've worked something out." She didn't tell Cynara that Delmore had been reluctant to offer his services; it had taken quite a bit of maneuvering on her part, plus her knowledge of the kind of pleasure that would make him amenable, but in the end he had agreed to help Cynara. Looking at the sudden eagerness in her friend's eyes, Sarah thought that the effort had been more than worth it.

"What is it?" Cynara asked, trying to keep the hopeful-ness from her voice.

"Well, it isn't much, and you might not like it after all." Encouraged by Cynara's expression, Sarah went on. "William's father is a solicitor, too. Sort of runs in the family, I guess. Anyway," she continued when she saw the impatience Cynara couldn't hide, "He—Delmore, Senior, I mean, has a client who needs someone to take care of her. I thought you might agree to that—until something else comes up, that is. There's only one catch—"

Sarah hesitated, and Cynara asked her to explain. At this point, she didn't care what it was; it was enough that she would have some means of employment at all.

"Well, this woman—her name is Hester Cord, I think—suffered some kind of tragedy a long time ago. William didn't say too much about it, except that her family was all killed at once, and she had collapsed because of the shock. She was in a hospital for a long time, and eventually recovered enough to be discharged, but she has to have someone to take care of her. It seems she—"

Again, Sarah hesitated, and Cynara nodded encouragingly, "Go on."

"From what William said—the woman is a little . . . strange."

"Strange? What do you mean?"

Sarah tapped her forehead. "Her mind went queer from the shock. Sometimes, she can be . . . difficult."

"Difficult?" Cynara realized that she was repeating everything Sarah said. "Do you mean she is . . . violent?"

Sarah shook her head quickly. "She isn't violent—just temperamental. That's why it's so difficult to keep people around her. William says she's had more nurse-companions in the past years than he can count. His father is about at his wits' end, trying to find someone who will stay." Sarah paused again. "I know it doesn't sound promising, Cynara, but it's the best we could do."

Cynara smiled as she squeezed Sarah's hand. "I'm grateful, Sarah, you know that. And it doesn't sound so bad—not after what I've been through." She smiled again, ruefully. "If this woman will have me, I'll be glad to try."

"Good! I'll tell William this afternoon, and he can made the arrangements."

They were interrupted by Doctor Engel, who frowned when he came in and saw Sarah sitting on the bed. "I thought I told you you had to rest, young woman," he said, glowering at Cynara.

"I was just leaving, doctor," Sarah said, rising. But before she left the room, she turned and winked at Cynara. "I'll come back and see you later," she said, tossing a grin at the doctor. "Just for a few minutes—I promise, Doctor Engel. Surely you can't deny us that?"

She sailed away before the doctor could answer, closing the door behind her. "Impossible young woman," Doctor Engel muttered, smiling in spite of himself. He turned to look at Cynara. "And, how do you feel today?"

Four days later, with the doctor's reluctant permission and a bottle of tonic he had prescribed, Cynara left Mollie's. She had to promise him that she would not try to do too much, and that she would eat a lot; she was far too thin, he insisted. Her injury was healing nicely and the headaches had gone, so he was forced to agree that further bed rest was unnecessary.

Mollie and Sarah were on the steps to see her off, and as Cynara said goodbye, she felt like she was leaving a haven. Thanks to Mollie, she felt rested and almost well again, and while she knew it was time to leave, she was reluctant to do so.

"Goodbye, Mollie," Cynara said as they clasped hands. "And thank you for everything you've done for me."

Mollie squeezed her hand. "If you decide to come back," she replied, smiling broadly, "You'll always have a place here—upstairs, that is."

Cynara was sufficiently recovered to laugh in response. "I'll remember," she replied, grinning. Then she turned to Sarah. "Thank you, Sarah," she said fondly. "I don't know how I'll ever repay you."

Sarah flushed, as always uncomfortable when receiving thanks. "Come back and see me," she said roughly. "Somehow I doubt that that Cord woman would appreciate me parading in and out of her house, or I would come and visit you."

"I don't care what she thinks," Cynara replied. "But I'll come—as soon as I can."

Delmore handed her into the trap he had driven to collect her, and they were off. Cynara turned back to wave, and the two women on the porch waved in return. As they turned and went into the house, Cynara had a strong impulse to ask Delmore to take her back. Suddenly she was nervous over the coming interview. What if Hester Cord disliked her? What if she refused to hire her? She knew little about caring for a semi-invalid; if Hester Cord asked about previous experience, what would she say?

"Nervous?"

Cynara glanced at Delmore; he had turned to look at her. "A little," she admitted.

He smiled for the first time, and Cynara saw that he was almost good-looking when he wasn't so somber. "Don't worry about it," he assured her. "Hester Cord is a difficult woman, but she needs you more than you need her. Everyone else my father has engaged for her has packed up and left within days. She's desperate."

Cynara forced a laugh. "Is that supposed to sound promising?"

Delmore flushed. "I didn't mean—"

How serious he was! She said quickly, "I know. Forgive me, please; I suppose I'm trying to make light of it because it means so much to me. I didn't mean to offend you."

"You didn't," he said, the smile returning. "I understand."

"William—"

He looked at her again. "Yes?"

"William, I . . . I want you to know how much I appreciate what you and your father are doing for me. I don't know what I would have done without your help."

The smile broadened. "I'd advise you not to be too profuse in your thanks," he said, with a heavy attempt at a joke. "After all, you haven't met Hester Cord yet."

"Well, young woman," the harsh voice said, "So you're the next incompetent my solicitor has decided to foist upon me." The gold-headed cane rapped sharply on the floor. "Come here and let me have a look at you."

Cynara glanced quickly at Delmore, who tried to smile encouragingly. She went forward to where Hester Cord sat in the high-backed chair, trying to force her features into some semblance of calm. Hester's chair was placed with its back to the window, shadowing the figure within, but leaving the light to shine fully on Cynara, making her feel even more at a disadvantage. She waited, trying covertly to see the woman whose eyes she felt so sharply on her.

"Turn around," the rough voice commanded.

Cynara obeyed, tightening her lips when the woman addressed Delmore. "She doesn't look very strong, William. And what's happened to her face? Is this your idea of a joke?"

"Certainly not, Miss Cord," he responded stiffly. "Cynara is—"

"Cynara is it? What kind of name is that?" Hester demanded peevishly. "I shall call her Rosslyn—if I decide to keep her, that is," she added petulantly. "You—" the cane pointed in Delmore's direction "—may wait outside, while I ask her a few questions of my own."

"Yes, Miss Cord." With another encouraging smile at Cynara, Delmore bowed and left.

The door had barely closed behind him when Hester ordered, "Come closer. What is it? Are you afraid of me?

Most of my so-called companions have been, you know. All nuisances, if you ask me, and I suppose you're no better. If I need someone to take care of me, what makes you think you deserve the job?" she asked suddenly, catching Cynara off guard.

"Well, I—"

"Don't stammer, girl!"

The cane banged on the floor again, and Cynara winced, memories of Myles rising up in her. She saw the darkened summerhouse, the cane swinging viciously at Evan . . . She swallowed, thrusting the memories from her mind, trying to collect herself enough to reply. Hester Cord continued before she had a chance to speak.

"Delmore tells me you were a convict. Ah—that surprises you, doesn't it? Did you think me such a foolish old woman that I wouldn't inquire about your background?"

"No, I—"

"Of course I did. And I'm not so sure that I want someone with a criminal record taking care of me. How do I know you won't go berserk and murder me in my bed?"

In spite of her nervousness, Cynara felt her temper begin to rise. The accusation was so patently ridiculous that she snapped, "If you believed that I would do such a thing, why did you consent to this interview?"

"Well, well." There was satisfaction in the voice. "Showing a little backbone at last. You're not quite the pudding I thought you were."

In another confusing swing of mood, Hester Cord continued, before Cynara could respond, "If I decide to keep you—and that is by no means certain—I will expect you to be responsible for carrying out my orders and managing this household. I have two other servants, who, if they are not watched constantly, would be most happy to bleed me dry. You will keep an eye on them. Secondly, you will attend me every day; occasionally, if you have served me well, I might allow you a half day off. Your wages will be minimal; in your position, you should be grateful for a roof over your head and food to eat. You will have the room next to mine, in case I need you during the night. I don't entertain, and I don't go out, except for an occasional turn in the garden. I will expect that you keep to yourself; I don't want strange people running about the house. Is that understood?"

"Yes," Cynara answered evenly, praying that her conflicting emotions were not betrayed by her voice. What an impossible woman she was! How could she endure her every day, with no hope of getting out, even for a few hours? But then she hadn't much choice, she thought bitterly. Would it be more to her liking if she were forced to earn her way on the streets, or at best take up Mollie's offer of an upstairs bedroom?

The harsh voice interrupted her thoughts. "Send Delmore in. I wish to speak to him again."

Cynara went to the door and beckoned to Delmore, who had been standing in the corridor, waiting anxiously. He entered, casting a quick glance at Cynara.

"Don't bother trying to find out from her," Hester Cord said from the depths of her chair. "She doesn't make the decisions, and neither do you. I do. And I have decided to give her a try."

Delmore smiled in response, but Hester's next words whipped the smile from his face. "And if there's any trouble, young man, I'll hold you personally responsible. I realize that you've diddled your father in this matter—I wonder how pleased he will be to find that you've saddled me with a convict."

"I beg your pardon, Miss Cord," Delmore said stiffly. "But my father and I discussed fully Miss Rosslyn's possible employment with you. I did not attempt to hide any of the facts, as you suggest. And as for Miss Rosslyn being a convict, I—"

"Never mind, never mind. I told you I would try her— that's all that matters. Show yourself out, young man. I have a few more things I wish to discuss with Rosslyn."

Cynara held out her hand to Delmore, whispering, "Thank you. I'm very grateful for what you've done for me."

Delmore took her hand. "I hope everything—"

"Why are you whispering?" Hester demanded peevishly. "I detest whispering; it's unutterably rude. Take yourself off, William, and give my regards to your father. Tell him he should have come himself—I don't pay him the retainer I do to have him shirk his responsibilities. Tell him that!"

"Yes, Miss Cord." His tone was properly deferential, but he raised his eyes to the ceiling and shook his head. Cynara smiled as he lifted his hand in farewell, and she watched him go quickly to the front door before he turned to wave at her again.

The door had scarcely closed behind him before Hester snapped, "Come here and help me out of this chair. I thought he would never leave!"

Cynara tightened her lips in exasperation as she went to obey. Hester leaned heavily on her arm when Cynara helped her to rise, and for the first time she was able to view her new employer closely.

Hester Cord was a woman in her mid-sixties, Cynara judged from her stoutly corseted body and the veined and gnarled fingers that clutched her arm. She was no taller than five feet, but her small stature was more than compensated for by her arrogance and air of authority. She was dressed in unrelieved black, a black lace cap perched on thin white hair that was incongruously frizzed into a youthful fringe over her forehead. But it was her face that held Cynara's attention: lined and sagging at the chin, it was nevertheless a strong face, with a hooked nose over a thin-lipped slash of a mouth. There were spots of rouge over each cheekbone, a dusting of powder that did not hide the raddled cheeks—a vain attempt to recapture the youth she had lost, and which was still evident in her black and sunken eyes. Those eyes held Cynara's now, and Cynara saw that they radiated displeasure.

"Well," Hester demanded, "Do you like what you see?"

Cynara started, realizing belatedly that she had been staring. Embarrassed, she said nothing, and Hester snapped, "When I ask a question, girl, I expect an answer!"

"Yes, Mrs. Cord."

"*Miss* Cord! *I* never married!" The black eyes transfixed her again. "Have you ever married, girl?" she demanded.

Cynara swallowed. "Yes," she answered quietly, helping the woman walk to the door.

"Well?"

"My . . . my husband died," she answered, praying that Hester would leave it at that.

"Just as well," Hester replied callously. They had left the room, and now Hester gestured toward the stairs. "Never had any use for men," Hester continued, puffing slightly as they climbed the stairs. "None, that is, except—" Hester stopped abruptly, her hand going to her heart.

"What is it?" Cynara asked, alarmed. Seeing a blank, unfocused look come into Hester's eyes, she looked around wildly for help as the woman stiffened under her hands.

"They were all I had," Hester said, her lips moving one over the other. "They were all I had. I saw it coming . . . I watched it creeping closer and closer . . . closer and closer . . . "

Hester's voice became shrill, her expression blank with horror as she relived some terrible inner vision. The stout body shook in Cynara's arms, the woman's hands became claws, tearing at the air. Her mouth opened and closed, as though she were gasping for air.

Cynara was terrified. What was wrong with her? Was she having a stroke, some kind of seizure? She opened her own mouth to cry for help, and Hester turned on her, her clawed hands digging painfully into Cynara's shoulders. "Do you see it? Do you see it? Red, red, nothing but red!"

"Miss Cord! Hester!" Cynara cried, trying to balance both herself and the other woman before they pitched to the floor below. "It was a long time ago—a long time ago! It isn't happening now!"

In her fear, she was babbling, saying the first thing that came into her head. The sight of Hester's blank, horrified face so close to hers, the empty, straining eyes, increased her terror. What should she do? She couldn't leave her while she ran for help. She didn't even know if anyone was about; no one had answered her call.

"Miss Cord," she said, trying to control her shaking voice. "Miss Cord—do you hear me? Can you hear me? It isn't happening now. Oh, please . . . "

"What? What?"

To Cynara's immense relief, the blank expression suddenly left Hester's eyes. "It's all right," Cynara said softly. "It's all right."

"All right? What's all right? What are you doing, clutching me in this fashion? Really, girl, you will have to learn to be more careful. You could have caused us both to fall down these stairs. Come along, help me to my room."

Cynara stared at her, bewildered. She shook her head; she was beginning to understand why none of the former companions had stayed; Hester's transformation had been sudden and frightening. When Hester had grabbed her, the strength in those twisted hands had been enough to send them crashing to the floor below. She felt beads of sweat breaking out on her forehead at how narrowly disaster had been averted.

"What is the matter with you, girl? Why are you staring at me so rudely?"

Taking a deep breath, Cynara forced herself to answer calmly, "I'm sorry, Miss Cord." Hesitantly, she added, "Do you feel all right?"

"Do I feel all right?" Hester repeated impatiently. "Of course I feel all right. Why do you ask such a stupid question? Stop dawdling and help me to my room. After that, you can bring me my tea."

Was it possible that the woman didn't realized what had happened to her? Cynara was reluctant to mention the incident, for fear of inducing a repetition of that frightening scene. Wordlessly she helped Hester negotiate the rest of the stairs, and went with her down a carpeted corridor to the door Hester indicated. With a sigh of relief, she settled the woman in a chair by the window, receiving instructions as to the location of the kitchen.

"And tell that woman, Bella, to mash the tea properly today!" Hester called out when Cynara went to the door. "I detest that insipid stuff she makes."

"Yes, Miss Cord."

Cynara went down the stairs again, still shaken. Turning left at the foot of the stairs, she went toward the kitchen, wondering if she should send for the doctor. Hester seemed to have recovered with no ill effects, but she could not be sure. Perhaps a doctor could tell her what was wrong with the woman, or if there was some way to prevent the same thing from happening again. Remembering the abruptness of the attack, or whatever it had been, Cynara shivered. What if Hester did have a stroke during those terrifying seizures? What would she do then?

Thinking that the cook, Bella, might be familiar with Hester's attacks Cynara resolved to ask her opinion. If Bella agreed, she would send for Doctor Engel.

But the kitchen was empty when Cynara pushed the baize door open, and Cynara glanced around, seeing the same evidence of neglect and carelessness that she had noted about the rest of the house. Remembering Hester's remark about her servants, Cynara thought that the first chore she would undertake was to have the house properly cleaned. Running her fingers along the edge of the kitchen table, she grimaced when the surface felt sticky under her hand. She would start in the kitchen, she thought, but in the meantime, Hester wanted her tea, and where was Bella?

As if in answer to her unspoken question, the back door opened, and a thin woman with a sharp face entered. She was carrying an empty basket, which she clutched defensively as she stared with suspicion at Cynara.

"Hello," Cynara said. "My name is Cynara Rosslyn, and I've been engaged to look after Miss Cord. She sent me for the tea tray."

The woman grunted, placing the basket on the table. "It isn't ready yet," she replied sullenly.

Determined to make a show of friendliness in spite of the surly expression on the woman's face, Cynara offered, "I'll be glad to help, if you will show me where the things are."

"I don't need any help."

"As you wish." Deliberately, Cynara folded her arms across her waist, returning the woman's stare with a calmness she didn't feel. But she knew that if she were to assume command of the household, as Hester had ordered, it would be fatal for Bella to succeed in intimidating her from the start. Judging from the condition of the kitchen, Bella had taken advantage of the woman upstairs for far too long.

Cynara stood silently, her eyes going only once to the clock over the stove, her attitude indicating more than words that she expected Bella to make the tea as requested.

Bella's lips twisted as the silence dragged on. At last, with an impatient jerk of her head, she went toward the stove where the kettle simmered. Reaching for the pot, she banged it down on the sideboard and began making the tea.

"Is there any cake?" Cynara asked when Bella had completed the task. "If not, perhaps—"

"It's cake, is it, that you want?" Bella turned to glare angrily at Cynara, setting the tray down on the table with a clatter. "I have enough to do without worrying about cake for tea, if you want to know!"

Cynara refused to respond to the woman's open hostility. She said calmly, "Then perhaps a little bread and butter." Her glance was even as she looked at Bella. "I assume there *is* bread and butter?"

Bella took a deep breath. Without another word, she stomped to a cupboard, jerked out a loaf of bread, and taking a knife from the rack, began hacking at it furiously. Slamming down the plate she had piled with the uneven slices of bread, she went to the pantry, returning with a bowl of butter, which she also slammed onto the tray. Her expression was defiant when she looked at Cynara.

"Thank you," Cynara said coolly. She picked up the tray, exiting with as much dignity as she could manage, refusing to give rein to her temper. Bella stared angrily after her.

Once in the corridor again, Cynara leaned shakily against the wall, her anger forgotten. Balancing the tray on her hip, she thought that she had won the first battle with Bella, but she knew it was only the beginning. How that woman would react to the news that Cynara was now in charge of the household, she could only imagine. Her dealings with Bella could only be unpleasant, unless she could find a way to get on her good side—if she had one, Cynara thought wryly.

As for Hester, Cynara wasn't sure yet what her reaction was to the woman. She suspected that underneath the arrogance and petulant demands, Hester Cord was a frightened old woman, who had been taken advantage of by the people who had been hired to serve her. In her suspicion of everyone, her irrascibility had emerged as her only means of protection. She was difficult—if not impossible—to please, and yet Cynara had already begun to feel sympathy for her. She had seen for herself the terror in Hester's eyes, the deep fear that she tried to hide. Something in Cynara responded to that fear, for she had been afraid so often in the past herself.

Mounting the stairs, Cynara resolved that as long as she was here, she would do her best to protect Hester, to see to her comfort. She knew it wouldn't be easy; even now, Hester was calling out sharply to her for being late with the tea. But as Cynara placed the tray before her, she knew that she would stay as long as Hester Cord would have her. For the first time in a long while, Cynara felt useful and needed, almost peaceful in her new resolve. It was a feeling she had thought never to have again, and she welcomed it.

CHAPTER TWENTY-FOUR

VINCENT LECROIX WAS worried about Evan. At first, when Evan had returned from that impulsive chase to Tamoora, Vincent had merely been concerned. Evan had glowered for days, his temper so short that everyone, at home and in the office, had almost tiptoed around him for fear of incurring his wrath. Restraining himself with effort, Vincent had kept silent, telling himself that if Evan wanted to confide in him, he would. But when a week had passed and Evan grew even more withdrawn, more tightlipped than before, Vincent became anxious. Had something awful happened? Vincent knew that he would have heard if any of Evan's investments had turned sour, or if he was in trouble financially, but there had been no whisper of disaster in that quarter. And yet, from the way Evan was acting, whatever was wrong had to be catastrophic.

After three weeks of silence, Vincent was tempted to come right out and ask Evan what troubled him, but every time he nerved himself to ask, he held back. He wouldn't be an interfering old man, he told himself. Yet whenever he saw Evan's set face, the dark eyes that seemed to burn with anger, or worry, or pain—Vincent couldn't be sure which it was—it was more difficult for him to maintain his self-imposed silence.

Finally one night Vincent could keep quiet no longer. After a dinner of Evan's favorite dishes, which the cook had spent hours preparing, only to have everything remain almost untouched, Evan had retired alone to the library. Vincent had noted with alarm that while Evan ignored the meal in front of him, he had filled and refilled his wine glass, drinking vast amounts that plunged him deeper and deeper into that black mood he had sustained for weeks. Making a sudden decision, Vincent finished his own port and went to the library; he would ask Evan if he could help, and that would be all.

Opening the door quietly, Vincent paused on the threshold, staring in dismay at the sight of Evan sitting by the fireplace. Evan hadn't even heard him come in. Thinking himself alone, he sat slumped on the edge of a chair, elbows on his knees, supporting his head with his hands. The whole picture was one of complete dejection, and Vincent was about to move forward, when to his utter amazement, he thought he heard a strangled sob break from Evan's lips.

Stricken by the sound, Vincent didn't know whether to go to Evan or leave the library as quietly as he had entered. He stood there helplessly, watching the young man who had become almost a son to him, and he cursed his helplessness. He didn't know what to do to alleviate the pain he saw so clearly in every line of Evan's body.

At last Vincent decided that it would be best to leave him alone. He knew that Evan would be embarrassed to be seen like this, that he would resent Vincent's presence when he so obviously wanted to be alone.

He was about to turn away when Evan chanced to look up. Their eyes met, and Vincent felt his heart lurch when he saw tears in Evan's eyes. He looked away quickly, forcing himself to move calmly to the sideboard where he poured himself a drink.

"Evan," he said quietly, "is there anything I can do?"

Evan gave no answer. He moved from the chair to stand by the fireplace, staring moodily at the floor, one arm resting on the mantle.

LeCroix gestured with his glass. "Whatever it is, I'll be glad to help you in any way I can. You know that, of course."

Evan was still silent, and LeCroix, after looking once more at his face, began to leave the library. He had almost reached the door when Evan said, "Vincent."

"Yes?"

"Vincent, I'm afraid I do need your help," Evan said in a low voice. His hand clenched into a fist, and he slammed it down on top of the mantle with such force that the china figurines spaced along its length rattled before settling back precariously to their former positions.

Moving away from the fireplace, Evan began to pace back and forth, and Vincent watched him in silence, trying not to be alarmed. Evan had lost weight these past weeks; Vincent had been aware of it, but never so much as tonight, for Evan's face was gaunt and drawn, and there were dark circles under his eyes. In times of stress or worry, the scar on his face seemed to stand out, giving him a satanic appearance that was furthered by the burning intensity in his eyes. Those eyes seemed to bore into Vincent as Evan stopped his pacing abruptly and turned to him.

"Do you remember the day I went out to Tamoora, after Thomas Hale died?"

Vincent nodded. How could he forget?

"I went there for a purpose. Oh, not what you think," Evan said quickly when he saw Vincent's dismay. "Hale was dead; he was nothing to me anymore."

Evan paused, closing his eyes. After a moment, as though he couldn't stand still, he resumed his pacing, more agitated than before. "I went there to see Hale's wife—widow," he said finally. "I wanted her, Vincent. I was going to take her away."

Still Vincent said nothing, obviously trying to suppress his astonishment, and Evan moved violently away. Yes, he thought bitterly; he had rushed off like some besotted fool, never thinking that Cynara might not want him to spirit her away. He had been so involved with his own feelings that he hadn't given a thought to hers. And even now he hadn't told Vincent the whole truth; he wasn't sure he understood his complex emotions himself. He wanted Cynara, yes; he wanted her as he had never wanted any other woman. His longing to hold her, to touch her, was unbearable at times; he could think of nothing else but Cynara. Had she but known, she could have mastered him with a lift of an eyebrow, a movement of a finger. He could see her now, smiling provocatively, tilting her head up at him, her eyes green smoke, offering promises that only she could keep. She could be dressed in sackcloth, he thought, and he would still be wild for her, for his desire knew no bounds. She had called to him in the ageless ways of a woman, sure of her power, and he was compelled to respond. She would be all things to him, passionate, loving, tempestuous. He would never know what to expect of her, and that was her fascination. She could be purring kitten one instant, savage tigress the next.

He didn't know how he knew these things. It was enough that the knowledge was there, teasing him, plaguing him, increasing his desire and anxiety to fever pitch. He couldn't rid himself of his dread, his certainty that something terrible would happen to her if he didn't find her. He had to find her; he could not lose the only woman in the world who meant life to him.

Vincent watched Evan, still recovering from his surprise at Evan's announcement. He had seen for himself that women were immediately attracted to Evan; he had always envied—just a little—that dark charm, the sexuality that Evan possessed without even realizing it. But Evan had never seemed particularly interested in women, except in that they satisfied the demands of his body. It was as though he had no use for them beyond a purely physical need.

In any other circumstances, Vincent would have been amused at the thought that a woman had captured Evan at last—Evan, who had been able to enjoy the women he bedded, but who had been able to walk away so casually the next morning, forgetting them until next time. But Vincent was not amused now; he had seen the agonized look in Evan's eyes, and he was alarmed. What was it about this one woman that caused Evan such pain? He felt a rush of protective anger against this unknown creature who had driven his friend into one of the blackest moods LeCroix had ever seen upon him, but he waited silently until Evan spoke again.

"She was gone when I got there. She disappeared without a trace." Evan's voice became even more strained. "I've had a man out looking for her, but—" He stopped, going abruptly to the sideboard where LeCroix had left the decanter out. Pouring a large measure of brandy, Evan drank it quickly and poured another before turning back to LeCroix. "I have to find her, Vincent," he said intensely, "before something happens to her."

LeCroix took a deep breath, motioning Evan to a chair. "Perhaps you had better tell me the whole story, Evan," he said quietly. "Then we'll see what we can do."

Evan ignored the offer of the chair and took up his pacing again. Tersely, he related the steps he had taken after discovering that Cynara had disappeared from Tamoora: the talk with Gerald Whitley, the buying of Cynara's transport papers, his hiring of a man named Boswell for her. But Boswell had not been able to find her, and Evan didn't know what else to do.

"Why didn't you come to me sooner?" Vincent asked, staring down at the amber liquid in his glass.

Evan made a gesture with his hand. "I didn't want to bother you with it. I thought I could find her myself." Moodily, he threw himself into the chair opposite LeCroix, running his fingers distractedly through his hair. "I've failed. It's utterly hopeless."

Vincent looked up. "Not necessarily. I think there are a few avenues open to us yet."

"What?" Evan asked bitterly. "I've tried everything I can think of."

"Well, let me think on it," LeCroix replied. "Boswell isn't the only man around." He smiled slightly. "I might know a few tricks myself."

It seemed that Vincent had been modest. Within a week he came home one night, very pleased with himself. He met Evan in the hall, and said immediately, "I think we're on to something, Evan. One of my men just told me that he thinks he saw a young woman of Cynara's description working at Michael's Inn—you know the one; it's halfway between here and—"

"I know it, Vincent," Evan interrupted tersely. "Did he say when he saw her?"

"I gather it was recently, but—"

"But what?"

"He isn't sure, Evan. Evan—where are you going?"

Evan barely paused on his way out the door. "Where do you think?" he threw over his shoulder.

"Wait for me!" This time Vincent had no intention of allowing Evan to dash off by himself. He had heard of the inn and knew it was a disreputable place, patronized by rough customers.

Grunting with exasperation, Vincent followed Evan to the stables. There was no time to call for the carriage; Evan was in a fever of impatience to be gone, barely able to restrain himself while a horse was saddled for LeCroix. As soon as Vincent had mounted, Evan wheeled his horse out of the yard and was galloping off down the road.

"Evan!"

Reluctantly, Evan pulled his horse to a slower gait, allowing LeCroix to catch up to him. "There's no need to wind the horses," LeCroix said severely as he came abreast. "We'll get there soon enough—if we can find our way in this blasted darkness."

"I know the way," Evan replied grimly. "And you don't have to come along, you know."

LeCroix shot a quick glance at him. "Don't I?"

Evan was silent. He knew why LeCroix was coming with him, and while part of him resented his presence, another part was forced to admit that Vincent had cause to worry. His behavior over the past month had not inspired confidence, and he was suddenly ashamed.

The ride to the inn seemed endless to Evan, who was forced to a slower pace than he wished. He held his horse to a trot but the urge to push the animals faster was almost unbearable. What was Cynara doing in a wretched place like that? Recalling the one time he had been there, Evan tightened his lips; certainly that was no place for a woman—especially Cynara. Remembering the owner of the place, Evan grimaced. The man was as bad as the customers he served; if he had laid a hand on Cynara, Evan would kill him where he stood.

What would he say to Cynara when he found her? It didn't matter, he thought irritably: she had no business even being near such a wretched place. His mouth tightened. He could just imagine her reaction to his rushing in and dragging her out of there, but he would deal with that later. His only concern right now was that he had found her; everything else was unimportant. Somehow he would manage to explain, to make her understand. He refused to think that she wouldn't want to be found by him; uppermost in his mind was that his long, agonizing search was over.

At last they spied the lane that led to the inn. As they turned into it, LeCroix reached out and grasped Evan's arm. "Easy, lad," he said softly. "I'm not the fighter I was in my younger days."

Evan managed a tight smile. "I hope it doesn't come to that, but if it does . . ." He shrugged.

LeCroix sighed. From the look on Evan's face, he knew there was going to be trouble.

They dismounted and tied their horses to the rail. Evan, without waiting for LeCroix, bounded up the steps to the entrance and pushed open the door. He stood on the threshold, his eyes searching the crowded and smoke-filled room, until his glance came to rest on Ben Knowles. Without looking to either side, Evan started forward, and so savage was his expression that the men parted silently to let him through.

Knowles was behind the bar. Evan noticed that the man's hand and arm were bandaged, but his mind barely registered the fact; his eyes were on Knowles's face.

"Where is she?" Evan asked, his voice hard. "Cynara Rosslyn."

There was a flicker of response in Knowles's eyes, quickly gone, but it was enough for Evan. He was sure now that this man knew where Cynara was.

"She? I don't know who you mean, mister."

"I think you do. I want to see her—now!"

The innkeeper shrugged his shoulders, spreading his hands in an uncomprehending gesture. "I still don't know who you're talking about," he replied roughly.

Evan moved so swiftly that he surprised Knowles. Leaning across the bar, he grabbed a fistful of the man's shirt, forcing him forward, until their faces were only inches apart. "Tell me where she is," he said. "I'm running out of patience."

Knowles tried to rear back. He was not as tall as Evan, but he weighed a great deal more. Sure of the outcome in any contest between himself and Evan, Knowles laughed. "You must want her pretty bad, mister—"

Evan's hand twisted. Knowles felt the shirt tightening around his neck, but he was still too confident to be intimidated. "Hey—" he started to object, but Evan's grip tightened even more, choking him.

"You've got five seconds to tell me where she is."

"I tell you, mister, I don't know who you're talking about!"

Knowles reached up with both hands, trying to free himself. He could feel the blood pounding in his head, and he wondered for the first time if the man would try to choke him to death right there. Alarmed, he realized that he could not break Evan's grip.

The pressure around his throat abated suddenly, and he was gasping for air when he felt Evan's hands on his shoulders. To the amazement of everyone in the room, Evan pulled him off the floor and across the bar. He half fell to the floor on Evan's side of the room before he realized what had happened.

"Are you going to tell me or not?"

Knowles, in spite of his size, quailed before the murderous fury he saw in Evan's face. "I don't—"

"You'd better tell him, Ben," someone shouted from across the room.

"Shut up, you!" Knowles snarled.

The exchange gave Evan the proof he needed. "Your time is running out, mister," he said softly.

Frightened, Knowles reared back. "What's she to you?" he snarled. "She was nothin' but a—"

Evan's fist smashed into his face, knocking him backwards. He cried out, putting his hand to his mouth, spitting out blood. Evan advanced on him again. oblivious to LeCroix, who was trying to push his way through the stupefied crowd, calling his name.

Knowles saw Evan coming toward him once more, and his face blanched. Grabbing the bar, he slithered backwards, groping for balance. Evan followed inexorably, and Knowles said, "Look, mister—"

Evan hit him again. He was like a madman, his face a mask of rage, his eyes black holes in his face. Knowles had never seen anything like it, and he was terrified. "Tell me where she is," Evan said.

Knowles had reached the end of the bar. Glancing around wildly, he saw that none of the men there would offer to help him. Some were actually grinning, their hands hooked into their belts as they watched. Desperate, knowing that he stood alone, Knowles saw a bottle of rum on the counter. Grabbing it, he smashed it against the bar, feeling a surge of power now that he held a weapon in his hand. The broken edges of the bottle glinted in the lamplight as he brandished it in Evan's face.

Evan ignored the threatening gesture. His eyes never left the innkeeper's bloody face; he had not even flinched when broken glass sprayed around him. A piece of the glass had flown up, cutting his face, but he did not notice it. He was aware only that Cynara was here, and because Knowles was the worst of men, a bully and a coward, Evan suspected the worst. Cynara would never have the strength to fight this bull of a man, and the thought of Knowles's hands on her soft flesh, his brutal mouth ravaging hers, drove Evan forward in a mindless rage.

Fear made Knowles reckless; lunging at Evan, he aimed the jagged end of the bottle directly at his face. His hand was arrested in midair as Evan grabbed his wrist. Standing over him, Evan forced Knowles's hand backward. The pain was excruciating; his fingers numb, Knowles was forced to drop the bottle. It fell to the floor between them, shattering, and still Evan did not move. Inexorably he forced Knowles's hand backwards as the man tried vainly to free himself. He was truly frightened now; never had he seen such cold fury in any man's eyes. Evan drew back his other arm, and Knowles cringed, crying out in anticipation of the blow to come.

"Stop! Oh, please—stop!"

A slight form came running from the kitchen, moving fearlessly between the two men. Evan started as he felt small hands on his arm, trying to free Knowles's wrist from his grasp. Blankly, he looked down and realized that it was a woman. There were tears running down her face as she struggled ineffectually, trying to make him let go.

"Oh, please," she cried again. "Please stop!"

The woman's desperate cry penetrated the blind rage that had gripped Evan. Dropping Knowles's arm, he moved back a step, leaving Knowles huddled against the bar, gasping for breath.

The woman looked up at Evan's face, her own contorted as she raised her hands pleadingly. "I'll tell you what you want to know," she sobbed. "Only, please leave him alone. He's been hurt already, can't you see that?"

Evan glanced contemptuously in Knowles's direction, his lip curling as Knowles grabbed at his bandaged arm. The bandage hadn't prevented him from trying to attack him with the broken bottle, Evan thought coldly, as his eyes went again to the woman's face. "Where is she?" he asked.

The woman wrung her hands. "I don't know—no, wait!" she cried as Evan moved toward Knowles again. "She was here, but some people came and took her away. I swear it!"

"Who were they?"

"I don't know," she wailed. "A man and a woman. I never saw them before. Please believe me!"

She had grabbed the lapels of Evan's coat, hanging on to him as she sobbed. "They took her away the other night," she gabbled. "They had a fancy carriage . . . with a coachman . . . Oh, please, no more trouble! That's all we know. Ask anyone here!"

Evan glanced around at the silent crowd. Several of the men who had been there the night Cynara was taken away nodded sheepishly. One of them, realizing that the fun was over, offered, "It's true, mister. I saw it."

Grinding his teeth together, Evan asked, "Where did they go?"

The man shook his head, looking questioningly at his companions, who shook their heads also.

"Evan!" LeCroix appeared suddenly at his side, grabbing onto his arm. "Evan, let's go. We can trace her from here. *Evan!*"

Evan glanced slowly around the room again, and as before, his expression made everyone uneasy. "If I find you're lying to me," he said, his voice low but somehow carrying to the far corners of the room, "I'll be back." As he said this last, his eyes came to rest on Knowles, who had remained motionless at the end of the bar. "The woman saved your life," he said. "Remember that."

Evan turned and walked from the room, leaving a thick silence behind. Outside, he ripped the reins from the rail and threw himself into the saddle. Wordlessly, he and LeCroix turned their horses in the direction of Sydney once more, and they had gone several miles before Evan broke the silence. When he spoke, his voice was so low that LeCroix could hardly hear him. "I'll never find her. She could be anywhere by now. Anything could have happened to her out here . . ."

"We'll find her, Evan," LeCroix said quietly, trying to be reassuring.

But Evan shook his head, and when he urged his horse forward a few paces, LeCroix let him go, making no effort to catch up with him.

CHAPTER TWENTY-FIVE

EVAN WAS WORKING at his desk, trying to concentrate on the figures in front of him, when Vincent burst into his office. LeCroix had such an air of excitement about him that Evan half rose from his chair, daring to hope for the first time in the two weeks since they had left the inn that there was some news of Cynara. At this point, Evan thought, he would have seized eagerly even the most meager scrap of information.

"What is it?" he asked, as LeCroix came to the desk and leaned over it, brandishing a slip of paper under his nose.

"I told you we would find her!" LeCroix crowed triumphantly. "I knew we just had to give it time!"

"Where is she?" Evan tried to grab the paper, but LeCroix snatched it away, throwing it jubilantly into the air.

"Not so fast, lad! Let me tell it in my own way!"

"Vincent—"

"In good time, lad, in good time. God, I can't believe it! After all these months, and she's been practically right under our noses the whole time!"

"All these months," Evan repeated blankly. "But—"

"Hester Cord! We've finally found Hester Cord!" LeCroix shouted.

Evan had been so preoccupied with Cynara that he had forgotten Hester completely; it took him several seconds to remember, and when he did, he tried to express the interest that LeCroix seemed to expect of him. But he was deeply disappointed; he had been so sure that Cynara had been found. Trying not to show how defeated he felt, Evan forced a smile.

LeCroix saw the effort Evan made, and his elation disappeared. He had thought that the news of Hester would cheer Evan a little, but he had been too optimistic. Dejectedly he retrieved the paper from the floor and put it on top of Evan's desk. "The address is there," he said quietly.

Evan made an effort to thank him. "I know how hard you worked to get this, Vincent," he said. "It's not that I'm ungrateful; it's just that—"

"I know, lad. I know. I thought this would help, but . . ." Vincent hesitated. "These things take time, Evan. Look how long it took to find Hester. Australia is a big country—"

"We don't even know if Cynara is still in Australia," Evan said, feeling that black depression settling on him again. It was as though Cynara had disappeared completely, and he had the hopeless feeling he would never find her.

Moving away to the window so that LeCroix could not see his expression, Evan thought of Cynara as he had seen her last at the ball at Tamoora, and he closed his eyes in pain. She had looked so lovely, he thought, so incredibly beautiful. Why hadn't he taken her away then, he agonized. He should have followed his urge to carry her away from there, riding swiftly through the night, feeling his arms strong around her, her slender weight leaning into him as his horse galloped back to town and safety. He would have taken her somewhere—anywhere—so they could be alone.

His pain was unbearable as he pictured it, and Evan bowed his head. Would he ever find her again?

"I'm going to Mollie's tonight," Vincent said suddenly. "Why don't you come along?"

Neither of them had visited Mollie's for some time: Evan because he had no interest, Vincent because he felt guilty at leaving Evan behind. But the idea of going there tonight had just occurred to him; if nothing else, a visit to Mollie's might help Evan take his mind off his disappointment. He looked inquiringly at Evan, his face falling when Evan shook his head.

"No, Vincent. I don't feel much like Mollie's tonight."

"Come on, lad. It might do you some good."

Evan started to shake his head again, but at Vincent's crestfallen expression, he abruptly changed his mind. "All right, all right. I'll go."

"Good!" Vincent exclaimed, slapping Evan on the back when he came around the desk to join him. "Maybe Sarah can cheer you up!"

"I doubt it," Evan replied darkly as he reached for his hat and coat.

"What's the matter, love?"

Evan started. He had been so absorbed in his thoughts that he had forgotten Sarah's presence in the room. She sat beside him on the sofa, watching him closely, her expression worried as he looked apologetically at her.

Reaching for her hand, Evan squeezed it. "I'm sorry, Sarah. I'm afraid I'm not very good company tonight." Bending his head back, he rested it against the sofa, closing his eyes wearily.

"Is there anything I can do?"

Evan shook his head, barely noticing that she had gotten up to come around to the back of the sofa. He felt her hands on his shoulders, massaging his taut muscles, and despite his tenseness, he began to relax. Taking a glass of whiskey from the table beside him, he sipped it slowly, feeling some of the tension leaving him as Sarah continued to knead his shoulders.

"Does that feel better?"

He nodded, and her hands moved down to his chest, slipping inside his shirt. The touch of her fingers against his skin was pleasant and he felt a stirring of desire. With one arm he reached around, grabbing her by the waist, pulling her around the sofa to hold in his lap. She raised her mouth for a kiss, and he responded, kissing her lightly, and then as her mouth became more demanding, with increasing desire. His hand moved to her breast, then followed the line of her hip and thigh as she reclined beside him. He felt the firm flesh under his fingers, and abruptly he grabbed her close to him and kissed her urgently. She answered with the passion that had always aroused him, but tonight something was wrong. The brief flare of desire he had felt moments ago vanished; try as he would, he could not recapture it, and he lifted his head.

"I'm sorry, Sarah. I think I'd better go."

"What is it, Evan? Did I do something wrong?"

"No, no." He forced a smile for her, and kissed the tip of her nose, putting her gently aside. "I just have too many things on my mind, I guess."

"Well, we don't have to go to bed," Sarah said tentatively as he made a motion to rise. "We could . . . we could talk."

To her gratification, he did not laugh at her suggestion, as so many men would have. He sat back again, regarding her seriously. "What do you want to talk about?"

"Oh, I don't know." Sarah cast about in her mind for a topic of conversation. She had not seen Evan for several weeks; she had missed him, and she didn't want him to leave her so soon. She had admitted to herself long ago that she loved him, but she had kept her feelings to herself. Evan enjoyed her, she knew that, but she also knew that he didn't love her—and never would. She had vowed to be content with the fact that he came to her regularly, for she knew that no good could come of a declaration of her feelings for him. A relationship such as theirs would be frowned upon by the circles he was destined to move in, and she would not be the one to hold him back. She would never forgive herself if she did, and she did not want to hold him to her out of a sense of guilt.

But Evan was looking at her curiously, waiting for her to answer, and because she was afraid of betraying herself, she said the first thing that entered her mind. "I saw a friend of mine a while ago—one of my shipmates, actually," she said, laughing nervously. She was aware that Evan, despite his pose of interest, had begun to drum his fingers absently on the arm of the sofa. "Mollie was very interested in her when I brought her here—she thought she would be a good addition to the house. You would like her, too," she added impulsively, reaching across to refill the glass he held from the decanter on the table. "Her name is Cynara, and she—"

"*What!*"

The word exploded from him at the same instant the

glass shattered from the convulsive grip of his fingers. Appalled, Sarah saw the blood trickling between his fingers, and she sprang up as he did. "Evan! Your hand!"

Evan looked down blankly at his hand, dripping blood and whiskey on the rug. "Never mind that!" he rasped. "What did you—"

But Sarah had run to the dresser, returning quickly with a cloth which she proceeded to try to wrap around his hand. "Evan, you're hurt—"

"Never mind!" Almost savagely he jerked away from her, then took her by the shoulders, oblivious to the fact that his blood was staining the wrapper she wore. Frightened, Sarah tried to pull back from him, stunned by the look on his face.

"You know Cynara?" he demanded harshly.

"I . . . I . . . yes," Sarah stammered. "I told you—she was with me on the ship."

"And you brought her here?"

"Well, yes . . . She was . . ." Sarah stopped. For some reason, she did not want to tell Evan that Cynara had been injured. "Yes," she said, as calmly as she could. "She was here—"

"She's gone!" To Sarah's amazement, Evan actually groaned aloud, his fingers tightening on her shoulders until she winced.

"Evan, you're hurting me—"

Evan looked down blankly at his hands, gripping Sarah until his knuckles showed white against his skin. His eyes widened, and he dropped his hands to his sides. "I'm sorry, Sarah; I didn't mean to hurt you."

Sarah watched him warily, rubbing her shoulder, as he sank down onto the sofa again, his head in his hands. The blood from the cuts dripped down the back of his hand, but he did not notice, and now Sarah quietly retrieved the cloth and took his hand from his face, wrapping it gently. Sitting down beside him, she forced him to look at her, and felt her heart sink when she saw his ravaged face. So Cynara was the woman, she thought, the woman whose memory had tormented him these past months. She should have known.

For a treacherous instant, Sarah was tempted not to tell him where Cynara had gone. She, Sarah, loved him, too, she thought; how could she tell him, knowing that she would lose him? But the impulse passed as quickly as it had come. She could not keep the knowledge from him after seeing what she had seen in his face.

"Evan," she said softly. "I know where she is."

She felt like a sword had gone through her heart when she saw the hunger in his expression. Turning away from him, she continued quietly, "She's working for a woman named Hester Cord—"

"Hester Cord!"

Again, Sarah was astonished at Evan's reaction. He was staring at her in stupification. "Yes, Hester Cord," she repeated. "Why, do you know her?"

Suddenly, Evan started to laugh, a wild sound that alarmed Sarah even more. "Evan, what is it?"

"Oh, it's too long a story to explain," Evan said, throwing his head back and laughing jubilantly. "It's just so ironic, that's all! If only we had known—"

His laughter stopped as quickly as it had begun when he chanced to see her face. Soberly now, he grasped Sarah's hand and said, "Thank you, Sarah. You don't know how long I've tried to find her. It's been a nightmare . . ."

Sarah tried to smile. Ironic, she thought. Yes, it was. Evan had been pursuing Cynara, and she had known where she was. She tried to tell herself that she was happy for him—happy for them both—but to her horror, she felt tears coming into her eyes. She stood up quickly and reached for the decanter to pour herself a drink. She felt the need to get drunk, to drink herself senseless so that she would never wake again. The impulse frightened her; she looked distastefully at the glass she held and put it back on the table. It was then that she noticed Evan looking at her with sudden knowledge in his eyes, and she flushed painfully as she looked away from him.

"Sarah. . ."

"It's all right, Evan. It's all my fault; I should know better than to get mixed up with my . . . my customers." She used the word deliberately, praying that it would return the situation to its proper perspective. She didn't want to prolong this emotional scene; in a few moments more she really would cry, and that would be disastrous.

He came to stand behind her, his hands, so rough before, now gentle on her shoulders. Closing her eyes, she allowed him to pull her back against him. He put his arms around her, turning her to face him, but she could not look up at him.

"Please, Evan—just go . . ."

"Not yet . . ."

He lifted her in his arms, carrying her gently to the bed. As he lay beside her, she asked, just once, "Are you sure you want to do this? You don't have to—"

He knew he didn't have to make love to her. He couldn't explain himself why he wanted to. Perhaps it was because Sarah had always been more than just a bed partner; she had cared for him, tended him when he was hurt, soothed him when he was angry or depressed. He couldn't simply leave her now, as though she had been nothing to him. Despite his wild impatience to be gone, to find Cynara, he owed this last night to Sarah, and he would give it to her gladly. He could never repay her for what she had done for him, but perhaps this last time with her would help her realize how grateful he was. No, more than grateful, he thought sadly. If it hadn't been that Cynara was in his mind, his blood, his heart, he might have been happy with Sarah. He wanted to show her this, to let her know what she meant to him.

Stopping her protests with a kiss, he took her in his arms, more gently, more tenderly than he ever had before. His hands moved over her rounded body, seeking the places he knew would give her pleasure, until she moaned and strained against him. Lightly, his fingers brushed her nipples, feeling them become taut and swollen, and he lowered his head to kiss them, his lips then leaving her breasts and traveling slowly down to her soft stomach and beyond.

Sarah clutched his hair, pulling him up again, her lips clinging to his, her tongue deep inside his mouth. Her hands were on him, stroking, caressing; her legs wrapped around him, holding him close as they rolled over the bed. As he entered her, she opened wide to receive him, her muscles tensing and relaxing, her hips moving sensuously, drawing him further inside her.

They thrust against each other, hands sliding on sweaty skin, mouths locked together, and as they reached the too swift climax together, tears filled Sarah's eyes. She would remember this moment always; it would be the last time she would ever have him.

CHAPTER TWENTY-SIX

"WHERE IS MY FAN? What have you done with my spectacles? Why is nothing in its place?"

Cynara paused before answering, trying to suppress her irritation. "The fan is on the table beside you. Your spectacles are on your forehead."

Hester reached up, felt the spectacles perched there, and lowered them to her nose. Picking up the fan, she began to ply it rapidly, muttering, "Why is it so hot? There is no air in here. Open the window."

Cynara sighed. Looking across at Hester once more, she thought impatiently that if the woman hadn't insisted on wearing her good black bombazine today, she wouldn't be so warm. But she had insisted, and now she sat there, draped in that heavy, elaborate gown, wondering why it was so hot. Compressing her lips for a moment, Cynara forced herself to answer calmly, "The window is open. Perhaps after I finish cleaning the room we can walk in the garden for a few minutes. Would you like that?"

"Hummph. I suppose it's better than sitting here roasting like a fowl on a spit. Hurry, girl—I'd like a walk in the garden before I melt."

Shaking her head, Cynara finished making up the bed. Hester allowed no one else in her rooms, and so it had fallen to Cynara to keep order in here, as well as supervising the rest of the house. The past few weeks had been even more difficult than she had imagined, and sometimes she questioned the wisdom of her impulsive decision to stay. But she had only to look at the lonely old woman to know she had made the right decision after all.

Not that it had been easy, she thought, remembering the battles she had had with Bella, the orders and counterorders issued in a rapid stream by the demanding Hester. Still, she had found satisfaction in bringing order into Hester's life.

Under Cynara's direction, the surly Bella had cleaned the kitchen until it shone. With the help of the daily maid, Penny, Cynara had cleaned the rest of the house from top to bottom. She had discovered, to her surprise, that the furniture, once the accumulated dirt had been wiped away, was of good quality; there had even been an Aubusson rug under the grime in the small drawing room. The house now sparkled with quiet elegance, and Cynara was proud of her efforts.

To her impatient amusement, Hester had said nothing about the changes she had wrought, but Cynara knew that those sharp black eyes missed nothing; several times she had even caught Hester staring at her with a grim expression that on anyone else would have indicated disapproval, but was probably as close as Hester could come to looking pleased.

Nor had Hester's manner toward her changed; she was still the autocratic, harshly demanding woman of that first interview. But Cynara noted that once or twice Hester had called her by her first name, rather than by the condescending "Rosslyn", and Cynara had to be satisfied with that, hoping that in time the woman would learn not to be suspicious of her, as she seemed to be of everyone else.

There had been no real repetition of that frightening episode on the staircase that first day, but Cynara watched Hester carefully, always afraid that it might happen again, and there had been a number of times when she thought it was about to.

All in all, Cynara thought as she smoothed the coverlet into place over the bed, she was almost happy here during the days. She was always busy, and she had even grown fond of the woman sitting impatiently in the chair, although she often wondered why.

But there were nights when she lay awake, tossing restlessly, until she was forced to get out of bed and creep out to the garden to sit under the stars. Those were the nights she could not get Evan out of her mind. She had seen him once since leaving Tamoora, and her thoughts kept returning to that occasion, tormenting her. It had been an afternoon when Hester had finally given her a few precious moments to herself and she had decided to visit Sarah. Mollie had greeted her warmly, pressing her immediately to have tea, and Cynara had accepted, asking after Sarah. She learned that Sarah was with a "patron," but should be free soon, and she and Mollie had passed the time in light conversation, Cynara relating a few incidents which she could look back on with amusement of her time at Hester's.

At last Sarah had come down, and as they greeted each other, Cynara had chanced to look out the front window. Evan's back was to her as he mounted his horse and rode away, but she had recognized him at once. An actual physical pain had shot through her as she realized that he was the patron Mollie had mentioned, and it was all she could do to control her chaotic emotions as Sarah chatted away gaily, mercifully oblivious to Cynara's anguish. Thankfully, she hadn't much time left for a visit, and she had escaped before Sarah noticed anything wrong, but as she walked quickly back to Hester's, she thought she would burst into helpless tears right there on the street. Sarah hadn't mentioned Evan, but Cynara had seen her flushed face and sparkling eyes, and she knew that joyousness of Sarah's had not only been because her friend was happy to see her. It was unfair— horribly, hideously unfair—that Sarah had Evan, when she herself had dreamed of him, longed for him! In her thoughts she had traced every plane of his face, every line of his body, until her own body ached for him. Sometimes she could actually feel his hands on her, hard and demanding one instant, light and tender the next. Oh, she wanted his hands on her; she wanted his lips covering every inch of her body; she wanted to feel him inside her, hot and swollen, driving, thrusting, lifting her to dizzying heights of abandonment. She longed for these things with the full passion of a woman, and if such thoughts were shameful, she didn't care. In her need for him she would do anything, just to have him love her.

But now—now it was too late. The moment she had seen
him at Mollie's, she knew that he had forgotten her. He had
found Sarah, and he would never want her now. Sarah was
so experienced, so sure of herself in the art of love-making,
while she . . . Cynara closed her eyes, feeling small and
ignorant and foolish with all her imaginings. Even through
all the sordid and degrading experiences she had endured at
the hands of other men, she still knew so little. Why would
Evan, who had everything he could want in a woman like
Sarah, even spare a thought for her?

The night she ran away from Tamoora she had debated
trying to find him, going to him for help, but she had been
too ashamed, too humiliated by all that had happened to her
since she left England. And then, after what Ben Knowles
had done to her, she knew that she could never go to Evan.

Her pride had taken hold again; she could not seek him
out, knowing that at best he would find her an object of
pity; at worst, a woman to be scorned. If he had ever
indicated by one word, one action, that he felt anything at all
for her, she might have swallowed her pride and asked for
his help. But he had done nothing; not even that night on the
veranda when he had spoken her name had she believed
him. In fact, she had convinced herself that it had all been her
imagination. No. She had told herself before that Evan was
lost to her, but she knew that he had never before been so
unattainable. He would never want her now.

"What are you standing there dreaming about, girl? I
don't pay you to gawk, but to work!"

Hester's harsh voice interrupted her thoughts, and
Cynara started. Staring blankly down at the feather duster
she held and couldn't remember picking up, she turned to
see Hester glaring at her. "I'm sorry, Miss Cord. I just—"

"Don't bother to explain. I can see from that fatuous
expression on your face that you're dreaming of some
young man. Well, it's just a waste of time, girl. Let me tell
you—"

Hester stopped, and Cynara saw with horror that blank

expression come into Hester's eyes. Hurrying forward, she almost lifted Hester bodily from the chair, speaking urgently. "Miss Cord, let's have that walk in the garden now. The fresh air will do you good. Miss Cord—*please!*"

To Cynara's vast relief, Hester turned on her irritably, her eyes once more sharp and penetrating. "Don't pull me about like that, girl! What's the matter with you? First you stand there woolgathering, and then you're all in a rush. Leave go my arm and fetch my cane!"

Cynara let out the breath she had been holding and moved to obey. Thankfully the crisis had been averted, but inside she was trembling in reaction. She must manage to speak to the doctor soon, she thought; the strain was beginning to tell on her more than Hester.

Hester insisted on negotiating the stairs alone, but Cynara followed closely behind, prepared to reach out and catch her should she fall. Hester was never steady on her feet, despite the aid of the cane, and Cynara had learned to watch her carefully without appearing to do so. Hester was a proud woman; she allowed assistance only when absolutely necessary, and then she accepted Cynara's offer of help impatiently, as though humoring her.

Hester paused at the foot of the stairs, one hand gripping her cane, the other grasping the newel post. She turned as Cynara came down beside her. The black eyes held Cynara's for an instant, and then she said gruffly, "Thank you."

Her voice was so low that at first Cynara wasn't sure she had heard correctly. When she realized what Hester had said, she was surprised; Hester had never expressed gratitude in any form to her before.

Her surprise must have been evident on her face, for Hester waved her hand impatiently. "You know to what I refer," she said stiffly.

Cynara was astonished. This was the first reference Hester had made to these strange attacks of hers, and Cynara realized that she only pretended to be unaware of them. How awful it must be for her, Cynara thought; never knowing when that horrible blankness would come over her.

Instinctively Cynara knew that the less said about it, the better. Inclining her head to acknowledge the comment, she said nothing. When she looked at Hester again, the familiar peevish expression had returned and the woman snapped, "Well, don't just stand there, girl! I thought we were going to walk in the garden."

The garden at the back of the house was small, enclosed on all sides by a high brick wall for privacy. As they entered the enclosure, Cynara was struck again, as she had been the first time she had seen it, by its resemblance to a true English garden. While there were brightly colored Australian flowers here and there, there were also beautiful roses, rhododendrons nodding in the shade of willow trees at the far wall, and a scent of lavender in the still air. There was even a birdbath, but splashing in the water were not the English songbirds she was accustomed to, but brightly colored finches and an occasional brilliantly green budgerigar that swooped down from the eucalyptus trees crowding the other side of the wall. As Cynara looked at the garden, she felt the familiar ache of homesickness and thought again that Australia was too harsh and unyielding, too empty and vast. She longed for the cool greens and lavenders, the gently rolling hills of her homeland.

Her feelings must have shown on her face, for Hester, in an unexpectedly soft tone, said, "The garden reminds you of England, doesn't it?" She glanced around fondly, her voice wistful. "It has the same effect on me. Of course, I had it planted when I came to this house, you know. I wanted something to remind me—I've always hated Australia," she added, her voice turning harsh again.

Cynara spoke up hastily, afraid that Hester would be reminded of whatever it was that provoked her attacks. "Why don't we walk to the sun dial and back again? Soon it will be time for tea."

Hester waved her away irritably. "I don't need any help

walking around my own garden, girl. Go on about your business and leave me alone for a while. In fact, go to the kitchen and tell Bella that I wish tea cakes served today, and cucumber sandwiches. I'm expecting a guest for tea, and I want things served properly for once."

Cynara looked at Hester in surprise. This was the first time Hester had mentioned a guest, and she was annoyed that she hadn't been informed before.

Hurrying off, Cynara tried to hide her irritation at Hester's secretive habits. In the next half hour she managed to persuade Bella to make the requested cakes and sandwiches as she polished the tea service and washed the delicate china cups and saucers she had found at the back of one of the kitchen cupboards during her first days at the house. Penny had been instructed to dust the drawing room and make sure everything was in order, and after that there was barely enough time to escort Hester from the garden and seat her in her favorite chair before the door knocker sounded.

"Penny, will you answer that, please?" Cynara asked as she handed Hester her fan and placed her cane where she could reach it easily.

Penny shot her a frightened look; it was rare that this house received a visitor, especially one who required all this advance preparation, and she didn't seem to know what to do. Cynara nodded encouragingly, and Penny, after straightening her cap and adjusting her apron as best she could, went down the corridor to admit the visitor.

"You don't have to remain," Hester said roughly. "Just make sure the tea is served and then you can wait in your room until I call you."

To Cynara's astonishment, Hester seemed nervous; her fingers plucked at her fan, and she shifted uncomfortably in her chair at the sound of voices in the hall as Penny admitted the visitor.

"I'll stay if you wish," Cynara offered.

Hester waved her hand. "No, it isn't necessary."

"Very well. I—"

"Miss Cord," Penny said from the doorway. "Mr. Calder is here."

Cynara's back was to the door as she faced Hester. At the sound of the maid's introduction, she stiffened. No! It couldn't be! She felt the blood rush to her face and drain as swiftly as it had come. It was some seconds before she was able to turn around.

He was there, standing on the threshold, towering over the small maid as she waited for his hat and gloves.

"Mr. Calder?" Penny said hesitantly, holding out her hand to receive the articles from him.

Cynara was aware that Hester made some movement at her side, that she said something, but Cynara did not look at her. Her glance was held by Evan, and it seemed that there was no one else in the room but the two of them. The irrelevant thought flashed through her mind that she wished she were wearing something other than the simple cotton dress that Hester had outfitted her with, and then she flushed at the absurdity of the thought. What did it matter what she was wearing? She couldn't move; she could only stand there, staring like a fool.

Evan was similarly transfixed. His hand was arrested in the act of handing his hat and gloves to the maid, and she was forced to tug them gently from him. He was unaware of the action.

They stood there, staring at each other from across the room, and so strong was the current that leaped between them that Cynara was shaken. Her lips parted, and she spoke his name. "Evan . . ."

Evan took a step forward, and the spell, if one could call it that, was broken. As the light fell fully on his face, Cynara was shocked into immobility by the piercing scream that rose behind her.

The scream sounded again, breaking Cynara's horrified trance. Looking down, she saw in one glance that Hester's eyes were blank, staring emptily before her with that expression Cynara had come to dread. The woman's lips were slack, but issuing from her mouth was one shrill cry after another. Raising a hand that trembled violently, Hester pointed to the stupified Evan. She half rose from her chair before Cynara could stop her, and as she swayed from one side to the other, she cried, "No, no! You're dead. I saw you die! Oh, God—it can't be!"

With every word, Hester's voice rose higher and higher, until her shrieks seemed to echo off the walls, surrounding them all with that terrible noise. Evan moved swiftly forward, but at his approach, Hester slumped back into the chair, covering her face with her hands. "No! No! Stay away from me!"

Penny stood frozen in the doorway; behind her was the gaping Bella, who had rushed from the kitchen, sure that someone was being murdered. Evan glanced quickly at Cynara, and they both looked down at Hester, aghast at what they saw.

"I'll send for a doctor," Evan said quickly.

"Yes, yes," Cynara answered, going to her knees in front of the woman, trying to cradle her in her arms.

"No doctor! I won't have a doctor here!" Hester shrieked, taking her hands from her face and beating at Cynara with her fists.

"All right, all right," Cynara soothed, trying to hold on to the flailing hands and keep Hester in the chair at the same time.

Hester broke from her, pointing to Evan again. "Take him away!"

"Yes, yes." Cynara hardly knew what she was saying. She was scared out of her wits by the transformation in Hester, and she glanced up blankly at Evan.

"What is it? What's the matter with her?"

"I don't know," Cynara answered fearfully, trying to control Hester's frenzied movements. "She's had these attacks before—"

"Go away!" Hester shrieked. "Get away from me!"

"Cynara—" Evan averted his glance from the struggling woman, speaking urgently to Cynara. "I have to talk to her."

Talk to her! Was that all he could think of? She wanted to leap up and beat at him with her fists, pummel him unmercifully for the blow he had just dealt to her pride. She had dreamed so many times of the moment when she would see him again, and now that he was here, all he could say was that he wanted to talk to Hester!

Oh, she hated him, despised him! What a fool she had been to waste time on stupid daydreams, on idiotic fantasies of being loved by him. He had no feeling for her, no desire for her; it was all a product of her own fevered imagination. God! she could kill him right now for making her feel so ridiculous and exposed in her need for him!

She wanted him to leave and never return. How could she ever look upon his face again without remembering the times she had wanted him, the pain she had suffered just thinking about him? Her cheeks flamed with the utter shame she felt, and she shouted, "Can't you see that she is in no condition to talk to you? I think you should leave—now!"

"Yes, yes!" Hester moaned, clutching Cynara. "Get out!"

Evan looked at Cynara's white face, at Hester's hands gripping Cynara convulsively, and his expression changed. He had been about to reach for Cynara, but seeing the blazing anger in her eyes, he stepped back. What had made him say such a ridiculous thing? He didn't want to talk to the crazy old woman; he wanted to sweep Cynara into his arms and carry her away from this place. The woman's shrieking had unnerved him; he hadn't been prepared for this violent storm of emotion. He had planned—oh, what was the use, he thought furiously. Everything had gone wrong, and there was no putting it right with Hester sobbing and wringing her hands and clinging to Cynara, taking all her attention. Christ! Would nothing stop that hideous howling?

In his agitation, he again said the wrong thing. "Do something with her, Cynara. I want—"

"I don't care what you want!" Cynara cried. "Get out!"

He had been about to tell her that he wanted to see her alone; he wanted to tell her how he had searched for her, and now that he had found her, he couldn't bear to lose her again. God, but she was magnificent! Standing there, her slim body taut with anger, her breasts heaving, her cheeks stained rose, Evan could not control his desire for her. Involuntarily, he took a step toward her, but she stopped him with the hard jade flash of her eyes.

"Get out, Evan!" she said, her small fists clenched at her sides.

He halted, reading the contempt in those huge eyes. Desire was replaced instantly by rage—at Cynara, at Hester, at this abominable ruination of his plans. Infuriated, he growled, gesturing toward Hester, "I'll come again. Tell her that."

"Is he gone? Is he gone?"

Kneeling by Hester's chair again, Cynara forced herself to answer. "Yes, he's gone. Come, I'll take you to your room now."

Her voice shook in reaction to the scene with Evan; she didn't know whom she was angriest with: herself, or Evan, or Hester—for being the cause of it. In this moment, she almost hated Hester, and it was all she could do to help the woman out of the chair, when she wanted to scream her fury and disappointment into Hester's face. Why, *why*, did everything seem to conspire to drive her and Evan further apart? She could have wept with frustration, recalling that horrible scene. How could he have done that to her?

Somehow she managed to get Hester upstairs and into bed. But Hester would allow neither Bella nor Penny near her, so it was Cynara who was left to bathe the raddled face and massage the woman's cold hands.

When Penny, her eyes wide, brought the hot water bottles Cynara had requested, she did not move from her position by the bed, but said, "Leave them, please. And have

Bella make a cup of strong tea for her."

"Yes, miss." The girl's tone held a new deference. Until now she had been easily influenced by Bella, and had responded sullenly whenever Cynara asked her to do something. But now, after seeing Cynara handle the situation almost calmly—when she and Bella would have been at a loss—her manner was almost respectful. She even sketched a curtsy before leaving the room.

Cynara didn't notice the change in Penny. Looking down at Hester's white face, she wondered if she should call a doctor despite Hester's protest. But a doctor might bring on another attack, and Cynara didn't want to go through that again. She had been frightened badly just now; it had taken all her will power to calm herself enough to take charge. But what had caused it? Evan had seemed to remind Hester of someone—but who could it be? Why should his appearance provoke such a terrifying reaction? This last attack had been far worse than the others, and now she wondered if it was really because of Evan, or simply because the storm had been building and she hadn't realized it. What should she do?

"Fetch my Bible. . ."

Hester spoke without opening her eyes, groping blindly for the book Cynara brought from the table and placed into her hands.

"Leave me."

Cynara hesitated, wondering if it was safe to leave her alone. Hester opened her eyes and glared at Cynara, still standing by the bedside. "Didn't you hear me?" she rasped. "I want to be alone."

"Miss Cord," Cynara said tentatively. "Don't you think it would be best to call the doctor?"

"What for? I had a bad turn, that's all. Nothing for anyone to be upset about."

"But—"

"I won't have a doctor in this house, and that's final! All they do is poke and pry, and never have any answers." Her voice lowered slightly, and she added, almost to herself, "It was just seeing him again that startled me, that's all."

"Seeing him again?" Cynara was confused. "Do you mean that you know Evan—Mr. Calder?" She asked the question hesitantly, unwilling to provoke another violent reaction.

But Hester's expression suddenly became sly, and she refused to answer. Cynara was forced to leave her alone, but as she paused at the door to look back at the figure in the bed, she wondered for the first time if Hester was more than a difficult, troubled old woman. Could it be that she was insane?

No. She answered her own question with a shake of her head. Hester was no more insane than she was, but still . . . There was something here that must be explained. Hester had been terrified, almost as though she had seen a ghost coming to life before her eyes. Now she seemed almost too calm, too much in control. In fact, Cynara thought as she noticed the cunning expression on the woman's face, it was almost as if she were plotting something.

Uneasily, Cynara left the room and went down the stairs toward the kitchen. She resolved, whether Hester wished it or not, that she would talk to a doctor herself, and soon.

"Send for him, Rosslyn. I want to see him after all."

It was several days after Evan's disastrous visit. In spite of her vow, Cynara had been unable to get away long enough to see a doctor. Now Hester, as if she had completely forgotten her reaction, was ordering her to send for Evan again.

"Do you . . . do you think that's wise?" she faltered, dreading the thought of another nightmarish confrontation.

"I'll decide what's wise, young woman! I told you to send for him. Do so immediately!"

Cynara bowed under the fierce gaze of the old woman. "When would you like to see him?" she asked stiffly.

"Today, of course! There's no time to waste. Invite him for tea."

"It's very short notice. Suppose—"

"Oh, he'll come, Rosslyn. Never fear—he'll come. Now bring me my breakfast. Suddenly I find that I have an appetite after all."

Cynara brought the tray to the bed, but as she leaned over to place it by Hester her hip brushed the bedside table, and the Bible that Hester kept on it fell to the floor. Quickly Cynara bent to retrieve it. But her hand was arrested in midair when she saw that it had fallen open to the frontispiece. There, elaborately inscribed, was a family tree, and the name that struck her eye was one she had run into before: Aron Ward.

"*Give me that at once!*"

Hester fairly snatched the book from Cynara's hand. "How dare you pry into my private possessions!" she screamed.

"I'm sorry," Cynara said dazedly. "I didn't mean to—"

"Get out!" Hester shrieked. "Get out and leave me alone!"

But Cynara was unable to move. She was remembering the night of the ball at Tamoora, and Thomas Hale saying so casually to Evan, "You resemble . . . Sean Ward . . ." As if it were happening again in front of her, she saw pictured in her mind Evan's explosive response to another of Hale's statements, "Sean had a son. His name was Aron . . ."

Cynara looked blankly at the furious woman in the bed, wondering why Hester's Bible would contain the name Aron Ward.

"Miss Cord," she said slowly. "Who was Aron Ward?"

"Get out! I won't answer your questions! You have no right to pry!"

Unmoved by the woman's show of temper, Cynara continued to stare thoughtfully at Hester. "Who was he?" she repeated.

The fury vanished abruptly from Hester's face, replaced instead by the sly expression she had worn for several days now. "All in good time, Rosslyn; all in good time." And then she startled Cynara further by uttering a high laugh. "Just send for Mr. Calder," Hester ordered, biting with relish into a piece of toast she had spread thickly with jam.

"He and I have much to talk about!"

Cynara had no idea what the woman meant, but she was beginning to have her suspicions. There was some relationship between Aron Ward and Evan and Hester Cord. And somehow Lyrebird Manor was concerned as well.

As Cynara left the room and went toward the stairs again, she suddenly remembered having seen a lyrebird once on the grounds at Tamoora. She had only seen it briefly, but she had been able to make out the feature that had given the bird its name: that graceful tail shaped exactly like a lyre. She recalled thinking at the time that it was no coincidence that Lyrebird Manor was named after an Australian bird: that its garden, which Rosie had told her had once been famous, had been planted to imitate that shape as well. Why? What did it all mean? And how was Evan involved?

Thoughtfully, Cynara gave Penny the note that Hester had written and addressed to Evan, and told her to ask one of the lads at the stable to deliver the message. She wondered if Evan would come at Hester's invitation. But of course he would, she thought; he had been too anxious before to talk to her; he would not ignore the summons now.

Moving away from the doorway, Cynara went toward the kitchen to tell Bella that another tea would be required for this afternoon. But as she entered the kitchen, she couldn't help wondering what effect Evan's visit would have on Hester this time. Hester had deliberately invited him, but still Cynara dreaded the thought of another scene.

That wasn't the entire truth. As much as she was concerned for Hester and her reaction to Evan, Cynara knew that it was her own reaction to him that she was worried about. She stood at the sink, trembling at the thought of seeing him again. She couldn't: she couldn't take the chance of betraying herself—as she surely would have done, had it not been for Hester. She would contrive some excuse; she would not be present when Evan was admitted. It was too much to ask of her; she would not make a fool of herself again. Plunging her hands into the soapy water she had added to the sink, Cynara began washing the delicate china for tea.

CHAPTER TWENTY-SEVEN

"NOW THEN, YOUNG MAN, sit down and we'll have that talk I promised. Just the two of us." Hester motioned to Cynara, who had been forced to bring in the tea cart because Hester had found a sudden objection to having Penny serve. Cynara stood now, her eyes trained steadily on the floor, beside Hester's chair.

"Leave us, girl," she ordered, observing Evan covertly. She was immediately satisfied by the flash of anger she saw in his face at her deliberately contemptuous tone, and Hester smiled to herself before continuing, "I do not care to have my . . . servants . . . listening to my private affairs. It's such bad training, isn't it?"

Again she was rewarded by that angry expression. She had chosen her words carefully, wondering if her instincts had been right about these two. People might say she was just an addled old fool, she thought, but she still had her wits about her, and could use them profitably. It hadn't been so difficult, after all, she thought smugly, to judge the reaction of these two young people, especially for an astute observer like herself. One had only to glimpse Cynara's face when she saw Evan Calder to know that this was the man who troubled the girl's dreams. Hadn't she heard, more than once, Cynara calling out to him in her sleep? Hadn't she observed Cynara pacing in her room when she thought Hester was asleep?

It had been unfortunate, Hester thought, that she had had one of her attacks the last time this young man was here, but she was stronger now, more prepared to accept his startling resemblance to Sean. It had been a shock, that last time, seeing him. For a horrible instant she had actually thought that Sean had returned from the grave. But now she knew how foolish she had been, dwelling on what had happened so long ago. The shock of seeing this young man had cleared her mind, and for the first time in years, she knew that she was free of those hideous memories of Sean dying, and the rest of her dear family being destroyed in that fire. She was able to think now . . . and to plan.

And what plans she had! She had been forced to wait until today to determine young Calder's reaction to Cynara, but now that she knew she had been right about them both, she could move forward without hesitation. She watched Evan closely as Cynara went stiffly from the room, and as she observed him, she could almost read his thoughts.

Evan forced himself to remain seated in the chair as Cynara left the room, aware of Hester's sharp black eyes on him. But even if Hester hadn't been there, he realized that he would not have followed Cynara. She had avoided his glance from the time he had entered the room, and now he was furious with himself for being so sure of her. What had he thought, he asked himself bitterly—that she would fall into his arms at the mere sight of him? What a fool he had been! Cynara had acted as if she were completely unaware of him, and if it hadn't been for this miserable old hag sitting opposite him, he would have demanded—what? That she declare her feelings for him? Oh, but she had made it perfectly clear just now, hadn't she, that she felt absolutely nothing for him. Nothing at all. She hadn't even deigned to acknowledge his presence by so much as a nod.

He thought of all the weeks when he had been out of his mind with worry, trying to find her. And now that he had found her, she refused to acknowledge his existence. What an amusing contretemps, he thought wrathfully, forcing his attention away from Cynara and onto the woman in front of him. He saw that she was smiling slyly, and this increased his anger. With an effort, he willed himself to be polite, knowing that he could not afford to offend Hester Cord at this point, before she told him what she knew.

"I appreciate your seeing me after all," he began. "I wanted to talk to you about—"

"Oh, I know what you wanted to talk about, young man," Hester interrupted calmly.

Evan stared at her. Could it be that he had misjudged this old woman after all? The sharp black eyes regarded him steadily, and now he saw cunning intelligence there —instead of the empty, faded gaze he had expected after his first disastrous attempt to see her. He would have to watch his step, he thought; this woman was no fool.

"Of course I know," Hester said, reaching toward the cart to pour two cups of tea. Smiling again, she gave Evan one, indicating the milk and sugar and lemon on the tray. "But first, I think we should be civilized and have our tea. Sean was always a great one for ceremony—"

Evan choked violently on the tea he had just drunk. His face crimson, he reached for a napkin, and Hester continued, as though there had been no interruption, "But of course you wouldn't know Sean, would you? He died before you were born." Hester stirred her cup delicately with a silver spoon. "You do bear an uncanny resemblance to him, though; it quite startled me when I first saw you. You must forgive an old woman. Sometimes such surprises can do strange things to one's mind." Laughing deprecatingly, she added, "For a moment, I actually thought you were Sean himself. Silly of me, wasn't it?"

"Miss Cord—"

"Oh, do call me Hester, please. Would you care for some of these cakes? Perhaps a sandwich? No?"

Evan shook his head impatiently. "Thank you, no. Miss Cord—Hester—" he amended when she shook her finger playfully at him "Tell me—"

"Oh, there's plenty of time to talk about Sean later," Hester interrupted. "Or Aron, for that matter. All in good time, young man, all in good time. What is more important at the moment, I think, is the proposal I have for you—or rather, Cynara and I have for you."

"Proposal?" Evan's tone was cool; he was struggling to control his anger, trying not to offend her. But she was more wily than he had imagined, and he realized that he would have to make a great effort not to lose his temper. At the moment, he wanted to reach across and shake the information out of her.

"Yes." Hester's expression took on a coyness that was

repulsive to Evan. Forcing himself to appear politely interested, he waited for her to go on. "Cynara would have told you herself, but she thought that I could manage much better. You could say that I am acting as a—what is the word?—a go-between."

"Go on." With every passing minute, Evan became more annoyed. What kind of game was this woman playing?

Hester put down her cup and wiped her lips delicately with her napkin before putting that aside, too. Clasping her hands in her lap, she stared evenly at Evan, and said, to his utter stupefaction, "You think my nephew, Aron Ward, was your father, don't you?"

Evan was unable to move, to speak. So it was true, he thought exultantly; this woman was actually Aron's aunt, sister-in-law to Sean Ward. He hadn't dared believe it was true until he heard it from her own lips.

"Yes," he answered as calmly as he was able, "I do. But I need proof—"

"Ah, yes. Proof. Well that, young man, is going to be a little difficult to obtain, I'm afraid."

"What do you mean?" he asked evenly. If she thought she could keep the knowledge from him now that he had come this far, she was mistaken. She would discover that he did not intend to give up simply because things were "difficult." His expression hardened as he looked around the room. Obviously Hester was not short of funds, he thought as he appraised the furnishings quickly, but she wanted something from him. If it wasn't money, what was it?

"What do you want, Hester?" he asked, bringing his glance back to her face again.

Hester frowned. "There is no need to be so blunt—"

"Isn't there?" Evan sat back in his chair, regarding her steadily. "I have the impression that while you have the information I seek, you want something in return from me. What is it?"

Hester waved her hand. "You're mistaken, young man. It isn't *I* who wants something from you."

"Who then?"

Sighing, Hester looked down at her hands again. "You realize, of course, that I am only an old woman, easily influenced—"

Evan doubted the truth of this statement; he had seen for himself that there was iron in her; that she knew fully what she wanted, and intended to have it. But he said nothing as she glanced up at him, allowing her to continue without interruption.

"Easily influenced," she repeated, "By those who serve me well. After all, I have no family; I am alone. It seems the least I can do for someone who has proved herself invaluable to me. . . ."

Hester sighed again, and Evan wondered impatiently if he would be forced to listen to these cloying sentiments all afternoon, if she would ever get to the point. "And?" he prompted heavily.

Hester straightened in her chair. "Well . . . even though I assured Cynara that there was no cause for her to be concerned over . . . what happened . . . that last time you were here, she was very worried, and so—and so, I was forced to confide in her a bit more than I intended."

"Miss Cord," Evan said, trying to keep the impatience from his voice, "I don't mean to be rude, but where is all this leading?"

"I'm coming to that, young man!" Hester said sharply, glaring at him. "When Cynara learned why I was so upset, she insisted that I not tell you until certain conditions were met. There now! I've told you."

Evan ground his teeth. "You haven't told me anything. What conditions are you talking about?"

Hester appeared uncomfortable. "Well, Cynara feels that the information you want should be withheld until you marry her and take us both back to England."

"What!"

"I admit the proposal does sound a bit—cold," Hester said hurriedly. "But that is the way Cynara wants it, and since I've grown quite fond of her, I promised I would agree. It's such a little thing after all, isn't it?"

"A little thing! My God!"

"There is no need to swear, young man," Hester said severely.

"I don't believe Cynara would want such a thing," Evan said flatly, when he had recovered somewhat from his angry surprise. "It isn't like her at all."

"Isn't it? How well do you know Cynara, young man?"

Evan was silent at this thrust. How well *did* he know her? Was it possible that she could be so scheming, so . . . cold?

Aware of Hester's sharp eyes on him, Evan shifted in the chair. Hester had planted a seed of doubt in his mind, and as much as he tried to dismiss it, he could not.

"I want to speak to her," he said abruptly. "I'll ask her myself if this absurd proposition is her wish."

"I'm afraid that's impossible," Hester replied calmly, ignoring the suffused face opposite her. "I knew that you would be . . . disturbed, so I think it's best that you should have some time to consider the idea. You can let us know—" Hester tapped the arm of her chair thoughtfully "tomorrow."

"Tomorrow! I can give you my answer this moment!" Evan ground out. "No! How could either of you imagine that my response could be anything else? I will not be blackmailed into marrying anyone, not even Cynara!"

"There's no need to shout," Hester said calmly. "However, I realize how startled you must be—"

"Startled! That's putting it rather mildly, isn't it?"

"I suggest that you think it over very carefully. After all, quite a bit is at stake, isn't it?"

"Is it? How do I know that? You haven't told me anything yet, have you?"

"Well, let's just say that the ownership of the Lyrebird Manor is involved. I would say that might make a difference in your decision, wouldn't you?"

"The ownership of Lyrebird Manor?" Evan repeated. "What does the Manor have to do with it?"

Hester smiled. "That's just another of the things you would be interested in learning, I think. What do you say, young man—tomorrow?"

Evan's expression hardened. "I can force you to tell me, Miss Cord. There are ways—"

"Oh, don't threaten me, young man. I assure you I am not afraid."

"Cynara might be—"

"I don't think so. She's quite determined, you know. I've given her the proof, but I know she will deny it unless you fulfill your part of the bargain."

"It occurs to me that you are more involved in this scheme than you care to admit," Evan said heavily. "Could that be?"

Hester lowered her eyes, but inside she was shaken. So much depended upon his believing that she would not give him the information he wanted until they were all safely in England; even more depended upon her approach with Cynara herself. But Hester had not dreamed of returning to England all these long years to lose sight of her objective now. With the tenacity of those obsessed, she was able to face Evan calmly when she looked up at him again.

"Mr. Calder, I am an old woman—do you think I would be able to force you to do anything?" With an effort she rose from her chiar, indicating that the interview was over. "I'm very tired now. Shall we meet again tomorrow?"

She extended her hand, and Evan was forced to take it. But his fingers barely touched hers, and he strode from the room without giving a reply to her question.

Leaping down the steps, he threw himself onto his horse. There was a violent pounding in his head, and his chest was tight. How could Cynara have betrayed him this way? It was as though he didn't know her, had never known her. He had been taken in by her, played for a fool. How could he have imagined that any woman willing to marry Thomas Hale was guileless?

Writhing inwardly, he thought how sorry he had been for her when he learned that her marriage had been a sham—how protective he had felt toward her! He had been frantic when he had believed her lost in the bush somewhere, an easy prey for bushrangers, and he had instituted that frenzied search, sure that if it was he who found her everything would be all right. He laughed harshly at the thought. Cynara was well able to take care of herself after all, it seemed. She had the ability, as Oliver had often said, of falling on her feet. Like a cat.

Uncharacteristic self-pity washed over him as he remembered his dreams of Cynara. He had pictured himself coming to her rescue, like some idiotic knight on his charger, sweeping her off her feet, carrying her away to safety. Instead, he now found himself in the role of supplicant, and the thought infuriated him.

He wheeled his horse away from the house, but as he rode back to the office, his thoughts were not concerned with Hester or Aron, or even Hester's odd remark about Lyrebird Manor. He was obsessed with thoughts of Cynara, and the further he rode, the more enraged he became. He forgot that he had intended to ask—to demand—that she marry him; he forgot that he had spent weeks searching for her for that very reason. The fact that she had betrayed him, that she had tried so deviously to coerce him into marrying her preyed on his mind until he thought he would explode with anger. She was a clever woman, Cynara; she must have guessed at once how much he wanted the answers only Hester could give; she must have known how important those answers would be to him. But why had she attached those absurd conditions to her proposal? Why would she demand that he marry her? It didn't make sense, he thought, unless . . . Unless there was more at stake here than he had imagined.

He thought about Hester's remark concerning ownership of Lyrebird Manor. Was it possible that Cynara thought to enrich herself through him in some way? He had seen for himself that she was greedy enough to accept Thomas Hale's proposal of marriage, thus assuring her the comforts Tamoora had to offer. But she had lost Tamoora;

she had been left with nothing. Could it be that she intended to try again—this time through him? Was she so avaricious that she would force him to marry her in order to obtain what she had lost before?

If his pride hadn't been so wounded, if he hadn't felt so utterly betrayed, he never would have believed that greed was Cynara's motive. But because he was humiliated and chagrined and hurt, he wanted to hurt her as well. It was wrong, and deep inside him he knew it, but he couldn't stop himself. If she so desired marriage, he thought savagely, he would marry her. But she would have his name and that would be all. Once they arrived in England, and he had the information he wanted, she wouldn't even have that. He would seek a divorce immediately. She would pay for her treachery, and he would see to it that she paid in the way that would hurt her the most—through her pride. In the end, he would have what he wanted, and she would have nothing.

His decision made, he tried to convince himself that he had every right to repay her in her own coin; he would reward treachery with treachery, he thought, trying to feel satisfaction. But as he gave his horse to the boy who stood waiting for it in front of the office, Evan realized that something had been destroyed in him as well that day. He had expected too much from her, and he was both enraged and disappointed that she had failed him. He had imagined her to be more than she was, and the realization that she was like the rest after all wounded him more deeply than he was willing to admit. For the first time he had acknowledged his love, his need of another person, and she had taken that love and made it contemptible. He would marry her, he thought, but never again would he be so vulnerable. Whatever feeling he had had for her was gone.

Speaking to no one, Evan went to his office and closed the door behind him. Ignoring the papers piled on his desk, he went instead to the window, staring sightlessly at the busy street below. He stood there, motionless, for a long time, his face without expression, before he turned at last to his desk and the work that awaited him.

CHAPTER TWENTY-EIGHT

". . . AND SO, TOMORROW you can tell Mr. Calder yourself that you accept his offer of marriage," Hester concluded. "It is decided; there is nothing more to say."

Cynara looked at Hester in stupified amazement. She had remained silent throughout this outrageous one-sided conversation simply because she could not believe what she was hearing. And now, incredibly, Hester had not only finished speaking, she obviously expected no argument in return. It was equally obvious, for the moment at least, that Cynara could not give her one; she could only stare dumbly at her, prevented from speaking by her disbelief.

It was inconceivable to Cynara that the two of them, Hester and Evan, had so blithely disposed of her future without so much as a nod in her direction. What was even more infuriating was that both had assumed that she would not dare to object. Hester wore a self-satisfied smile that indicated clearly to Cynara that she was not required to speak in her defense. "It is decided; there is nothing more to say," Hester had said. Well, as far as Cynara was concerned, there was a great deal more to say—if only she could manage to overcome this tremendous anger that threatened to choke her at any second.

Cynara had been sitting on the edge of her chair, gripping the arms so tightly that her fingers ached; now she sprang up and moved to the window, unable to face Hester for the turmoil of her thoughts.

How calmly Hester had sat there and informed her that she and Evan had struck a bargain between them—Evan would marry Cynara, and then take both her and Hester back to England. How simple it was! All she had to do was to give her consent—no, she needn't even do that, Cynara thought wrathfully. If she refused, Hester had made it clear that she would contact the authorities. Because Cynara was still a convict, she would be compelled to do whatever Hester wished—unless, of course, she preferred to take her chances in prison for willful disobedience. Oh yes, it was all very simple; all she had to do was marry Evan and everything would be fine.

The only problem, Cynara thought bleakly, was that Evan had been forced into this marriage just as surely as Hester was trying to force her into it. Oh, Hester had told her that Evan had readily agreed, but Cynara knew him well enough to realize that Hester must have offered him something in return, something he couldn't refuse. He would never have agreed otherwise; he was too proud and too stubborn to be forced into anything without some gain to himself. That being the case, she thought as her anger grew again, she couldn't marry him—she wouldn't marry him! They would end up hating each other—that was, if Evan didn't despise her even more than before for being at the center of this crazy old woman's plans. But why did Hester want them to marry? That was the question Hester refused to answer.

"I won't do it," Cynara said from her position at the window.

"I think you should reconsider, girl," Hester replied sharply. "Didn't I make it quite clear that you had no choice?"

"Oh yes. You made it perfectly clear," Cynara retorted. "But all the same, I won't do it. The very thought is absurd!"

"Your defiance is not only ridiculous, it is useless as well. Perhaps you don't realize—"

Cynara tossed her head. She was through deferring to this mad creature; she was not going to marry Evan no matter what threats were used against her. In fact, if she had known what was going on in the drawing room this afternoon, she would have burst in and confronted them both herself. How dare they trade her back and forth like a sack of potatoes in the market place! It was despicable, monstrous!

But as much as she tried to sustain her anger, she felt herself giving way to tears instead. She lifted her head, blinking rapidly, trying not to cry. She had believed Evan to be different from other men; she had thought that he was at least . . . honorable. Now it seemed he was like all the rest, considering only himself, not caring whom he hurt in the process. If only he had come to her on his own, everything would be so different. If he had proposed to her himself, she would have been delirious with joy. Even now, despite her anger and disappointment, her treacherous mind contemplated marriage with him, and she cursed her weakness.

Oh, she could see him in a hundred different ways: tender, passionate, adventurous—calling her to ways of lovemaking that she had never even dreamed of. She would follow his lead, abandoning herself to him, offering herself for his pleasure, accepting him as he gave of himself in return. They would be as one . . .

Oh yes, she wanted that, and more. She longed to be loved by Evan; she longed for . . . What did it matter what she wanted, she thought angrily. Wishing would not change things; the fact was that Hester, for some obscure and ridiculous purpose of her own, had demanded that Evan marry Cynara, and Evan had agreed. Her dreams were ashes at her feet, and nothing would ever be the same because Evan had not come to her.

Turning to Hester suddenly with a demand of her own, Cynara asked, "Why do you insist on this marriage? It doesn't make sense."

"I'll thank you not to take that tone with me, young woman! I have my reasons for not telling you at this time. It is not your place to question me!"

Cynara stared at her. "Not my place!" she repeated unbelievingly. "You're talking about my life—my future!"

"Your future is in my hands, girl. Who gave you a place here? Who took you in when you had no where else to go?"

"That does not give you the right to—"

"It gives me all the right I need!" Hester snapped. "Don't

forget—you came here on a transport ship. You are under *my* care now—my protection! As your guardian, I can do as I think best for you."

They glared at each other, Cynara too furious to reply. Then, waving her hand dismissively, Hester stated, "This distasteful interview is over, girl. I've told you what you must do, and I expect you to do it without further protest." She looked at Cynara from under lowered brows, adding, "I must admit that I expected better of you, Cynara. You're acting as though I've done you a great wrong, when in fact the opposite is true. It is obvious now that I was premature in expecting gratitude, and you have wounded me deeply by your defiance. But . . . my decision stands. I will require your presence tomorrow at tea. You may give Mr. Calder your acceptance then."

Dismissed, Cynara swept from the room without looking back. In her own room she threw herself on the bed. Staring up at the ceiling, she tried not to cry. She was helpless, and she knew it. Her thoughts raced back and forth, seeking a way out, but in the end she always returned to the one fact she could not ignore: the law did not look kindly upon someone who had already run away from one sentence. She knew that if she refused to follow Hester's orders, she would be opening herself up to a serious charge, with an additional imprisonment added to the first. She had no choice: she must marry Evan.

Groaning, she rolled over and put her face in her hands. Why had Evan agreed to Hester's proposal? Why? It wasn't like him to be forced into anything, she knew, so there had to be a reason why he had consented so readily, something she hadn't considered yet. But what?

Angrily, Cynara threw herself off the bed to begin pacing back and forth, trying to think. She knew that it couldn't have been any love for her that decided Evan. Oh no, she thought bitterly; the few times she had seen him, or been with him, he had either been angry with her or treated her with scorn. He had made it quite clear that night in the lyrebird garden exactly what he thought of her, and evidently he hadn't altered his opinion of her since then—not if he could entertain the thought of marriage to her simply because a crazy old woman had demanded it in exchange for something else. That alone showed his contempt: if he had felt anything at all for her, he would have refused Hester outright. Any man of honor would have, Cynara thought wrathfully. But then, she had seen for herself that he was not honorable; he was too ambitious, too driven. No, whatever reason Evan had for agreeing to this marriage, it wasn't because he loved her. Loved her! And to think that she had imagined herself in love with him! How she despised herself now for all those nights when she had lain awake, thinking of him . . . wanting him . . .

With a cry, she threw herself into a chair, hugging her arms around her body, as if in pain. How could she have been so foolish, so . . . so despicable . . . as to imagine herself in love with a man like Evan? Rocking back and forth, she began to cry in earnest, the tears running down her face as she forced herself to admit the end of a dream. She had loved him once, but now all she felt for him was contempt, loathing. He was contemptible—and so was she, for harboring such absurd fantasies. In that moment, she despised herself as much as she did Evan.

But perhaps the situation was not lost yet, she thought suddenly. Straightening, she dropped her arms from around her waist as an idea occurred to her. She had to marry him, she thought; there was no choice in that. But maybe there was a way to turn the circumstances to her advantage. Perhaps through Evan she would have her revenge against Myles.

She had not thought of Myles for some time. But now, at the thought of him, her eyes narrowed. Myles was ultimately responsible for everything that had happened to her. If he hadn't lied about what had happened that night, she would never have been transported to Australia; she would not have been forced into that bogus marriage with Thomas

Hale. She would never have had to suffer Ben Knowles—
and she wouldn't be in her present situation.

Yes, she thought, smiling fiercely to herself through her
tears. There had to be a way to use Evan to get back at
Myles. If she was Evan's wife—and this time she would
make sure that the ceremony was a valid one—she would
find some way to make Evan help her. She would use him
to force Myles into court, to make him confess what he had
done to her.

Sitting taller in the chair, Cynara considered the idea,
finding it more to her liking the longer she thought about it.
If she had to marry Evan, at least she would salvage something of the situation by avenging herself on Myles. She
would become Evan's wife, since she must, but she would
take his name and whatever he had to offer her, and that
would be all. He had destroyed any feeling she had for him
in the past; now she would feel no compunction at using
him as he intended to use her.

Her decision made, Cynara rose calmly from the chair
and went to the washstand to wipe away the last trace of
tears. Looking in the mirror as she smoothed her hair,
Cynara paused to stare at her reflection. She was eighteen,
and no longer a girl; her birthday had passed unnoticed a
few months ago. Staring at herself, she saw that her expression was hard, remote. The same green eyes looked back at
her but she saw the wariness there, and the hurt. The change
in her had been inevitable, she supposed; her experiences
had taught her not to trust people.

Still, the woman who looked back at her from the mirror
was someone Cynara didn't know, and she had to admit
reluctantly that she didn't care for the change.
Cynara the girl was gone; in her place was a woman who
had learned to trade any chance of happiness for a dream of
revenge that she knew would never bring her joy, only a
cold satisfaction. Was it enough? It would have to be.

With one last look at herself, Cynara turned away. Going
downstairs to help prepare the evening meal,

Cynara knew that she would not allow herself to be so vulnerable ever again. She would never love anyone as passionately as she had loved Evan, she thought; she would never love anyone again. For the first time she understood a little why Hester was so suspicious, so mistrustful of everyone, even those who tried to be kind to her. Perhaps Hester, like Cynara, had learned long ago that to be trusting was to open oneself to unnecessary hurt.

Turning in the direction of the kitchen, Cynara thought that only her desire for revenge and the fulfillment of that desire would sustain her throughout the long, empty years ahead. She had learned, with a vengeance, that love was only for the young and inexperienced, the dreamers who had no grasp on reality. She thought now that she was finished with dreaming; her feet were firmly on the ground, her heart locked away where no one would ever reach it again.

Evan arrived promptly the next afternoon at four. When he was ushered into the drawing room by the awed Penny, who had spent a great part of the evening before exclaiming about how handsome, how assured he was, Cynara was sitting calmly on the sofa next to Hester's chair.

She had planned through a long sleepless night exactly what she would say to him, the words she would use to accept this offer of marriage, the contempt she would allow him to hear as she gave her own agreement. But now that he was here, her carefully prepared speech fled from her mind, and she stared at him in angry silence as he acknowledged Hester. Her anger increased when she saw the cold disdain in his face as he murmured her name, and it was only by a fierce effort that she remained in her chair. She wanted to spring up and confront him openly, demanding to know why he had consented to this ridiculous farce of a marriage. Only Hester's presence kept her still. Her eyes flashed as he took a seat opposite her, and she glanced away, unable to look at him any longer.

How dare he appear so calm, so unmoved, when her own emotions were shrieking inside her, demanding release! Her fingers itched to slap that handsome face that expressed so much and so little at the same time, and she joined her hands in her lap, vowing not to give way to emotion. She would be as cold as he.

Hester gestured for her to pour the tea, but Cynara ignored her. The thought of the three of them acting out this mad charade over the teacups revolted her. She turned her face away, disregarding Hester's impatient exclamation at her refusal. To her satisfaction, she saw Evan make a brusque gesture when Hester offered him a cup she had poured herself, and Cynara thought savagely that he was not as complacent as he appeared to be. Watching him covertly, she saw that he actually appeared uncomfortable, and she was coldly amused. So, she thought, he is beginning to wonder if he has done the right thing after all. Now that it is too late!

Coolly she turned back to him. "You appear distressed, Mr. Calder," she said, with deliberate scorn. "Could it be that you are reconsidering your offer, after all?"

Dark eyes met stormy green. "Not at all, Miss Rosslyn," he replied, matching her tone. "My offer still stands—does yours?"

Briefly, she wondered what he meant. But then she dismissed the remark, thinking that he was trying to anger her by attempting to make her share the blame for this hideous situation. Icily, she inclined her head. "Of course," she answered. "There was never any doubt, was there?"

She did not see the quick expression of pain cross his face at her reply; she only saw the sneer that had replaced it when she looked up again, and this infuriated her even more.

Hester, who had been watching them both closely, now said brightly, "Perhaps you would like to be alone for a few minutes. Cynara, why don't you show Mr. Calder the garden?" Hester turned to Evan. "It really is beautiful at this time of year—imagine, roses in November! I never have become accustomed to the reversal of seasons here in this accursed country. November will always be winter for me, I'm afraid. But you go on, both of you."

"I haven't the time," Evan said, rising.

Hester affected disappointment, but actually she was relieved. She did not trust these two alone: all one of them had to do was say something inadvertantly, and her plans might be wrecked before they had begun. "Oh, what a pity," she said, looking up at Evan. "Perhaps another day—?"

"I think not. I have already taken the liberty of booking passage on the next ship sailing for London. We leave in two weeks—"

"Two weeks!" Hester exclaimed. "But that scarcely gives me time to—"

"I didn't think there would be reason for delay," Evan interrupted coolly. "Surely you realize that I am anxious to return to England, now that this matter has been settled to everyone's . . . satisfaction."

"Yes, yes," Hester answered hastily. Now that she thought about it, she did not want to delay either; anything could happen if Cynara and Evan were alone together for any amount of time. "I understand," she replied. "But my house . . . I won't have time to make arrangements for it—"

"That will be taken care of," Evan said caustically. "My associate, Vincent LeCroix, has offered to help in any way he can. If you wish to sell the house and no buyer can be found before we leave, he will assume responsibility. You need have no worries on that score."

"How kind," Hester murmured. But she did not care for his tone. Had he guessed that something was amiss? Devoutly, she prayed not. Once they sailed, however, it would be too late for him to do anything about it.

Evan now turned to the silent Cynara. "We will be married the day we sail," he said coldly. "I trust that is satisfactory to you—?"

Wordlessly, Cynara inclined her head. How like him, she thought wrathfully, to make arrangements that suited only his own purposes! She told herself not to speak, not to ruin her pose of indifference, but in the next minute, his words brought her out of her seat to glare at him.

"I have also made arrangements for you to draw on my account for anything you need in the way of a . . . trousseau."

The disdainful tone of his voice angered Cynara even more. "How kind," she answered coolly. "But quite unnecessary. I wish nothing from you, Evan."

"Nonsense!" Hester exclaimed. She had no intention of providing the wherewithall for a new wardrobe. "You must have some new things, Cynara," she urged. "And if Mr. Calder is generous enough to—"

"I won't accept a cent from him!" Cynara interrupted fiercely.

"I'm afraid you will have to," Evan said, adding condescendingly. "That is, unless you have resources of your own . . ."

"You know I don't!" Cynara snapped, her face crimson. "But how like you to remind me of it!"

"It's just that I will not have my . . . my wife . . . dressed like a servant," Evan answered, his voice as cold as Cynara's expression was fiery. "If you have no particular woman in mind, I'm sure I can find a seamstress for you."

Cynara was so outraged that she almost choked. "I will find someone myself," she ground out at last, knowing that if she did not, Evan was fully capable of carrying out his threat. How she loathed him for compelling her to accept his charity! She could have scratched his eyes out and laughed while doing so.

Evan seemed unaffected by the fury in her face. Calmly, he said, "As you wish. Order whatever you like, but be sure that you are suitably attired when next we meet."

How dare he speak to her like this! "Yes, sir," she said, her tone expressing her icy contempt of him. "And is there anything else you desire? Perhaps you can order that as well!"

Their eyes met like a clash of swords. She saw his lips tighten, but he was more adept than she at checking his temper, and he did not answer her directly. Instead, he went to the door, where he paused. "I'll send word when we are to sail. Until then, don't expect to see me; I have my own concerns to attend to. I will not have time for foolish . . . pleasantries."

Foolish pleasantries! In the space of a few seconds, several caustic comments rushed through her mind, but this time Cynara bit back the words. Turning swiftly away from him, she thought furiously that if she had needed any further proof of his disregard for her, she had it now. How dare he patronize her—how dare he! If this was going to be his attitude in the future, she would not go through with this abominable marriage. She wouldn't do it, no matter what threats were used!

But she did go through with it after all. On a bright day at the end of November, with the cicadas singing in the gum trees beyond the open window of the magistrate's office, Evan slipped a plain gold wedding band on her finger and they became husband and wife.

Cynara, in a spirit of rebellion that even Hester's loud protests had been unable to quell, wore a dress she had ordered herself. Dark blue linen, it was utterly plain, without flounces or trim, the only color being a small ruching of lace at the high throat and at the end of the long sleeves. It was too somber a color for the time of year and certainly for the occasion, and Cynara knew it, but she didn't care what anyone thought. If she had dared, she would have chosen black, as befitted her feelings on this day; only the thought that Sarah had promised to see them off on the ship had kept Cynara from following her first inclination. She had satisfied herself with the blue, ignoring the shocked expression on the seamstress's face.

But her defiance had proved useless; Evan had not even noticed how she was dressed, let alone what color she wore.

In fact, she thought irately, the only times he had glanced at her were those occasions in the ceremony when he was compelled to do so. Now that the magistrate had made his pronouncement, Evan ignored her completely. There was no tenderness here, no gentle and chaste kiss covering passion between bride and groom after the wedding vows were said. Cynara and Evan stood together, but as far apart in spirit as if they had been at opposite ends of the room, as they received the congratulations of Hester and the man Evan had introduced to her briefly before the ceremony as Vincent LeCroix.

Vincent LeCroix, it appeared, had arranged for a small reception at his home after the wedding. It was apparent that he had done so without Evan's knowledge, for when he mentioned it, Evan's face darkened, and he answered curtly, "It isn't necessary, Vincent."

"Nonsense, lad!" Vincent said, a shade too heartily as Cynara's face flamed at Evan's deliberate rudeness. She started to apologize, but Vincent stopped her with a smile that held genuine warmth. "It would be an honor for me, Mrs. Calder," he said softly.

Mrs. Calder. It was the first time she had been addressed by her new name, and Cynara winced. Impossible to believe how she had longed in the past to share Evan's name; now that it was hers, all she could think of was that it was wrong. Everything was wrong, ruined. She wished desperately that she could call back the words that had bound her in marriage to this stranger who still glowered at Vincent LeCroix.

In an effort to make up for Evan's discourtesy, Cynara said, too quickly, "Please call me Cynara."

Vincent smiled and bowed, but not before she had seen the puzzled expression in his eyes as his glance went from Evan to her.

"I hope you do not object to this small gift of a wedding reception," he said. "If you would rather not—"

"I'm delighted," Cynara said swiftly. "It's very kind of you to have thought of it."

"Then it's all right?"

Cynara smiled. "Of course." She took the arm he held out to her without looking at Evan again. "Thank you, Mr. LeCroix. You must excuse Evan's rudeness," she added deliberately. "I'm sure he did not mean to be so unkind."

LeCroix looked over his shoulder at the frowning Evan and said hastily, "Shall we be off, then?"

Fortunately the ride to LeCroix's home was a short one. Only Hester seemed unaware of the uncomfortable silence that descended upon the small party, and she chattered blithely during the entire ride. With both Cynara and Evan maintaining an icy silence, Vincent was forced into conversation with Hester, and Cynara saw that he was as relieved as she was when the carriage halted in front of the house. She felt the beginnings of a fearful headache, and she wondered if she could endure the afternoon until it was time to leave for the ship. The ship. Cynara closed her eyes, dreading the thought of the long voyage ahead of her. Already it seemed interminable to her. What would she and Evan do to each other, confined together for the five months or so it would take before they arrived in London?

Vincent LeCroix seemed determined to interject a note of cheer into the dismal wedding party. As soon as they had entered, he ordered his butler to preside over the lavish buffet that had been arranged on the sideboard in the drawing room. Hester needed no encouragement to begin; she hobbled imperiously over to the buffet and commanded the man to fill her plate, after which she seated herself and began to eat ravenously, ignoring them all.

Cynara had no appetite, but Vincent looked at her so anxiously that she forced herself to select a few of the cold meats and some of the carefully displayed fruit, wondering how she was going to eat at all. There was a lump in her throat; an ache of tears that she had held back from the moment Evan had turned away from her. She wished suddenly that she had confided in Sarah, the one time she had managed to see her these past hectic weeks. But she had been too proud then to confess her doubts and misgivings, and it was too late now. But now, too, she remembered that Sarah had been distinctly uncomfortable with her on that one brief visit, so it was doubtful that she would have confided in her anyway. Sarah had denied that anything was wrong but Cynara wondered all the same why Sarah seemed so distracted, so nervous with her. Looking down at the gold ring on her finger, she had the sudden urge to rip it off and fling it away from her across the room.

Vincent was at her side, looking at her with a concerned expression since he saw that she hadn't been able to eat anything on her plate. Forcing her thoughts away from Evan and what might have been, Cynara said the first thing that came into her mind. "You have a beautiful home, Mr. LeCroix."

"Thank you." LeCroix was pleased at her comment, glancing fondly about the room as he smiled. But then the smile disappeared, and he said, "I would have liked the opportunity to get to know you, Cynara. But it seems . . ." He stopped, his face coloring.

"Yes?"

LeCroix waved his hand. "It was nothing. I had hoped that Evan would not be in such a rush to leave, that's all."

Cynara's expression hardened. "He has his reasons, I'm sure," she replied, her eyes going to where Evan stood across the room, drinking champagne as if it were water.

LeCroix followed the direction of her glance. "Yes," he sighed. "But I thought it would be nice to have you two young people here, even for a short time. The house will seem so empty after Evan leaves."

"You're fond of him, then?" Cynara heard herself asking softly.

"Oh, yes," LeCroix answered. "I'm very proud of him; he has done well for himself."

"Evan was always ambitious," Cynara said shortly.

LeCroix nodded. "Yes. But that is not necessarily an undesirable trait, Cynara. And now he has you to—temper that ambition."

"I'm afraid Evan does not listen to me, Mr. LeCroix," Cynara replied, too curtly. "He goes his own way, and I will go mine."

LeCroix looked at her strangely, and Cynara regretted her impulsive remark. She said quickly, "I wish you were coming with us, Mr. LeCroix."

"Ah, well. Someone has to stay behind and take care of business here," he said, pleased at her comment nevertheless. "But perhaps you will return here some day."

Cynara smiled noncommittally, but she wondered if that was true. Would they return? Would Evan want to leave England? What did it matter, she thought dully. She was concerned only with having her day in court with Myles; after that, she would have accomplished her objective, and there would be nothing to look forward to at all. Tears sprang into her eyes at the thought, and although she tried not to let LeCroix see, he looked at her with concern.

"Have I said something to distress you?"

"No, no," she replied quickly. And then, to her horror, for she had not meant to say it at all, she heard herself blurting, "It's just that it seems so . . . so hopeless . . ."

"Hopeless?" LeCroix seemed confused. "What do you mean?"

Appalled at herself for confessing her innermost thoughts, Cynara tried to recover. "I'm sorry, Mr. LeCroix. I shouldn't have said that. I . . . I must be overtired . . ."

Evan chose that moment to start toward them from across the room. Cynara, seeing him walking purposefully in their direction, knew that she could not face him like this, and she said quickly, "Forgive me, Mr. LeCroix. It must be the heat; suddenly I feel faint. Is there a room where I might rest for a few minutes . . .?"

"Of course."

Ignoring Evan, who was advancing upon them with a frown, Cynara allowed LeCroix to take her arm. In his concern for her, Vincent did not see Evan approaching, and to Cynara's relief, they were able to escape the room without speaking to Evan. LeCroix helped her up the stairs to a cool, dim guest room. He left her at the door, asking, "Can I send one of the maids to you? Perhaps you would like—"

"No, I'll be all right," Cynara replied hastily. "I'm sure . . . I'm sure it's just the excitement. You understand—?"

"Of course. It isn't every day that a young woman gets married—" He stopped, flushing, obviously remembering too late that she had gotten married before, to Thomas Hale. "Well, then," he finished uncomfortably. "If there is nothing . . ."

"Thank you, Mr. LeCroix. You've been very kind."

Alone in the room, Cynara went toward the bed, but she did not immediately lie down. Instead, she stood with her hands covering her face, trying desperately not to cry. She could not face Evan with swollen eyes, she thought, and yet—how could she bear it, seeing that cold contempt in his face every time he looked at her?

She had made a dreadful mistake, she thought, dropping her hands to glance wildly about the room, as if searching for a way to escape. If she left now, she could disappear through a back door without anyone seeing her, she thought frantically. Evan could seek an annulment, and this horrible thing they had done to each other would be undone before it had gone any further. Her thoughts were so chaotic that she actually took a step toward the door, intent on getting away from Evan before he realized that she had gone. But then she looked up and saw Hester, frowning at her from the threshold.

"What is the matter with you, girl?" Hester demanded, seeing Cynara's wide eyes and frantic expression. "Why aren't you downstairs? We have to be at the ship in exactly thirty minutes."

Cynara took a step back, her hand at her throat. Desperately she tried to think, to marshal some argument that would convince Hester she could not go through with this. But she couldn't think at all; she could only stand there, shaking her head, unable to explain.

"Get control of yourself, Cynara!" Hester said sharply. "You're not some timid bride, suffering from nerves. I insist that you pull yourself together and come downstairs with me at once. Your husband is waiting."

Her husband was waiting. Vincent LeCroix was waiting. They were all waiting for her to make some kind of decision. But what choice did she have, after all? She had said the vows of her own free will; she herself had spoken the words that bound her in marriage to Evan Calder, and she had to take the consequences.

Abruptly the frantic, trapped feeling that had gripped her vanished, and she was herself again. Taking a deep breath to steady herself, Cynara saw a mirror on the wall and she went to it on the pretext of examining her appearance. Avoiding the sight of the pale face reflected there, she smoothed her hair and adjusted the lace at her throat. When she turned back to Hester, her expression was once again neutral. "I'm ready now," she said quietly.

Hester gave her a sharp look, but she said nothing more. In silence, the two women descended the stairs just as Evan and Vincent entered the hall. LeCroix was coming to the docks with them, and Cynara was grateful. With him there, she would not have to speak to Evan; she would have that much more time to steady herself.

Trying not to think of the moment when she would have to face Evan alone for the first time, Cynara accepted her cape and bonnet from the maid and tied the bonnet ribbons under her chin with hands that had begun to shake again. Vincent gave her arm a reassuring squeeze as they re-entered the carriage, but this time even Hester was silent during the journey to the ship, and Cynara was too tense to make conversation. She wanted to thank Vincent for his kindness, but she was afraid that if she spoke she would burst into tears.

But Vincent looked as glum as she felt, and Cynara saw from the corner of her eye that Evan's expression was cold and remote. He could have been alone in the carriage for all the notice he gave anyone else.

Fortunately, Sarah was waiting for them when they arrived. Cynara took one look at her and almost burst into tears again. Blinking rapidly, she noticed that Sarah had tears in her eyes as well, and as they clung to each other for a moment, Cynara whispered, "I hope I'll see you again, Sarah. . ."

"And I . . ."

Then Sarah said a strange thing. Before she turned away to say goodbye to Evan, Sarah met her eyes and whispered, "Be happy—for both of us, Cynara. Please . . ."

Cynara was so startled at the urgency behind the remark that she stared blankly as Sarah held out both hands to Evan. Be happy for both of them, she repeated in her mind; what did Sarah mean? And then she happened to see Sarah's face as she spoke to Evan, and suddenly she knew. The swift shadow of pain crossed Sarah's features as she said goodbye to Evan, and Cynara realized with a pang that Sarah loved him. It was there in her face to read, despite her efforts to hide it, and Cynara wondered bleakly why she hadn't realized it before. If she hadn't been so preoccupied with her own problems, she would have guessed. If she had known, perhaps she could have done something, said something!

"Sarah—" she began.

But Sarah had already hurried off to the waiting trap. With a brief lift of her hand, her hat shading her face so that Cynara could not see her expression, Sarah stepped into the vehicle. And then she was gone without giving Cynara a chance to explain, and Cynara stared after her, her own expression bleak.

Cynara did not dare look at Evan; she was afraid of what she would see in his face if she looked. Was he in love with Sarah, as she was with him? Cynara didn't want to know. But she had no more time to think about it, for Vincent had grasped her hands, and was kissing her cheek. She turned dazedly to him, and to her astonishment saw that there was the glitter of tears in his eyes.

"Be good to each other," Vincent whispered. "You are better suited than either of you know. . ."

"Vincent," Cynara said impulsively, "Will you do something for me?"

"Of course."

"Will you . . . will you explain to Sarah—about Evan and me? I mean . . ." She stopped, unable to go on.

Vincent smiled sadly. "She knows, Cynara," he said softly.

"But—"

"Sarah knows it wasn't meant to be," Vincent insisted quietly. "She didn't want to stand in Evan's way; she will get over it."

"Will you tell her—" Cynara blinked back tears "that I didn't know?"

Vincent nodded again. "I'll tell her, but I think she knows that already."

Cynara turned away, fumbling for a handkerchief. She wouldn't cry, she muttered fiercely to herself; she wouldn't!

She could not watch the leavetaking between Evan and Vincent, but as she wiped her eyes, she saw that Evan offered his hand, and that Vincent took it. And then Vincent clasped Evan to him for an instant, and to her amazement, Evan did not try to pull away from him. Vincent muttered something to him that Cynara didn't hear, and then he had stepped back, murmuring a farewell to Hester, who had stood waiting impatiently.

"I'll let you know how things come out," Evan said to Vincent, his voice rough with emotion.

"I'll expect to hear from you, lad," Vincent replied, shading his eyes with his hand. "Have a care . . ."

Evan nodded, and then abruptly he climbed down the ladder and was seated beside her. Looking up, she saw that Vincent was waving at them, and she raised her own hand in response. How she would have liked to have known him better, she thought. He looked so sad, so lonely, standing there by himself, waving to them as the boat pulled away toward the looming presence of the ship waiting in the bay.

Would she ever see him again? She found herself wishing fiercely that she would, and she turned to Evan, intending to ask him. But at the expression on his face, she remained silent. For the first time the hard lines of his face had softened slightly as he raised his hand in a last farewell to the solitary figure on the dock, and Cynara realized that he was struggling with some emotion of his own. She watched Evan, and wondered what Vincent LeCroix had meant to him. Would she ever know? Would they ever reach any level of communication, of understanding, that would enable her to ask him? She doubted it.

As Vincent's figure dwindled and became small with the increasing distance between them, Cynara felt a heavy sadness descend upon her. It was a sadness for herself and Evan, for what might have been. They could have had something rare, something precious, but now . . . now it could never be. Too many memories stood between them—from that night in the lyrebird garden to the scene in Hester's drawing room, it seemed that everything that had happened in between had only driven them further apart. They were married; they shared the same name; but that was all, and there would never be anything more between them.

Cynara looked out over the water at her last glimpse of Sydney. Suddenly, as if in a nightmare, she saw Myles's face superimposed on the terraced landscape and its sandstone buildings, and it seemed to her that she could hear his high, shrill laughter of satisfaction over what he had wrought.

PART III

CHAPTER TWENTY-NINE

"AH, HOME AT LAST!" Hester glanced around with satisfaction, accepting as her due the curtsies of the three maids who waited in the hall, acknowledging the inclined head of the housekeeper and the deep bow of the woman's husband, the butler. She had sent a letter from Australia as soon as she knew she was returning to her home in Suffolk, and now her piercing gaze raked every corner of the entryway as she made sure that the house had been properly readied for her return. A distant cousin of her mother's had been allowed to live at the house since Hester's parents had passed away some years before. The cousin had died last year, and the house had been kept with only a skeleton staff since that time. But now she was home, and she intended to see that her home was properly maintained while she was in residence.

Cynara had entered after Hester, and now she stood gaping at the sight before her. The house was a soft rose-colored brick on the outside. Within, everything was shining and immaculate, the evidence of quiet wealth all around. Cynara had suspected before that Hester was far from poor, and now, catching sight of the thick pearl-gray carpet and muted blues of the drawing room opposite the entry, she wondered why Hester hadn't returned years before. From just this glimpse of the furnishings, and the obvious deference of the waiting servants, it was obvious that Hester had had the means to make the journey. Cynara wondered why Hester had allowed a cousin to preside over this luxury when it could have been hers.

Puzzled, Cynara looked at Hester, and was again struck by the woman's energy. It had taken them hours to make their way from London, where they had stayed for several days after disembarking from the ship. Cynara was almost too tired to stand after the constant jolting of the hired coach that had brought them here, but Hester did not seem to feel the debilitating effects of the journey, for she was issuing orders briskly as she waited for Evan to come in.

He had been supervising the unloading of their baggage from the coach, but he came into the hall at that moment, and Hester turned imperiously to him.

"What do you think, Evan? Aren't you glad now that you accepted my offer to stay with me?"

Evan was tired and irritable. Barely glancing at the shining parqueted floor of the entryway, the curving staircase with the elaborately carved bannister that led to the upper floor, he chose not to answer, but turned to Trent, the butler, instead.

"I would like a brandy," he said abruptly.

"Certainly, sir." Trent inclined his head. "If you will follow me . . ." He gestured toward a corridor to their left.

Without a backward glance, Evan walked away, leaving the two women standing in the hall. Cynara bit back an angry comment as she watched him go, but Hester chuckled fondly. "Isn't that just like a man?" she asked, her eyes following him.

"Hester, I'm sure you must be exhausted," Cynara said. "I know I am. Why don't we go to our rooms, and—"

"You go along," Hester interrupted irritably. "As for me, I think I'll join Evan in that brandy."

This was not a new occurrence. During the long, confining voyage, Hester and Evan had taken to sharing an after-dinner brandy, leaving Cynara to make her way to the cabin alone. She hadn't minded at first, not after the bitter quarrel she and Evan had engaged in so soon after they had boarded the ship. As time went on, and the after-dinner brandy had been extended to late afternoon conferences with wine, Cynara had become more and more lonely. It was almost as if the two of them were deliberately excluding her. What they found to talk about, Cynara didn't know, and after a while she hadn't cared. In fact, she had learned to hope that these sessions went on as long as possible; she hadn't wanted Evan near her any more than was absolutely necessary.

One of the maids, introducing herself as Marie, offered to show her the way upstairs. Cynara followed gratefully, suddenly longing for bed and a sleep that she hoped would refresh her and enable her to cope with this new situation.

The maid had been instructed to take her to the master suite—a cruel joke on Hester's part—and when she opened the door and waited respectfully for Cynara to precede her into the room, Cynara was at once pleased and dismayed by the sight before her. Glancing away from the huge four poster bed set against one wall, Cynara went instead to the window seat. From there she could see gentle, rolling hills dotted here and there with grazing sheep.

How she had longed for a sight such as this! But now, having it before her, she felt only disquiet instead of the peace she had longed for. The restful landscape in front of her was marred by the knowledge that beyond the first slope to her right was Lyrebird Manor. They had passed the beautiful and distinctive gates that led to the Manor on the way here, and it was then that Cynara had realized why Evan had so readily accepted Hester's invitation.

Only when Marie had gone did Cynara relax from her stiff pose. Sinking into a chair, she put her head back and closed her eyes. It seemed impossible that she was actually here again, that the long voyage was over and Australia had been left behind.

The past five months had been worse than she had imagined—oh, not the voyage itself, she conceded; compared to the conditions she had suffered on the transport ship, this last journey was almost a luxury. No, it hadn't been the long months of travel that had wearied her; it had been the strain of maintaining a surface relationship with Evan for the benefit of the other passengers.

Thinking now of the scene she and Evan had engaged in only hours after boarding the ship, Cynara knew that any hope she had entertained of making their marriage viable had been shattered with Evan's first question. He had asked, quite softly, "Are you going to tell me now, or do I have to wait until we reach London?"

Cynara remembered the scene so clearly that it could have taken place only yesterday instead of months ago. She had paused in the act of unpacking her few things to stare blankly at him.

"What do you mean?" The ship had weighed anchor, sailing down the coast at sunset, and was now on the open sea. Unaccustomed to the rolling motion under her feet after so much time on land, Cynara grabbed the edge of the cupboard for balance as she looked at him.

The single lamp cast shadows on his face as he stood there in the cramped space, only a few steps from her. Was it only the flickering light that made him seem so satanic in that moment? She wanted to look away from him, but she could not; she seemed impaled by those dark eyes. "What do you mean?" she had asked again when he did not answer.

"There is no longer any need to play coy, is there, Cynara?" he had demanded harshly. "I've fulfilled my part of the bargain; now I expect you to fulfill yours."

Her temper rose in response to his sneering tone, and she said sharply, "Any bargain you made, Evan, is between you and Hester. I suggest you speak to her."

Although she had expected it, she was still unprepared for the anger she saw in his face. Alarmed, she watched his hands clench into fists, and her heart began to pound. For the first time, she was frightened of him, and she heard herself say quickly, "I don't know what you're talking about, Evan. What bargain?"

"It doesn't suit you to play dumb, Cynara," he ground out. "Hester told me—"

"Hester!" Her fright turned again to anger, and she repeated scornfully, "Hester! And what did she tell you, Evan?"

He advanced a step toward her, and she cried, "Don't come near me until we settle this, Evan! I'm warning you!"

He was so surprised that he stopped. Looking at her, he saw that her expression was wild, almost as if she were seeing not him, but someone else. But then her gaze became focused on him again, and she drew back from him, asking once more, "What did Hester tell you?"

"She told me," he said heavily, "that you had persuaded her not to tell me what she knows about Aron Ward—and Lyrebird Manor. It was your idea," he said, his anger growing again at her blank expression, "that I marry you and take you both back to England before she told me what I want to know." He took a step toward her again, his face menacing. "I'm through playing your little games, Cynara—I want to know now!"

But Cynara had heard only part of what he said. Appalled, she stared at him before choking out, "She told you that I insisted upon marrying you? And you believed her?"

"Why shouldn't I have?" he snarled. "I saw for myself to what extent you were willing to . . . to sell yourself to Thomas Hale. Why should it have been any different with me?"

Cynara was so enraged that for an instant she couldn't speak. Then, without thinking, she raised her hand and slapped him full across the face. "How dare you speak to me like that!" she hissed as he staggered back. "How *dare* you talk to me of prostituting myself to get what I want!"

She had raised her hand again, so furious that she intended to strike him once more, to slap that disbelieving look off his face. But in the next instant her wrist was imprisoned in his strong fingers. Infuriated, she tried to pull away from him, but he held her fast. He pushed his face close to hers, forcing her to bend backwards in an attempt to get away from the blazing light in his eyes.

"Are you trying to say that this absurd marriage was not your idea?"

"I had nothing to do with it! How could you believe that I would willingly marry you!" she spat, still seeking to free her wrist.

"You bitch!"

He dropped her arm so suddenly that she fell back,

striking her hip on the edge of the cupboard. Wincing with pain, she lifted her head to glare at him. "And why did you marry *me*, Evan? Wasn't it because you wanted something from Hester? You have no right to call me names!"

Both furious, they stared at each other, until finally Cynara hissed, "You won't find out anything from me, Evan, because I don't know anything to tell you. Hester is the one to confront—obviously she keeps her secrets well."

"If I ever find out that you know and aren't telling me—"

Cynara tossed her head. She was too angry to be frightened of his threats. "Don't worry about that, Evan." She added, deliberately taunting him, "But it does surprise me that you were duped—I would have thought that you would have suspected it from the first. *I* had no choice—"

"What does that mean?" he snarled.

"Hester threatened me with further imprisonment if I didn't marry you. What threat did she use on you? Or was it only your own ambition and greed that made you agree to a marriage that is obviously as distasteful to you as it is to me!"

But Evan did not seem to hear her last remark; he was staring at her strangely. "What did you mean about further imprisonment?" he asked, in a strangled tone.

"You know very well what I meant!" Cynara cried. "Don't tell me you didn't know about my being a convict! I'm sure she told you all about it!"

Evan passed a hand over his eyes. "Oh, God," he muttered. "I can't believe. . ." He saw her wild stare, and he shook his head. "I told Hester, in the first letter I sent around, asking to see her, that you were . . . free."

"Free?" Cynara repeated. "I don't understand!"

Swallowing, Evan was unable to meet her eyes. "When I found out what Hale had done, I—I bought your papers. I told Hester that, so she knew. . ." His voice trailed off.

"You what!" Cynara rounded furiously on him, so angry that her eyes blazed. "Why didn't you tell *me*!" she cried.

"I thought . . . I assumed that she had told you . . ."

"Well, she didn't tell me! My God! How could you have done this to me?"

"God damn it! I told you I thought—"

"I don't care what you thought! Can't you see what you've done? If I had known—oh, God, if only I had known, I wouldn't have been forced to marry you! She couldn't have threatened me!"

They stared at each other in a sudden awful silence, aghast. They had been tricked, maneuvered by a cunning old woman, moved about as though they were chess pieces on a board. In that first horrible instant of recognition they turned away from each other, appalled that they had fallen so easily into Hester's trap. Each felt like a fool, and, ashamed that the other was witnessing their humiliation, their anger turned not to Hester, who had plotted against them, but onto each other. Pride reared its head, and the moment of understanding and forgiveness vanished like a puff of smoke. When they looked at each other again, they were like two combatants on the field of battle, each trying to hide from the other his tumultuous feelings of shame and betrayal.

"Get out!" Cynara cried, lifting her hand. "Get out and don't come back! God—how I hate you! How I hate you both!"

Evan actually flinched at her words, but he did not move. Cynara, wanting him only to be gone so that she could surrender to the tears gathering in her, rushed toward him to push him out the door. Instinctively, he grabbed her, gripping her arms to defend himself against her attack.

"Let me go—you're hurting me, Evan!"

But he couldn't let her go. Despite his own rage and humiliation, something had happened to him the moment he touched her. The more she struggled, the stronger the feeling grew. Blood pounded in his veins, there was a swelling in his loins. Looking down at her flashing eyes, he thought that she had never looked so beautiful to him as in this moment when she fought to get away from him.

"You're my wife," he said harshly, "Or have you forgotten that?"

"I'm *not* your wife!" she shouted furiously. "It was all a trick! Let me go, Evan!"

"Not yet." He hardly knew what he was saying; he seemed to be mesmerized by her nearness, by the slim body straining against his arms. "If I never come near you again, at least I will have claimed my rights as a husband this one time."

Aghast, she stared at him. "You wouldn't dare!"

He didn't answer. Couldn't answer. Her nearness was intoxicating, and he couldn't have stopped himself even if he had wanted to. Bending his head, he kissed her.

The touch of his lips was like fire. Cynara struggled against him, her hands pushing vainly against his chest. The pressure of his mouth increased, and he held her so tightly she couldn't move. His mouth was seeking, demanding, and despite her fury, she felt herself responding. A tremor raced through her, and suddenly she was caught up in a wave of desire so strong that she sagged against him. Without being aware of it, her arms wound around his neck and she pressed her body into his. She heard his sharp intake of breath, heard him whisper her name.

The time for denial was past. In this moment there was only their need for each other, the surrendering of will to desire, the passion that must be spent. Whatever happened in the future, this time was theirs and they forgot everything else in their urgency.

She felt her hair come loose as Evan pulled the pins from it, and then he was burying his face in the thick fall that tumbled to her shoulders. Groaning, he said her name again, and then he lifted her and carried her to the bed.

She never knew whether he had undressed her or whether she had helped him. Nor did she know when he shed his own clothing. She only knew she felt her nakedness against his, the warmth of his body as he slid over hers. She ran her fingers through his hair as he held her tightly against him, and pulled his head down to hers. Their lips met and Evan uttered a wordless sound as his hands found her breasts. She arched against him and he rolled to the side, taking her with him. She felt the hardness of him against her, felt his legs pushing hers apart, and she moaned.

This, she thought dazedly, this was what it was like to be loved. She felt lifted, transported, breathless, and she wanted to prolong this moment forever. "Evan," she whispered, "wait . . ."

But he was beyond hearing her. Caught up in his own delirium, he was conscious only of her slim white body under him, of her breasts against his chest, of her legs enclosing his. His passion for her was uncontrollable; he was lost in her, drowning in the touch and scent of her. He had denied himself too long; all his senses screamed at him to take her, and he didn't hear her second, frightened protest.

His movements above her increased in frenzy, and Cynara tried to draw back. Where was the tender, gentle lover of moments ago? Without warning, memories of other men who had used her so roughly flashed through her mind, and for a terrible instant, Ben Knowles's face was superimposed on Evan's. She cried out in real fear, trying to push Evan away.

Evan didn't realize that her frantic movements were the product of terror and not desire. He felt her writhing under him, and his passion increased to fever pitch. Driving into her, he uttered her name as the climax came rushing toward him, and then seconds later, it was over.

He fell against her, panting, and it was some time before he realized that she was crying. The sound of her weeping startled him; he lifted his head and looked at her in stupefaction. "What—"

"Get out," she said between clenched teeth. "Get out!"

He stared at her, unmoving, unable to comprehend this sudden change in her from passion to contempt. He could not know that she felt ashamed and humiliated because her

passion for him had seemed to change him into all the other
men who had taken her, as he had, forcibly. Turning her
head away from him, she began to cry again. Was he really
like all the rest? Couldn't he understand that she had been
frightened, that other memories haunted her? If only he had
stopped to reassure her, to hold her until she was no longer
afraid. But he had not, and in her mind he was no better than
the others who had been so engrossed in their own feelings
that they did not care about hers.

Her pride would not allow her to explain, and Evan,
rousing from his stupifaction, did not ask for explanations.
Remembering his own behavior, the desire that had blinded
him to everything but his own need, he was ashamed of
himself. Christ! he thought; he had nearly raped her. He
recalled now that she had cried out in protest at one time,
but he had ignored her, too consumed by passion to pay
heed to anything but the chaos that raged inside him. His
shame increased, and he flung himself away from her.

Dressing quickly, he could not look at her. When he
finally pulled on his coat, he went to the cabin door, and in a
strangled voice he said, "I think that it would be better if I
take Hester's cabin for the rest of the voyage, and she share
this one with you."

Without waiting for her answer, he strode out, slamming
the door behind him. An hour later, Cynara was surrounded by Hester's hastily assembled baggage, trying not
to weep in front of Hester's disapproving and curious expression. Cynara and Evan had remained estranged for the
entire voyage, the barrier between them that had begun to
crumble with their first coming together rising higher than
before, built of misunderstanding and false pride.

Cynara passed a hand over her eyes. Rising, she walked to
the window again, surprised to find that while she had sat
there thinking, the afternoon had shaded to dusk. The huge
trees outside the window cast shadows over the pane, and
she turned away to light the lamp. Had she fallen asleep?
Where was everyone? The house was too quiet, and Cynara

shivered as she went to the door. She heard a gong sound as she descended the stairs, and realized with a start that it was dinner time. Where had the afternoon gone?

Hester was just going into the dining room as she reached the foot of the stairs. The long table was set only for two, and as Cynara seated herself, she wondered where Evan was. But she had no time to ask, for Hester lifted the silver bell by her plate and gave it a shake. Instantly, Trent appeared, followed by a maid carrying two covered silver dishes. The maid put one dish on the sideboard, removed the cover of the other and offered it to Hester. Hester gave herself a generous portion of the sliced beef, and the maid moved to Cynara. Cynara shook her head: she couldn't eat.

"You must have something!" Hester exclaimed impatiently.

"Not now." Cynara refused the second platter as well, and the maid moved away to bring additional dishes from the kitchen. Trent came forward with wine, and Cynara allowed him to fill her glass before she asked, "Hester, where is Evan?"

Hester paused in the act of lifting her laden fork to her mouth. "He isn't here."

"I can see that. Where is he?"

"He went back to London."

"London!" Cynara was unable to conceal her astonishment.

"He had business to attend to." Hester washed down the food in her mouth with a swallow of wine. She looked at Cynara critically before lowering her head to begin eating again, but she said nothing more.

Cynara was silent as well. She would not ask, she thought fiercely, what business it was that had taken Evan away so soon after their arrival. But she thought to herself: Now it has begun. He had threatened to leave her alone, and he had done so, barely waiting until they had entered the house before he made his departure.

Briefly she wondered what the servants thought about

this strange behavior, and then she shook her head impatiently. What did it matter what they thought? If he had remained, the fact that their marriage was one in name only would soon have been obvious. Hester's gesture of giving them the master suite had been an empty one, for Evan would never have stayed with her there, even if the servants gossiped their heads off. Too many hateful and hurtful words had passed between them for the rift ever to heal.

But did she want it to? Cynara didn't know. She thought back again to that night they had faced each other so furiously, when he had coldly informed her that he would take a cabin to himself. She had been so angry and so hurt over the way he had treated her that she had been glad he had decided to leave her alone. She hadn't cared then—did she now?

Abruptly she rose from the table, excusing herself curtly before going out. She was aware that Hester's eyes followed her as she left, but she didn't pause. Let Hester think what she would, Cynara thought angrily. If she hadn't meddled in something that was none of her affair in the first place, perhaps . . .

Cynara thrust the thought from her mind. Useless now to wish that she and Evan hadn't quarreled; futile to hope that either of them would ever forget how it had ended. She knew she could never forget; the hurt and humiliation of that night would be with her always.

But there was another memory of that time that she would remember as well, and though she was loath to admit it, she knew she would never forget the passion that had taken hold of her from the moment his lips first touched hers. Even now something in her responded to that memory, and she felt a stirring deep inside her as she recalled the sensation of his naked body against her. She had wanted him—oh yes, she had wanted him, with all her heart and senses and emotions. But then other memories had risen up to haunt her, and she had become afraid. Would she always remember those other encounters—would those hideous memories forever make her freeze when a man touched her?

Opening the doors that led to the terrace, Cynara stepped outside, allowing the cool night air to flow over her flushed face. She shouldn't have let herself be forced to marry him. It had been a mistake from the beginning, and they had only made it worse by refusing to speak of that night.

He hadn't even said goodbye to her, she thought suddenly, resting her cheek against the post at the end of the veranda. He didn't even have the courtesy to say goodbye. He had left without a word, and it was obvious now that their relationship was meant to continue as it had begun that night on the ship. It would always be this way, she thought: passing each other without speaking, living in the same house without acknowledging each other's existence. Would he even return from London, she wondered suddenly. What did he intend to do there?

Cynara realized abruptly that Hester had come out onto the terrace. Reluctantly she turned toward her, and Hester murmured, "Isn't it wonderful to be back in England again?"

Cynara had no wish to be drawn into conversation. She answered curtly, "Yes, I suppose so. But it's getting late . . ." She began to move toward the door, but Hester stopped her with an imperious wave of her hand. "What is it?" Cynara asked impatiently. She was in no mood for one of Hester's lectures tonight.

"Why are you unhappy, Cynara?"

Cynara stared at her, unable to believe that Hester could ask such a question. "I think it's obvious, Hester," she began stiffly.

"Oh yes, it certainly is," Hester replied, staring straight at her. "But it's your own fault, you know. If you—"

"Hester," Cynara said firmly, trying to control her temper. "I don't care to discuss my happiness, or lack of it. If you will excuse me—"

"No, I won't. If nothing else, you can do me the courtesy of listening until I finish what I have to say."

Cynara waited, her lips tight.

"It's your fault that you and Evan are . . . at odds—"

"My fault!" Cynara was indignant. "That's absurd!"

"No, it isn't. You don't understand Evan. You've made no effort to try. I think you should—"

Cynara's indignation changed to anger. Understand him! Even the thought was ludicrous! With an effort, she managed to say coolly, "Isn't it too late for advice, Hester? What understanding do you expect me to show when you lied to make me marry him?"

"Lied to you? How can you accuse me—"

"You knew I was no longer a convict when you told me I had to marry him or face another prison sentence."

The statement hung heavily between them, and in the silence that followed, Cynara saw the flush that spread over Hester's cheeks. If she had needed confirmation of Hester's lies she had it now. The woman couldn't meet her eyes. The resentment she had been holding back for so many months burst from her now, and she leaned forward, the words pouring from her in an angry torrent. "Yes, you lied to me! I don't know what you told Evan to make him marry me, but I suppose it doesn't matter, does it? You got what you wanted"—her arm made a sweeping gesture that included the house in back of them—"and that was the only thing that was important to you. You were able to come home, weren't you—although God knows why you didn't just tell the truth in the first place! But no—that was too simple, wasn't it? You didn't care that you had ruined our lives—Evan's and mine—by forcing us to agree to this horrible charade of a marriage!" Cynara took a deep breath, staring directly into Hester's eyes. "And now you have the effrontery to tell me that I don't understand Evan. Well, let me tell you, Hester—I understand him better than you ever will!"

Hester tried to speak, but for the first time, she actually quailed before the blazing fury in Cynara's eyes. Her hand went to her throat, her fingers trembling, but Cynara, once aroused, had no pity.

"You're a selfish, greedy old woman, Hester!" Cynara hissed. "Why didn't you simply tell Evan what he wanted to know? It would have been so much more honorable than what you have done!"

Hester backed away a step, fumbling for the chair behind her. Sinking into it, she looked up at Cynara and said, "I thought..." She swallowed. "I thought that if I told him, he wouldn't bring me home ... I couldn't come by myself—there was no one I could trust ..."

Cynara told herself not to weaken at the stricken look in Hester's eyes. Turning away from her imploring expression, she said coldly, "But you didn't even ask him, did you? You went ahead with your own plans, and didn't care whom you hurt in the process!"

For the first time in their association, Cynara heard a pleading note in Hester's voice, but she would not turn around. "You don't understand, Cynara," Hester implored. "I thought we could be a ... family."

"A family!" Now Cynara did turn back to her. "You lied to both Evan and me, you tricked us, and you thought we could be a family!"

Hester actually winced at the incredulity in Cynara's voice. "I know it was a ... a foolish thing to wish, Cynara," she whispered. "But I had lost one family, and—"

"And you thought to manufacture another?"

The scorn underlying Cynara's question was too much for Hester. Dropping her eyes, she mumbled, "After all, he is my great-nephew. I thought—"

"I don't care what you thought!" Cynara raged. "You had no right—what did you say?"

Hester looked up again. "I said Evan is my great-nephew," she repeated weakly.

Cynara stared at her. "Does Evan know that?"

Hester shook her head. "He only suspects."

"Then why in God's name haven't you told him? Is that what he wanted to know? Is that why he agreed to marry me—to find out?"

A small measure of the autocratic Hester returned in response to Cynara's rapid questioning. "There are things even you don't know or understand, Cynara," she replied stiffly.

"What things?"

"The time isn't right," Hester announced obscurely. "I must be sure."

About what? Don't you think you have meddled enough, Hester? If you are truly Evan's great-aunt, surely he has a right to know!"

"I'll tell him soon."

"When?"

"When I think it's time for him to know," Hester replied maddeningly.

Cynara was sarcastic. "And when will that be?" she demanded. "After he has done something else you want?"

Hester rose from her chair. "I must be sure that no violence will be done," she replied, with dignity.

"Violence?" Cynara felt a stab of apprehension. She knew all too well the extent of Evan's temper, and suddenly she was uneasy. "Why should there be violence?"

"Good night, Cynara."

"Hester—"

"Good night."

Short of physically detaining her, Cynara was unable to stop her as she walked from the terrace, moving slowly as she leaned on her cane. As Hester disappeared from sight, Cynara shivered. Suddenly the air was chill and she was cold. Wrapping her arms around her for warmth, Cynara stared at the doorway through which Hester had gone. Why should Hester be afraid that the knowledge of their relationship would provoke violence from Evan?

Cynara shook her head, puzzled. Should she tell Evan herself? But something within her shied away from the thought. Closing the terrace doors behind her, Cynara slowly mounted the stairs after Hester. She knew that Evan was adept at concealing the rage that seemed to burn within him, but she had seen him near to losing control, and she did not want to be the one to unleash the fury he had so far held in check. If Hester was apprehensive about telling Evan, perhaps she had good reason to be.

Cynara undressed and then put out the lamp and climbed into bed, but it was a long time before she slept. She was unable to forget that strange conversation with Hester. Reviewing it again and again in her mind, she was forced at last to admit that she did not understand the implications of what Hester had said.

But as much as Cynara tried to avoid the real reason that kept her awake so far into the night, it was there, in the back of her mind, gnawing at her. Despising herself for not being able to thrust the image from her thoughts, Cynara kept picturing Evan in the arms of some woman he had found in London—some nameless, faceless creature who would give him what he desired. She told herself again and again that she wouldn't care if Evan took a mistress—or a hundred mistresses, for that matter—but in her heart, she knew it was a lie. She wanted to be the woman who excited Evan; she wanted to be the one his arms ached to hold. Only she would satisfy him; there would be no one else for him. It would be her lips, her body, he sought. Every other woman would be as nothing to him, for she alone would have the power to keep him. Her hands would make him wild with desire; her lips would sear his skin, inflaming him with passion; her body would drive him to ecstasy. Oh yes, given the chance, she could have loved Evan in such a way that he would never have looked at another woman.

But Evan had given no sign that he wanted or needed her, she thought bitterly. And now she was here alone, and Evan was gone. Would he return? Would things be any different even if he did? Turning her face into the pillow, Cynara choked back a hopeless sob.

CHAPTER THIRTY

EVAN WOKE WITH a start. The girl's warm, soft body next to him shifted position. She threw an arm over his chest and moved closer to snuggle against him in her sleep. For a moment he lay there, enjoying the feel of her against him, thinking sleepily that it was Cynara he held. And then he saw the glint of blond hair in the early morning light, and he knew it wasn't Cynara at all. In fact he couldn't even remember what this girl looked like, nor her name, and he irritably removed his arm from around her bare shoulders and sat up. The girl murmured something as she slept, and Evan reached across and drew the covers over her again.

God! He shouldn't have drunk so much last night, he thought as he went to splash cold water on his face. His eyes burned, and the ache in his head increased when he bent over. He ran his fingers over his jaw and knew that he would have to have a shave before facing the banker, James Melburn, with whom he had an appointment at nine o'clock. Frowning at his haggard reflection, he turned away to dress.

The girl still hadn't awakened when he finished dressing, and Evan stared briefly at her before pulling some pound notes from his pocket. He left them on the dresser and walked softly to the door.

What was the matter with him, he wondered as he let himself out of the hotel room. He had spent lavishly the night before in an effort to forget the problems he had left behind; he had picked up the girl somewhere along the way, and they had returned to his room and spent a good part of the night making love. He should feel rested and relaxed. Instead he was irritable and annoyed, and what was more, he couldn't even recall that he had enjoyed himself at all.

Damn her! he thought angrily. Cynara was like a disease, a fire in his blood. No matter how hard he tried to convince himself that he could walk away from her at any time, he knew it wasn't true. Sometimes his desire for her became unbearable, and he was driven, as he had been last night, to satisfy his hunger with another woman, trying vainly to find in someone else what he had lost. He searched for Cynara in every woman he met, and now he realized that the only reason he had taken that girl back to his hotel was that her eyes were green, like Cynara's. He remembered that much, at least, and despised himself for his weakness.

But the girl wasn't Cynara, no matter how he had wanted her to be, and he was left with this agonizing emptiness that nothing could fill. Only Cynara had the power to satisfy him; only she called to him with her siren's song, beckoning him to taste the sweetness of her lips, to feel the softness of her skin and the lushness of her body. No other woman could do so, for he would always remember that he had had her once.

But that memory, as much as it aroused him, also brought with it a sense of shame. That first night on the ship he had literally forced himself on Cynara, and even now he cringed at the thought of it. What had possessed him? He had never acted that way before. He couldn't believe, even now, that he had done such a thing to any woman, much less a woman who had become his wife only hours before.

There was no excuse for what he had done. What did it matter that she had hurled those accusations at him, that she had screamed at him to stay away from her? He should never have allowed himself to become so impassioned that he had attacked her. And that was the only word for it: attack. Thinking about it now, he felt his face grow hot.

Added to his shame was the knowledge that because he had been hurt by her, he had wanted to hurt her in return. She had scorned him; she had told him that she never would have married him if she hadn't been forced into it. Forced into it. That had come as a shock. He could remember even now how he had gaped at her. But he hadn't believed her; he had thought that she was trying to exonerate herself, and he had been so furious that he had . . . he had . . . raped her. God! He must have been utterly insane!

But she had stood there, those huge eyes of hers flashing

green fire, and something in him had snapped. Desire had flooded over him like a tide, and the way she had lifted her head, her hair tumbling around her shoulders, her slim body vibrating with anger and indignation, had aroused him to the point of madness. The result was humiliating to think about even now. When he had stood there, threatening so manfully that he would leave the cabin to her, almost hoping that she would refuse to let him go, she had glared back at him and hadn't said a word. He had seen the fierce anger in her eyes, her utter contempt for him and what he had done, and he had known in that moment that he had lost her. She would never forgive him, and deep inside, he knew that he couldn't expect her to. How could he, when he couldn't forgive himself?

Those months on the ship had been torture for him—seeing Cynara every day but never able to approach her, to tell her he was sorry. Every time he got up the nerve to speak to her, she turned away, her disdain clearly written on her face. In the end he had said nothing, and the gulf between them had widened with his silence . . . until he knew that he could never cross it with words. But the seemingly interminable voyage had ended, and because he was as proud as she was, their estrangement was complete. If she had given him the slightest encouragement, the smallest sign that she was willing to listen to him, he would have swallowed his pride and gone to her. But she had given him nothing, and now it was too late.

And that damnable Hester, he thought irritably. In a way, she was responsible for everything. If she hadn't lied to them both, if she hadn't bribed him into marrying Cynara, none of this would have happened. He had been furious when he discovered how he had been duped, and he had blamed Hester entirely. Now he realized that the reponsibility was his, and he was even more enraged. He hadn't been compelled to accept Hester's conditions; he could have refused outright. He *should* have refused, no matter what she offered him.

To his surprise, once he got over the worst of his anger at

Hester, and boredom had set in, he found her a witty and wily companion—someone to pass the hours with as the ship churned through the endless miles of ocean. He knew that she was holding something back from him, some vital piece of information about Aron Ward. Although he tried many times during those long months on the ship to make her reveal what she knew, she had cunningly changed the subject every time, until he was so infuriated that he refused to ask her any more questions. He would not beg, he vowed stubbornly; he would not put himself in the position of supplicant. If Hester wanted to tell him, she could do so. If not . . . He shrugged. Now that he was in England again, he had his own plans for John and Myles and Lyrebird Manor, and whatever he would accomplish would be done alone.

Looking up at the gray stone facade of the bank where the hack had deposited him, Evan felt a stirring of excitement. In a few more minutes, he would know if his plan would work. If he succeeded, he would soon be the owner of Lyrebird Manor, and nothing else would matter.

Silently he thanked old Oliver for the information that had led him here without having to waste valuable time trying to locate the bank on his own. Evan had gone to see him at once, and as old as Oliver Lindsay was, his mind was still quick. Evan suspected that he had known right away why he wanted to know which bank John Ward used.

"But how did you know about the mortgage on the Manor?" Oliver had asked, trying to contain his excitement at seeing Evan again.

Evan had shrugged. "It was something you told me a long time ago, about John overextending himself," he had answered. "I suspected that he was in trouble financially, and I thought he might take a loan, using the Manor as collateral."

"You've learned much in the time you've been away," Oliver had replied softly, with pride.

"Yes."

"You've done well for yourself, then?"

The question was asked tentatively: Oliver was aware

that Evan did not care to have his privacy invaded. Evan had smiled briefly. "Yes," he said again. "I've done well. But I was also fortunate to have a good teacher—" he nodded in Oliver's direction, and the man coloured with pleasure at the compliment. "And I met Vincent LeCroix. He helped me get a start."

"Ah, yes. Vincent LeCroix. You mentioned him in your letters." Oliver smiled self-consciously. "I kept them all, you know," he said shyly. "I'm glad you kept your promise to write."

"I told you I would." Evan was embarrassed by Oliver's obvious gratitude.

"Can you stay for a while?"

Wincing inwardly at the eagerness in Oliver's voice, Evan shook his head. He reached out to touch the old man on the shoulder. "I have to get back to London immediately," he said. "But I'll be back soon, and then I will come for a longer visit."

"Where are you staying?" Oliver tried vainly to cover his disappointment.

"At the Cord house, when I'm here."

Evan was unprepared for the swift shadow of fear that crossed Oliver's face. "The Cord house?" Oliver said, glancing away from him. "I thought the owner died last year . . ."

Watching Oliver closely, Evan replied, "The man wasn't the owner; he was only a distant cousin, I believe. The real owner is a woman named Hester Cord. I met her when I was in Australia. We came back together . . ." He did not mention Cynara; he was too interested in observing Oliver's reaction to Hester's name.

When Oliver said nothing, Evan added casually, "Did you ever hear of Hester Cord, Oliver?"

"No, no." Oliver's response was a shade too quick, and Evan looked at him again, causing Oliver to add hastily, "Of course I knew Edgar and Cecilia Cord; they were the owners of the house in Eric's time. But I thought . . . I thought there was no close relative to claim the house when they passed away."

Oliver's voice trailed off at Evan's expression. "Apparently, no one was aware that Hester was still living in Australia," Evan said softly.

"I . . . I suppose not," Oliver answered, faintly.

The old man looked away from him again, and once more Evan felt that Oliver was deliberately withholding something from him. But he couldn't go into it now; he had taken too much time as it was, and the hack was waiting for him back at the road. He rose, and Oliver stood with him.

"Will you . . . will you come back soon?" Oliver asked tentatively.

Evan met his glance. "Of course. We have much to talk about, Oliver."

Oliver nodded, an expression of resignation in his faded blue eyes. "Yes," he said quietly. "I suppose we do."

As he appproached the bank, Evan recalled that strange conversation with Oliver. Once inside he asked a clerk for the office of James Melburn. As the man led the way toward a heavy carved door, Evan felt his nervousness return. The next few minutes would determine if all his hopes and plans had been in vain, and he took a deep breath before walking across a vast expanse of burgandy-colored carpet toward the man rising from his desk. Evan offered the man his hand, and as he introduced himself, he felt a surge of confidence. He could not fail.

"I'm afraid your request is somewhat—irregular, Mr. Calder," James Melburn said at last.

Melburn was not what Evan had expected. He had had a vague image of the prosperous banker as stout, with a congenial expression on a round, bewhiskered face, and this man was none of those things. Instead, he was tall and so thin that his clothing, as well tailored as it was, seemed to hang loosely from his frame, and he had no whiskers.

Indeed, except for a scanty fringe around his narrow skull, he had no hair at all. Everything about him was spare except his eyes, which were a startling deep blue. Those eyes held Evan's glance and their expression was penetratingly sharp.

"May I ask how you came to learn that we hold the mortgage on the estate known as Lyrebird Manor?"

"I had a conversation with the man who was once steward to the Ward family," Evan replied smoothly. "During the course of his remarks, I deduced that John Ward was in need of some financial help. I came here prepared to offer my assistance."

James Melburn was silent, studying the young and handsome face opposite him. It was a face that gave nothing away, he thought; the young man's reasons could be the ones he stated, and then again, they might not be. He would have to move cautiously here; after all, there were ethical considerations involved, even if Evan Calder could be the answer to his problems regarding that boor, John Ward. At the thought of the man, his expression became grim. He had no liking for John Ward; he considered him a scoundrel, and worse, a wastrel.

"And what assistance do you intend to offer, Mr. Calder?" Melburn asked finally, realizing that he had been staring.

Evan's glance was level as he returned the banker's stare. "I am acquainted with Lyrebird Manor," he said. "And I know that the estate is in need of repair. I assume that the mortgage was taken out to facilitate that repair, but it seems nothing has been done." He paused, waiting for Melburn to make some comment. It had only been a guess on his part, and now he needed confirmation before he proceeded.

Melburn nodded cautiously. It was true; John Ward had borrowed money for the stated purpose of making improvements; then he had borrowed again when the first loan had proved to be insufficient—or so he had said. Melburn had driven out some time ago to assess the nature of those improvements, and could find very little evidence that anything had been spent on the place itself. He had been outraged. If this was the way the man intended to go on, the bank would soon have to foreclose, especially since it was obvious that John Ward would have to borrow even to repay the interest on the first notes. As president he had no intention of throwing good money after bad, and yet . . . He had not wanted to saddle the bank with a burden he would be unable to get rid of. The new owner, if he could find someone to buy the Manor, would find himself hard pressed to make the estate productive again, considering how Ward had let it go to ruin while he pursued—whatever he pursued. Melburn pursed his mouth, thrusting the thought aside. It was no business of his what John Ward spent his money on, except where the bank itself was concerned. But now here was this young man, calmly stating that he had visited the place and would not be averse to buying the notes. Why?

He asked the question, noting that Evan's eyebrows rose in surprise. "I'm not here as a supplicant, Mr. Melburn. As I see it, it is none of your affair if I want to buy the estate only to abandon it to the owls and the mice. Once it is mine, if I decide to accept such a heavy responsibility, I can do as I wish with it."

"Very true." Melburn nodded solemnly. This man, young as he was, seemed astute . . . and very clever. Melburn found himself admiring these qualities, since he believed he possessed them in good measure as well. He decided to make a clean sweep of the situation, since it seemed unlikely that he could find another buyer. "It is true that in a short time I will be forced to call in the first of the notes on Lyrebird Manor," he said slowly.

"And is Mr. Ward able to meet them?" With an effort, Evan kept the eagerness from his voice. He regarded the man opposite him with a neutral expression.

Melburn's own expression stiffened. "I really am in no position to say, Mr. Calder."

Evan waited, saying nothing.

Melburn stared evenly at the young man sitting so assuredly opposite him, and now he said, "Of course, quite a bit of the land surrounding the estate is valuable. The bank could do quite well with that land . . ."

"That's true," Evan agreed calmly. "But only if the bank wishes to invest a great deal of money in improving that land. As it is now, it would need recultivating for crops; reseeding for pastures, not to mention—"

Melburn was irritated that Evan had seen through his ruse. "I'm aware of all that," he said curtly.

"Of course." Evan inclined his head politely, waiting for him to continue again.

"If you assumed the mortgage, I'm sure Mr. Ward would want a guarantee."

"What kind of guarantee?"

Evan's voice was soft, but the banker was aware of the iron underlying his tone, and again he felt a stirring of admiration. The young man was no fool, he thought, but he did have an obligation, however distasteful, to do his best for John Ward.

"Well, I know that Mr. Ward would want the opportunity to buy back the mortgage, should he decide to do so," he answered.

"And with what would he do it?" Evan asked smoothly. "If he is unable to pay the due notes to you, how could he possibly repay me? No, Mr. Melburn, if the mortgage cannot be met by John Ward, he would have no guarantee from me."

Melburn was aware of the increasing hardness in Evan's tone. But as Calder's uncompromising statement exactly matched his own feelings in the matter, he sat back, trying not to show his approval. He would not offer such a guarantee himself, he knew. If the man could not repay one set of debts, it was ridiculous to expect that he would repay another.

"There is one more thing, Mr. Melburn," Evan said abruptly. "John Ward must not know that I am the man who has taken over the mortgage."

Melburn's eyebrows rose. "But it is only right that he should—"

"No. My offer is between the bank and me. If you cannot keep that in confidence, I will withdraw—"

"Let's not be hasty," Melburn said quickly. "I'm sure we can work something out."

"There is nothing to 'work out.'" Evan's face was uncompromising. "It will be the way I want or not at all."

Melburn appeared about to object, but then he sat back. If the man didn't wish his name to be known, what did it matter to him? Still, it was strange, and it occurred to him again that there was something wrong here. As clever as young Calder was, Melburn had read something in his expression just now, and he wondered if the young man carried some sort of grudge against John Ward. It wouldn't surprise him if he did, Melburn thought grimly, recalling how he himself had detested the man on sight.

James Melburn was a practical man, and he valued this characteristic in himself. He wouldn't have risen to the heights he had in the banking world without being a realist, and he decided it was none of his concern if there was a feud between John Ward and Evan Calder. He had the bank to consider, and in this case, the bank would benefit; if Calder wanted the Manor, and John Ward was unable to meet his payments, then he had no choice. In fact, he was relieved that the troublesome matter of Lyrebird Manor would soon be out of his hands.

Melburn rose. "I will let you know, Mr. Calder," he said noncommittally, although he had already made his decision. "John Ward has until the fifteenth of the month. After that—" he shrugged slightly "we will see. If Mr. Ward defaults . . ."

The implication was clear, and as Evan took the hand offered him, their glances met, and Evan knew that he had won Melburn's support. Victory was so close that he could almost touch it, and yet he did not allow himself to betray his exultation. Keeping his expression carefully neutral, he said only, "I will expect to hear from you, Mr. Melburn."

Melburn inclined his head and then pressed the buzzer under his desk, summoning the clerk to show Evan out.

Evan concealed his fierce joy until he was safely within the confines of a cab. But after he had given directions to his hotel, a savage smile of triumph broke out on his face, and he could no longer hide his exhilaration. He was sure that John Ward would not be able to meet the notes when they were due; all he had to do now was wait until the fifteenth—two weeks away—and Lyrebird Manor would be his. He laughed aloud. He would celebrate tonight to mark the occasion. What did it matter that he did not yet hold the deed to the Manor in his hands? He would, soon enough. He had told himself that he would not fail, and he had not!

Abruptly, Cynara's face flashed into his mind, and he tried to thrust aside the sudden wish that she were here with him to share this moment of victory. Despite himself, he pictured them together, celebrating with champagne and a sumptuous meal in the hotel, and after that . . . Closing his eyes, he tried to shut out the fantasy of a willing Cynara in bed, of her smooth, long-limbed body, her round breasts, her mouth parted for his kiss. The image was so strong that he thought he could actually touch her; if he opened his eyes he would see her there, laughing, beckoning to him.

And then the cab jolted him to one side, and as he reached out to balance himself, the image disappeared, and he was alone again. Cursing and groaning at the same time, Evan told himself savagely that he would allow no thoughts of Cynara to ruin this evening. He would go back to the hotel and see if that girl was still in his bed. If she was, he would celebrate with her; if she had gone . . . He shrugged. There were always other women who were willing.

But the thought of Cynara had dimmed his pleasure and he could not recapture his former jubilation. He would have his victory celebration anyway, he thought fiercely, as he paid the hack and entered the hotel. Why should he care that Cynara was not here with him? He tried to feel anticipation over the coming evening, but his mood had suddenly fallen flat, and his face was almost grim as he mounted the grand staircase and went toward his room.

CHAPTER THIRTY-ONE

NOW THAT THE damage had been done, Cynara wished uselessly that she had never allowed her curiosity to overcome her. Staring down at the Bible she held in one hand and the letter she had found inside the pages in the other, she bit her lip. Too late now to pretend that she hadn't seen either, and she stood indecisively in the center of Hester's sitting room upstairs, wondering what had possessed her to pry into Hester's private affairs. She had come here so bored with her own company that she had thought to persuade Hester to take a drive. The Bible had been lying open on the table in the empty apartment and the temptation had been too great. When she lifted the book curiously, the letter had fallen out. Now she had seen both, and she knew why Hester had guarded the Bible so carefully all these months.

Her eyes ran down the family tree inscribed on the frontispiece, and she saw the name Eric Ward at the top. Eric's name was followed by those of his sons: Sean, Michael and James, and below Sean's name was that of his son, Aron, and his daughter, Ann. Cynara had had a glimpse of this family tree before, the one time she had handled Hester's Bible, but then she had not seen the one inscription that riveted her attention now. Under Eric's name, three words leaped out at her, and she could no longer ignore the significance of those words. For under Eric's name, written in faded ink, was the simple phrase: *of Lyrebird Manor*. Eric Ward, of Lyrebird Manor. And the eldest of Eric's sons was Sean, and Sean's oldest son was Aron.

Cynara stared at the letter she held in her other hand. The date was twenty years ago, and it was written by Aron Ward, visiting Lyrebird Manor, to his parents at Lyrebird Hill, Australia. She had scanned the letter once, but now she read it again. She had been too stunned to absorb the contents on the first reading, but now as her eyes raced over the hastily scrawled lines, she felt her anger and disbelief growing at the same pace. How could Hester have kept this letter from Evan? Certain sentences caught her eye, and she knew she had found part of the secret surrounding Evan's birth: "I know you will be disappointed that you were not here for the wedding, but there is something strange about John Ward, and we were forced to keep our marriage a secret. I will tell you why when we return . . ." And then further down: "Jenny is a wonderful girl, and we have reason to believe that she is with child—so soon! Only two months after the wedding! If the child is a boy, we have decided to call him Evan . . ."

Frowning, Cynara looked up again. So Aron Ward had married a girl named Jenny, and at the time of the letter they were expecting their first child. But the marriage had been kept a secret—why? Why hadn't Aron wanted John Ward to know? And then, even as she asked the question, Cynara knew the answer, and she felt a chill. She knew why Hester had guarded this secret so well; it should have been obvious to her from the first.

But now—now that she knew, she felt herself growing exultant. She would tell Evan at once, and together they would face Myles. She almost laughed aloud at the thought, picturing Myles's face when he learned that Evan had a right to a share in the Manor. She would have her revenge on Myles after all, she thought excitedly. Who knew better than she how selfish and grasping and greedy Myles was? How devastated he would be to discover that he must share his inheritance with his enemy, Evan! And she would be there, to see it all! She could imagine the scene even now, and a fierce satisfaction crossed her face. She hugged both the Bible and the letter to her, wondering how she could get a message to Evan to tell him to return at once.

"So now you know. I hope you're satisfied."

Cynara whirled around, the color rushing to her face when she saw Hester in the doorway. Guiltily, she looked down at the letter and the Bible she still held, but it was too late to deny what she had done, even if she had wanted to. They stared at each other, until finally Hester stepped into the room and shut the door behind her. Her movements were slow; there was a sag of defeat about her shoulders as she hobbled forward toward Cynara.

"What are you going to do about it?"

Cynara looked at the woman in puzzlement. She had expected Hester to be furious with her, as she had every right to be, but the resigned tone in the woman's voice made her uneasy.

"Well?"

"I'm going to tell Evan, of course!" Cynara replied, wincing inwardly at the defensive tone in her voice. "What else did you expect?"

Hester looked at her, and the disappointment in her face made Cynara even more uncomfortable. "Well, what did you expect?" she said again, belligerently.

"I expected you to see beyond your own concerns, for once," Hester replied. "But I can see that's too much to ask."

Stung, Cynara said angrily, "That isn't fair, Hester. You don't understand—"

"Don't I? I understand more about you than you think, Cynara. But I had hoped that you would be unselfish enough to consider someone beside yourself. I see now that I was mistaken. You're determined to let petty jealousies and childish ideas of revenge ruin your life—and Evan's."

Cynara stared at her, too furious for a moment to speak. When she did, her voice was choked. "You know nothing about my motives, Hester. How dare you say such things to me!"

"I dare because I care a great deal about Evan—more than you do, obviously." Hester held out her hand. "May I have my things back?" she asked, with dignity.

Sullenly Cynara folded the letter and inserted it between the pages of the Bible. She gave the book back to Hester.

Hester accepted it, her eyes never leaving Cynara's face. Then she said abruptly, "There is something I want you to see."

Leaning heavily on her cane, still clutching the Bible to her chest, Hester turned her back on Cynara, obviously expecting her to follow as she slowly led the way to the attic stairs. Cynara hesitated. She was angry with Hester, and angry with herself for being so upset over what Hester had said to her. What did Hester know about her own private thoughts? Had she betrayed herself without being aware of it? Wincing at the thought, Cynara sighed in exasperation. She wasn't interested in whatever it was that Hester wanted to show her, she told herself stoutly, but the same curiosity that had led her to pick up the Bible impelled her to follow the woman down the corridor to the steep flight of stairs at the opposite end.

Hester was waiting for her, and without a word, she gestured to Cynara to precede her. They went up the stairs, and Cynara tugged at the door leading to the attic. It was stuck, but finally she managed to open it, and now it was Hester who went by her, leading the way.

A fan-shaped window admitted enough light for them to see, and Cynara followed between heaps of discarded furniture and trunks and crates that littered the floor space. Hester made straight for an area along one wall where the shapes of picture frames were discernible under a protective canvas.

Still maintaining her pained silence, Hester took one end of the canvas and motioned Cynara to take the other. Several paintings, one of a horse and hound, another of a pheasant in flight, met her eyes as they pulled the cover away, and Cynara looked at Hester. Was this what she wanted her to see?

"It has to be here," Hester muttered. She bent over, pushing the first of the paintings out of the way, seeking something in the stack behind. At last, with a satisfied exclamation, she dragged a heavy frame from the back of the pile and turned it toward Cynara.

Cynara gasped. Even though the painting was dark with age, and spotted from lack of care, the figure therein was easily discernible. Cynara looked at it again, and it was as if she were staring at Evan. It couldn't be, she thought in confusion, and yet there were the same dark eyes, the same arched brows and high cheekbones and lean jaw. Even the mouth was the same—no, not quite, she conceded. Where Evan had an arrogant set to his mouth, the man in the painting seemed to have a more amenable expression, as though his nature was not as stubborn, as fiercely proud as Evan's. And now she noticed something else: the man in the portrait was older than Evan, by about ten years. Even so, the resemblance was astounding, and she raised her eyes. "Who is he?"

"Sean, of course," Hester answered testily, as though Cynara should have known. But she did not look at Cynara: she was staring intently at the portrait. "The ring," she muttered. "I forgot about the ring!"

Cynara glanced back at the painting. The artist had painted Sean Ward standing with his arms folded across his chest. She had not noticed it before, but now that she looked closer, she saw the heavy gold ring on his finger. Against the dark fabric of Sean's coat, the design of the ring was clearly visible. It was in the shape of the lyrebird, two heavy ropes of gold forming the arms of the lyre, and surrounding the more finely wrought chased gold that made up the other feathers of the tail. The bird's head was turned sideways, and an opal, or what appeared to be an opal, formed the eye. So great was the artistry of the craftsman who had made it that the bird seemed almost a living thing.

"It's beautiful," Cynara said.

But Hester appeared not to have heard her. She was mumbling to herself, "I forgot all about it. I should have remembered—"

Confused, Cynara stared at her. "What?"

"That ring—" Hester pointed at it with a shaking finger— "was designed by Eric. It was intended as an heirloom, handed down from him to his oldest son. Sean wore it, and then just before he sent Aron to England, he gave it to him. Solid gold, it was, and executed by one of the finest goldsmiths in Paris. I wonder what happened to it. If we knew . . ." Hester broke off, turning away abruptly, as though she had said too much.

"What is it?" Cynara asked, following her quickly as Hester made her way through the maze in the attic. "Why should the ring be important?"

Impatiently, Hester turned to glare at her. "Whoever possessed that ring was never without it. If we knew where the ring was, we would know what happened to Aron, wouldn't we?"

Before Cynara could ask her what she meant, Hester had started down the stairs, her cane thumping heavily on each step. What had happened to Aron? Cynara wondered. She had been so excited about her discovery of the letter that she hadn't given it much thought. If she had wondered about it at all, she had assumed that both Aron and Jenny had simply died. Was there something sinister about Hester's comment?

"Hester—" Cynara followed rapidly, closing the attic door behind her. "Hester, what did you mean just now? Did something happen to Aron?"

Hester shook off Cynara's restraining hand. "I don't know," she muttered.

"But you must know!"

"I tell you, I don't!"

"I don't understand."

"Nor did anyone else," Hester said darkly. "It wasn't like him—I knew that boy; he was like my own. It wasn't like him."

Hester edged away from her, and again Cynara put her hand on the woman's arm. "What wasn't like Aron?" she insisted.

"He disappeared," Hester replied, her voice flat. "That letter was the last anyone ever heard from him."

Pulling away, Hester retreated down the corridor, and this time Cynara let her go. Disappeared! she thought. With a new bride, and a child on the way? It didn't make sense; not after she had seen the letter he had written. Aron had obviously been in love with Jenny; he was excited about the coming child. Would the man who had written a letter such as that simply have disappeared?

A sudden thought occurred to her, and she rushed after Hester, reaching her at the door to her room. "Hester, did . . . did anyone try to find Aron, to learn what had happened to him?"

Hester gave her a withering glance. "Of course. Did you think that we would just let him go?"

"And?"

"Nothing. My sister, Emily, tried to do what she could, but—"

"What about Sean, Aron's father? Surely he—"

Hester's face became pinched. "Sean had died some months before," she answered.

"Sean died before Aron disappeared?"

"Yes."

The thought that had occurred to her before was stronger now, and with it came a sense of dread. But she must be careful not to let Hester see anything in her expression, and she made a fierce effort to control the muscles of her face. Her voice deliberately neutral, she asked, "Did John Ward know about Sean's death?"

"Yes," Hester said again. There was a faraway look in her eyes, and in spite of her own preoccupation, Cynara became uneasy. Did that look indicate the beginning of another of Hester's attacks? To her relief, it seemed not, for Hester continued, steadily enough, "Naturally, we sent word to Aron—he was at Lyrebird Manor at the time—that his father had died. Shortly after that, we received that last letter from him. The letters must have crossed in transit, because there was no mention of his father. Emily and I thought that he would return home once he knew about his father, but when he did not, and we didn't hear from him, Emily wrote again, asking John to send him home."

The sense of dread increased in her. Cynara managed to say, "And?"

"John wrote, informing us that Aron had left straightaway, when he heard about Sean. He was surprised at Emily's letter; he assumed that Aron was already home. But no one ever heard from Aron again . . ." Hester swallowed, and then her voice became even more harsh. "I suppose you must know the rest, since I've told you this much. There was a fire, one of those dreadful bush fires; Emily and her daughter, Ann, perished in that fire. I . . . I had gone to visit some friends, and was on the way back when I saw the fire. It . . . It was too late to save them."

Cynara bit her lip, watching Hester closely. She had never before mentioned the fire, and Cynara was worried that the memory of it would bring on another attack. But Hester saw her staring at her anxiously, and she said, "I'm all right. I lived with that memory for a long time, but now . . . There was nothing I could have done—was there?"

Hester looked at her, almost pleadingly, and Cynara said quickly, "Of course not. It was a terrible thing, but it wasn't your fault. You couldn't have known . . ."

"No, I couldn't have known," Hester repeated, that absent look in her eyes. Fumbling, she put out her hand and opened the door to her apartments.

"Hester—"

"I'll be all right," Hester muttered. "I want to be alone for a while now."

"Are you sure?"

Nodding impatiently in response, Hester entered the room, closing the door firmly behind her. Cynara stood there for a moment, indecisive. She put her ear to the door, but only silence greeted her, and uneasily she moved off down the corridor.

She was too restless to stay in the house. Too many things had descended upon her at once; she needed time to sort out her thoughts. She would go for a walk, she decided; perhaps an hour or two alone would help her digest what she had learned today. She must make some kind of decision about whether or not to tell Evan what she knew. It was obvious that Hester wouldn't tell him, and now Cynara wondered herself what would be the best course. For the first time she understood Hester's comment about being sure no violence was done once Evan learned the circumstances of his birth. She shivered. What would Evan do if he ever found out? But did anyone have the right to keep the truth from him? Fetching a shawl, Cynara let herself out the front door, and head down, frowning in concentration, she began to walk down the drive.

Cynara paused at the edge of a clearing for breath. She had walked further than she had intended, too preoccupied to notice the distance. Now she was tired and thirsty; the afternoon was warm, and she hadn't needed her shawl after all.

Ahead she saw a small cottage under the trees and walked toward it, thinking to ask for a glass of water and a chance to rest for a minute before she started back. As she approached, an old man came around the side of the cottage carrying an armful of kindling, and Cynara raised an arm to hail him. But her greeting changed to a cry of alarm as he tripped over something and went sprawling on the ground. Cynara rushed forward to help him. "Are you all right? Are you hurt?"

Dazed, the man looked up. "I think so," he answered. He tried to smile, but winced instead when he tried to sit up.

"What is it?" Cynara looked at him anxiously and saw his torn sleeve and a smear of blood along his arm. "You're hurt!"

He looked down. "Just a scrape; it's nothing," he said, obviously embarrassed.

"Let me help you—" Cynara assisted him to his feet, brushing off the dirt from his shirt, surreptitiously trying to see if he was hurt anywhere else.

"Well, I must say, I could have chosen a more graceful way of making your acquaintance," he said, laughing self-consciously.

"I'm sorry—my name is Cynara . . . Calder."

The laughter died abruptly from his eyes. "Did you say—Calder?" he asked, his voice high with surprise.

Cynara nodded, thinking that she might as well admit it now; the whole neighborhood would know soon enough anyway, if they didn't already. Resolutely she refused to think of the reaction at Lyrebird Manor, and she smiled slightly, "Yes, Cynara Calder," she repeated. "My . . . husband is—"

"Evan!" the old man said breathlessly. "Why didn't he tell me? Oh, this is wonderful!"

"You know Evan?"

The man laughed again, with genuine delight. "Know him! Oh, indeed, I do! Come in, come in, my dear—" he took hold of her arm, his spill forgotten as he propelled her along toward the open door of the cottage. "I'll make us a cup of tea, and you can tell me about yourself. Oh, this is wonderful!"

Ushering her inside, he gestured toward a chair, and then bustled off to the kitchen. Seconds later, she heard the clatter of cups, the sound of the kettle banged hurriedly on the stove, and she smiled. He poked his head around the doorway, and said, somewhat abashed, "I'm sorry—in my excitement, I forgot to introduce myself. My name is Oliver Lindsay."

"I'm pleased to make your acquaintance, Mr. Lindsay," Cynara replied, trying not to smile at the wide grin on his face.

"Oh, do call me Oliver, please!"

"May I help with the tea . . . Oliver?"

"No, no. You just sit there. I'll be right out."

He dashed off again, and Cynara thought with pleasure what a delightful old man he was. Had Evan ever mentioned him? She was sure he had not; she would have remembered.

He returned quickly, carrying a tray that held the tea things and a plate of bread and butter. Setting down the tray, he passed a cup across to her, and as she accepted it, she said, "You really should do something about your arm."

"Oh, it's all right. It was a just punishment for not watching where I was going. I was daydreaming, I guess. I'm not usually so clumsy." Waving away her concern, he changed the subject. "Tell me," he said eagerly, "When did you and Evan marry?"

"It was some months ago," Cynara replied carefully. She was not sure she wished to speak of her marriage, but she added, "In Australia. We just returned to England a week or so ago, and came to stay—"

"At Cord House. Yes, I know. Evan told me."

"Evan told you? You've seen him then?" Annoyed at the sudden leap of her heart at the thought that Evan had returned from London, Cynara forced herself to ask, more calmly, "When?"

If Oliver noticed the hope that sprang into her eyes, he gave no sign. "I believe it was the night he left for London. He didn't have time to stay long," he added, almost apologetically. "He was in a rush."

"Yes," Cynara said, her tone hard. "He would be."

Oliver gave her a curious glance, and Cynara flushed. Bending her head to avoid his eyes, she sipped her tea.

"Cynara . . ." Oliver said musingly, after a small silence. "What a beautiful name. It means 'beauty surrounded by thorns,' doesn't it?"

Surprised, Cynara looked up at him. "Yes. How did you know that?"

Oliver answered with a smile. "I studied some Greek a long time ago," he answered. "I always loved the sound of the language, even though to others it sometimes has a harsh ring. I tried to teach Evan a love of language," he continued, his smile deepening, "but I'm afraid Evan was always more interested in the practical."

"You were Evan's tutor?" Cynara's tone indicated her astonishment.

"No, not exactly. I tried to teach him what little I knew,

but there was never enough time. It was rare that he could get away from the Manor for more than a few hours . . ."

Oliver's voice trailed off, and he reached abruptly to pour himself another cup of tea. But Cynara had seen the sudden sadness in his face, and now she leaned forward. "Tell me about Evan," she said softly. "I . . . I know so little about him."

Their eyes met and Cynara wondered that she felt no embarrassment over her confession. Oliver held her gaze intently, and Cynara knew that her own expression was wistful, and again she didn't feel any discomfort that Oliver could read her feelings. She gazed back at him, and she knew that he would not laugh at her, or deride her for asking a total stranger about the man who was her husband; his face was sympathetic, full of understanding. She smiled tremulously, and Oliver reached out and covered her hand with his own gnarled fingers.

Then he began to speak, and as his voice flowed quietly over her, Cynara realized that she had known nothing of Evan. Nothing at all.

By the time Cynara left the cottage, it was late afternoon. She would have to hurry if she wished to get home before dark, and she quickly said goodbye to Oliver.

"Please, let me walk part of the way with you," Oliver said. "I would feel better seeing you home safely."

Cynara smiled, but shook her head. "I'll be all right," she answered. "I know the way now."

"You'll come back and visit me again?"

Oliver tried unsuccessfully to mask the pleading tone in his voice, and Cynara took his hand. "Of course." She hesitated for a moment, then added quietly, "You have given me much to think about, Oliver. I want you to know that I'm grateful."

A fleeting shadow crossed his face, and for the first time he appeared uncomfortable. He seemed about to say something, changed his mind and said instead, "I'm so glad we have met, Cynara."

"I am, too, Oliver." Cynara's response was genuine. To cover her sudden emotion, she gestured sternly to Oliver's arm, which she had insisted upon bandaging before she departed. "You take care of yourself," she ordered. "No more tumbles about the yard."

Oliver raised his hand in farewell, promising to be more careful in the future. Cynara waved in response, and then she turned and walked quickly from the clearing toward the road Oliver had pointed out.

She had meant to hurry, but once on the road, her steps slowed, until she halted completely. Thinking about what Oliver had told her, she sat down on a tree stump at the edge of the road, and stared despondently at her hands, laced loosely together in her lap. She should have known; she should have realized long before now—before Oliver had to tell her—the reason Evan was the way he was. The evidence had been there before her eyes from the first day she had entered the stableyard at Lyrebird Manor. She had seen the antipathy on Jacob's face, the scorn in Jimmy's expression. She should have realized then. But she had been too preoccupied with her own feelings, her own recent loss and the upheaval in her life to pay any attention to what Evan was going through. Even later, when she had observed for herself the way Myles and John treated Evan, she should have understood. But she had not; she had been willfully blind, and now she was deeply ashamed. All his life, Evan had been humiliated and treated with derision—if not actual cruelty. He had fared worse than the lowest servant. Even the horses at the Manor were treated with more kindness than Evan had received. Was it any wonder that he had rebelled? And in rebelling, he had closed off his feelings, his emotions, to make himself less vulnerable. Oh yes, she understood it now. She had done the same thing herself. Her own resentment had flared to the point of hatred, even after only a few weeks at the Manor—how much more deeply had Evan's resentment and hatred been felt after so many years?

Dejected, Cynara forced herself to get up and move on.

But as much as she tried to shut out the things Oliver had told her, his voice continued in her mind as she walked slowly home. She could hear him telling her of incidents that had occurred in the past; things that she did not want to remember now. He had spoken simply, trying to cover his own emotion, of how Evan had suffered, and as he talked, Cynara had felt her own shame and guilt growing, until she had to stop him. Too many things had assailed her that day; she could not listen to any more without breaking down completely.

Twilight was upon her; she began to hurry. But as she walked quickly toward Cord House, she wondered for the first time why John had treated Evan as he had. She hadn't thought to ask Oliver; she had been too stricken at what he was telling her to bring up the question. But she considered it now, and suddenly the reason came to her, and with it, that sense of dread she had felt when speaking to Hester. John must have discovered Aron's marriage to Jenny, and knew that Evan was the legitimate child of that marriage. He must have been afraid that Evan would eventually claim a share of the Manor as his inheritance.

But if that were so, why had he kept Evan at the Manor at all? Wouldn't it have been safer for him to have sent Evan away, where there was little chance that Evan would learn about his parents? And then she thought that there was little danger for John after all: Jenny was dead, Aron had disappeared. Who would tell Evan? Far away in Austrailia, Sean had died, and his family, with the exception of Hester, whose mind had been turned by the tragedy, had been burned to death. There was no one left to watch out for Evan's interests, and John had seized his opportunity.

But someone must have known, she thought. Oliver had lived at the Manor during that time, and yet her tentative questions about Aron and Jenny had been met with a blank stare by Oliver. Omitting any mention of who Evan's father might have been, Oliver had only said evasively that Jenny had died in childbirth. Evan had been cared for by another of the maids at the Manor until he was eight: as a child he had called this woman his grandmother, and he had not understood why she, too, had deserted him at such a young age. When Evan had turned eight, John had dismissed her from his employ, deciding that Evan no longer needed the care of a surrogate mother.

Why had Oliver been so evasive? Did he know more than he was willing to say? And if he did, why did he feel he must keep his knowledge a secret? Cynara had seen for herself that Oliver loved Evan: it had been evident in his face, his voice, his manner. If he knew anything, why would he keep silent, realizing that Evan's welfare was at stake?

Her head pounding with unanswered questions, Cynara turned into the drive that led to the house. As she walked up the graveled expanse, she saw one of the grooms run from the stable to take a horse from someone at the front door. Her heart leaped in her chest, and she had to will herself to check her steps when she wanted to race ahead. Evan was home! Even though she was still some distance away, and dusk was gathering, she would know him anywhere: no one else stood that way, no one else walked with that easy air of command and assurance. He said something to the groom, who nodded happily, and then he turned and went into the house. Cynara approached slowly, willing her heart to stop its frantic bounding. With an effort at control, she mounted the steps calmly and entered the front door after him.

He was still in the entryway, giving his hat and coat to Trent. At the sound of her footsteps, both men turned, and Trent bowed, murmuring a greeting. Evan said nothing. Their eyes met, and to her distress, Cynara dropped her gaze first. She didn't know what to say to him: she hadn't expected his return so quickly, and now, seeing him here, with all she had learned today, she was confused.

"Hello, Evan," she said finally. She was dismayed: she had not meant to sound so distant, so cold, but the damage had been done. Evan's eyes were cool as he returned her greeting.

"Is Hester here?" he asked.

"I . . . I don't know. I just returned myself."

He did not ask her where she had been, or how she was, and despite the longing she had felt for him when she saw him standing on the front steps, she was irritated at his manner. He had been gone for over a week: was that all he could say to her?

Trent, sensing the sudden animosity that sprang up between them, answered quietly, with an apologetic glance at Cynara, "I believe Miss Cord is in the drawing room, sir. Dinner was to be served shortly, unless you prefer to have it held back . . .?"

"No, no," Evan replied impatiently. "Just continue everything as planned."

Trent glided off, and to Cynara's outrage, Evan did not give her a second glance. He strode off in the direction of the drawing room, leaving Cynara standing in the hall by herself.

Eyes narrowed, she looked after him. She wanted to dash forward, demanding—what? That he notice her, that he speak to her? Despising herself, Cynara realized that the moment when she could have said something had passed, and it was her own fault. But the admission only increased her anger, and instead of going after him, she turned toward the stairs. She would not follow him, she thought furiously. It would be just what he would expect.

But once alone in her room, Cynara regretted her own stubbornness. What was the matter with her? She had spent the long walk home from Oliver's cottage thinking of Evan, rehearsing what she was going to say when she saw him again. She had promised herself that she would be willing to—to humble herself, to apologize for her past actions: she had told herself that she would be the first to begin a new relationship with him. Now that she understood a little what he had suffered in the past, she would tell him that she had been wrong, too quick to judge. Oh yes, she thought scornfully, she had planned exactly what she would say to him. But when she had seen him standing there, looking at her but not really seeing her, her carefully prepared speech had fled from her mind. She had sensed, once again, that barrier between them, and she had not been able to make herself speak. No, she couldn't tell him her feelings: far better for them to remain apart than to see his cold amusement—or worse, she thought suddenly, his pity.

Infuriated with him, angry at herself, she threw herself into a chair, her head in her hands as she heard the dinner bell. She couldn't face him, not with Hester listening to every word. She would not go down to dinner: she would stay in her room like the coward she was.

The minutes ticked by, and although she knew that he would not come to her, still she started at every sound in the corridor outside her door. Did she really believe that he would want to know why she had refused to join them at the table? One minute she found herself wishing fiercely that he would: the next, she prayed that he would stay away.

An hour passed. Surely they had finished dinner by now: had they been so involved that they hadn't even noticed that she wasn't there? Gritting her teeth, Cynara told herself that she was acting like a spoiled child, wanting to be persuaded. This was ridiculous, jumping at every sound. She would go to bed.

She was tying the belt of her dressing gown when she heard the tap on her door. Sure that it was Hester, coming at last to investigate, or to give her another lecture, she called permission to enter.

To her dismay, Evan came in, carrying a tray with covered dishes. He set the tray on a table, and said, "Since you did not deign to join us, Hester thought you should have a tray here."

"I'm not hungry, thank you," she said stiffly.

They stared at each other, and all at once Cynara was conscious of her hair falling loosely to her shoulders, and that she wore only a thin nightdress under her dressing gown. Pulling the sash of the robe more tightly about her waist, she snatched up a ribbon from the dressing table and tied her hair back, wondering why she felt less vulnerable, less exposed after doing so. Why had Evan brought the tray himself? Why hadn't one of the maids come instead?

Grabbing her shawl from the chair where she had thrown it earlier, she folded it and went to the chest to put it away. She must say something, she thought, to break this awful silence. "I trust you had a pleasant stay in London?" she said, at last.

"More profitable than pleasant, I would say," he answered, his voice cool.

Oh, why didn't he go? Her back to him, she could see him in the mirror, staring at her, and because his scrutiny made her even more nervous, she whirled around and cried, "What do you want, Evan?"

Want? How could he tell her that he wanted her? She was staring at him angrily, her eyes brilliant, her slim body taut. Desire rushed through him as he saw the rapid rise and fall of her breasts under the dressing gown, and he wanted to rip away the material to gaze at her naked body.

Restraining himself with great effort, he forced himself to answer her coolly, deliberately goading her to give him time to control himself. In another minute, he *would* reach for her, and that would be disastrous.

"Want?" he repeated. "Why nothing. I thought it only polite to visit my—my wife, after my absence. There are some proprieties we should observe, after all."

"It's a little late for that, isn't it, Evan?" she answered, trying to keep her voice steady. She would die of shame if he once suspected that it was taking all her will power to stop herself from rushing across the room to him. "After all," she continued, swallowing hard, "it's no secret that we . . . we do not have a conventional marriage."

"And whose fault is that?"

Was he actually trying to blame her for this situation? She felt her temper rise, and she welcomed her anger, for it enabled her to put aside her other emotions. "I don't care to discuss whose fault it may be," she said stiffly.

Dismayed, she saw him take a cheroot from a silver case in his pocket. Raising one eyebrow questioningly, he gestured with it, and she nodded tautly. Deliberately taking his time, he trimmed the end and rolled it between his fingers before he finally put it to his mouth to light it. Cynara watched the process, one part of her mind noting the easy grace of his movements, the other wishing that she had never allowed him to enter the room. His evening dress— black coat and trousers, white silk shirt and blue waistcoat—accentuated his dark coloring. He was easily the most handsome man she had ever seen, and despite herself, she remembered the touch and feel of that hard, strong body under the clothing. Fascinated, she watched his hands, and the memory of those hands on her made her weak. What was the matter with her? she wondered wildly. She wanted to scream at him to go; she wanted to beg him to stay.

With great effort, she looked away from him. She would never let him know how she longed for him; she couldn't bear another rejection.

"What would you like to talk about then?" he asked, resuming the conversation as though there had been no strained silence.

"I don't think we have anything to say to each other, Evan."

"Don't we?"

Why did he persist in asking her these questions? He was mocking her, deliberately taunting her, and she refused to answer. The ache of repressed tears was in her throat, and she could feel them gathering in her eyes. She averted her head again, hoping that he had not seen.

"Damn it, Cynara—"

He broke off, as surprised at his outburst as was she. Startled, she looked quickly at him, and saw that he was struggling with some emotion of his own. This time it was he who turned away. He said, his voice thick, "Good night, Cynara."

She could not let him go. His name burst from her before

she could stop it, and he halted at the door.

He looked over his shoulder at her, and in that instant, she saw the longing in his eyes that he was not able to hide. Her heart leaped in response. "Evan . . ."

She was never sure how it happened, but all at once she was in his arms, and he was holding her tightly against him, murmuring incoherently. He pulled the ribbon from her hair, raising fistfuls of it to his face. She clung to him, her eyes closed and her arms around him, enjoying the feel of his hard body under the broadcloth of his coat.

Oh, the times she had dreamed of this moment! Even now she couldn't believe it was happening. Raising her head, she saw him draw back at the same time to look at her, and she began to tremble at what she saw reflected in his eyes. Grasping her chin in his strong fingers, he lowered his head, murmuring her name once more.

The touch of his lips on hers sent a shock through her. Though his kiss was gentle, tender, she sensed the passion in him, and she responded to it. Her mouth parted under the increasing pressure of his lips, and she did not withdraw as his tongue probed hers.

She stiffened once, for an instant, when his hand touched her breast; she remembered other men, other rough hands on her body. But Evan's caress was like no other; she put her hand over his and held it there, wanting him to touch her, desiring the contact between them.

He uttered a groan at her gesture, his other hand reaching for the sash of her robe. He slipped the dressing gown off her shoulders, leaving her clad only in the thin nightdress she wore underneath.

His hands were more insistent now. Raising the hem of her nightgown, he slid his hands under it, straining her toward him. They pressed against one another, moving in unison as he kissed her again, more deeply than before. She felt the hard bulge of him against her thighs, and the contact aroused her even more.

Now it was she who was insistent. Her mouth never

leaving his, she swiftly unbuttoned his coat, and then his shirt, helping him out of both. The skin of his chest was firm under her fingers; she ran her hands lightly over his shoulders to his back, glorying in the feel of him.

With another groan, he lifted her from the floor and carried her to the bed, whipping back the bedclothes in one motion before depositing her gently on the sheets. She watched him hungrily as he tore off the rest of his clothing, and he stood by the side of the bed, naked, for an instant before he lay down beside her, his body lean and lithe, every muscle taut.

There was no embarrassment in her as he raised her nightgown and lifted it over her head to fling on the floor; she felt no shame as his eyes took in every detail of her body. Gently, his fingers traced the fullness of her breasts, the line of her hip as she faced him; she trembled when his hand lingered on her stomach before dropping still lower. At that touch of his hand, she pulled him toward her, and their lips met again in a fierce hunger that shook them both. He rolled over on top of her, and she took his weight gladly, lifting her hips, encircling him with her legs, guiding him inside her. Then they were moving together again, her fingers digging into the flesh of his back as she sought to draw him deeper and deeper inside. His lips moved from her mouth to the wildly beating pulse at the hollow of her throat, still lower to her breasts and the nipples that had become erect at his first touch. The rhythm of their movement increased, and he slipped his hands under her, murmuring her name over and over.

For the first time with a man, Cynara felt the throbbing of pleasure that seemed to begin at some point in her belly and spread like a roaring tide all through her body. She clutched Evan convulsively, her hands moving over him, feeling the straining of his muscles, the slipperiness of sweaty flesh against her own. She wanted to sustain this moment when they were locked together, but the forces in her body demanded release, and she knew that his need was as great as her own. Their tempo increased to a wild, feverish pitch, and she was compelled to rise with it, transported suddenly by a glorious sensation that lifted them both at the same moment into utter and complete abandon. She cried aloud, an animal sound that burst from her throat, as she strained with him toward fulfillment. Her body was not her own; they clung together fiercely, each dissolving into the other, and at that moment, when the shuddering climax surged in both of them, they were truly one.

Too soon, it was over. Evan lay on top of her, still holding her tightly, his breath coming in gasps. When he made a movement to roll away from her, she held him still; she didn't want to lose this moment, when they were both trembling with the aftermath of spent emotion, still joined together. Her body felt light, as if she were floating; she didn't want to move, and she didn't want him to move.

Finally Evan raised his head. Balancing himself on one elbow, he looked down at her, and she saw the same wonderment in him as she felt herself. He began to say something, but she put her fingers across his mouth; she wanted no words to spoil the warm mood of this moment. Right now there were just the two of them; all the problems and decisions and things that had happened in the past were held at bay. It was as if they had closed themselves off from the rest of the world, and while she knew it must end soon, she wanted to postpone the time when explanations and discussion were necessary. It was futile, but she wished that she could stay like this with him forever, that there was no necessity to leave the tender and loving shelter that covered them now. But as soon as the wish was made, she knew that it had to end, and so she spoke.

"Evan . . ."

The single word broke the spell, if one could call it that, and Evan shifted slightly away from her. She turned her head to look at him, biting her lip, wondering how to begin. His dark eyes were close to hers; she could see herself, a tiny image, reflected in their depths. There was tenderness in his eyes; the first tenderness she had seen in him, and all at once, she knew she could not speak.

But Evan, a lazy curiosity aroused, looked at her questioningly. "What is it?" he murmured, and then he put his mouth against her throat.

She closed her eyes. Even now, when her first passion had been spent, the touch of his lips against her skin aroused her. She felt the stirring of desire and she reached for him again, then stopped herself reluctantly. No matter how much she wished to forget the problems that had raised a barrier between them in the past, she knew that they would never be free to love each other until they faced this thing that had kept them apart. She could start by mentioning her meeting with Oliver, she thought. That would at least bring them onto common ground, and hopefully they could proceed from there. Surely they would be able to talk to each other now, after sharing these glorious moments together!

Taking a deep breath, she began softly, "Evan, I met someone today . . ."

Evan's tone was absent; he had begun to caress her once more. "Who?"

"Oliver Lindsay."

She felt him stiffen beside her; his hand stopped its gentle tracing of her shoulder, and she looked anxiously at him. Then, dismayed by the expression in his eyes, she said quickly, "It wasn't what you think, Evan. I met Oliver by accident—"

His withdrawal was even more abrupt this time; he jerked away from her and sat up. "And what did Oliver tell you?" he asked, his voice dangerously low.

Bewildered by his reaction, Cynara stammered, "He . . . he didn't tell me anything. We just talked—"

His mouth twisted, he cast a look at her over his shoulder and then turned away again. "So," he said harshly, "that's why you were so amenable to this . . . this love scene. Oliver enlisted your—pity."

"No, no!" she cried, appalled. "It wasn't that at all!" She

sat up also, clutching the sheet around her. "That had nothing to do with—"

But Evan would not listen to her. He threw his legs violently over the side of the bed and stood up. She gaped at him. What was wrong? What had she said?

"Evan, where are you going?" she cried as he snatched his clothing from the floor and threw it on. "Listen to me! I didn't—"

"I should have known," he muttered, grabbing his shirt and ramming his arms into the sleeves.

"You should have known—what?"

"That there had to be a reason for your sudden change of attitude," he said, almost snarling at her.

Her alarm at his behavior changed to anger at his accusation, and she flung herself out of bed, furiously grabbing her robe to put around her. "You're behaving like a child! What difference does it make what Oliver told me? You're being ridiculous!"

She hit home, but not in the way she had expected to. He drew himself up, glaring down at her coldly.

"All right—deny that that foolish old man's ramblings had anything to do with what happened tonight," he demanded. "You've never been like this before—what changed your mind, Cynara?"

She swallowed. What could she say that he would believe? "Oliver loves you, Evan. He was only trying to help—"

She shrank back again at the cold fury on his face. "Oh, I see," he said, his voice deadly with anger. "And because you felt sorry for me, you decided to allow me your bed. Well, I won't be patronized, Cynara, by anyone—and certainly not by you!"

"Patronized! How dare you accuse me of such a thing!"

"What else is there?"

They glared at each other, and Cynara could not speak for the indignation choking her. Her fingers itched to slap his face; she wanted to beat at him with her fists, to make him understand how unjust his accusation was. She wanted to shout at him that her need, her desire for him had swept everything else from her mind. But she did none of these things; she saw the arrogant lift of his lips as he stared at her, and she was silent.

Evan was silent as well, obviously struggling to control his own violent emotions. He took a deep breath, then reached for the doorknob. "I thought so," he said coldly. "Good night, Cynara."

"Evan, wait!"

But he was gone, the door slamming behind him, and she could not make herself go after him. Uttering a sound that was half groan, half sob, she stood in the center of the room, her hands clenched. How could everything have gone so wrong? How could they have reached such heights of passion, only to descend once again into suspicion and accusation? Cursing Evan's volatile nature and her own pride that had kept her silent, she threw herself onto the bed, clutching a pillow to her face, trying to stifle the tears that choked her.

CHAPTER THIRTY-TWO

CYNARA WOKE THE next morning with a headache. Dragging herself out of bed, she went to the window and saw that it was a beautiful morning. The sun was shining through the trees and the birds were singing cheerily. Cynara regarded it all with a sour expression; she would have preferred to see the sky low and gray, the birds huddled silently in the branches outside the window.

Muttering to herself, she began to dress, wondering how long she could avoid seeing Evan. Bitterly she reflected on the irony of the situation: where before she had spent days longing for his return, now all she wanted was for him to go away again. Dreading the thought of facing him, she buttoned a pair of walking boots, realizing too late that she should never have mentioned her chance meeting with Oliver Lindsay. She should have known what Evan's reaction would be, but she hadn't stopped to think about it then, and she was paying dearly for that mistake now.

Sighing, Cynara went quietly downstairs and out the front door. Wincing at the memory of their quarrel, Cynara cursed her own ineptitude the night before. She should have said something: she should have made some effort to explain. Instead, she had reacted as she always did when confronted with that glacial expression she hated on him. She had lashed out furiously, and nothing had been accomplished except to make them even angrier with each other. But now, in the light of day, she saw clearly what she should have said and done, and she was disgusted with herself that she had failed so miserably.

She came to a path that led off the road toward a small wood, and she turned into it, still preoccupied with her thoughts. She had just entered the line of trees when she heard hoofbeats behind her, and she looked over her shoulder, thinking at first that Evan had followed her. But it was not Evan, and when she recognized the figure astride the horse, her heart stopped for an instant, and then resumed again with a rush. Glancing around quickly, she searched for a place to hide, but it was too late. Horse and rider were advancing rapidly on her and she could only wait as he approached.

Myles reined the horse in almost under her nose, forcing her to step back quickly off the path to avoid being trampled. "Well!" he exclaimed, staring down at her from the animal's back. "If it isn't Cynara!"

Cynara did not trust herself to speak. Trying to ignore him, she moved away. Myles spurred the horse to the side, effectively blocking her way, and she looked sharply at him.

"Let me pass, Myles!"

"Oh, surely you don't intend to rush off! Why, it's been —what? Almost three years since we've seen each other. We have a lot to talk about."

Cynara saw the avid look in his eyes, and she wished suddenly that she had told someone where she was going. She did not trust Myles, and they were alone in these woods, the trees screening their presence from the road. "We have nothing to talk about!" she said, striving for calm.

"Oh, I think we do." Myles swung his leg over the saddle and dropped to the ground beside her. He tottered for an instant as his misshapen foot refused to take his weight, and he looked quickly at Cynara, his face reddening.

He hasn't changed, Cynara thought distastefully, except to put on even more weight. His blond-white hair still covered his round head in tight curls, his face with the small, almost bud-shaped mouth still wore that petulant expression. He was regarding her with a malicious glint in his tiny blue eyes, and Cynara shivered. He has changed after all, she realized; he's more evil than before.

"I had heard that you were back," he said. "In fact, I had thought to pay a call—"

Repelled, Cynara did not answer. She tried once more to move around the horse, but again Myles blocked her way. She was beginning to be frightened in spite of her revulsion;

she did not care for the look on his face. It was as if he were undressing her with his eyes, and again she was conscious that they were alone here, and that no one knew where she had gone.

"What do you want, Myles?" she asked curtly.

He cocked his head to one side, studying her. "I think," he said softly, "that I made a mistake the first time. I've often thought that, you know."

"What does that mean?" She heard the shrill note in her voice with alarm; she must not let him see that she was afraid of him.

"I should never have sent you away," he mused, still staring at her. "Do you know that you're even more beautiful than the last time I saw you?"

She did not answer. Her fear and mistrust were growing steadily; with an effort, she just prevented herself from glancing over her shoulder, seeking a way to escape.

"Yes," Myles continued. "I should never have allowed Mama to influence me in that hasty plan to send you away." He smiled, nastily. "She hated you, you know. She would have done anything to get rid of you."

"You both were successful," Cynara replied shortly.

"Ah, yes. But now that she is gone, we won't have to worry about her, will we?"

"Gone? What do you mean?"

"Oh, Mama died last year. It was her heart."

He waved his hand negligently, and Cynara stared at him with horror. She had despised Cornelia Ward, and she could not be sorry that the woman was dead. But Myles—Myles was her son! How could he speak of his mother's death so casually? He was a monster, a grinning, evil toad of a man. His lack of remorse increased her fear of him, and she watched him warily as he absently slapped the reins against his open palm.

"Yes," he said softly, studying her again with that appraising stare. "I've often wished that I hadn't sent you away. But I don't plan to let you go again."

"Let me go!" she echoed disbelievingly. "What makes you think—"

"I always get what I want, dear Cynara. You should know that. And I've decided that I want you."

Appalled, Cynara stared at him. "You're mad! You can't mean that!"

"Oh, but I do."

She could see that he did mean what he said, and again she was stunned. Forcing back her fear, she said quickly, "I'm afraid that you will be disappointed this time, Myles. I—"

"You won't disappoint me, Cynara," he interrupted softly. "There are ways to make you do what I want."

"Not this time, Myles. Oh no, not this time," she said sharply. "I'm not at your mercy any longer. I'm—"

"Married," he said, glancing contemptuously at the gold band on her finger. He nodded. "Oh yes, I know all about your marriage to—Evan," he continued, his lips twisting as he spoke Evan's name.

"Well, then, even you can see—"

Myles waved his hand. "A small inconvenience. Besides, I rather fancy taking Evan's wife away from him. He doesn't deserve you, you know."

Cynara's mouth was dry. This wasn't real, she thought wildly; she couldn't be having this insane conversation with Myles. "Whether he 'deserves' me or not," she choked, "there isn't anything you can do to change it."

"Isn't there?"

He was staring at her again, the blue of his eyes almost hidden in the fleshy folds of his lids. As she watched him, she saw the tip of his tongue appear between his teeth, and she looked away, only to snap her head back again when he spoke.

"I don't think there will be any trouble with Evan," he said, "Especially when you tell him that you're going to leave him."

"I'll do no such thing!"

"Oh, I think you will. Either that, or—" He shrugged.

"Or what?"

"Let's leave that, shall we? Why bring up unpleasant threats?"

Cynara had no doubt that Myles was capable of anything to get what he wanted. But this time she was on surer ground, and she spoke quickly, telling herself that she must not let him gain any advantage over her. "Your threats are futile, Myles. I think there's something you should know before you assume that I will do what you want."

Lazily, Myles raised an eyebrow. "And what is that?"

"Simply this: I know that Evan has a right to Lyrebird Manor."

He became alert. "Absurd!" he scoffed.

"Is it?" She had seen that behind his pose of indifference, he was shaken, and now she pressed further. "I know that Evan's father was Aron Ward, and that he was married to Jenny Calder." She looked steadily at him, and although she wasn't sure of this herself, she added evenly, "Unless you cease your childish threats, I will tell Evan to press his claim, and have you and your father evicted."

Myles's aplomb deserted him for an instant, and Cynara saw the leap of fear in his eyes. But he recovered quickly, and she knew that her sense of triumph had been premature. "You can't prove that," he said menacingly.

"Can't I?" It was Cynara's turn to be scornful. "I happen to have a letter from Aron to his parents, telling them about the marriage. I will take that letter to court if I have to!"

To her dismay, she saw that he was unaffected by her declaration. Grinning at her, he was sure of himself once again. "A letter!" he said disdainfully. "What does that prove? What does anything prove, without Aron himself to substantiate it? After all, he disappeared many years ago, and no one knows what happened to him, do they? Do you suppose any court will accept a letter as evidence?" He laughed. "A daring attempt, Cynara, but foolish. I can't blame you, though, for trying." The laughter disappeared abruptly from his face. "Don't think to threaten me again,

Cynara," he said dangerously. "In fact, if you try to take this little matter before the courts, you will have to do so alone. I won't lose my home, but Evan . . . Evan might lose his life. Do you take my meaning?"

Cynara swallowed: she understood him very well, "Evan is strong enough to fight you, Myles," she said. "You can't hope—"

"He can't be on guard all the time," Myles sneered. "There will be some time when his back is turned, and then—" Myles made a vicious motion with one hand, and Cynara shrank back.

Myles appeared not to notice her movement; he was staring at his hand, still clenched into a fist. "Now that I think about it," he said musingly, "It might be better to eliminate Evan, after all. He stands in the way of too many things—you, my home—" he looked up and grinned, his eyes glittering "My peace of mind. I've always hated him. He's been a thorn in my side for years. Why not get rid of him now?"

Horrified at what she saw on his face, Cynara stared at him. "How can you speak like this?" she whispered, aghast. "You don't know what you're saying!"

"Don't I? The more I think about it, the more the idea appeals to me."

"In the name of God, Myles! You can't—"

"Can't what? Kill him?" Myles grinned at her again. "His life means nothing to me, Cynara. Does it to you?"

"Myles—" she began desperately.

"Of course, there is one way to save his life," Myles said softly, as though she hadn't spoken. "You can come willingly to me, and I will forget about Evan. It's up to you, Cynara."

He grabbed her so suddenly that she had no chance to move away. Once again, she felt the surprising strength in his sausagelike fingers, once again she was trapped in the circle of his powerful arms. Rearing back, she tried to break free; even in her horror, she felt the trembling of his body, and she knew, as she had known from the first, what he wanted.

Myles laughed at her futile attempt to free herself. "Is this how you are going to repay me for sparing Evan's life?" he jeered.

His face was too close to hers. She pushed against him, trying to put some distance between them, and he laughed again, making smacking noises with his thick lips. "Perhaps you need a little time to reconsider. I wouldn't want you to think me unfair."

He released her abruptly, and she staggered back, even more repelled than before. Her skin seemed to crawl where he had touched her, and she wrapped her arms about her waist, trying to control the shaking of her body. Myles watched her for a moment, smiling to himself, and then he turned and mounted his horse, grinning nastily at her from the saddle. "You have until tonight to decide, Cynara. If you come to me, I'll leave Evan alone. If not—" He shrugged, lifting the reins.

The horse began to move forward, but Myles jerked it to a stop again, adding, almost as an afterthought, "I wouldn't discuss this little meeting with Evan, if I were you. We both know what a temper he has, and he might not think it sporting of me to spirit away his wife. I'm sure you can think of something to convince him—can't you?"

Cynara did not trust herself to speak. She was more afraid of him than before, for she had seen the evil light in his eyes, his absolute disregard for anyone but himself. She knew that he could kill Evan without a second thought. Helplessly she looked up at him, her revulsion showing plainly on her face. Myles, far from being angry at her expression, was amused instead. He chuckled.

"I will give you until tonight," he said. "Ten o'clock. We will meet in the garden—by the summerhouse. You remember the summerhouse, don't you?" he added, his face cruel.

"I remember it," she heard herself say, her voice without inflection.

"Ten o'clock, then?"

He did not wait for her answer. Spurring his horse, he rode quickly away as Cynara stared after him. Trying to tell herself that it would have done no good to fight him, to declare that she would not do as he asked—that she would tell Evan despite what he had said, Cynara waited until he had disappeared. He was insane; she had seen it in his eyes, she had felt it in his manner, and Cynara shivered. Myles was even more dangerous than before, she thought desperately. Once he had been a spoiled, petulant boy who threw tantrums when he did not get what he wanted. Now he was a grown man, and the evil that had always been in him had grown as well, until he recognized no restraint. He was frightening.

Biting her lip, Cynara began to walk slowly back the way she had come. She could not tell Evan about meeting Myles, and yet if she didn't tell him, what was she going to do? Myles had not spoken lightly about killing Evan; she knew that he was unbalanced enough to do anything to get what he wanted. But why did he want her? She didn't know: she thought that Myles himself probably didn't know. How could she go to him tonight? Even the touch of his hands had revolted her, made her almost physically ill; she felt hysteria growing at the thought of his body violating hers. She couldn't do it; couldn't surrender to him. And yet, how could she not?

Trying to quell her rising despair, Cynara thought furiously, trying to find a solution that would check Myles and still protect Evan. But no matter how she considered it, in the end there were only two choices: stay with Evan and risk his life, or go to Myles and protect Evan. Even as she spoke aloud to herself, repeating the words, she realized how melodramatic they sounded, and yet . . . She had seen Myles's face, she had heard the eagerness in his voice, and she knew that he would not hesitate if she crossed him. It occurred to her that she had only to tell Evan what Myles had threatened, and he would take care of Myles himself. But Evan, no matter how enraged, would confront Myles openly. No, she couldn't tell Evan, she thought desperately. She could not take the chance that he would be hurt.

Somehow she managed to get back to the house, although she couldn't recall a step of the journey. When she let herself in the front door, she saw with dismay that Evan was descending the stairs before her, a scowl on his face. He had seen her come in; it was too late for escape. Fighting down the desire to run from him so that he wouldn't see something was wrong, she forced herself to stay where she was as he came toward her.

If Evan noticed her distraught manner, he gave no sign of it, and Cynara tried to get hold of herself. Now she was almost glad they had quarreled the night before; if he thought she was acting strangely, he might assume she was still angry. But it was an effort to lift her head and face him: only the thought of how important it was for him to suspect nothing gave her the strength to look at him. Now that she knew what she had to do, she hoped that she could carry it through before she broke down completely.

"Where have you been?"

His cold tone gave her the impetus she needed. She had always hated it when he spoke to her like that; she now stiffened. "I went for a walk."

"I've been looking all over for you."

She saw the intent expression in his eyes, and she felt herself wavering. If only she could tell him about Myles; what a relief it would be. No! she told herself fiercely, deliberately picturing what would happen as a result of her cowardice; no, she couldn't tell him. She must make him think that the breach between them was final; she must, if she wanted to save his life.

Willing her voice to steadiness, she said, "I didn't realize I needed your permission to leave the house."

She had intended to anger him, knowing that would make it easier for her to say what had to be said. To her dismay, she saw him make an effort to control his temper, and she was alarmed. What was wrong? Why hadn't he

responded in his usual manner—especially now when she
wanted him to? Annoyed that he had disappointed her, she
now became angry with him, and she welcomed the feeling.
If she was angry, she wouldn't have time to think about
what she was doing, what she had to do.

"Evan," she began. "There is something—"

"I would like you to—"

They spoke at the same time, and now that she hesitated,
she lost courage again. Gesturing, she indicated that he
speak first.

"I would like you to take a ride with me," he said, after a
pause in which he stared curiously at her. "There's something I want to show you."

Her first inclination was to refuse. She didn't want to go
anywhere with him; she wanted to stay right here, so that
after she told him she was going to leave him she could run
to her room and lock herself in. She couldn't let him see how
she despaired over what she must do.

But she knew that in spite of her convictions, she would
go with him. This might be the last time she would see him
or be alone with him, and she could not deny herself this last
farewell.

She said, finally, "All right, Evan. When do you want to
leave?"

"Right now."

He had ordered his horse harnessed to the trap. As the
vehicle was brought around to the front door and they
stood waiting, Cynara could not look at him. She was
conscious of his presence beside her; she remembered the
touch of his hands the night before, the feel of his body over
hers, and remembering, she closed her eyes against the pain
that assailed her. Never to touch or hold him again, never to
feel his lips on hers—how could she bear it?

"Cynara?"

She opened her eyes, startled to see the trap in front of her,
a groom waiting respectfully by the horse's head. Evan
handed her in, and then climbed inside himself, lifting the

ribbons to signal the horse. The groom saluted smartly as they went by and Cynara forced herself to nod in response. They moved briskly down the drive, and although the circumstances were entirely different, Cynara was reminded forcibly of the first time she had seen Evan. The vehicle then had been an old farm wagon, the horse a plodding work animal, but for a moment Cynara was thrown back to that time, and she felt bitter tears coming to her eyes. If only things had been different, she thought fiercely—if only she and Evan had been older, or a little wiser, they might have been able to resist the forces that had kept them apart, and were driving them even further apart now.

But now it was too late, and it was futile to reflect on past mistakes. The past was gone, and there would be no future for them; Myles had seen to that. Cynara knew that she should speak at once, before she lost her nerve again.

Turning to Evan, she saw that he was as preoccupied with his own thoughts as she had been with hers. She opened her mouth to speak, and then closed it again. She had not paid any attention to the direction in which they were going, but suddenly she realized that they were traveling toward Lyrebird Manor. The consequences of a confrontation between Myles and Evan frightened her, and she said sharply, "Evan, where are we going?"

Evan started, as though he had forgotten her presence beside him. He turned to look at her, and at his expression of surprise she realized that she had revealed her fear to him. Averting her head, she tried to control her own expression, but the thought that Myles could appear at any moment made her even more tense. "Evan, please stop," she said faintly.

But he had already signaled the horse, which obediently halted at the side of the road. Springing down off the seat, he raised his hand to help her alight, but she pretended not to see the gesture. Now that the moment had come when she must tell him her decision, she couldn't allow him to touch her; any contact between them would weaken her resolve, and she must not let that happen. Thinking again of Myles's face when he uttered his threat, she stiffened. As long as she could keep Myles in mind, she could tell Evan what she had to.

Frowning, Evan stepped aside as she climbed down unaided. "Cynara—"

"What was it you wanted to show me?"

Again, he was startled by her manner. It was obvious that he was puzzled by her peremptory tone, for his mouth tightened. He began to say something, changed his mind, and finally asked, "Will you walk with me?"

"Evan, there is something—"

"Will you walk with me?" he asked again, quietly.

She didn't want to walk with him; she wanted to turn and run away from him—anything to avoid the next few minutes, and the fierce quarrel she was sure would follow. But there was no running away; she had to tell him before tonight, before Myles made good his threat. Her face bleak, she nodded, and Evan tethered the horse to a bush by the road.

She didn't wait for him. Moving swiftly up the slope he had indicated earlier, she followed a sheep track that wound its way to the top. Tears blinded her; she couldn't see where she was going and she stumbled several times, each time hurrying forward again lest Evan catch up to her. The thought that he was close behind unnerved her; she thought desperately that if she didn't speak to him soon, she would not be able to speak at all.

There was a small stand of trees near the crest of the hill and Cynara paused there to catch her breath and try to compose herself. She must speak calmly, neutrally, if she was to succeed in convincing him; there could be no violent display of emotion. A slight breeze blew over her, and she lifted her flushed face to its coolness, determined not to cry. When Evan came up beside her, she was able to face him, thankful that her eyes were dry. He would never know the effort this cost her, and she bitterly congratulated herself on her control. But then Evan spoke her name, softly, and she realized how precarious that control was. His tone was almost tender, as it had been the night before, and Cynara felt a wrench inside her. Why had he never used that tone before last night? Why hadn't she?

"Cynara," he said, "We have to talk."

It was impossible to delay longer. Any further hesitation on her part would only be more hurtful to both of them. Her heart was hammering painfully against her chest, and yet she must appear distant, aloof. How could she do it?

"It's past time for talking, isn't it?" she managed to say finally.

"Is it?"

He had reached for her hand, but she moved away. Breaking a branch from the tree, she began pulling the leaves from it with great deliberation, as though she hadn't heard him. "I really don't think we have anything to say to each other," she continued, "Except—"

"You can say that after last night?" The softness left his voice; his tone sharpened.

Cynara shrugged. She did not answer, leaving him to interpret the gesture as he would. From the corner of her eye, she saw him stiffen. The last vestige of tenderness had gone from him, and he was the Evan she had known before, harsh and bitter with unspoken emotion. Now it was easier for her; if she could maintain this pose of indifference, she would be able to convince him.

Looking up at him again, she began to speak. But before she could say anything, he grabbed her by the arm, pulling her forcibly up the distance to the top of the hill. Flinging out his arm in a savage gesture, he ordered her to look at the sight below.

She had known from the moment he stopped the horse at that point on the road what it was that he wanted her to see, but she was unprepared for her violent reaction as she gazed down. To her right stood Lyrebird Manor, and behind the house, clearly etched in detail from this high vantage point, was the lyrebird garden. She saw the curving arms of the lyre formed by the line of yews, the four beech trees at the center appearing from this height like long, graceful feathers. Everywhere in the garden was a profusion of growth, the spring flowers already blooming in untended masses of color. Staring down at it, she realized suddenly that she had hoped it would not be the same—as she was not the same. But she saw that it remained unchanged. She had actually once admired the garden for its wild beauty, but now she hated the sight of it and all it represented.

Averting her glance as a wave of bitterness assailed her, she looked at Evan. He had moved a few steps away from her and was staring fixedly at the sight below. When she saw his expression change and become almost savage, she knew he was thinking, as she was, of Myles, and she became alarmed.

"Evan—"

He did not appear to hear her. He stood alone, the wind ruffling his black hair, lifting it away from his face. His eyes were shadowed again, his mouth a thin, bitter line. She took a step toward him, and stopped. He looked up then, and their glance held.

"There it is, Cynara," he said harshly. "And it will soon be mine. Mine! Oh, how I have longed for this day!"

Her alarm turned to fear. There was something almost demonic about the way he stood there, his face dark with triumph, and she wondered if he could possibly have discovered he had a right by inheritance to a share of the Manor.

"I don't . . . understand," she faltered.

Evan took a step toward her, and she wanted to shrink back at the ferocity on his face. "As of the fifteenth of this month, it will be mine," he said, his voice rough. "I intend to buy the mortgage, Cynara, and after that I will foreclose. Everything I have, all my money, will be used for this, but in the end, the Manor will be mine!"

She backed away from him. This was worse than she had thought! If he ever realized that part of the Manor was his by right . . . But she could not complete the thought even in her mind. It was impossible, she thought frantically; what was she going to do now? What could she say? But there was no time to think, for Evan was continuing, and she could only stare at him, speechless with shock.

"I want you to share it with me, Cynara," he said.

"Share it with you!" Her voice was shrill; with an effort, she lowered it, forcing herself to remember her purpose. "I'm afraid that's impossible," she said, more calmly.

His eyes narrowed. "Impossible?" he repeated. "Why?"

She thought of all the times she had dreamed of the day when Myles would suffer. She had planned to use Evan to avenge herself, and yet now when he had offered her a share in his triumph, she knew that all her plans and hopes and dreams were meaningless. What did revenge mean to her when she was about to lose the man she loved?

Knowing that she was about to destroy the fragile link between them, she forced herself to answer, a part of her surprised that she could sound as cold and as harsh as she wanted to be, when her own pain threatened to choke her. "It's impossible," she said, "because I'm leaving you, Evan, for . . . for another man."

Sick at heart, she watched the color drain from his face until only the scar, an angry thin red line, was visible. She wanted to look away from him, from the utter disbelief and rejection she saw in his face, but she could not. He tried to speak and failed, tried again, but the blow had been too sudden, too unexpected. He stared at her uncomprehendingly.

Now her fear for him, the thought of what Myles had threatened to do if she did not leave Evan, came to her rescue. There was no other consideration but his safety, she thought desperately; if nothing else, she could give him that, even if he never knew it. She said, praying that he would believe her, "Our marriage was a mistake, Evan—a dreadful mistake! We both know that. I see no sense in going on. I—"

He advanced upon her, grasping her by the shoulders, his fingers digging into her flesh, but she did not feel the pain. Terrified by his expression, she tried to struggle away, but he held her tightly.

"Who is he?"

Fighting to control her fear, she cried, "What difference does it make?"

"Who is he?"

She had never seen him like this; it was as though he wished to strike her down, and for an instant she actually thought he would. His hands tightened upon her.

"*Who is he?*"

The pain was excruciating: in his rage he had almost lifted her off the ground. He was like a man possessed, and she wondered frantically what to tell him. But would he believe anything less than the truth?

"I won't tell you!" she cried. Oh, if he would only let go of her, she might be able to think! Should she tell him it was Myles? What would he do if she did? The thought flashed through her mind that if she told him, his pride might compel him to leave here, to abandon his possession of the Manor. She had to answer; his fingers were like talons, numbing her shoulders. Dare she tell him what he wanted to know?

"Tell me."

"All right! All right!" she shouted at him, fear and pain forcing her to take the risk. If she had misread him . . ."It's Myles! Myles!" she shrieked.

He dropped her so suddenly that she staggered. Reaching out, she grabbed on to a branch for balance, not daring to look up, dreading what the knowledge had done to him. But when she sensed no movement from him, she forced herself to glance at him, and what she saw on his face made her cringe. She had never thought to see that look of pure anguish that gripped him now as he stared at her. She felt her own pain take hold of her like an iron hand, and though she tried to speak, she could not. Every nerve in her body screamed at her to go to him, to tell him that everything she had said was a lie, and yet she compelled herself to remain still. She had done what she had set out to do; she could not undo it now. She prayed that she had been right in assessing the fierce pride that was in him. If not, she knew that he would go after Myles to kill him. Closing her eyes, she waited.

A stark silence vibrated between them, the only sound his labored breathing as he struggled for control.

At last he spoke, and the sound of his voice was worse than the silence before. "You whoring bitch! I should have known the reason you were so anxious to get back here! All the time it was Myles—from that night in the garden, when you pretended you needed help. What was the plan, Cynara? Was Myles supposed to kill me, or was it only intended to drive me away?" He laughed harshly, and the sound chilled her even more than the tone of his voice. "Whichever it was, it doesn't matter now, does it?"

He paused, and when she dared to look at him, she saw that his eyes were terrible; they appeared like black pits in his white face. "What is expected of me now, I wonder?" he continued, his voice ragged with fury. "Am I supposed to do the gentlemanly thing and step aside? What is it you want me to do, Cynara, now that I've gone to all the trouble of returning you safely to the arms of another man?"

He didn't mean it, she thought wildly; it was only because he was hurt that he accused her of plotting with Myles. She wanted to tell him that he was wrong, that if he stopped to think, he would realize that she couldn't have planned anything with Myles because she had been sent away from the Manor herself. But she could tell him none of these things; it was better that he believe what he had said, for then he would leave without a backward glance. She started to say something, but he hurled an epithet at her that made her cringe again.

"Say something, damn it! Tell me I'm wrong!"

She closed her eyes at the pain she heard in his voice. "I hate you for bringing me back, Evan!" she cried. "I—"

"You wanted it as much as I!" he shouted. "You couldn't wait to get back, could you—to him! Well, I wish you luck, the two of you. You deserve each other—a cringing whore and a half-man! God! How you disgust me."

Abruptly, he turned away from her, his hands clenched at his sides. Cynara stared at his stiff back for a long moment, then with a cry she whirled around and started down the hill without looking back. By the time she reached the foot of the slope she was running, her skirts lifted high, as though she were fleeing from the devil himself.

The horse stood waiting patiently between the shafts of the trap, but Cynara did not stop. Sobbing, gasping for breath, she ran on until the curve of the hill hid her from sight. Only when she was sure that Evan could no longer see her, did she throw herself on the ground. Burying her head in her arms, she began crying, uncontrollably. She had won, but even the knowledge that Evan would not go after Myles was no comfort. She thought of the house and the garden she had seen from the top of the hill, and she knew that she could not surrender herself to Myles. She hated that house and those who lived there, she hated them for what they had done to her, for what they had forced her to do to Evan. Through Myles and John, she had lost the one thing that mattered most to her. She would never forget; the memories would be with her always, and whenever she looked at Myles, she knew she would remember the first and last glorious night with Evan, and how it could have been.

Another wave of convulsive sobs shook her, and she uttered a cry. Grabbing a fistful of hair in each hand, she bit down hard on her lip as she remembered the pain in Evan's eyes. Evan . . . Evan . . . Her own anguish hammered at her, and she bent double with it, knowing that it was only the beginning of pain, and that she would never be whole again.

Evan stood where Cynara left him. Only when he had heard the sound of her running footsteps did he turn to watch her go. His eyes on her, he followed her flight until she disappeared around the curve of the hill and was lost to view. It wasn't until then that he turned back to his contemplation of the house below him. Now that he was alone, with only the wind and one lone hawk circling high in the sky above him, he allowed his desolation to surface. His mouth tightened in an effort to control his emotion, but the pain was too great, and he had to force himself to remain where he was. He wanted to run after her, he wanted to grab her and shake her and make her tell him—what? That she had lied? But he could not doubt that she meant what she said; he had seen the contempt for him in her eyes, he had felt her shrinking away from him.

His eyes stung, and he looked up quickly, forcing himself to follow the movements of the soaring hawk, trying to control his feelings of rage and disbelief and grief. He had lost her, he thought, and the admission brought with it a greater anguish. And he had lost her to Myles. Myles! Just the thought of Myles had the power to drive him mad, and an expression of such hatred crossed his face that his lips actually drew back from his teeth. His hands clenched into tight fists again, and he brought his head down sharply to stare once again at Lyrebird Manor. Bitter memories came back to him, and he let them come. He wanted to remember all of it, savoring the full depth of his hatred, so that the final victory over Myles would be that much sweeter when it was accomplished.

He laughed, and the sound was harsh even in his own ears. To think that he had brought her up here, like a lord surveying his kingdom, trying to impress her before he declared that he loved her. What a fool he had been to think she had changed in her feelings for him, when all the time she had been planning to leave him for Myles. He tried to laugh again, but the sound he uttered was a strangled sob, and he gritted his teeth. He would not give in to the pain that hammered at him whenever he thought of her. He . . . would . . . not . . .

He knew that she had hoped he would simply go away and leave them alone; he had seen it in her face when she had defiantly shouted the name of her—lover. She had taken a great risk, revealing that name, and he knew she was aware of it. How clever she was, he thought bitterly; how sure she had been of his reaction. She had guessed right—at first, he thought savagely; his initial response had been to rush down the hill and kill Myles with his bare hands, but that urge had passed as quickly as it had come, and then he had been so disgusted and revolted that he had almost told her she could have Myles and the Manor and all be damned. Oh yes, she was cunning; she had calculated what his reaction would be, and he had given it to her. But not now—oh no. Not now.

His first towering rage had passed, and he was able to think more clearly. The idea of abandoning the Manor left him. He would not so easily be convinced to give up his revenge. He had not struggled, had not taken chance after chance in Australia, building up his last few shillings into the amount of money he needed to buy the Manor, to give it all up now. No, not even for Cynara could he just walk away.

His decision made, Evan turned abruptly and strode down the hill. He did not glance in the direction Cynara had gone; he didn't care where she went now or what she did. Untethering the horse, he climbed into the trap and urged the animal into a fast trot back the way he had come. He told himself that Cynara had ceased to exist for him, but every beat of the horse's hoofs seemed to echo inside his head, increasing his desolation. The empty road stretched before him, and despite his fierce command to himself to forget his loss, his feeling of betrayal, he knew that it was only a matter of time before he was compelled to give in to the pain that tore at him whenever he thought of Cynara . . . and what might have been.

CHAPTER THIRTY-THREE

EVAN PAUSED IN THE stableyard at Cord House only long enough to hand the horse to the groom with orders to saddle another mount for him immediately. Ignoring the man's curious look, he went raging into the house by the back door and straight up the stairs to change his clothes. He did not glance at the closed door of the master suite as he went by; he knew Cynara could not have arrived before he did, and in any case, he told himself savagely, he intended to be gone before she returned.

Striding down the corridor, he flung open the door to the room he had used the night before, and saw with satisfaction that his riding clothes had been cleaned and pressed and were hung carefully in the wardrobe. He changed in seconds, and was on the way downstairs again when he heard Hester calling to him. He paused. He had forgotten about Hester. Now he would have to devise some sort of explanation for his hasty departure. Cursing under his breath at the delay, he walked quickly in the direction of the sitting room, and halted on the threshold when he saw Hester sitting in one of the chairs by the window.

"Oh, Evan," she said. "I heard you come in just now. Is . . . is something wrong?"

She had seen the dark expression on his face, and was staring at him anxiously, but he felt only impatience at her concern. The old woman was too nosy by half, he thought in annoyance; he had no intention of explaining himself.

"I'm leaving for London again," he said curtly.

"When?"

"Right now." He made a move toward the doorway. "Goodbye, Hester."

"Evan, wait!" Hester was startled. "You've only just come last night!" she exclaimed. "You said you were staying a week or more!"

"I've changed my mind," Evan answered, out of patience. He was in a hurry to go before Cynara returned; he had to get out before he saw her again, or he might not be able to make himself leave at all. Exasperated, he made another move toward the door, but again Hester stopped him.

"Why do you have to leave in such a rush?" Hester glared at him over the rim of her spectacles. She had been working on a piece of embroidery, and now she threw aside the square of linen. "Did you and Cynara have another quarrel?" she demanded.

Despite his resolve, he stiffened, and Hester pounced. "Tell me about it."

"There's nothing to say, Hester. Now, if you don't mind—"

"I'll talk to her myself," she announced maddeningly. "There's no reason for the two of you being at loggerheads all the time. It makes me uncomfortable."

"Perhaps you should have thought of that before you brought us together," Evan replied, his voice hard.

"Oh, really! You know you're suited to each other. Is it my fault that you're both too stubborn to see it yourselves?"

"We're not as suited as you think, Hester," Evan answered coldly. "You might ask Cynara to explain the reason why."

"I'd rather ask you, Evan."

"I don't want to discuss it," he said stiffly, in a fever of impatience to be gone. "Goodbye, Hester."

"Evan—"

But he was gone, shutting the door behind him. Outside, he mounted his waiting horse and spurred the animal quickly into a canter. The startled horse leaped forward, bits of gravel flying up from its hoofs to strike near the window where Hester had come to stand. He did not turn around to see her standing there, staring after him with a bemused expression, shaking her head.

It was late afternoon by the time Evan stopped to rest. He had some distance to go yet, but he had no desire to punish his horse for his own impatience. Besides, now that he was away from Cord House, away from Cynara, what was the hurry? Suddenly, the thought of London, with its grime-filled, crowded streets, the pall of gritty smoke hanging in the air, repeled him, and when he saw an inn by the side of the road, he turned in.

A lad came running forward to take his horse, and he instructed the boy to feed and water the animal lightly after rubbing him down; he did not intend to linger long. The lad nodded solemnly, his eyes widening in surprise when he caught the coin Evan flipped him. It was not every customer who paid him so handsomely, and he shouted his thanks as he led the horse toward the stable at the back.

When Evan entered the tavern, he saw with relief that it was almost empty. Two men sat at one oak table, sipping ale and talking desultorily. Ignoring their curious glances, Evan seated himself as far as possible from them; he did not wish to engage in conversation, for his mood was blacker than before. When the proprietor brought him his ale, Evan paid for it without looking up, and the man departed, leaving him alone to stare morosely into the contents of the tankard, his thoughts far away.

Now that victory over John and Myles was so close at hand, he felt a depressing sense of anticlimax, and suddenly it seemed too much of an effort to complete the journey to London to see James Melburn. No, what was he thinking? Of course he had to go. He couldn't abandon his plans now, after so much work; it was out of the question. He had directed all his energies toward possessing the Manor; he couldn't give up now, just because his dream of revenge had gone flat, like champagne the day after a party.

Rubbing his eyes with one hand, Evan sat hunched in his chair, angry with himself for not making plans for the future. He had not really thought beyond the time when he would own the Manor; it had been enough for him to anticipate that day alone. Vincent had told him once that it was dangerous to be single-minded in pursuit of a goal, that a man must have something else to go on for, but Evan had laughed at the warning and focused his attention on his plan to the exclusion of everything else. Everything else, he thought—even Cynara. He had had his eyes on his goal, and hadn't seen what was going on under his nose. Could he have stopped her involvement with Myles? Would he have done so, if he could?

Of course he would, he told himself savagely. But he had been too blind, too complacent, to pay heed to the danger signals: from that first quarrel on the ship, when he had asserted so manfully that he would leave her alone in the cabin, she hadn't objected: she had seemed almost relieved. And then, when they had finally arrived at Cord House, and he left immediately for London, she had let him go without a word.

He took a long swallow from the tankard, banging it down on the table again. He had been so sure, that night when he had gone to her suite, that she felt the way he did. But that night had meant nothing to her, after all, and he had been a fool to think it had.

How could he have been so wrong? Had he been so inflamed with his own passion that he had not noticed hers was feigned? But he had seen nothing but that lithe body waiting for him. She was matchless, every line perfect, every curve flawless. She knew how to excite him: every movement had been tantalizing, seductive. The memory of her hands on his body, of her long legs wrapped around him, of her straining muscles as she drew him inside her, brought a rush of blood to his head, a throbbing to his loins. He had never loved a woman like Cynara: he never would again.

As much as he tried to blame her, he knew the fault was just as much his. In his arrogance he had assumed that once his dream of owning the Manor had been attained, he would turn then to Cynara. He had told himself that when he had something of value to offer her, he would be able to tear down the barrier between them and make her . . . happy. Happy. Sneering at himself for his self-deception, he realized that he had thought only of himself. How could he expect her to understand, to forgive, when he couldn't forgive himself for his own blindness, his absorption in something that was meaningless after all?

Evan closed his eyes and pictured Cynara as he had last seen her: eyes shimmering with unshed tears, hair blowing in tendrils about her white and strained face. Even then she had been beautiful to him, and pain stabbed him again as he thought of her. It was useless to tell himself that he could simply walk away and forget her: he knew that even if he never saw her again she would be with him always, in his mind and in his heart.

More despondent than before, it was several moments before he realized that someone had come up to him. He glanced up and stared. His eyes met those of a young and very pretty girl who was looking down at him with an arch expression that indicated she was not as young as she appeared to be. When she saw that she had his attention, she smiled coyly. Without invitation, she drew up another chair and sat beside him.

"My name is Daisy," she said, her voice husky. She leaned forward, deliberately, her full breasts straining against her tight bodice. She smiled again, enticingly.

Evan kept looking at her, and what he saw was not displeasing. He was not overfond of plump girls, but for an instant he was almost tempted. Perhaps he did need someone warm and willing, eager to please, right now. Then, impatient with himself, he shook his head. He was in no mood for lovemaking, however casual.

"Another time, Daisy," he said.

Disappointed, the girl sat back, and Evan relented enough at her expression to pull a gold sovereign from his pocket, hoping she would take it and go away. Suddenly, he wanted very much to be alone.

The sovereign disappeared quickly. With a smile of thanks, Daisy tucked it into her bodice, but instead of leaving him, she continued to sit there, staring at him.

Evan was not aware that Daisy had stayed: he was deep in thought once more, assailed by doubts that had ridden with him all the way here. Had he done the right thing, leaving so precipitately? The nagging thought that he had taken the coward's way out struck him again, and he wondered if he should have stayed to talk to Cynara again. Then, wincing, he tried to reassure himself that he had taken the only course open to him, pride or not. He couldn't force Cynara to stay with him: if she was determined to leave him, how could he hold her against her will? He knew himself well enough to realize that he couldn't have stayed there and accepted the fact that Cynara was leaving him for Myles. Myles. Even now he could not make himself believe that Cynara truly wanted Myles. She knew him: she knew the sort of man, or half-man, that he was. It didn't make sense to him, knowing Cynara as he did. Or did he know her at all? Draining the tankard of ale, he reflected bitterly that she was an enigma to him, that he had never really understood her.

"Women are incomprehensible sometimes, aren't they?" a soft voice said in his ear.

Startled, Evan looked up. He had forgotten Daisy completely, but he saw now that she was looking at him with sympathy in her round blue eyes. He grimaced, nodding in spite of himself. "Yes," he said briefly.

"Would you like to tell me about it?" she asked. "Perhaps I can help."

He shook his head, once. "No," he answered, just as briefly as before. "It's done: there is nothing to talk about."

Daisy was silent for a moment. Then, tentatively, she put her hand on his arm, and said, with greater sympathy, "You love her, don't you?"

Again he was surprised at her perception. He looked away from her in confusion, down at his hands, which were clutching the empty tankard until his knuckles showed white. With effort he relaxed his grip, but Daisy had seen that convulsive gesture, and she smiled sadly. "Go back to her," she said softly.

"I—can't." Roughly, he jerked his arm away from her grasp.

"I see."

"Do you?" he demanded, almost savagely. "I wish to hell I did!"

She rose with a quiet dignity that was somehow not incongruous with her overblown appearance. "Perhaps," she said, looking down at him, "You understand better than you want to admit. Could that be?"

She waited a moment, but when he did not answer, she moved off without another word. Swaying her hips, she crossed the room and laughingly accepted the offer of the two other patrons to sit with them. Throwing a glance over her shoulder at Evan, she tossed her head, and then turned her back to him.

Well, he deserved that at least, he thought ruefully, gesturing for another tankard of ale. But when it came, Evan did not touch it; he was wondering if Daisy's remark had any merit.

Frowning, he considered what Daisy had said. Did he understand Cynara's behavior more than he wanted to admit? He shook his head, trying to dismiss the idea as absurd. But then he thought of that tempestuous scene on the hill, and he wondered whether he had missed something after all. Had there been some clue that in his anger and hurt he had overlooked? Eyes narrowed in concentration, Evan tried to remember exactly what they had said to each other. And then from somewhere in the back of his mind he heard Cynara crying: "I hate you for bringing me back, Evan!"

His eyes narrowed even more. He pictured her as she had stood there, her head lifted defiantly, face white, hands clenched at her sides. Why would she hate him for bringing her back if she intended to leave him for Myles?

Grimacing, he recalled his own hateful words. He had accused her of plotting with Myles that night in the garden, when he had heard her call for help. He had hurled his charge at her, believing it himself in that moment, because he had been too enraged to think otherwise; because he had *wanted* to believe it. But now . . . Now, he wondered. If Cynara had been in league with Myles, why had she been sent away in the first place? Why had she been accused of some fictitious crime, and then transported? Why?

His head in his hands, Evan tried to reconstruct the events of that night. There could only be one reason why Cynara had been sent away, and that was because she represented some kind of danger to Myles. But what? Unless . . . unless her terror had been real that night; that she *had* been calling for help from the summerhouse. What had happened after that fight between Myles and himself? He had gone, quickly, as soon as Cynara helped him to the stables—he hadn't waited to corroborate her story. She must have told John and Cornelia that Myles had tried to rape her, and that he, Evan, had gone to help—with the result that Evan had attacked their precious son, and that that son had almost killed him. But there had been no one to witness her statement; it had been her word against Myles's, and he could imagine now what Myles had said in response. He knew only too well the ingenious lies Myles could invent on the spur of the moment to protect himself. Hadn't he lived for years taking the blame for things Myles had done? There had been incidents too numerous to recall now. If he had been there, he would have realized the futility of trying to reason with John and Cornelia, who had always believed that their son could do no wrong. But Cynara had not known that it was useless to defend herself against Myles; she had tried to tell the truth, and she had been sent away to protect Myles.

But now . . . what about now, today?

The thought occurred to him so suddenly that he froze, hardly daring to move while his mind raced ahead. Myles, he thought; Myles was behind all this. He didn't know why, or what he wanted, but he knew that he must have threatened Cynara in some way. That was why she had been so frightened when he told her he was going to buy the Manor; that was why she had finally revealed his name. She wanted Evan to get out, to leave—but why? Why? What had Myles threatened her with? What would Myles want. . . ?

He thought back over the years, recalling now that everything he had ever had of his own, Myles had taken from him, either by lies or by force. Myles had always had a compulsion to possess the things that were Evan's, from a whistle Oliver had carved for him to a pup he had found tied to a tree. And Myles had destroyed them all—his pleasure was not in the objects themselves, but in taking them from Evan.

What did he have now that Myles would want to possess? Not the Manor; he couldn't know that Evan was negotiating to buy his home. But if not the Manor . . . Evan stiffened. God! How could he have been so stupid? It wasn't the Manor; it wasn't anything as worthless as that. Myles wanted the most valuable prize of all—he wanted Cynara!

Evan stood up so suddenly that the chair crashed to the floor behind him. He ran for the door, shouting to the lad to bring his horse around. Seconds later, as the boy stared after him in bewilderment, he raced out of the yard, tearing back the way he had come. Glancing up, he saw that the sun was low on the horizon; too soon it would be dark, and the going would be slower. He could not afford to waste any more time. It would be late as it was before he reached Cord House, and a sense of urgency was hard upon him as he urged the horse to a faster pace. Cursing himself for being such a fool, cursing Cynara for not telling him the truth, he closed his eyes briefly, forcing himself to believe that he would make it home before something happened to Cynara.

Evan had rarely prayed before; now he found himself offering up a silent and desperate prayer that he would be in time. The horse, as if sensing the frantic haste of his rider, stretched out. They pounded down the road, running at breakneck speed. Oh God, Evan thought, let me get there before it's too late . . .

CHAPTER THIRTY-FOUR

"CYNARA, WHERE HAVE you been? I've waited two hours for you! Do you know Evan is gone again? But of course you know—you drove him away! How could you? Do you know what you've done, girl?"

Cynara looked dully at Hester, who was glaring at her from the threshold. Hester stared at her a moment longer, then she hobbled stiffly into the room, prepared to deliver another rapid-fire volley of accusation. She had followed Cynara from the front door, up the stairs and into the suite, denouncing her all the way, but Cynara was too exhausted, too emotionally spent to care. She turned away from Hester now to stare unseeingly out the window.

Behind her, Hester's harsh voice jabbed at her again. She did not hear the words, only the sound, a shrill chatter that scarcely registered. She had finally managed to drag herself home after stopping to wash her face in a small stream. But her tears had come again in spite of that, and she had sat by the brook for a while, trying vainly to get a grip on herself, asking herself what she was going to do. But she hadn't been able to think of anything but that terrible scene with Evan. Every time she pictured him as she had last seen him, his eyes almost black with rage and pain, the scar on his face an angry red slash, his jaw so set that a muscle leaped spasmodically under tight skin, she had begun to cry again.

Finally there had been no tears left in her, and she sat quietly until the last shuddering sob had ceased. Only then had she been able to think clearly, and to decide what she was going to do. She thought at first that she would simply go away, disappear. But she knew the instant she thought of it that the idea was impossible. She could not leave without striking back at Myles for what he had forced her to do. If there was only some way to threaten *him,* she thought; if she could learn something that would stay his hand against Evan, she would be free to go. She knew so much, more even than Evan, about what had happened long ago to prevent him from claiming his birthright, and yet, it was too little. Myles had sneered at her efforts to intimidate him by revealing her knowledge of Aron and Jenny's marriage. Under his scorn she had sensed fear. There had to be something else, some vital piece of information that she lacked.

There was only one person who could help her. She knew that he was hiding something; she had sensed it yesterday, but she had not pursued it, not wishing to upset him. But the time for consideration had passed; if she didn't press him now, it would be too late.

Glancing at the clock on the mantle, she saw that it was almost four, and she was alarmed. She hadn't much time.

"Cynara, are you listening to me? Have you heard anything I've said?"

To her surprise, Hester was still there; she had forgotten her completely. She looked at the woman blankly, and Hester responded with an outraged expression.

"You haven't heard me at all!" she accused. "I'm trying to tell you that Evan is gone, and it's all your fault!"

Cynara sighed. "Is it?" she said dully. "Yes, I suppose in a way it is."

Hester gaped at her, speechless for once. It did not last long. "How can you be so complacent about it?" she screeched. "This isn't some stranger we're talking about! Evan is your husband!"

Cynara shook her head. "Evan was never my husband," she said. But he was, she thought; for a few minutes last night, here in this room, he had been her husband. Resolutely, she put the thought from her mind; she couldn't allow herself to think of that now.

"What are you saying? Are you mad? What's got into you?"

Cynara was impatient to be gone. Aware of the clock ticking away, she didn't want to waste any more time arguing senselessly with Hester. She went toward the door.

"Cynara, where are you going? Cynara!"

She went down the stairs, Hester's voice pursuing her loudly as she tried to follow. "Cynara, I don't understand you! Cynara—come back here at once!"

But Cynara, with a lift of her hand, was gone, leaving the frustrated Hester gripping the bannister and glaring angrily after her.

Oliver's greeting was warm, if surprised, when he opened the door at her knock. He immediately invited her in and asked if she would like tea, but Cynara shook her head.

"Oliver, I've come to ask you something," she said, seating herself in the chair he indicated. She grasped her hands tightly in her lap.

"Certainly. Any thing you wish, my dear."

His kind expression was almost her undoing. Forcing control over her wavering emotions, she said, more shakily than she had intended, "I want you to tell me about Aron."

"Aron?" he repeated, his glance shifting uneasily away from her. "I don't—"

"Oliver," she said, measuring her words carefully, "I know that Aron and Jenny were married—"

"Oh no!" Oliver raised his hand, violently shaking his head in denial. "Jenny was a poor girl, led astray—"

"No, Oliver," Cynara said firmly. "They were married. I have the proof. Why did you lie, Oliver? Why did you allow Evan to believe he was illegitimate?"

"I . . . I . . ." Oliver dropped his head into his hands, covering his face as Cynara continued relentlessly.

"You knew, Oliver—didn't you? How could you do that to him? You said you loved him, and yet you kept silent, knowing that you were depriving him of his birth-right, of his inheritance. Why did you keep it from him, knowing that he was entitled—*entitled!*—to a share in the Manor?"

Oliver lifted his head, his face agonized. "You don't understand!"

"Tell me."

Her tone was harsh, demanding, and Oliver closed his eyes. "I was trying to . . . to protect him . . ."

"From what?"

Again, her voice was remorseless, and Oliver flinched. She could not weaken now, she told herself; she must not. Resisting the impulse to take his hand, Cynara repeated her question, forcing him to look at her.

"You don't understand," he said once more. "There were reasons—"

"What reasons?"

"Why bring it all up now?" he cried, wringing his hands. "It was so long ago!"

"Oliver, I need to know!"

His head sank down on his chest as he covered his face with his hands again. "I can only tell you that part of the answer lies in the beech trees in the garden," he said finally, his voice so low that she had to strain to hear him.

"The trees?" Cynara tried vainly to keep her impatience from her tone. "Oliver, that doesn't make sense!"

She could hear him sobbing behind the screen of his fingers, and she was alarmed. "Oliver, look at me."

He shook his head. His voice was muffled again when he repeated. "The trees. That's all I can tell you."

She was afraid that she had pushed him too far. He seemed to have shrunk in size, huddling in his chair, his thin shoulders shaking. Again, she felt that stab of pity for him: he was an old man: she shouldn't have pressed him.

Rising, she put a hand on his shoulder. "I'm sorry, Oliver," she said quietly, "But I had to try. If Evan ever discovers the truth—" Her voice shook slightly, and she had to pause before she could continue. "I'm going to see John Ward," she said more evenly, "And tell him that I know the truth about Evan's birth. He has to make some kind of an offer to Evan: he *must* be made to see that. If I have to, I'll tell him that Evan intends on buying the Manor—"

Oliver looked up. "You can't go to John Ward," he said frantically. "You don't know him!"

"Oh yes, I do," Cynara replied grimly, thinking of that night he had come to her room at the Manor. With an effort, she thrust the memory from her mind. "I have to see him, Oliver."

"No, no! You can't!" Oliver actually shook with fear. "John Ward is a dangerous man. If you go to him with threats, there is no telling what he might do!"

"I'm not going to threaten him, Oliver," Cynara said, to calm him. "I'm simply going to tell him—"

Springing from his chair, Oliver grabbed her hands. "Please," he begged. "Don't go!"

Cynara tried to disengage herself. She saw the terror in his eyes, and despite herself, she responded to it. "I have to go," she said, her own voice shaking. "If I don't, Myles will—" She stopped abruptly. She didn't want to burden Oliver with the threat that hovered over her like an evil black shadow.

Oliver's terror increased. "Myles will—what?"

"Nothing, Oliver: it's nothing," Cynara said quickly. "I will take care of it myself—tonight."

She left him then, before he could reply, and as she hurried from the clearing, she didn't look back. There was a path to the right of the cottage, and she took it, walking swiftly, too aware of the gathering darkness. She had to reach Lyrebird Manor before she lost courage: if she stopped to think about John Ward and what he might do, she would never be able to face him. Even now, the idea of seeing him again made her quail inside, and she forced herself forward. There was nothing left to do.

It was dark before she reached the Manor. She had followed the path blindly, sure only that it led in the direction of the house. When the trees thinned abruptly and she stepped out into the open, she saw the bulk of the stables in front of her, with the garden to her right and the house itself a great looming shadow before her.

She stopped for a moment, telling herself that she wasn't

frightened. But now, with the house so close, her heart began to hammer painfully inside her chest, and she knew that she was terrified. It all seemed so impossible, and she found herself wishing irrationally that Evan were here with her. But he wasn't here: she had taken such pains to assure that he wouldn't be, and now she had to do this by herself and she realized too late what a fool she had been. Oh, why hadn't she told Evan the truth? Now she had to face John Ward alone, and she wasn't sure she could do it.

Would John believe her? Cynara clenched her hands. He *had* to believe her: the fact that she knew about Aron's marriage to Jenny Calder must be enough to convince him. She wished suddenly that she had told someone beside Oliver where she was going, what she was going to do. But who was there to tell? Hester? What could Hester have done? There hadn't been anyone she could turn to for help: she was alone.

Closing her eyes at the thought, she stood stiffly, taking one deep breath after another to try to calm herself. So much depended on the interview with John Ward, and yet she could picture him laughing at her, as Myles had done, telling her that Aron was the only one who could prove anything, and that Aron had disappeared long ago. If only, she thought desperately, she had been able to find out more about him: if only she knew what had happened to him . . .

The garden, dark and full of shadows, was to her right, and now she thought of what Oliver had said about the trees. She frowned. She remembered those trees. In the center of the garden, four of them, one surrounded by three others. What did it mean? How did the trees hold the secret, as Oliver had said?

Suddenly, almost as much to postpone the moment when she would have to meet John Ward as to find out what Oliver had meant, Cynara started toward the entrance to the garden. Giving a quick look around, to make sure no one had seen her, she darted to the side. Her footsteps sounded loud in the silence as she crossed the terrace. She paused, glancing up at the bulk of the house, observing the lighted windows, praying that no one would come to investigate. But only silence greeted her, and after a moment, she entered the garden.

The yews made a high, dark screen over her head, but even though it had been almost three years since she had last visited the garden, she knew her way as well as if it had been only yesterday. The gravel path crunched under her feet as she hurried forward, and the sound reminded her of that last terrible night in the summerhouse. She shook her head: she could not think of that now.

Then her feet found the path that circled the trees in the center of the garden, and there they were in front of her, tall, dark shapes rustling with the night breeze. The moon was full and the leaves on the trees were spangled with silver light. The sight reminded her of something, and she searched her memory, trying to think of it. There was something familiar about the play of moonlight and shadow on these trees; she had seen it before, somewhere . . .

And then she remembered it. There had been a painting in the salon at Tamoora of one of the most romantic trees in Australia: the beech. Gerald Whitley had commented upon the painting once, when she had stood there staring at it, wondering what it represented. Now she recalled what he had said, wondering why she hadn't thought of it before. The trees in the painting were very old—Gerald had told her that they had existed before the Romans came to Britain—and the artist had taken full advantage of the romantic story surrounding this tree. He had painted it in moonlight, giving it an ethereal quality that enhanced the tale of the tree growing in a fairy ring. As the one tree aged, a number of offspring grew up from the roots and formed a thicket around it, so that each trunk was encircled by a guard of relatively young and vigorous trees. It was almost as though an aging warrior were surrounding himself with his best and strongest young braves.

But why should she think of that story now, except that this stand of trees reminded her of that painting? Frowning,

Cynara circled the path that led around the trees. The oldest of the trees, surrounded by three other, deliberately planted in that fairy ring . . . Suddenly Cynara saw pictured in her mind the frontispiece of Hester's Bible, and the names written there leaped into her mind. Eric—the patriarch of the Ward family—and his three sons: Sean, Michael, and James. But Michael and James had both died in childhood, and there had only been Sean to carry on the Ward name. There had been no mention of John Ward: she was sure of it. But the solicitor, Abel Bertram, had told her that John Ward was Eric's grandson: that was why he had inherited Lyrebird Manor.

She frowned again. If John's father had been one of Eric's sons, there would be five trees in the garden, not four.

Did that mean what she thought it did? The four trees here in the garden could merely have been planted for decorative purposes: they didn't have to be symbolic.

But Eric Ward had been a man for symbols, she thought: the garden itself was one, designed after Sean had gone to Australia. Then there were the huge iron gates at the entrance to the Manor, with the same pattern of the lyrebird. And the ring had been fashioned in the same motif. Eric had obviously been intensely interested in Australia, and things Australian. It seemed reasonable that he would use the Australian beech as a symbol, as well.

If that were true, she thought, then John had no right at all to the Manor. And if John had no claim—the Manor belonged solely to Evan!

Her sense of triumph disappeared as quickly as it had come, and now all her earlier fears returned in full measure. If she had guessed right, the situation was even more dangerous than before. All this time she had believed that Evan was entitled only to a share in the Manor—now it seemed that he had been cheated out of much more. No wonder John had treated Evan so brutally: he had been afraid that Evan would somehow discover the truth!

The realization that John Ward was the usurper gave her no pleasure: it only increased her fear. If Evan ever learned what John had done to him . . . She shivered, closing her eyes as she pictured Evan's rage. Somehow she must make John listen to her: she had to force him to get out before Evan realized that he had sole claim to Lyrebird Manor. She didn't care about John or Myles: she cared only for Evan, and what he might do.

"So. You couldn't wait until ten o'clock, after all. I had no idea you were so anxious to come to me, Cynara."

She whirled around at the sound of his voice. Her hand went to her throat defensively, and Myles laughed. She could see his face, a round white disk in the moonlight: she saw that, as always, he carried his cane. He leaned on it now, casually, watching her as she struggled to speak.

"You're mistaken, Myles," she managed to say at last. "I came to speak to your father."

"My father?" he repeated mockingly. "And you thought to find him here, in the garden?"

Cynara tried to control her fear. But she was only too aware that she was alone with him, and that this time Evan was not here to help her.

She forced herself to speak calmly. "I came to tell him," she said, as steadily as she was able, "that he must give up the Manor."

He stared at her in silence. Then he laughed shrilly. "You must be mad!"

"No, Myles, I'm not mad," she said, gaining confidence when she saw that she had shaken him. "But your father was, to think he could get away with this forever. Oliver told me the answer was hidden in the trees—:"she raised her hand to point to the dark shadows behind her"—and it was. I know the secret, Myles, and if—"

Myles had followed her gesture, and now he laughed again. "What secret is that?" he jeered. But his glance had sharpened, and he was no longer leaning so casually on his cane.

"There are only four trees, Myles," she said. She was trying desperately not to be afraid of him, but in spite of her efforts, her voice shook again as she continued. "Eric only had three sons," she said. "That's why there are only four trees: one for each of his sons, one for himself."

"A romantic notion," Myles interrupted haughtily. But the mockery was not as evident in his voice as it had been before. She saw him grasp the cane more tightly, and she tensed. She remembered only too well the strength of his thick arms, and she watched him warily. "And you think this means something?" he continued. "What a fool you are!"

"It means that your father has no claim to the Manor." She was more wary of him with each passing minute. She didn't trust his quiet calm; she had been prepared for a violent outburst.

"No claim! My father owns the Manor, Cynara—or have you forgotten that? And I—I will inherit after him!"

"No. No, you won't, Myles," she said quickly, as he took a menacing step toward her. "And I'm not the only one who knows."

"Oh, come now. You'll have to be more convincing than that!"

She backed away as he took another step toward her. "There are records, Myles—records to prove that Eric only had three sons—and . . . and there is the letter from Aron—"

Myles advanced again. "Are we back to that?" he asked, with contempt. "I told you that so-called letter was useless."

She could feel the low wall surrounding the trees pressing against the back of her knees. "Useless or not, I'm going to tell your father."

"Oh, I don't think so," Myles answered lazily.

His tone fooled her; she wasn't prepared for the swift jab of his arm that knocked her against the wall. She lost her balance and before she could catch herself, Myles was on top of her. She began to scream, but he grabbed her by the throat, trying to force her to the ground.

Panic-stricken, she clutched the wall, twisting away from him. She kicked out with one foot, catching him on the shin of his bad leg; the leg and foot gave way, and he crashed into the wall beside her. She didn't hesitate; while he was scrambling to right himself, she shoved him away from her, pushing violently away from the wall at the same time.

Flinging herself forward, she tried to run, but her heel got caught, and she felt herself falling. And then Myles was behind her, grabbing her by the waist, pulling her back toward him. His hand was at her bodice, tearing at the material, and she screamed.

The sound pierced the silence of the garden, and Myles stiffened. "Shut up!"

She screamed again, trying to break away from him, but he held her fast. She clawed at him, and he cursed loudly as her nails raked his arm.

His grip slackened for an instant, and she swung her arm wildly, hitting his shoulder with enough force to stagger him. Again his clubfoot gave way, and he went down on one knee.

He was up again before she could move, and this time he held his cane in his hands like a club. She saw the heavy gold ball on the end flash in the moonlight as he waved it back and forth in front of her face, and she caught her breath. He was between her and the path, the wall was behind her, and there was no place to run. She was trapped.

Myles released one hand from the stem of the cane to wipe his mouth. His eyes glittered as he advanced upon her, and she dropped her glance from his face to the cane. If only she could manage to get it away from him, she thought desperately; if she could get possession of it she might have a chance.

She started to circle him, but Myles saw her intention, and he lifted the cane high in the air. "You won't get away from me this time," he said. "Oh no, not this time."

CHAPTER THIRTY-FIVE

"WHERE IS SHE, Hester? God damn it—tell me now!"

Stunned, Hester stared at the thunderous Evan. He had burst into the house just as she was crossing the entryway, and through the open door she could see his horse, lathered with sweat, standing loose outside. Switching her glance back to Evan, she said tremulously, "I . . . I don't know. What is all this about, Evan? You look so—"

He actually advanced upon her, his expression fierce. "I don't have time for games," he said harshly. "Tell me where she is."

Truly alarmed, Hester stepped back. "She went out, some time ago. I don't know where. Evan—please. Tell me what's wrong!"

"I have to find her!"

Something had happened: she could tell by his face. He wasn't angry: he looked—frightened. Hester's alarm increased; she had never seen him this way, and suddenly she was frightened herself. Making a rapid decision, she said quickly, "Evan, come with me. There's something I have to tell you."

"I haven't time."

Without waiting to see if he followed, she turned and went toward the sitting room. Thank God she had left the Bible there; she didn't think she could climb the stairs in this condition. Now that the moment had come, she felt faint, her heart sending up a clamor inside her breast.

Fortunately he had decided to come with her, and when the door was closed, she lifted the Bible from the table, opened it to the front, extracted the letter, and gave both to him before sinking weakly into a chair.

He looked blankly at her, and she gestured. "Read it," she said. "It's from your father."

"My father!" Rapidly, he scanned the letter, then looked at the open Bible, frowning. When he glanced up again, the expression on his face was more than she could bear, and she closed her eyes.

"Yes," she said faintly, "it's true. Aron was your father." She opened her eyes again, forcing herself to look at him. "I didn't tell you before, because I—I was afraid . . . for you . . ."

Evan looked down at the Bible again. He had grasped the implications at once, and he was stunned. Gesturing, he choked, "But if this is true, it means that I—that I . . ." Savagely, he slammed the book shut. His eyes blazed with rage.

"Yes," she said simply.

"Why didn't you tell me before?"

She quailed before the look on his face. "I was afraid you would do something . . . rash . . ."

"Rash! When I think of all the years—of John Ward, and what he did to me . . ." He stopped, too enraged to continue. Violently, he threw the Bible down on a table. It slid across the top and fell to the floor with a crash, but neither Evan nor Hester heard it. She was struggling out of her chair, trying to reach him as he turned swiftly and headed for the door.

"Evan—wait!" she cried after him. "You can't go to him like this! Evan, please!"

Her frantic voice followed him as he raced out the front door and vaulted onto his tired horse. He had a glimpse of Trent rushing to help her as she staggered after him. She spoke quickly to the butler, and the man turned a white, frightened face in his direction.

He didn't stop. Almost blind with fury, Evan spurred the horse around. It wasn't until he had reached the road again that his mind cleared enough to remember his original intent; hesitating for only a second, he turned the horse to the left, in the direction of Oliver's cottage. John Ward would have to wait; he had to find Cynara first. But as he galloped up the path, he found himself thinking more of John than of Cynara, and he ground his teeth together at the realization of what John had done to him. He would kill him, he thought; with his bare hands, he would kill him!

The lighted window of the cottage was a yellow beacon in the dark woods. Evan reined the horse in and was out of the saddle before the animal had stopped. Flinging himself through the door, he took in the empty room at a glance, and groaned aloud. Where in *hell* was Cynara? Where could she have gone? For that matter, he wondered frantically, where was Oliver? They wouldn't have gone to the Manor, he thought wildly, and yet it was the only place left.

He was just about to dash out again when an envelope on the table caught his eye. His name was written on the front in large black wavering letters, and Evan hesitated. He didn't have time to stop, and yet there was something about the quality of that writing that made him pause again. Swearing, he crossed the room and tore open the envelope.

His hope, that Oliver had taken Cynara away somewhere to safety, was abandoned as he started to read the letter inside. The cramped lines were difficult to decipher, and here and there a blot of ink obliterated a word, but Evan saw what it was at once: a confession and an explanation.

Aware that each minute he delayed increased the danger for both Cynara and Oliver, Evan nevertheless stopped a moment, forcing himself to calm down and think. The information contained in this letter was so explosive that he had to take time to assimilate it all before he went rushing off to confront John Ward.

Oliver wrote that he had been employed as steward at the Manor the same year Sean left for Australia. Oliver had been there; he had witnessed it all, Evan thought in amazement. And yet he had kept the secret all these years—kept it so well that Evan had never suspected how his own life was interwoven with the people Oliver mentioned now. He felt a blind surge of anger against the old man; he read more rapidly.

When Sean had gone, after a bitter argument with his father, Eric, bereft of his eldest and only remaining son, had taken in a ward, an orphan named Richard. Richard had never been formally adopted by Eric, and this had rankled. Eric insisted that the estate be held in trust for his errant son. As the years went on and Eric aged, Richard assumed more and more responsibility, always resenting that he had no legal claim to the Manor. He had taken over completely when Eric died, and by then it was generally assumed that Sean would never return to England. Richard married; his wife bore him a son—the present John Ward. When Richard was killed in a carriage accident, it was John who assumed control. When Sean sent his son, Aron, to England, the envy and resentment John had learned from his father had erupted . . . into murder.

Evan looked up from the letter. The mystery of Aron's disappearance was finally explained. Evan knew at once what Oliver intended to do.

There wasn't much time. He had to get to the Manor before Oliver confronted John Ward. Groaning again, Evan realized that Cynara must have gone with him, for support. The two of them, Oliver and Cynara, against a man who would be like an animal at bay—the thought spurred him to action, and he stuffed the letter into his pocket and dashed outside again.

The horse stood with its head down, sides heaving, and Evan cursed. He would have to go by foot, rather than take the longer way by the road with the horse. But hadn't he spent years traversing this path through the woods, to Oliver's cottage? Years of coming to the old man, who seemed to be all he had in the world? And Oliver had betrayed him . . .

Evan took a grip on himself. Oliver hadn't betrayed him, he thought fiercely; the old man had risked his life to save Evan's. He set off at a run down the path, praying that he would be in time.

The path ended at the back of the stables, but Evan skirted around to the front of the house, bursting violently in the front door. He saw a light under the closed library door, and he strode in that direction, taking a deep breath to steady himself. If Oliver and Cynara were there with John, he would have to be careful. He knew only too well now how dangerous John Ward was, and Evan would have to get them out of there before John did something desperate. This was between him and John Ward, as it had always been, he realized now. He would take care of Myles later.

Evan paused a moment outside the door, trying to get

himself under control. It was useless; his rage pulsed through him like a black tide, and he hoped that he would have enough restraint not to strangle John the moment he saw him.

When he threw open the door, John was sitting at his desk. He was alone in the room, and Evan saw it at once. An alarm went off in his mind. Where was Oliver? Where was Cynara? But there was no time to wonder; as soon as he saw John, everything else was obliterated from his mind in a rush of hatred.

John looked up in annoyance at being interrupted. But when he saw Evan standing on the threshold, the color drained from his face, and he half rose from his chair.

"Sit down, John," Evan said. "It seems we have a lot to talk about."

"Get out! How dare you come in here unannounced? I'll have you thrown out at once!"

Evan advanced. As he came forward more into the light and John saw his face, his own face paled even more. He made a convulsive movement toward the bell rope behind him, but Evan's voice arrested his hand in mid-air.

"I wouldn't, John."

John paused, beads of sweat breaking out on his forehead as Evan leaned over the desk. The lamp shone on Evan's face from below, casting sharp light and shadow across his set jaw and dark eyes. John pushed back into his chair, his own eyes wide and straining. "Get out!" he choked.

Evan appeared surprised. "Get out?" he repeated, and something in his voice made John draw back farther into the resisting chair. Evan continued, and his voice, if possible, was even colder than before. "Get out of my own house?"

John did not care for the smile that curved Evan's lips. "Your house?" he croaked. "I don't know what you mean!"

Evan leaned forward. "Don't you?"

He had found out, John thought with desperation. Somehow he had found out. The fear he had lived with for years flowed through him now, and without being fully aware of it, he began sliding his hand toward the top drawer of the desk, where he kept a pistol.

Evan moved so swiftly that John cried out more in surprise than with fear. Whipping an arm across the desk, Evan grasped John's wrist with fingers that were like iron.

Dark eyes bored into his, and John cringed. "I know what happened to Aron, John. My father—Aron."

John jerked in his chair. His wrist already felt numb; he tried to pull away from Evan's hold. He couldn't move his arm.

"You can't prove anything!" he cried. "You can't prove it!"

"All those years," Evan said, ignoring him, speaking almost musingly. "All those years I believed you had a right to the Manor. You told me so enough times, didn't you? Oh yes, you made me believe it was true, in a thousand different ways. You had your methods, and I had to believe."

John was distracted by Evan's tone. In his fear, he did not see Evan's narrowed eyes. "Of course it was true!" he gabbled. "My father was—Eric's son!"

"Your father was a liar. He had no more claim than you have!"

"That's a lie!" Evan's grip tightened even more, and John gasped. "That's a lie," he repeated, but with less conviction.

"Tell me about Aron," Evan said, his expression savage.

John cowered, the sweat dripping freely now from his face. "I don't know what happened to Aron!" he cried. "You have to believe me! I don't know!"

Violently, Evan jerked him out of the chair. John fell awkwardly across the top of the desk, trying to pull back. He could not free himself: Evan seemed to have the strength of ten. His face distorted with terror, he looked up at Evan, and what he saw in his face made him even more terrified. He actually sobbed.

"Oh, God—let me go!" he blubbered.

"You didn't let Aron go, did you? You had no mercy then—why should you deserve it now?" Evan paused. When he spoke again, his voice shook with rage. "I could kill you," he said. "I could kill you. Just as you killed Aron."

John broke. Consumed by fear, in terror for his life, he dissolved into tears. Evan, disgusted, threw him back into the chair, where he huddled, his hands over his face, tears gushing through his fingers. "I had to kill him," he sobbed. "I had to, don't you see? My father worked all those years to have the Manor—I couldn't let it be taken from me. He always told me we deserved it, and we did—it should have been ours! And then . . . and then, Aron came, and I knew I would lose it unless I did something!"

John dropped his hands, his face a blank, staring mask. He looked up at Evan, but he didn't really see him; his mind was turned inward, as if he were reliving it all over again. "I didn't mean to kill him," he whispered. "I didn't. Not then. But we were in the garden—that accursed garden!" His eyes focused briefly on Evan. "I should have destroyed it long ago; I never could stand the sight of it!"

John's face became blank and he continued, in a singsong voice that made Evan's skin crawl. "I knew Sean was dead; I had Emily's letter. But I hadn't told Aron yet. Oh, no. I had to wait for the right opportunity, you see. All I had to do was get rid of Aron. But he was suspicious. We had words—there in the garden. I was afraid someone would hear. And so . . . I killed him."

John laughed suddenly, a mad sound that made Evan frown. He watched John closely, but it seemed that the man was unaware of him. He continued; it was as if once started, he couldn't stop. "And then Jenny Calder came to me. Oh, I was so sure everything had been taken care of, until she told me she and Aron were married, and that she was to have a child. She asked me if I knew where Aron had gone—he had left without a word to her, you see." John laughed again, and Evan took a step toward him: the expression on John's face was eerie; he didn't trust that look.

John still seemed unaware of him. "She showed me her marriage lines, to prove that she and Aron were married, and I took them and threw them into the fire. Who would believe her—a servant girl—over me, the master of Lyrebird Manor? Once the marriage lines were gone, she had no proof, don't you see? I was safe."

He tried to focus on Evan, but he was still held in the grip of his private terror. Evan did not relent when he saw John's slack face, the saliva drooling from his lips. He had no pity; he had to learn the rest.

"But you weren't safe, after all, were you?" he said. "Someone else knew what you had done."

John rocked back and forth in his chair. "Ah, yes," he said, almost to himself. "Oliver. Oliver knew, I remember now. I made a bargain with him. He was fond of Jenny, don't you see? He wanted to protect her. I said she could have the child, and we would keep it here. She had only to keep silent. Yes, that was the bargain we made. It worked out well, didn't it? I had you where I could keep my eye on you, and you never found out. No, you never found out."

Frowning, Evan watched him as he continued to rock in his chair. His eyes were open, staring, his hands loose in his lap. He appeared to have retreated into some private world of his own; when Evan cautiously approached him and waved a hand in front of his eyes, John did not blink. His only reaction was to begin humming, a tuneless sound that raised the hairs on the back of Evan's neck.

"John—" he began.

Suddenly there was a piercing scream from outside. The windows in the library were open; Evan heard it clearly. He stiffened. "What the hell—"

The scream came again, louder this time, vibrating with terror. Evan's head snapped up. He was out the door and running down the corridor before the sound died away. He forgot about John, forgot about everything but the fact that Cynara was in the garden, screaming for help.

As he reached the entrance to the garden, he heard the sound of a scuffle and another cry, muffled this time, and he headed toward the center. Leaping over flowerbeds, vaulting over everything that stood in the way, Evan raced toward the sound of the fight. He heard Myles cry out in pain, and then shriek again in anger. There was a third voice added to the din, and Evan recognized it as belonging to Oliver. He leaped forward, and then stopped, frozen for an instant, when he saw three figures silhouetted in the moonlight.

CHAPTER THIRTY-SIX

"THERE IS NO ONE to help you this time, Cynara," Myles said. "You won't get away from me now!"

Cynara did not answer; her entire attention was focused on Myles. He had raised the cane even higher, and now she moved back, feeling her way cautiously lest she stumble off the path and give him the advantage.

"Why not be sensible, Cynara, and give up? You know you can't beat me alone."

"She isn't alone, Myles."

They both jumped at the sound of the voice coming at them through the darkness. Myles whirled around, and Cynara cried out when she saw the slight figure of Oliver Lindsay step from the shadows onto the path. He appeared so old, so frail, with the moonlight shining down on his white hair. Why had he come? What was he doing here?

"Come here to me, Cynara," Oliver said.

She obeyed at once, giving the stupefied Myles a wide berth. "Oliver—" she said anxiously.

"It's all right," he answered.

Myles had recovered. "What the hell do you think you're doing, old man? You have no business here!"

"Not with you, Myles, no. With your father, yes." Oliver's voice was calm; only Cynara was aware that he was afraid; his fingers, which had grasped hers, were shaking.

"Whatever you have to say to my father, you can say to me!"

"Ah, yes. As the father, so is the son. But are you man enough to accept this?"

Suddenly there was a glint of gold in the palm he held out toward Myles, and Cynara gasped. She recognized the ring instantly; it was the same one she had seen in the painting. The lyrebird ring—where had Oliver gotten it?

"Do you recognize it, Myles? Surely your father told you about the ring. He was frantic to find it, after he—"

"Give that ring to me!" Myles screamed. "Give it to me!"

Oliver shook his head. "No, Myles. I've saved it all these years, as insurance against this night. I'm going to see your father, as I should have done long ago."

"Oliver—" Cynara said worriedly when he took a step forward.

He turned his head to look reassuringly at her, and in that moment, Myles attacked. She saw his rush an instant before he reached them, and she shouted a warning, trying to push Oliver out of the way. She was too late. Myles had launched himself toward them and all three crashed to the ground. Cynara heard Oliver give a grunt of pain as he fell, and it was then that her fear left her.

She must protect him somehow.

With a cry Cynara leaped up and pounced on Myles, trying to pull him away from Oliver. Springing onto his back, she sought to topple him over, but he was like a madman, ignoring her as his fists flailed at Oliver. Oliver groaned once and then lay still. Myles straightened, Cynara still clinging to his back, and now he whirled around, trying to reach around to pull her off. She tightened both arms around his neck, and Myles uttered a choked cry. His fingers tore at hers, and she felt herself giving way. When he flung her to the ground, she tried to scramble to her feet, but he was too quick for her. Enraged, screaming incoherently, he threw himself on top of her, his hands closing around her throat, choking the breath out of her.

Bright sparks shot before her eyes as the pressure of his hands increased. Clawlike, her own hands came up, trying to pry his fingers away, but he wouldn't let go. She couldn't breathe; a darkness blacker than the night around her began to close in at the edges of her vision, and she knew that she had only seconds left. She pushed at him, but he was relentless, and her arms were suddenly too heavy, too weak, to lift.

Abruptly the pressure against her throat was gone, and she looked up to see a shadow behind Myles. He was lifted up and off of her, and flung to one side. Cynara closed her eyes; now that her throat was free, she tried to take in great mouthfuls of air, but every breath was fire on her bruised throat. Gasping, she put one hand underneath her, her only thought to reach Oliver and try to get away before Myles attacked again.

"Cynara—"

"Evan?" she choked.

"I'm here. Cynara, are—"

Then there was a shadow behind him. Cynara uttered a strangled sound, trying to scream, gesturing frantically. It was a nightmare; she had seen the same thing before, in the summerhouse. Her vision cleared, and she could see Myles standing over Evan's unprotected back as he bent over her. She saw him raise the cane high over his head to bring down on Evan. She couldn't scream, she couldn't make a sound: she could only watch in horror as the cane wavered in the air, and below it, Myles's contorted, mad face as he held the weapon. With an effort that took all her strength, she reached up and shoved Evan out of the way just as the cane came crashing down.

She heard the whistle it made in the air, saw it descending, incredibly, in slow motion, to smash harmlessly on the ground between them. The stem snapped with the force of the blow, the heavy gold top flying up into the air. Seconds later, she heard Myles utter a cry, and then she felt, rather than saw, him sink slowly to the ground beside her. At that moment she heard another sound, and she stiffened. It was the noise of a gun being fired, and it came from the house. Then there was silence—broken only by her laboring gasps for air, and Evan saying urgently, "Cynara, Cynara—my God! Are you all right?"

His eyes searched her face, his hands moved frantically over her body, trying to find out if she was hurt. She couldn't speak; her throat was swollen with tears.

"Christ! If he hurt you—"

She managed to take a breath without feeling as though it were liquid fire. "I'm all right, Evan," she gasped. "But Oliver—"

Oliver was lying on the path, off to one side. Cynara

burst into tears at the sight of his pain-contorted face, his hand grasping convulsively at his shirt front. They both knelt quickly beside him.

Evan lifted him up, so that his head and shoulders were cradled in his arms. "Oliver—"

"Don't say anything," the old man gasped. "I have to tell you . . ."

"Oliver," Cynara begged, on the other side of him. "Don't try to talk. We must get a doctor—"

Oliver shook his head, and the movement brought on a fit of weak coughing. "Later . . ." he panted. "I must . . . tell Evan . . ." He brought his hand up, pushing it toward Evan. The ring he held gleamed in the darkness, and he said faintly, "I . . . I saved it for you, Evan. It was your father's ring . . ."

He began coughing again, and Evan met Cynara's eyes over Oliver's head. She nodded, and Evan looked down. "Oliver, there will be time later to talk," he said, his voice ragged with emotion.

Oliver grasped Evan's coat. "Yes," he whispered. "But . . . whatever happens . . . you were like a son to me. I . . . I did the only thing I could . . . It was wrong; I see that now. But I wanted to . . . protect you. Say you . . . forgive me . . ."

"There's nothing to forgive, Oliver," Evan answered, his voice breaking again.

"I . . . love you, Evan . . ."

"And I—"

Oliver sighed. His eyes closed, and his hand relaxed its grip on Evan's coat. His head rolled to the side, toward Evan's shoulder, and Cynara uttered a cry. "Is he . . . is he . . ."

Evan shook his head. "No," he said fiercely. "But we have to get a doctor right away."

Gathering the old man in his arms, Evan lifted him as easily as if he were a child. He looked toward the house, and then away again, and then seemed to make up his mind. He started toward the Manor. And why not, Cynara thought wearily, as she stumbled to her feet to follow: he owns it, doesn't he?

She glanced only once in the direction where Myles lay unmoving. The crimson gleam of blood was evident on his face, and she wondered coldly if he was dead. But she couldn't make herself go over to look, and after a slight hesitation, she walked slowly after Evan.

It wasn't until she reached the terrace that she realized all the ground floor windows were alight, and that there was the sound of frenzied activity inside the house. A man she didn't know came running outside, almost knocking her down as he headed toward the stables. When he stopped to steady her, she saw that his face was blank with shock, and she asked him what had happened.

"It's the master," he gabbled. "He's been shot. Got to ride for the doctor," he panted. "Lord, what a night this is going to be!"

He ran off, and Cynara started quickly for the house. There would be questions, and she had to tell someone about Myles, still in the garden.

But when she was almost at the back door, she stopped. Let Evan take care of it, she thought wearily; suddenly she didn't seem to have the strength to go inside.

Backing away, she went toward the garden again. There was a stone bench inside, sheltered by the yews, and she slumped down on it. She couldn't leave yet, not until she heard if Oliver was going to be all right. After that, there was nothing to keep her here. Remembering how Evan had walked away from her without a glance, she thought again: no, there wasn't anything at all.

She heard a familiar harsh voice berating someone in the kitchen, and although she couldn't hear the words, she recognized the tone. Hester Cord.

Hester's voice faded, and now there was only silence. She wasn't sure how long she waited, but after what seemed an endless time, she heard the sounds of a carriage clattering on the front drive, and then there was silence once more. The doctor had arrived, and with him, ominous signs of rain.

Looking up, she saw that clouds had completely obscured the moon. She had lost her shawl sometime that night, and she was cold, but she could not make herself get up and go into the house. She could only stare emptily before her, waiting for—what? For Evan to come? But he wouldn't come, she thought; it was all over between them. Whatever brief flame had flared was gone, and she knew it.

She raised her head as the first drops of rain began falling, not caring as it came faster and faster, soaking her to the skin. What did it matter? What did anything matter?

"Cynara . . ."

He appeared suddenly beside her, his black hair already glistening with rain. She sprang up. "Oliver?" she asked anxiously.

"The doctor says he's going to be fine. He will need rest, but he'll recover."

"And John Ward?" she asked.

"He shot himself Cynara. He's dead."

Cynara let out a breath of relief, but the tension did not leave her. She was too aware of him standing there gazing at her. She said awkwardly, "Oliver did what he thought was right, Evan."

"I know."

"Well, then . . ." Her voice trailed off. She had begun to shiver, but not from cold. Why was he staring at her so?

"Cynara—"

She couldn't make herself look into his eyes. "Evan, I—"

"Don't say anything. Let me—I should have spoken a long time ago, but like a fool, I—" He stopped abruptly. "It doesn't matter," he said huskily. "Cynara, do you think . . ."

He stopped again. Now, when she forced herself to look at him, she could hardly see for the rain that fell in great drops, obscuring everything between them. But she could see his eyes, and what she saw there reflected what she felt, what she had always felt, from the moment when she had first seen him, an arrogant young man she had thought only an ignorant farm lad, and who had been more of a man than she had ever dreamed.

Evan made a motion with his hand, indicating the dripping garden, the rain-blurred house. "It doesn't matter, Cynara," he said. "None of it matters. The only thing that matters is you."

"Do you mean that? Oh, Evan—do you really mean that?"

He put his arms around her and held her close, and she could feel the trembling of his body, as her own was trembling. The rain beat steadily upon them, and Cynara lifted her head, quiet tears sliding down her cheeks to mingle with the raindrops. She raised her hands to his face, and his skin was warm and wet under her fingers. She saw with wonder the tears in his eyes.

"Evan, it was a lie about Myles," she sobbed, beginning to cry uncontrollably. "I never would have—"

He put a finger to her lips, silencing her. "I know . . . I know," he murmured. "Perhaps we'll talk about it sometime. It doesn't matter."

Tipping her head up, he said softly, "Cynara, will you marry me?"

She thought of her response to Hester only hours earlier: "Evan was never my husband," and in spite of her own emotion, she smiled. He had known it, too.

Head lowered, his eyes were on a level with hers, searching her face. She couldn't speak; her heart was too full. But her lips met his fiercely in answer, and when he swept her up into his arms, she laughed joyously.

There, in the garden, with the thunder sounding around them, and the wind rising, whipping her hair about her face, they surrendered to the love that had been too long denied. Evan's hands were warm on her rain-swept skin; his body was all the shelter she would ever need as he bore her to the grass. He was strong and hard as he entered her, and their mingled cries of ecstasy were carried away in the storm.